BLOODY
PARADISE

Get the Water Street Crime Starter Library
FOR FREE

Sign up for the no-spam newsletter and get *four* full-length ebooks—the thrillers **BLOODY PARADISE**, **FROM ICE TO ASHES**, **TROPICAL ICE**, and **SING FOR THE DEAD**—plus two introductory short stories by the author of **STAINED FORTUNE** and lots more exclusive content, all for *free*.

**Details can be found at
the end of *BLOODY PARADISE*,
or go here now:
mailchi.mp/waterstreetpressbooks.com/
waterstreetcrimemailinglist**

BLOODY PARADISE

JAME DIBIASIO

Water Street Press
Healdsburg, California

Published by Water Street Press
Healdsburg, California

Water Street Press paperback edition published 2018

Produced in the USA

Print 978-1-62134-310-3
E-Pub 978-1-62134-311-0
Mobi 978-1-62134-312-7

Cover design by **thecovercollection.com**

Typesetting services by **bookow.com**

For Mabel.

Acknowledgments

Jordan Dotson and Melanie Ho critiqued the manuscript. Elizabeth Trupin-Pulli found a home for it. Lynn Vannucci and her team at Water Street Crime midwifed it. They have my thanks.

A special shout-out to the Koh Samui gang: Chapman, Fok, Katherine, Mabel, Maggie, May and Shirley.

My depictions of the management and employees of the Samui Aquarium and Tiger Zoo are entirely fictitious.

Chapter 1

Guava Juice

THE pain in his right hand grew harder to endure as the airplane approached Koh Samui International. Trav was now certain he had broken it. He bent over in his seat, trying to capture the focus of his training: the breathing, the mantras, the discipline of violence in motion.

He imagined the sandbag, the circuit, the morning routine of chops and kicks. Tried remembering how it felt to tear through them, one by one.

The drugs had seen him through takeoff but now the changes in air pressure were popping his nerves back to consciousness. He tried to rock himself to a different place, somewhere away from the anonymous co-passengers, away from the stale announcements in Cantonese and Thai.

Think about the other guy. He forced the enunciation of a complete sentence in his mind. *At-least-you're-not-the-other-guy.*

The plane circled, cabin light alternating between white sun and ocean blue. It felt like purgatory. His breathing and mantras crumbled against the hurt that was now screaming out of his knuckles. As he imagined his training routine, breathing sharply with the movements in his mind, what he started thinking was *Car-o-line, Car-o-line.*

By now the pain radiated down to his elbow, possessed his entire arm. He couldn't even fumble for the airbag. He pushed his head against the upright plastic tray and vomited between his shoes.

A stewardess had wiped the detritus from his face with a wet towel; the first thing he noticed as he came to was an airplane antiseptic chill in his nostrils that burned down the back of his raw throat. Whoever had been traveling beside him must have managed to escape to another seat. The changes in air pressure as the plane had plodded in its circle had ceased and they were back at sea level, touching down. Or maybe it was the catharsis of throwing up. The pain was still there, but it had returned to a part-time throb, bearable so long as he touched nothing.

"Are you feeling better?" asked the stewardess, pronouncing his name as "Mister Meetcheng."

"OK," he said, but then remembered: "My bag. I passed out. Where's my bag?"

She blinked. "Your bag?"

2

Panic squeezed his guts. "It was here, under my feet? Where the hell—"

"Oh, I moved it...when you got sick." She raised herself up to open the luggage bin and hopped down with a dusty backpack. "This one?"

"Yeah," he sighed, "that's it." He reached for it but she put it back up top.

"We land now," she said, shutting the overhead bin with finality. "There's ambulance for you, but you must go through immigration."

Trav resigned himself to letting the bag remain up there, relieved it hadn't been opened after he had passed out. A kernel of paranoia in him wondered if, perhaps, it had been. The stewardess buckled herself into the fight attendant's jump seat a few rows ahead, her face passive. Trav willed himself to look out the window. Green hills sped by. Palm fronds, then the airport, a low-set huddle of wooden pagodas, surprising in its lack of formality.

Ambulance. What kind of questions would they ask him? He looked at his hand. It was starting to resemble an eggplant. No choice. The landing was smooth but a whiff of puke made him gag. The stewardess had wiped his face clean, but she hadn't managed to address the floor.

The usual bedlam. Everybody out. He wanted to get his bag but a fear of banging his hand held him back. The stewardess motioned for him to sit back down. Trav closed his eyes and breathed through clenched teeth. Not the most auspicious start to lying low. He was too brittle to really care, but caution prompted him to use his good hand to hide his face from the disembarking mob.

She guided an airport attendant pushing a collapsible wheelchair his way. "I can walk," Trav protested.

"Airline rule," the stewardess said.

"Sorry about the mess," he said as the attendant pushed him out, his good hand guarding the backpack in his lap.

"I'm happy you feel OK, Mister Meetch-eng."

I bet you are very happy, he thought, *to see the back of me.*

An open-top airport cart sped him to the terminal. Samui's airport boasted a friendly design intended to mimic a Thai garden, bursting with orchids, teak beams and open spaces. A whiff of scent perked him up. Someone handed him a glass of guava juice. Awesome.

The good vibe turned to panic, though, when he wondered what the immigration officer was going to ask. What if they wanted to search his backpack? Why does an American resident in Hong Kong show up on a direct flight to Samui, with no local fixed address or hotel booking, with a broken hand and a backpack containing one laptop and wads of Hong Kong dollars?

No doubt a phone call would reveal he had bought the ticket five hours ago at Chep Lap Kok with cash. Are you here to buy drugs, Mister Mitchell? Are you here to buy guns? Are you here to launder money, sir?

The truth might not cut it. *Actually I'm on the lam, Khun Immigration Officer. I know that sounds corny, and believe me, I'm just as surprised about it as you. But if you had just cost a Chinese triad boss face and money by knocking out his son cold, trust me, you'd have gotten the hell out of Dodge too. Deport my ass if you have to, but not back to Hongkers, OK?*

But that would of course lead to a few more questions that he would prefer not to answer. It could lead to something even worse: attention. If word leaked out...if whatever passed for the local press caught wind of a *farang* showing up injured and with stacks of cash, and that got published, and picked up, and written in the *South China Morning Post* or one of the Chinese papers...

Then Thailand wouldn't be a bolt hole. It would be a death trap.

He'd be safe in police custody, no doubt—safe from Kang. But he had a feeling that Thai jailhouses didn't provide such a lovely welcome. Didn't see the cockroaches or the cutthroats handing him a juice of guava.

They wheeled him in front of an immigration officer with an oil slick for hair. Thick brown fingers turned the pages of his passport. "Why you come to Thailand?"

No one had ever before asked him why he was coming to Thailand. A zillion tourists a year, what was the point? But now the immigration officer raised his thick eyebrows over his chunky face, and Trav realized he had no idea what to say.

The wheelchair must have saved him.

"Medical tourism?" the man proffered, glancing at the immigration form the stewardess had helped him fill out during the flight. Trav nodded, forcing himself not to glance down at the backpack in his lap.

The immigration cop grunted and pressed a stamp on his passport. "This way, Mister Meetch-eng," said one of the airline attendants as the other put some muscle into the wheelchair.

"My luggage."

"Yes, Mister Meetch-eng."

And there it was, on the carousel in an adjoining pagoda-like space of teak beams: his duffel. One of the airport attendants shepherding him through even carried it, everything that he now owned, everything he could carry, that and the contents of his backpack.

"I gotta change some money," he said, because he had no baht on him, and they wheeled him to the bank counter. He was careful to take out as much money from his backpack as he could with one hand without drawing notice. He hadn't been thinking, though, because the pile of baht he received in exchange was conspicuously thick. Trav braved standing up long enough to stuff bills into his pockets. He folded back into sitting position. "OK, let's roll."

An ambulance was waiting, a tiny toy-truck, along with a smiling woman who gave him a *wai* and wished him a pleasant stay. Trav's hand ached badly, but habit prompted him to extend it as they were lifting him into the back, which rejuvenated the splintering pain. Nausea took hold once again and they had to carry him onto a stretcher bed.

It took about twenty minutes to get to the hospital, and every teeny bump amplified the agony. But his stomach had settled and he found himself grinning like a maniac. *I made it into Thailand.*

Thinking about the other guy came easier now.

Chapter 2

Startled Cat

SHE knew what it was to get hit. The glow razzling off her cheek. The deeper, more substantial ache where the ring had struck. The jarred jawbone, still vibrating. Those were all the physical reactions, and Mazy felt alive to them all, but they didn't matter. She registered the sensation, the shock. The absolute indignity.

More than Gordon backhanding her, what outraged her was her response.

"But I'm a teacher," she complained. As though the only thing wrong was whether she'd have to show the students her scarred face.

It had been months since he had last struck her, and she had let herself believe that those days were gone, a mere artifact of memory. Like she had once believed of her foster dad—the third, final one. The one whose face she had willed out of memory, whose name she had consigned to oblivion. It had taken an effort, though, forgetting. It had involved an all-in commitment to just go numb. Getting smacked by Gordon frightened Mazy, because of what it might take to make her forget again.

Mazy mumbled an apology and walked down the villa steps, past the pool where Isaac was sunbathing, fingers jamming with the heavy bass lines growling from the speakers. She placed a palm over her stinging flesh, as if to hide it, and stepped onto the beach. Here, at the south end of the island, the water remained shallow far out to sea. The neighboring islands were close enough to make this more of a channel than an ocean, far enough to float there like a promise they needn't ever keep.

She slipped out of her flats on the sand and glided in.

They were on their third day on the island, at the beginning of what Gordon had billed as a month's break—oh and by the way, Ginger and Isaac are staying on. Don't worry, villa's massive, you can't even tell when they're around. Just a bit of work on the side...you just read a book, love, go for a swim, get a massage.

Can't tell they're around? Isaac sunning himself by the pool while blasting Coldplay on the outdoor stereo system? Ginger upstairs on the PlayStation, Grand Theft Auto IV again, shouting obscenities between the sounds of explosions?

She protested while he was upstairs watching soccer, West Ham versus Blackburn. That was probably where she had erred, interrupting the game, "the footy", even though it was just the highlights from earlier in the week. He tried to soothe her, but turned on a dime—or should that be a pence?—suddenly irritated by her insistence that a romantic getaway wasn't meant to include two of his cronies.

Mazy thought she had always maintained a reasoned detachment. She wasn't the nagging, clingy type. Gordon had often said he appreciated the way she trusted him. But this time she let a little whine into her complaint.

He had erupted. "Ungrateful cow!" Then wham, dropped her right there, spun her face first onto a sofa. "I take you on holiday for a month, pay for everything—food, massages, golf, the lot—and I'm here, in case you hadn't noticed, I'm here to get a job done. Denying meself all the luxuries."

"*But I'm a teacher*," Mazy mimicked herself in disgust as she strode further out into the channel. She had been walking for a few minutes but still the water only licked her knees. Out here there was just the sound of the wind, and a strange crackling, like a bonfire, as though waves and wind collided like kindling.

She felt it now, gnawing inside of her, that familiar impulse. Was her need for a drink her response to self-loathing? Or did she despise herself all the more because, God, she needed a drink now and there was only one way that was going to end.

The water abruptly went from her knees to her waist, soaking her tight denim shorts and lapping at her T-shirt. She was quite far from shore. Then, another few steps, and it was up to her breasts. She kept her gaze firmly on the islands, blue pyramids in the middle distance.

Just keep going, Maze.

The thought had just materialized like a shooting star enlivening the nighttime sky. Just keep going. The water tickled her collarbones. Splashes, somewhere behind her, but she took that step and the water was at her chin, salty spray stinging her eyes. Instinct kept her mouth shut and her breath held, but a few more steps and the current, already strong, would do the rest. There'd be no going back. She willed her legs forward and water got up her nose and she snorted. Then she was flailing and screaming because someone was behind her. Their arm locked around her throat, and struggling did nothing more than get her to choke on seawater. Gagging triggered other reflexes and she couldn't go any further.

Ginger was the one who had come to get her out of the water. His tree trunk of an upper arm swiveled her around. By the time she had stopped coughing, she tried screaming in protest, but her throat was ragged and her voice was lost to the wind. By now he had maneuvered her into shallower water, where he could leverage his bulk to drag her back. Ginger's meaty fingers squeezed her breasts.

"Get tired of Gordo, I'll give you what you need," he said.

"Fucking get off me." And then, pathetically, "If Gordon finds out how you've been touching me, he'll kill you."

11

"Aw, it's true love."

She stopped resisting and as the water depth fell away he stopped fondling her, and then let her walk sullenly by herself. Mazy strode back to land like a woman on a mission.

Gordon was contrite. He met her at the edge of the villa compound, on the grassy stretch between the infinity pool and the beach. "Don't be like that, Maze," he said. From his raised eyebrows and pleading hands, she recognized this was the closest to an apology she would receive.

"I just wanted to go for a swim," she said.

"I've got a treat for you. Hurry up and get changed."

She walked past him to the stairs of the main building.

"Where are you going?"

Mazy ignored him and made directly for the upstairs kitchen. He caught up just as she was pouring a splash of Coke into a tumbler of vodka. Gordon shook his head. "Not this again."

She gave him the finger, American style, and drank the glass. It hit her immediately, harsh and hot. Gordon took the empty glass from her hand and set it on the counter.

"Are you done now?"

Mazy wiped her mouth and nodded. "I'll go get changed."

Half an hour later, Mazy was guided into a big cage. "This way, pretty lady," said the trainer, beckoning. "Remember, put your arm like this. No other touch. Very safe if you follow the rule."

She bumped into a fat white man coming out of the cage, camera slung around his neck. Scuse me.

The trainer was a stocky man with a shiny bald crown. He dressed all in black: T-shirt, trousers, Wellington boots. One hand gripped a crop. He pivoted and placed the crop on the back of the Bengal tiger, soothing it with gentle words in Thai.

Mazy glided into the cage, her heart jackhammering. The tiger didn't turn to look at her—the trainer's crop touched its shoulder, and it seemed to accept this as a direction.

Gordon's treat: a trip to the zoo. Mazy hadn't any idea that such a thing existed on the island. Ginger had taken her around the cramped cages while Gordon and Isaac disappeared for "business". She couldn't fathom what on earth could make a zoo a place for Gordon's venture, but at this stage she didn't care. Right now her entire world was focused, laser-like, on this living, breathing, gigantic tiger that she found herself joining on a raised platform.

'Noble' didn't begin to capture the essence of this beast. Its fine paws were as big as the trainer's face. 'Ignoble' did a pretty good job of capturing the situation: a magnificent cat demurely letting humans come in, sit beside it and drape one arm around its torso, so that humans on the other side of the bars could take a quick photo of the conquest of a wild beast.

Things were pretty slippery for Mazy that afternoon. The trainer had to catch her before she stumbled too heavily against the tiger. She focused on its stripes, then on its chest, undulating in the sticky heat of the dingy cell.

"Careful, pretty lady."

She put her arm around the beast's shoulders, as instructed, but the horror and the magic of it collided and she couldn't stand acquiescing to this travesty. Mazy lunged forward with her other arm to give the tiger a loving squeeze and the next minute got lost in a blur. What she knew was that the tiger *barked*. A roar, yes, but it was really like a dog's bark, only a thousand times more intense. She was against the wall, her bones, her skin, her pores reverberating from that sound, then she was on the floor and the trainer was screaming in Thai. A scuffle, a ballet of black Wellingtons, and they dragged her out of the cage on her ass.

"She's going to spray!"

Mazy was hit by a smell so pungent that it made her gag. Human distress cries. A final roar-bark before another set of bars clanged shut. She was on the floor amid the crowd— Ginger was there, too, making a space for her. Looking up, she saw Gordon and Isaac, with a man she didn't recognize, a scruffy peasant-looking type in a janitor's green overalls.

The bald trainer blocked her view. "What I tell you about touching tiger? You lucky bitch, still living with both your hands." He snarled an order at the janitor and strode off.

"Someone get her off the bloody floor," Gordon said, walking away. The janitor followed Gordon as Isaac helped her to her feet.

"Phew, Maze, you stink something awful," Isaac said.

She was totally sober now, every nerve on alert. As she apologized to everyone, she saw Gordon standing apart. He patted the janitor on the shoulder, the janitor nodded; the man was openly staring at Mazy in wonderment, and in her hyperaware state she found the male attention familiar yet childish. "What are you looking at?" she challenged him. "Never seen a woman before?"

"Not one that smells of tiger piss," said Gordon, wrinkling his nose as the janitor scurried into the zoo's interior. "We're done here." He turned to Isaac. "Take her back, will you?"

"What, you're not going back to the villa?" Isaac asked.

"Course I am. Call a taxi. I don't want her stinking up the van."

Chapter 3

Man and Dog

IT was in Hong Kong that Trav made and spent
a lot of money for the first time in his life.
He wasn't a saver because he had become convinced that he had enough audacity and guts
to make a fortune. That's why he traded commodity futures, and why, against the mounting
evidence, he thought he was good at it. Au-
dacious and gutsy were Trav's preferred adjec-
tives; others might have used 'reckless'. He was
a quintessential American, though, living today
to the full and to hell with tomorrow—that was
the doctor's opinion.

"You are a lucky man, Mister Travis."

"Thanks, doc. Although I'd feel more lucky if
my hand wasn't covered in plaster."

"You can keep this X-ray. You see, here, the
break. Metacarpal number five. They call this a
boxer fracture. Did you hit something with your
hand?"

"I punched someone."

"Oh. Thai people, you know, we are Buddhist. Better to smile than to fight."

"I'll remember that next time I watch some Muay Thai. So why am I so lucky, doc?"

"This one single fracture, it's very clean. You won't need surgery. Right now there's no infection, but I don't want to take any chances. You'll need to take these antibiotics. Take the set, every pill, twice a day until you've finished the entire pack."

"And the cast, and the sling?"

"Come back in one week, and we'll take off the sling. Move your other fingers. Like this? Very good, Mister Travis. Exercising them is good."

"And the cast?"

"Six weeks."

"Six weeks."

"It's not long, Mister Travis, it's nothing. You keep this dry and don't put inside a stick or anything to scratch it, even if it itches. Otherwise we just give you a new cast, and start all over again. Benadryl or other anti-histamines can help prevent a rash. Keep the hand lifted like this or it will swell."

"And when we're done, will I be back to normal?"

"Oh yes."

"I can even box again? You know, fight?"

"Why would you want do that?"

"Sometimes, doc, a guy's gonna want to throw a punch."

"But then you will come back to the hospital, Mister Travis."

17

Trav left the hospital on his own two feet with his hand wrapped in a clean bandage and resting in a sling. He had paid for outpatient care with cash. He stood alone in the parking lot, holding his face up to the sun, feeling the sweat already beading on his skin. Keep the cast dry? On an equatorial island?

The hospital was spread out like a resort on the northern side of Chaweng, the main tourist center on Koh Samui, but was too far from town to walk. Trav hailed a taxi.

Chaweng hadn't changed in character but seemed to have expanded its tentacles through even more valleys. Trav rated this sprawl just a notch above a beachfront sewer. Shops selling tats to obese white women. Skinny brown teenagers cruising on mopeds, looking for the next hustle. White men, maybe sex tourists, gorging on afternoon Carlsbergs. Everywhere he looked, a flowing river of sunburned, tattooed Westerners wearing Crocs and straw hats.

No wonder Asians think we're all decadent. Look at these fat assholes.

Trav got off at a DTAC shop. First order of business was to get a mobile phone, which was easy. Second was to get lodging. Trav opened his wallet and fished out a dog-eared business card: Mr. Montri, house for rent, and the number. He'd kept this for over a year as a memoriam of Caroline, or more accurately of that kind of life—shared—that he once had. It was one of several things from those days he hadn't brought himself to throw away. He hadn't imagined he'd actually use it.

He dialed from the porch outside DTAC, fumbling with his left thumb with the card wedged between good fingers on his bad hand. The conversation was confusing, with the snarl of cars, bikes and tuk-tuks making it almost impossible to hear Montri, but the house was free. He'd better get down there to have a look.

Next order of business: transport. He rented a blue Honda scooter for a month. Cash. He felt a twinge of nervousness as his US driver's license data was typed into a computer—who knew what those triad bastards could track down. He decided not to ask the attendant for directions. He'd find Montri's place eventually.

The kid secured Trav's duffel to the bike with stretch cords. The backpack stayed on Trav's back. It took him a few tries to turn the key in the ignition with his left hand. Got it. He propped his right on the handlebar. Cast ran halfway toward his elbow. Beads of sweat dotted his skin. *Don't put inside a stick or anything to scratch.* Good luck with that, doc.

It took longer than he remembered, maybe because in the past he had made this trip in the air-conditioned comfort of a car's back seat, holding Caroline's hand with his perfectly good ones. The duffel balanced precariously behind him. It was too big for the bike, and he knew that driving one-handed wasn't safe, so he kept it slow. He left the helmet in its cache beneath the hind seat, preferring the sun and wind: *I'm in Thailand, man.*

Most of the route was pretty obvious, just following the island's ring road, skirting the cliff-lined coast. The stretch through Lamai was tedious, for this low-key village had morphed into a long, ugly strip dedicated to the tourist trade. Signs in misspelled English, German and Russian occupied every nook. 'Cheap Gassoline, Bt40.' 'Der Beste Thai-Massage in Lamai.' And everywhere, suggestions to buy land and build a condo.

He turned left off the highway. The road eventually emptied along a village on the beach, a quiet cluster of homes and restaurants on the shore side, a few shops and properties under construction land-side. This he remembered. He didn't know what this hamlet was called, but he had stayed here in a happier time, and he knew it offered the hideaway he needed.

At the far end of the hamlet, looming over the palm trees, stood a grey peaked roof shaped like a giant trapezoid. It was a villa, *the* villa, and anyone on its balcony commanded a view of the road and most of the village, like a castle lording over the fief.

Nestled in a copse of trees alongside the villa, facing the sea, was a modest wooden house on stilts. A giant painting of the unsmiling king and queen, resplendent in gold, capped its entrance.

He parked the bike and walked through a clutter of buckets and brooms that filled the entry, up the creaky wooden stairs to the veranda where the Montris operated a restaurant. He regarded the palms, the beach and the marine blue sea. It might take a while, but if there was a vista capable of easing the pain throbbing through his body and the panic stirring his gut, this had to be it.

Old man Montri and his wife were there, and one of the kids. Montri was the one in the family with the best English; he answered the phone, he dealt with the tourists. He led Trav down the other side of the restaurant onto the beach. Behind the restaurant, invisible from the road, was a small house, also raised on stilts, with a porch and a peaked tin roof. It appeared to be the domain of a dog, a big brown mutt, who didn't bother to raise her nose from the comfort of a cushioned rattan chair. The dog's eyes merely watched the old man unlock the door and show Trav inside.

Not much to it: yellow-green linoleum floors and a fluorescent light. Kitchenette, TV, table and sofa. Three doors—bathroom, two bedrooms, only one with air-con. Trav bargained a little but the price wasn't much to begin with. He opened his backpack, trying to obscure its contents but the plastered hand fumbled and out cascaded wads of baht. Old man Montri didn't have to say a word. His eyes betrayed his amazement.

Chapter 4

Gamma Trades

"FUTURES."

"Dude, it's me, Trav."

"What the—Trav? Are you for real?"

"Kar-wei, I just wanted to let you know I'm OK and say good bye."

"Let me know you're OK? Jesus, man, nobody round here gives a shit if you're OK. They're praying you're dead."

"I saw the news. WTI's been volatile."

"Volatile? Trav, man, your positions—are you aware how much you've lost?"

Trav stared at the sea impassively. "Couple of bucks?"

On the other end, Kar-wei, at the desk in Hong Kong, paused for breath. "You're almost five hundred in the hole."

Trav couldn't believe it. Five hundred million? "Wally OKed those positions."

"Not according to compliance."

"It's in the e-mails."

"Trav, listen to me." Kar-wei's voice fell to a whisper. "You know I gotta tell them I spoke to you, or it's my ass too."

"Sure, I understand."

"Man, you gotta get lawyered up."

"I'm out, Kar-wei. Something happened, I had to go."

"Yeah, I know something happened, you fucked up, man. They've shut down our desk. Three people lost their jobs."

"No, no. Something else. I was in a fight. It ended badly. What, you think I skipped town because of something from work?"

"That's what everybody says. They're using your name in the same sentence as Nick Leeson. Bloomberg's been calling all week. It's a shitstorm here, man."

"You think I left because of...of...market vol, because of gamma trades on West Texas Intermediate? You think I'm scared of *interest rates*?"

"Dickhead, we live our lives in mortal fucking terror of interest rates."

Trav was dumbfounded. "I had no idea, Kar-wei, you got to believe me."

"Where are you? Where you calling from?"

"Not Hong Kong. It's not safe."

"I gotta go, man. Listen to me and get a lawyer. The bank's coming after you."

"Kar-wei, thanks, man, and sorry."

"Don't call me again." Kar-wei hung up.

Trav scratched the dog behind her ears. It was morning, the tide was up and the current swift.

The kingfishers flashed brightly in the trees. Beyond the tidewater hovered blue limestone mountain-islands, utterly unmoved by Trav's puny fate. He felt very small then, a sensation he despised.

"I guess this is good material for the novel," he said to the dog, who didn't disagree.

Fleeing, though strange and scary, had been a typical decision for him. He always boasted he shot from the hip. Seat of the pants, he'd say. Thailand was a pretty known quantity to an expat living in Hong Kong—Key West to a New Yorker, so it had seemed like an easy choice. Late at night, as his worst decisions paraded through his memory, he'd wonder why he seemed incapable of thinking ahead more than one or two steps.

Sometimes he'd let his thoughts wander, all the way back to that night as a sixteen-year-old when a car bent around a tree and he became an orphan. From stunned boy to foolish man, going hell for leather, damn the torpedoes —name your cliché. He'd lay awake in the darkness thinking, *I'm a cliché. I'm a joke.* And come morning he'd try to feel like he was on the roller-coaster, waving his arms in the air, screaming his lungs out, because it beat sitting around with himself for company.

That ethos—*accelerate through life*—made this latest improvised move hard to take. Samui was paradise. Samui was quiet. Samui was for tourists who paid for simulated experiences instead of really living with danger. He missed the pace of the trading floor and the filthy banter with the guys. He missed taking clients out and getting hammered in Lan Kwai Fong. He missed the buzz of getting rich when the futures markets went into contango—he even missed his loudmouth boss, fat Wally—and wondered if they missed him, Travis Mitchell, the dumbass Houdini who'd pulled the disappearing act.

He missed the way his work had helped him forget Caroline, but he didn't miss the way coming home every night to an empty flat in Mid-Levels had reminded him of her. He hated those late-night reviews of his worst errors because so many revolved around her. She had tolerated his shit for longer than he had expected. Maybe it had been love.

He missed the training: the early morning workouts in the gym with Heinz and Master Lee. He missed the reliability of it, the discipline, the advances, the setbacks, the bruises, the abrasions, the blood on his knuckles. The tightness of the wraps cocooning his hands, not at all like this plaster cast that itched so much he bit his tongue to the point of pain. He missed using his hands—both of them. He was sorry he hadn't had the chance to say goodbye, but then Heinz, who credibly billed himself Asia's most dangerous martial arts trainer, would probably kill him now if their paths ever crossed.

Literally kill him.

Trav didn't miss Kang. Not one frickin' bit.

And he didn't ever let himself think about a young fighter named Chi-Man. All Trav had known about this guy was, first, his name, which initially had meant nothing to him; second, his record, which had been 12 wins, 4 losses (make that now 12 and 5); third, that Heinz had told him Chi-Man was meant to win; and fourth and last, that they had shared a mere eight minutes of combined time in the ring together, the first seven and a half of which had gone according to plan.

Caroline, Kang, Wally, Chi-Man...the absent parents, obliterated on the New Jersey turnpike ...

OK, his career in finance was over, and he didn't have the faintest idea of what country he'd even be in a few months from now. He'd always thought it would be easy to write a novel —that's what went through his head when he bolted from Hong Kong. Tell the tale. But now that he was here, he didn't want to think about any of that. Write what you know, they said, but he didn't want to go anywhere near what he knew.

Trav opened his Mac on the kitchen table a day after moving in. That didn't work so he tried it on the porch, but he felt bad about kicking the dog out of her favorite chair. Couldn't type much with just his left hand. Eventually he carried the Mac over to Montri's restaurant where he mostly spent his time, sipping Changs and occasionally ordering a bowl of tom yum or a dish of fried fish, gazing at the sea when he wasn't staring at the blank screen.

One night he buried the backpack beneath the porch. Next morning he found the dog had dug it up. Next night, he tried a copse of bamboo. Same thing. He considered hiding it atop one of the palms, but sometimes there were monkeys up there.

It took him the better part of an afternoon to carve out a hole in the bottom of the mattress in the guest bedroom using kitchen knives. He had to endure the babbling over loudspeakers the whole time.

The geckos honked at night; the roosters cawed in the early dawn; the man's voice shattered the morning calm. Always the same man, whose voice boomed through the village from a network of loudspeakers. The entire village was wired up and came alive several times a day with babble. For an hour or sometimes two, the man spoke, sometimes calmly, sometimes with the fervor of a sermon or a diatribe.

The villagers went about their chores without paying any attention, so far as Trav could tell. The water buffaloes, kept tied to the trunks of palm trees in the adjacent lots, didn't seem to mind the sermons one bit. Trav knew from his excursions that other nearby villages also had to endure these regular intrusions. There was no way to change the channel; there was no switch to turn it off.

At first it made him simmer but eventually he, too, was able to put the broadcasts into the background. They became his way of telling time and he stopped wearing a watch. There was the morning sermon that woke him up. There was another in the late morning, the blessed end of which heralded lunch. And some days there was one in the late afternoon. Did the islanders have seven days a week? Did they know what a weekend was?

After a week he went back to the hospital and the doc removed the sling. Five weeks to go for the cast. It was getting dirty and ragged along the edge, so the doctor trimmed it with scissors.

"This thing itches like hell."

The doc told him to take a blow dryer, put it on 'cool', and aim it along the crack of his cast. See if that did the trick. Trav didn't say anything back; there was no hair dryer at the house.

Trav tried going for an early morning jog. He didn't get far before the pain forced him to stop. Besides, the doctor had warned him off sports, because it made him sweat, which made the cast get wet and stink like a locker room. Trav practiced some of the yoga he'd picked up instead, some of the bends and twists. It wasn't much, but it was better than nothing, and if he did it inside the bedroom with the air conditioner running at full blast, he didn't sweat.

The only time the cast didn't drive him half crazy was when Montri let him join one of his boat tours. The old man owned a longtail boat, a long, narrow skiff that he used to sell rides to tourists. Montri stood in the back, one hand on the heavy propeller that doubled as a rudder, and Trav and the tourists baked in the late-morning sun. Once the boat cleared the shallows, Montri gunned it and the wind from skipping across the sea felt delightful, even if the ride was bumpy and the seat uncomfortable. Trav had been facing outward and it was only on the return that he realized how big the villa was, the way it lorded over the village. The top floor was open, front and back, and he could make out a figure crossing the living area. He had to look away, then, in case he glimpsed a ghost from his past life.

Montri had refused to accept his cash for the ride. The old man seemed to enjoy his company, although Trav couldn't fathom why. Montri, in his creole English, suggested Trav could come along again. The opportunity never emerged, however, and Trav spent more time alone in the rented hut.

His greatest accomplishment after the boat ride was learning to cook one-handed. Hardest was to make an omelet. He'd brought back two dozen eggs from the grocery store in Lamai. He probably smashed or dropped half of them before figuring out how to open them with his left hand. Then came the realization that he needed to turn the eggs over. The spatula felt alien to his available fingers. A lot of eggs ended up on the floor before he figured out how to flip them. Halcyon days for the dog, who immediately developed a taste for cooked eggs. When he finally aced it, he let out a childish whoop that sent her skittering out the door.

"It's all in the wrist, baby," he told her as she poked her nose back inside.

Trav never once again looked at the big villa or glanced at the compound walls or took his strolls that way.

Chapter 5

Mango Smoothie Surprise

MIDDAY, the loudspeakers crackled and the man's voice resumed its lecture to the village.

"What's he saying?" Trav was sitting on the wooden veranda, drinking a beer and looking at the calm straits instead of whatever drivel he had just typed on the Mac.

"Sorry?" It was the oldest son, the one who had spent time in Bangkok and spoke some English.

"The guy on the loudspeaker." He gestured expansively.

"Sorry," the son said with a big smile. Bigger the smile, less likely you were going to get a helpful response. Trav waved the kid away. He reread his work and vaguely grasped how far it was from anything good. No idea what day of the week it was, but he knew that time was nearing an inflection point. He could almost make a fist with his right hand. Soon he'd be free to scratch his right arm all the way to heaven.

He walked back to his house to take a whiz. It was OK to leave the Mac up there, he trusted the family to look after it. There were always a handful of tourists or locals, either on the veranda or at the tables on the beach, but the place was never crowded, and by dint of habit the corner table was acknowledged among the Montri clan as his.

Trav broke out a couple of dozen one-handed push-ups on the porch, under the puzzled eyes of the dog. A few stretches finished the impromptu workout. Feeling better, he shuffled towards the veranda, trying to figure his way around the stupid story he was trying to write. A woman was walking down the steps of Montri's restaurant to the beach, carrying a large mango drink. His chest stammered in recognition. Her, here. He'd have to hope she hadn't recognized him, but she glanced at him, too, and there was a questioning pause in her gait. She had long healthy legs, blue shorts about as short as they could get, and a flowing gauzy top. Dark hair bounced off her shoulders. Trav walked up to the veranda, not wanting to draw attention to himself with a sudden U-turn, while she meandered toward one of the concrete tables beneath the palms.

Trav took his usual spot, leaning the plastic chair on its hind legs.

Think, you idiot. You've been spotted by someone from Hong Kong. And that means your time here could be about to come to an end. He entertained a number of arguments along the line of "what are the odds" but knew that in Asia, expats traveled in similar circles and the odds were actually pretty good. *The villa, you dipshit.* The villa got a lot of traffic, including once his own. If he should be surprised he had but to remember it was going nearly a month on Koh Samui without encountering anyone he knew; it was only by sticking to the remote village that he had managed to remain hidden.

He also thought, with more hope than sense, *I wonder who she's with.*

Maybe he'd better do a reconnaissance mission, just to make sure the woman was really the one from Hong Kong. Not to check her out for any other purpose. *Definitely not.* He walked over to the counter where old Mama was watching a Thai variety show on a tiny TV, the volume turned low.

"Can I get a Chang please?"

Not yet lunchtime but he needed something to do with his hands—well, hand. He nonchalantly strolled to the beach-facing side of the veranda and leaned against one of the wooden pillars. He looked at the sea and the islands beyond. He regarded the clouds in the sky. He removed his shades and cleaned them roughly against the edge of his T-shirt. He put them back on and glanced down and to the left. Only two of the tables on the beach were occupied, one by a pair of Thais. She stared at him from the other and he felt another wham in his chest.

He pretended not to notice her and returned to his table. He stared at his computer screen without seeing a thing. He didn't look up when she eventually climbed the veranda steps. He kept his gaze squarely on those meaningless computer-screen scrawlings as he heard her ask for another mango smoothie. His hackles were up. He could sense her leaning against the counter, those long legs taking their time to reach the dolphin tattoos swimming around her ankles. She might have been regarding him.

"Must be good, whatever you're watching." American accent. Yep, it was her.

"Just trying to concentrate," Trav sort of mumbled.

Mama got the woman her mango smoothie but she didn't leave. "I know you. You're one of my students."

Fingered. It was almost a relief.

"From yoga," he said.

"Been a while. Where've you been?" There was a sneer in her tone.

"Around. Nowhere. Here."

"What's your name again?"

"Trav. Travis."

"That's right. You go by Trav."

"Mazy, right?" Like he didn't know her god-damn name.

"Yeah, but I go by Maze." She said it with such a wide smile that he couldn't tell if she was mocking him. She read his discomfort. "Oh well, see you later, Trav." She wafted toward the steps, her tight rear end wobbling a little, as if she were unsteady on heels. But she was barefoot. Not what you'd expect from a yoga instructor. Was she tipsy? As she descended toward the beach, she said, "Come over if you want some company."

How could she be tipsy on mango smoothies? Mazy. He'd been taking classes at the studio, part of the training recommended by Heinz. Mostly Indian brothers in there, one skinnier than the next, all of them able to fold like origami swans. You bet he took notice of the new instructor, with her skin and her accent and her tats and her everything. He'd had just a couple of classes with her, before the fight. And now she has to turn up here, in this back-of-nowhere village, and remember him.

Idiot. It might be useful to know who she was with. To figure out what his next move was going to be.

He wandered down to where she was sitting by herself in the shade of a palm. A dollop of orange mush brightened the sand and grass. As if she had poured most of the smoothie onto the ground. Which, judging by the near-empty bottle of Absolut that rested next to the expunged smoothie, was exactly what she had done, leaving just enough mango in the big glass to make the cocktail palatable.

"Is that lunch or breakfast?" he asked, sitting on one of the palm stumps that served as a stool.

"Neither. I'm on a diet."

"Have to admit, Maze, this isn't in keeping with your granola image."

"Fuck you."

"Hey, it's cool. I like it. You're going against the grain is all."

She picked up the vodka bottle. "I'm going *with* the grain, Trav."

"Yeah, I guess you are. So, how long you been here?"

"You saw me come in."

"I mean on Koh Samui."

"A couple of weeks. We're..." She gestured—and frowned—beyond his shoulder and he knew that meant the big villa. "We're very comfortable."

"It's a beautiful place."

"You should see it."

"I have. I mean, a year ago, about. I stayed there once."

"So now you're just...lurking."

"Lurking. Yeah. I'm staying nearby. Just chilling out. Who you with?"

"That's very weird, Travis. If you don't mind my saying so. First you stay at the villa, and now you come back to Samui and...you're a sneaky type."

He had no idea what to make of this. "Just living cheap."

"What are you doing lurking and sneaking?"

"Uh, not much. Taking time off from work. Working on that novel, you know?"

"A novel, wow. What's it about?"

"Financial thriller. You know, behind the scenes and stuff."

"What happened to your hand?"

"Hit by a car back in Hong Kong."

He couldn't tell if she bought the lie. Mazy kept her eyes on him as she slurped the last of her concoction through the straw. "Time for another smoothie."

"Want me to get it for you?"

She held the glass aloft. "What a gentleman."

He ran the errand. Waiting for Mama, he felt in a daze. Three sheets to the wind and still a knockout. Somehow kept her poise. He hadn't figured out if she was all Caucasian or Eurasian. White skin, black hair, eyes like lunar eclipses. Pert nose, cute as hell. He still didn't know. When he got back to her table he chucked out half the smoothie, and then handed it to her. She smiled at him as she unscrewed the vodka bottle and re-filled the cup. It gave him a hard-on, that smile.

"I don't like you," she said after the first swig. "You're sneaky smart."

"Funny, most people call me a dumb son of a bitch."

"Maybe they're wrong. Cheers."

They touched cup to beer bottle and he stumbled on what next to say. He told himself he needed to stick around, learn a little more. Not that he wanted to linger—or lurk. The two of them regarded the current and the lonely fishing boat and the blue islands.

"That's a big villa," he said. "You here with a big group?"

"It gets big at night. Who you here with?"

"Me? Nobody. I mean, nobody right now."

"The Lone Ranger." She squinted. "Is your nose crooked, cowboy?"

"Kind of a recent development."

"Makes you kind of ugly, you know."

"Thanks. You're gorgeous. Feel free to take that the wrong way."

"Just because I'm drunk doesn't—" She stiffened. Trav looked over his shoulder. A man was coming down the veranda steps wearing just camouflage shorts and a beard, murmuring into a cell phone. Like her, sculpted, not an ounce of fat, but even from here Trav could tell this guy's leanness was of a different type from Mazy's. Wound up tight, the boxer's wariness, black eyes that frowned. Not open like a *trikonasana*, the extended triangle pose in yoga that spread your chest wide and helped you breathe—coiled.

And those studs in his earlobes, big steel cylinders that created open holes you could stick a finger through.

The man snapped his phone shut and pocketed it. "So this is where you are," he said to Mazy. British accent.

"I just took a little walk along the beach."

Trav saw her grip the cup so tightly her knuckles turned white.

"Yeah, well, you can take a little walk back."

She stood up and said to Trav, "Nice seeing you, cowboy."

"Who's this then." The man gave Trav an efficiently cold appraisal.

"Just a tourist," Trav replied.

"I wasn't addressing you, was I? I'm asking you, Maze, who is this?" Trav wasn't good at taking apart English accents, but this one was kind of an overwrought cockney, if such a thing existed; street arch.

"Just a guy sitting here having a beer," she said.

Trav stood up as the man drew a step closer, the man's body wary and poised, looking for trouble. Trav instinctively loosened his arms and knees.

"Tourist," the man said to him. "Enjoying the sun and sand. Thousand baht for a shag. Fucking paradise. I always say you get what you pay for, but I'm going to offer you a bit of free advice, and I suggest you take it. Stay well away from me and what's mine or this island won't be paradise any more."

Trav raised his left palm in contrition. "No offense meant, buddy."

"Because I'm a reasonable man, and I know what a drunken slut she can be, none taken. Mazy, now."

She walked past Trav to the man, maintaining a straight line despite her three prodigious vodkas. The boyfriend put a hairy arm around her waist. "I missed you, darling."

"I'm sorry. I should have let you know I was going for a walk." She kissed the man as they walked arm in arm back along the beach.

Trav watched them thread through the sparse palm tree trunks, all the way down the beach, her head nestled on his shoulder. They walked along the low wall that framed the villa's sea front. At the steps leading up to the villa a third figure emerged, white and obviously hulking, even at this distance. He lingered on the beach after Mazy and the man disappeared into the villa compound, as though waiting for Trav to make a move.

Chapter 6

Catching Coconuts

L YING in bed, weak from nausea, Mazy indulged a daydream. It had begun as a real memory, of her running on the beach. She was flee-ing for her life—that was the nightmare part that still lingered, but as the dream crossed into something more aware, she focused more on the power of her body, the pounding of her muscles, the sure rhythm of her expanding lungs, the businesslike pumping of their heart engines.

Their? Yes, because he was alongside her now, in this dream, Travis. It was not a girl-ish rendition, no holding hands and kicking up surf. It felt very grown-up, as though she were dreaming of a man as a...a business part-ner, a man who with his cropped blonde hair and muscular, bronzed body exuded compe-tence (never mind his crooked nose). It was the escape that was the fantasy.

She eventually roused herself late in the day, resigned to the familiarity of a hangover. It felt bad to get up but it felt bad to just lie there, too. The room was chilled from a day's worth of air conditioning. Mazy walked naked into the en suite bathroom, wearing a skin of goosebumps. It took the water a while to heat up but the shower helped. She stood beneath the rain showerhead puzzling over why Trav had snuck into her head like that.

Dressed in shorts and a T-shirt, she slid open the glass doors, parted the drapes and stepped into the dry warmth of late afternoon. Outdoor speakers blasted Radiohead. The room she shared with Gordon—although *shared* was a generous term, because Gordon didn't really share anything—was the largest in the complex, set down at sea level alongside the giant infinity pool that served as the compound's centerpiece.

Across the pool, beneath the *sala*, a Thaistyled gazebo, she saw them playing a game of cards. Isaac and Ginger usually killed the time upstairs playing Grand Theft Auto. Maybe Gordon got sick of the noise. Isaac was about to play a card but both men paused to steal a look at her.

"Hey there, Maze," said Isaac.

Isaac styled himself a gentleman, relishing the little formalities even in the privacy of the villa. A white linen shirt hung loosely on his narrow ebony frame. He sported blue trunks, Italian loafers, and his hallmark white trilby with a black band. He was Gordon's chemist. When he wasn't at the lab, he helped keep an eye on the place, and on her, which he obviously relished, but in a harmless, naïve schoolboy way.

"Quit perving the boss's girl," said Ginger, born Chester Collins, a white beef-patty of a man boasting a new class-A sunburn almost as brassy red as his close-cropped hair. He wore tight black bathing trunks and flip-flops, showing off his body builder's physique. Ginger's piggy blue eyes squinted at his opponent, and, trying to sound like an American tough guy, he said, "I just wanted to piss you off before I killed you." The two of them were always reciting inane lines from Grand Theft Auto. "Jack to your eight-nine-ten, mate, and that's gin."

Ginger was normally stationed up top, where he could keep an eye on the road. If he was down here playing cards with Isaac, that meant Gordon had company and wanted privacy.

"Jammy bastard," Isaac growled as he threw a few baht on the table.

"Hey, guys," Mazy said as she headed for the sandstone stairs leading up to the top floor of the superstructure.

"Best not to go up right now," Chester said.

"You got anything to eat?"

"Crisps and Coke Zero."

She devoured a bag as they played another hand. "Keep standing there, Maze, you're killing his concentration," Ginger said as he picked up the jack of spades discarded by Isaac. "Three jacks to you, Mother Africa."

Isaac soured at this next loss of face. "What?"

Another GTA line: "Just think of this as so-cialism in action."

"No wonder Gordon says never trust a Scouser."

Ginger said, "Shut your gob and get on with your knitting, Granny."

Isaac shuffled, dealt. The sun fell behind the palms looming over the compound wall. The sky turned purple and the breeze picked up. The potato chips only served to sharpen her appetite.

"I'm going up," Mazy decided. She lifted Isaac's hat and kissed his forehead. It was a gesture she would have never granted Ginger. Both men were always ogling her, but differently, and she hadn't forgotten the way Ginger had fondled her. "That's for luck, Isaac."

"You work miracles, Maze," said a smiling Isaac, laying down cards. Now, faux Eastern European from the video game: "You think you're ready for me? Watch and learn. Caution: genius at work." He threw down three aces and Mazy rewarded him with a smile.

"Aww, puppy love," Ginger cooed, but there was nothing humorous in his voice. Mazy headed for the villa top. "You been warned," he called after her.

"I'll yell first." She climbed the flight of sun-toned sandstone steps. As her eyes peeked over the topmost one, her bravery expired. "It's me," she called, knowing how foolish it would be to simply materialize unbidden.

No answer. She walked to the top.

The upper level was one giant space beneath a vaulted ceiling. The sliding doors at both front and back were always left open, encouraging the breeze to flow from the sea through to the garden and driveway facing the land. Between the balconies overlooking both directions ran a series of furnished set pieces: sofas to watch TV, a dining table that sat eight, a bathroom, and a luxurious kitchen, with its own island counter surrounded by bar stools.

The maid, Lek, was at the sink washing dishes, while Gordon hunched over the island on one of the stools, pondering the mountain of coconuts that had taken over the countertop. Coconuts sliced this way and that, coconut water slickening the counter, the smell of coconut defying the ocean breeze. A chopper and a kitchen knife lay near his right hand, while in his left was what looked like a cross between a hair dryer and a drill.

Gordon held up coconut, his left hand setting down its bulky pistol-shaped tool. "Come here." As she approached he heaved the coconut at her, like a shot put. She caught it with a woomph, the husk biting her hands. "What do you make of it?"

Mazy held it up. "It's a coconut."

"It's reassuring to know the bleeding obvious never escapes you. What else?"

She turned it around and shrugged.

"Good." He ambled over to the sink, the maid side-stepping out of his path, and rinsed his hands. "I fucking hate coconuts."

45

Mazy walked past the kitchen table. The weapon was indeed a pistol; printed on the holster was 'Black & Decker Glue Gun – Electric Hot!'

"I came up to get a snack. I haven't eaten all day."

"Don't spoil your appetite. We're going out for dinner tonight."

That gave her a little jolt of happiness. "Good! We've been cooped up here all week."

"Well, we may have something to celebrate, and I expect you to dress the part."

She placed a hand on his shoulder. "Should I pick out something for you, too?"

"I'm wearing my Gucci blazer. But tell the lads not to overdo it, get all blingy."

"OK."

"The problem with blokes these days is they think dressing like a hip-hop rapper is style."

"I'll tell them to look sharp." She moved her hand to the back of his head and leaned in to kiss him, but he seized her wrist and his black eyes revealed no mirth.

"How do you know that man from the beach restaurant?"

"Who says I do? He's just some tourist."

"I say you do. You said to him, 'Nice seeing you.'"

"Gordon, you're hurting me."

"When you leave a stranger, you say, 'Nice meeting you.' When you leave someone you know, you say, 'Nice seeing you.' I'm not fucking deaf, Maze. Who is he?"

"Seriously, I don't know. I guess he must have been in one of my classes because that's what he said."

"So he lives in Hong Kong then."

"I guess so. He came up to me, Gordon, I didn't recognize him from Adam. Can you please …let go of my wrist?"

"What's his name?"

"I told you I don't know this guy. He introduced himself but I can't remember—ow! Travis. His name is Travis."

"Last name?"

"I don't know. Gordon, I swear I don't know!" She was now practically on her knees, Gordon leaning over her, two fingers clasped on her wrist's pressure points. He let her squirm for a moment longer then released her. She groaned and flapped her hand back to life. "That really hurt."

"What really hurts is that the woman who professes to love me lets herself get sweet-talked by one of her yoga students instead of telling him to sod off. What hurts me is this lack of loyalty."

"A girl can tell a guy to sod off nicely. Not everybody does things like you."

"Well, now you know. Next time no polite conversation, all right?"

"All right."

"That's my girl. How about a smile for Gordon? Yes, that's it, love, fantastic." He kissed her and tapped her bum. "I've got a few things to sort out up here."

Mazy was relieved to be excused. As she descended to the pool area, she focused on breathing through the nostrils, practicing her pranayama. *Don't come near me, cowboy. He now has your name.*

Chapter 7

Follow That Van

IT was nighttime by the time Trav drove back to the house. It wasn't very late, but in the tropics, once the sun goes down, the darkness is swift and complete. He had spent the day going through the motions of being a tourist, turning onto the dirt road behind the Buddhist temple in Lamai and heading for the interior. The Honda scooter struggled much of the way on the unpaved track, but traffic was sparse.

He stopped frequently to let the jungle and the hills envelop him with their spare silence. Buddhist statues and makeshift temples surprised from around corners, and he ate from a lonely stand an incredibly spicy bowl of glass noodles in dark beef broth, its fire making him sweat. He relished the pain and the noise of the wind when he drove—loved the way these things blocked out everything else.

Like the white-hot realization that Maze had seen him come out of his rental house and all her domineering boyfriend had to do was ask her about it.

Like the understanding that the boyfriend was a dangerous man. Trav had seen types like him, at the gym, in the ring. Pals of Heinz, men high on their physical prowess. Mazy's lover was not a man he wanted to cross paths with.

Trav barely made it back to Lamai in time to refill the gas tank. Mama and old Montri closed the restaurant at night, but there was a small open market across the street where they cooked the day's catch and the local men got drunk on whisky and gambled on the Premier League. Tonight there was also a Thai country band and karaoke.

He pulled onto the side of the road as he approached the market. He had a clear line of sight to the front of the villa. The gate was lit up at night, the exterior a bland yellow slate. Montri's beachfront restaurant was dark and still; his rental house lay behind it, out of sight. Trav idled the Honda's engine by the market's entrance, where the noise from the big TV screen showing Chelsea at Everton competed with a sappy country ballad.

There were one or two Westerners in the market, but it was a mostly local crowd. Children burst around him in play, levitating a cloud of dust. The gate was moving and Trav waited, not knowing for what. Looked like two of the villa servants, a Thai man and woman, walking in the parking area behind the sliding gate door, their silhouettes glowing red from a retreating vehicle. A soccer ball bounced in front of his bike and children fluttered in his line of sight. A van backed out from behind the villa wall, a stylish Toyota Alphard, tall and sleek and black as the nighttime sea.

You here with a group? he had asked her. "It gets big at night."

He watched the van head north toward Lamai.

Dude, you're laying low, remember? Then another voice within his conscience said, *And remember the way he bullied her on the beach, like she was a piece of property.* He remembered the bearded boyfriend's aura of violence, his egregious rudeness, the way he had dictated terms to her and Trav.

He walked the scooter in a tight U-turn. In the rear compartment was the helmet he never wore, and now he put it on and lowered the visor, white skin hidden. The van's red lights disappeared around a bend in the road. He drove back through the village and followed it.

They got caught in the traffic that thickened through the artery that defined Lamai. Trav thought he could make out the van, because of its size, but there was now a long queue of vehicles between them: taxis, tarp-covered pickups, Thai nuclear families propped up on a single motorbike. For the second time that day he angled around the monastery at the village's heart and crawled on, smelling his own fetidness, sometimes wiping his hands dry on his shorts when he had the chance.

Eventually the village lost cohesion and the van accelerated into altitude, the road now winding along the cliff edges, nothing but inscrutable ink beyond the occasional resort on the roadside. They could be headed to one of the fancy restaurants that lined the highway. Or heading further north to Chaweng, or for all he knew going a step further to the airport. Airport would be best, for if they were leaving Samui then Trav would be forgotten, but it also meant he'd never see her again.

Hold up, hold up, pal. Was that – yeah, that was the van, parking in front of one of the cliff-clinging resorts, red lights flicking on and off as it eased alongside the entrance. He didn't have the opportunity to stop here and the road bent abruptly. There was another restaurant just ahead. Trav signaled and turned around there, forced to wait for the traffic to thin before he could head back to the resort entrance where the van had stopped.

He spotted what he had hoped to find, a shoulder on this side of the road, landside. It connected to a small lane that climbed up the mountainside, toward the skeletons of half-built holiday homes. It provided plenty of space directly across from the waiting black van.

Trav pulled over and tried to observe them through the traffic. The van must have emptied because now its driver was edging it back onto the road, continuing north, probably to some nearby parking lot.

The passengers were just making their way inside, beneath the roof of a well-lit pavilion. He thought he saw three men, two Caucasians and one black, and a white woman in a shawl and skirt. Was that Mazy? One of the white guys was definitely the boyfriend, recognizable in his white linen suit thanks to the dark beard. He had only a passing notion of the other two men who walked with the swagger of fearlessness.

Another black van pulled up, this one smaller and carrying what looked like Thai passengers, and his view of the entrance was blocked.

OK, Marlowe, what's the next move?

He figured he had time to get something to eat, and went back to a hawker stall in Lamai that served crispy pork and noodles and provided a toilet. Then he was back on the shoulder of the same road, parked beneath the ghostly unfinished development up the hill, ready to pretend he had a flat tire, keeping the helmet on despite the stifling heat but the visor up so he could see. The waiting was deadly, the roadside filthy with exhaust and noise, and his wrist itched like crazy inside its cast. He was too scared to pace or stretch, lest he attract attention. He had to stand there and take it.

Chapter 8

Lady Song

Mazy was eager for them to start pouring the drinks. It was the only remedy available to her. She was careful not to overdo it and get sloppy, lest a careless remark trigger Gordon. Of course, these days she had no idea what might set him off. His tenor of confidence, which initially in its modest dose had proven attractive, had morphed into a paranoid ego trip. He stayed sharp, that much she knew.

Gordon had arranged for the resort's most private table, located at the far end of the restaurant, beyond the rows of bulbous red Chinese lanterns, down a set of stairs along the giant, smooth granite rocks that marked where cliff met sand. Waves washed up a few feet away from where the two waitresses busied themselves around their party. They were nine now, having been joined by two Thai men and three Thai women wearing cheap glitzy dresses and too much makeup.

Mazy kept quiet and tried to look like she was bedazzled by their surroundings. *Where the hell's that refill?*

It was a get-to-know-you occasion, business-men sealing the deal. The Thai men were Gor-don's contacts and seemed utterly out of place in this restaurant, while the women were ob-viously prostitutes who spoke pidgin English and clasped themselves noisily around Isaac and Ginger. The Brits dressed like men of the world, pinstripes substituting for class: Paul Smith or Armani silk shirts, thin pants and elegant shoes, Gordon even enduring a white linen jacket that had crumpled in the humidity. As ever, Gordon's precious Samsung phone lay on the table, a totem of his belief that someone extremely important was always just about to call.

The two Thai men were studies in contrast. The one called Tarrin boasted spiky hair, pock-marked cheeks and the air of a cocky street thug. He sported baggy hip-hop gear, a gold medallion and a garish baseball cap twisted to the side. One of the women was his, apparently; barely out of her teenage years, pretty by sheer dint of youth, she fed him with her spoon and squealed whenever he pinched her.

Jaidee, on the other hand, had the disheveled, confused look of a migrant worker. He refused to touch the expensive Bordeaux and ordered something called Lady Song, a whisky with a bouquet to tickle the most hardy of palates, as Maze discovered when he poured her the first shot; seated between Mazy and Ginger, Jaidee was the one male without a female companion. Mazy had removed her shawl, revealing her bare shoulders and their latticework of tattoos, and given him an encouraging smile. She took genuine pleasure in knowing, as she knocked back the drink, that accepting cheap local hooch amid Western luxury offended Gordon's snobbery. It occurred to her that she had seen this uneasy man, Jaidee, somewhere recently.

"Perhaps we should save the whisky for later," Gordon said, and proceeded to command the ordering of food.

Mazy suspected the Thais couldn't read English, and would despise whatever was laid before them. The Thai women whispered to the waitress, who brought them individual bowls of rice, the only food they'd touch that evening.

The Thai men picked apprehensively at the fish and the pasta, and kept mainly to their own tipples: Singha beer for Tarrin, Lady Song for Jaidee. Mazy nearly burst out laughing when Tarrin requested the usual Thai condiments of chili and fish sauce for the lamb shanks Gordon had ordered for him. The comedy came partly from the culture clash, but mostly at the way the whole embarrassment seemed to flummox Gordon. For once he couldn't scream "You stupid cunts," even though that was surely what he was thinking. Ginger and Isaac caught the mood, too, and raised the volume of their football banter.

"Jaidee, can I have another?" she said, stretching out her shot glass.

"Yes, time for a toast," Gordon said, raising his glass of wine. The only sound then was the gurgle of Lady Song leaving its bottle. "Right. It's been a most productive few weeks for all of us here on Koh Samui. Here's to the fortune we are about to make."

"To the big fuck money," said Tarrin.

"Too right, brother," Isaac intoned, "I loves the big fuck money."

"Cheers to that!" Ginger shouted.

The assorted glasses clinked, the Thai women smiling ignorantly, Mazy in a rush to down it.

"Hang on—Maze, hang on." Gordon reached into his jacket and pulled out a set of folded papers. "Get a pen from the waitress, there's a lass." Mazy signaled. "Now, we have already divvied up most of the benefits to our joint venture. But there's one last piece. And this will go to Mazy."

"Me?" she said, trying to sound as stupid as possible.

"Don't ask me to repeat myself." Gordon laid out a series of documents in front of her and snapped his fingers at the scurrying waitress. "Oi, I need a pen."

"What is it?"

"Well, love, this is a deed to a franchise of restaurants in Hong Kong which you are about to own."

Now she really did feel stupid. It felt as though the table, the waves, the bottles, the food—it was all receding in a rush and those papers were expanding to envelop her.

"I don't get it."

"No, you do get it. You get all three—the Chili Hut franchise. You know the one you like on Wellington? There's another in Causeway Bay and one in Sha Tin. They were going under, and you are now going to buy them with some of my money."

"Why are you buying Chili Hut?"

"We can't get enough of the fresh produce," Ginger snorted.

"Shut it, Chester. Look, love, just sign the bloody papers, yeah? You want to run a business, here's your chance. All taken care of."

"I have a business. I teach yoga."

"That's not a business," he fumed. "That's hardly a job at all. You've pickled yourself so thoroughly on this holiday I'm surprised you can touch your toes without chucking up. *This* is a business. Yours. Owned entirely by you. It's a pissing *gift*, for fuck's sake." The waitress arrived with the pen, which he practically grabbed out of her fingers.

Mazy was beginning to assemble the pieces and the last thing she now wanted was to put her name to a legal document that a prosecutor would wave in her face. Gift—yeah right. "Gordon, I don't know what to say."

"You don't have to say a bleeding word if you just sign it." He attempted to smile. "Although 'thank you' would be appreciated." He lifted her hand and wrapped her limp fingers and thumb around the pen.

"This is too much."

"Aw, Gordo, you've brought her to tears," Ginger said.

"That's brilliant, Gordon, you're a star," Isaac added. "Ain't he a star, Maze?"

"Yeah," she said, wiping away the wetness in her eyes. "So I guess this makes us all partners, hunh?"

"Absolutely," Ginger said, raising his glass.

"*Chokdee*," toasted Jaidee.

Gordon leaned his lips beside her ear. "You're not writing your name on that dotted line."

"I'm just...just—"

"We're out for this wonderful celebratory dinner in this posh restaurant with our new friends and I have just bequeathed you a new future. It is time to move from shock to gratitude. Hear me?"

She beamed a smile at the assembly. "Am I the luckiest girl on the planet or what?" Mazy scribbled her name on the first sheet.

"Anything for your happiness, sweet," Gordon said. "And here. Date it. It's the twelfth, bloody hell. And here. Now a kiss."

She kissed him and he raised his glass as his tongue parted her lips and the others let out a roar and clinked glasses once more. He held her tongue with his teeth for a long moment, but she knew better than to protest. He let her go and she gasped in pain. "Isn't she lovely," he said to them, shuffling the papers together. They went back into his jacket and the talk turned to Formula One. She heard the engines racing in her head, louder than any of the others could have imagined.

Chapter 9

The Burden of Management

GRATITUDE. It was something that Gordon expected, and its perceived absence perpetually amazed him.

Take, for example, his girl, Mazy, who was probably set to graduate with a first from the University of Ingratitude. But Gordon could handle this. She was a bird, and a septic, surely a losing combination. Two strikes against her, as her compatriot hillbillies would no doubt say. Even so, allowing for certain genetic dispositions beyond her control, he was increasingly regarding her as a surly, humorless cunt.

He had just paved the way to her entrepreneurial, money-making dreams, and here she is, standing—no, leaning against a pillar in the entrance to the resort, drunken cow—with a big spaced-out frown.

Gordon was starting to wonder what he had ever seen in her.

But gratitude was a fundamental problem across the board. Where was the appropriate level of displayed thankfulness from Isaac

Alika? Had Gordon not demonstrated a truly awe-inspiring level of humane compassion and open-mindedness toward this lost darkie? Not many whites would have taken him under their wing, regardless of his chemistry skills—not in Shoreditch. He had suffered a falling out with his own kind after being accused of snitching, unfairly as it turned out.

And where had Isaac been with the blacks anyway? Drinking Cristal from the bottle in the back of his stretch limousine, like an American rapper? No, that had not been Isaac's situation three years ago. And yet hadn't Isaac enjoyed that very experience just a month ago in Hong Kong, with a pair of Flippers grinding on him to boot? Yes, the lucky git, thanks to Gordon's entrepreneurial success. So where was the proper deference, offering to carry Gordon's things, opening doors for him, any of that bollocks?

Then there was Ginger. Fucking incredible lack of gratitude. But Gordon knew he should not have been disappointed. Ginge was from Liverpool, a Scouser, and there was nothing, no amount of breeding, that could cure that. Born a Scouse, always a scallie. Gordon had reckoned a natural-born thief would fit into his operation, but Ginger was more interested in lifting weights and admiring his pasty torso in the mirror than doing any real work.

Gordon kept him around mainly because he seemed to relish violence. This had come as a surprise, actually. Cracking lame jokes while picking someone's pocket seemed more the Scouse modus operandi, rather than sadism. But criminality in all its variety was in the city's genes. Ginger seemed to live for the moments when Gordon asked him to beat some lying bastard to a pulp.

Now, as the group assembled outside the restaurant for the ride into town, back to Gordon's particular subject of thought: gratitude. Was Ginger really appreciative of the lengths Gordon had gone to keep him out of jail? Examples were numerous but the most recent served his argument well: cleaning up after Ginger got a little carried away with a local tart. He and Ginger had dumped the body somewhere in the island's forsaken interior and Gordon had paid the mama-san in Chaweng enough to forget the girl had ever existed.

And yet here he was, Chester "Ginger" Collins, smoking Gordon's cigars and strutting around like he was on a catwalk. Was he keeping a lookout? No. Was he asking Gordon if there was anything further he could do to help? Ha! The problem with Liverpudlians, Gordon decided, was they all thought they were natural-born comedians. So why should a businessman of Gordon's stature—considerable, he believed, based on revenue, profitability and sheer fucking audacity—take a comedian like Ginger seriously?

The problem of gratitude was not one limited to the white race. Here was this farmer, Jaidee, who hadn't said a bleeding word all night. Just because he didn't speak English didn't make him a flipping mute, did it? And the gall, bringing along his own bottle of cheap firewater when Gordon had arranged for this posh meal, French wines, oysters on the half shell, steaks and frites...food, for fuck's sake, real food; food good enough that you didn't have to cover it in bloody chilies to make it edible.

Not that Gordon didn't like Thai food—it was marvelous stuff, but a man should appreciate the opportunity to try European cuisine for once in his pathetic life. When else had Jaidee, whose day job was literally to shovel shit, cleaning out the cages at the Samui zoo, ever tasted a goddamned Bordeaux? Well, never, and not tonight either, since this fool evidently thought Lady Song its superior. Gordon was already thinking of ways to cut the ignorant janitor out of the operation.

Which led him to the final member of their party: Tarrin. And here, Gordon had to admit, was a bloke who appreciated the meaning of gratitude. True, he dressed like a chav and sounded worse, braying American darkie slang words with that gay singsong accent. But Tarrin had turned out to be a true entrepreneur, a man of Gordon's mould, albeit one who had been consigned to Samui because of his linguistic limitations.

But now that Tarrin and Gordon had met—a chance encounter at Lumphini stadium in Bangkok, wagering on the boxing—their compatibility had been realized. Gordon had discovered a new Thai supplier, one that was organized and disciplined. Tarrin had found an international distributor who could elevate him from squabbling over one island's turf to the status of a national player.

Tarrin had not been a fan of the foreign food either, but he had taken a liking to the wine and generally seemed at ease, without taking the piss either. He had greeted Gordon with a respectful *wai*, and addressed him with the Thai honorific "khun". He remained appropriately tolerant of the snorts and chortles from Isaac and Ginger. He didn't offend his host by eyeing Mazy too obviously, but made it clear that he was impressed by her looks.

And at the end of the meal, he had turned to Gordon and said thank you, in English.

That was gratitude. That was respect.

And now Tarrin was really impressing Gordon, for as their two vans pulled into the narrow parking space between the resort, where the dinner party had gathered, and the busy road, he jutted his square little chin toward the traffic.

"That motorcycle," he said.

Gordon saw only the red taillight slide into traffic from across the street.

"Yeah, what of it?"

"Man fixing the tire when we come."

Gordon checked his watch. They had been in the resort for an hour and a half.

"Long time to repair a tire," he said to Tarrin. "You reckon we got a tail?"

Tarrin, not one given to smiling—the Thai stereotype was bollocks, Gordon was sure, as these were some of the meanest, capricious, greediest bastards he had ever met—dialed his frown down a notch. "Narc."

"Are you regularly followed?"

Tarrin shrugged.

"It must be that," Gordon said. "No one in Thailand knows me. It can't possibly be me, Tarrin." He fished out his smart phone from his pocket and turned on the camera. "This should scare him off."

But Tarrin had other ideas. "I check it out, yo."

Gordon winced at the *hommage à l'américain.* "It could be a complication if the local police connect you with me. We should call it a night."

"What?" Ginger said. "Boss, come on, we're just getting started." One of the Thai women was immersed inside the crook of his gigantic arm. "Me and Buppha here are having a good time, aren't we, darling?"

"Yeah," Mazy said, propped against a pagoda pillar, "we're just getting started."

"Shut it, the two of you. Where's your focus? Did either of you notice a motorcycle parked across the way when we got here? I buy you a civilized meal to celebrate a business deal put together solely through my acumen and instead of gratitude, instead of 'Oi, how do we help the boss out, how do we do our bleeding jobs,' no, it's get drunk and play with pussy."

"I thought we were celebrating," Isaac said, confused.

"Celebrating! Is that it, then, Isaac, you celebrating your great accomplishment? Your fucking flair for wheeling and dealing?"

Isaac bowed his head. "No, Gordon. Sorry."

"Sorry. You're sorry. Tarrin here spots a possible cop tail while you two are holding hands and skipping through the stupid streets of Lamai like a pair of nancy boys. Well, get your fingers out of each others' bums and stay alert."

"Will do, boss," Ginger said.

"And how about a fucking 'thank you', eh? A little appreciation for the fine food and wine I have charitably bestowed upon you, for fuck all, it seems. A little *gratitude*."

"We were, Gordon," Isaac pleaded. "We didn't know the evening was done, is all. Next place is on us."

"There's still time to catch some of the boxing," Ginger added. "Full stakes on us. Drinks after."

"Dinner was brilliant," Isaac said.

"And what about you?" Gordon snapped at Mazy. "I've heard words of contrition from my colleagues. You're my bird; everything I do is for you."

Mazy put her arms around his shoulders. "I know and I'm grateful. Please calm down, Gordon, no one's done anything bad." She kissed him and he let her, but it all felt perfunctory and he pushed her away.

"Don't get messy," he said to them all as he stepped into the van. "Come on, then. It's half-eight already."

In the other van, after one of the Thai women sucked him off, Ginger said, "He's starting to repeat himself. You notice that?"

"*A little gratitude*," Isaac mimicked.

"I tell you, mate, he's losing it."

"Maybe."

"'Maybe'? Are you blind?"

"Losing it don't mean he's lost it."

"True, bro."

"Yet..." Isaac hedged.

"Sure you don't want a bluey?"

"I'm good," Isaac said, easing his Thai woman off his lap without having done much beyond some fondling. "You're too heavy, darling."

"Whoever made Viagra made a mistake marketing it to old men. What they should've done is sold it to blokes our age. It's not for geezers making their biddies happy; it's a lifestyle choice for the modern male."

The two women moved up to the van's forward row of seats, behind the driver, adjusting their dresses.

Isaac said, "Keep doing these whores, you're going to get AIDS."

"Maybe you're right, Isaac. I should lay off the Thai birds for a while. Maybe go back to white ones."

Isaac shot him a dangerous look. "Don't go there."

"Don't go where?"

"Leave Mazy out of it."

"Who said anything about shagging Mazy? Although, now that you mention it, my friend,

I'm pretty sure she's been giving me that come-hither look."

"I'm pretty sure she hasn't. Don't stir the pot."

Ginger grinned at the night. "If I was you, mate, I'd fall out of love with the boss's girlfriend."

"I'm not your mate, Chester."

"Oh, I forgot. Like Gordo says, we're businessmen."

"That's right. We do this shit then find another island where we can buy our own villas and do whatever we like."

Ginger shrugged his enormous shoulders. "I do whatever, and whoever, I like already. You think Mazy takes it up the Gary?"

Chapter 10

Mazy Maintains Her Balance

Mazy had reached that wonderful equilibrium whereby she had drunk herself to the point she now felt reasonably capable and alert. She could maintain herself at this level for a while before she either drank herself to sleep or Gordon got fed up and locked her away, making her go cold turkey for the rest of the evening... or morning...or until the cycle was ready to repeat.

Right now, however, was a good place to be. It didn't hurt so much when she got slapped, but her mind was clear enough to remember it. Anyway, it wasn't the occasional physical abuse that made her need the drink. Bruises healed. At a sufficient state of pickling, she could be happy.

Gordon, look at him. They were sitting in the front row of a series of benches behind a wire mesh. Two lithe Thai kickboxers were hammering the bejesus out of each other in the cage as dusty men in the stands yelled and passed folded baht notes among their thin, gritty fingers. Gordo loved it all. He sat erect and slightly forward, jerking his lean frame in tandem with the punches and kicks in the ring, as though he were in there with them instead of wearing a linen Gucci blazer in the sluggish island heat. His dark eyes were lit with an excitement that came rarely to him these days.

He had once regarded her with that sort of intense devotion. Not long ago, either, and she had loved him for it.

Big mistake.

"Gordon, I need another beer."

"What, already?" His eyes never left the ring, and he made a tiny shadow upper cut motion. "Keep your hands up!" he shrieked at one of the combatants above the din of the drums, cymbals, and tinny clarinet that provided the constant soundtrack to the fights.

"I'm empty. I'll get you one?"

"Yeah, all right then."

"Tarrin, you need another?"

Tarrin, also absorbed by the fight, fingered his gold medallion and ignored her. His female companion kept her hand on his knee and didn't look Mazy's way.

"You got it," Mazy sneered at the rude Thais.

Mazy knew that she moved well when she was at equilibrium, even in heels. She sauntered toward the sad little bar at the rear of the tiny stadium, through a few rows of Western tourists in the expensive seats and past the rowdy local punters kept behind a wire mesh. Isaac and

Jaidee sat a little further back, an island of quiet gloom. Isaac fiddled with his trilby, head down, while Jaidee followed the action in the ring with a slack-jawed passivity. Ginger had been sent to look for a good nightclub and would be back soon, as the fight was the last one on the schedule: nine contests and, so far at least, one boxer hospitalized.

Mazy sailed past them all to the bar, holding a hundred-baht note from Gordon, her passport to a temporary nirvana.

"Maze."

He was stooped over the bar, his back to the arena. With his flip-flops, shorts and light-weight hoodie, from behind he looked like any other Western tourist. The hand in its sling rested unobtrusively on the bar. He was holding a plastic cup of beer with the other, and it was trembling slightly—Mazy in equilibrium could see many things. Equilibrium also muted her surprise.

"Cowboy, you following me?"

She meant it as a joke, and he shrugged, but his grin seemed forced. "Small world, I guess."

Mazy hazarded a backward glance, but Gordon and Tarrin remained focused on the fight. "You know, coincidence and all, it's not a good idea that we continue our acquaintance, Trav. I realize I'm the one who approached you there at the beach this morning, and if I gave you the wrong impression, because maybe I was a little drunk, then I apologize." She signaled to the woman behind the bar. "Can I get two beers, please?"

"Ask you a question?"

She looked over her shoulder again. "Make it fast."

"What are you doing with that guy? I mean, the way he treated you on the beach. I know it's none of my business, and I don't know you too well, but you don't need to put up with that."

Mazy considered him for a moment: crew cut, tanned, solid though not particularly good looking, especially with that bent nose. His sea-blue eyes betrayed nervousness. But he was standing here. Knowing that Gordon was crazy enough to have him beaten up, and him unable to defend himself with that broken wing. Standing here, milking a beer, looking right into her.

"You were right, what you told me this morning," she said. "You're not sneaky smart, Trav. You really are a dumb son of a bitch."

The bartender brought over two cups of beer and took Mazy's money.

"I kinda figured you weren't going to talk to me, not with Prince Charming around," he said, sliding a scrap of paper toward her along the bar. "It's my mobile number. I'm closer to you than you think. Call me if you need help."

Mazy left his offering there, dangling. "Help. You have some nerve."

The music, and the screaming of the punters, was reaching a frenzy; the fight's second round was nearing its conclusion, with one final round to go.

"Take the number."

She avoided his gaze, staring at the bartender instead. "I appreciate the sentiment, but it's best for both of us if you get out of here as quickly as possible."

The bartender pushed forward Mazy's change. Trav scrunched his bit of paper into a ball and flicked it into her hand scooping up the baht.

"See you around, Maze."

She knew better than to look his way. She turned the opposite direction with the money in her pocket and the beers cold in her hands, both of which nearly ended up all over Ginger's stripey shirt and alligator shoes. Where had he come from?

"Easy does it, Mazy," he said.

"Sorry, I didn't see you," she said, her heart beating wildly. Equilibrium! "What are you doing here?"

"Watch your tone, sweetie," he snarled down at her. He was standing close enough to peer down her halter top.

Mazy backed away. "You startled me is all."

"I just got here. Found a good spot for us to party. Fight's over?"

"One more round to go. Out of my way, I've got to get Gordon his beer." She sidestepped his clumsy attempt to pat her ass, trying not to think about the fact that Ginger felt emboldened to make such a crude move around his boss. He was right behind her, spurring her to walk too fast. Gordon and Tarrin were engrossed in an analysis of the fighters, using sweeping gestures to compensate for Tarrin's limited English. "Here you go, honey," she said, still a little breathless.

Not that Gordon seemed to notice. Taking the cup, he said, "Ginge, you're back."

"I've got a club all set up, boss. You're going to like this place."

They waited for the third round to finish and for the judges' split decision. Baht traded hands, Gordon sullenly paying the grinning Tarrin a few thousand, and the entire party of seven—two of the Thai hookers had been let go earlier—meandered out with the crowd.

They exited to a dark parking lot and some more undeveloped or abandoned construction sites enveloped by wild grass, beyond which stretched a small, garbage-strewn lake. Cars and motorbikes streamed into the main road headed into town to low-set buildings, some—the girlie bars, emitting a soft pink glow.

Ginger whistled and waved at the drivers, and their two vans rumbled to life across the parking lot.

Mazy stood behind Gordon, knowing not to touch him and waiting for him to take her hand, or not. She was at equilibrium and didn't care where they went next, so long as she could get a drink there. She didn't care if it involved more hookers and drugs and fake lesbian shows, because they'd have whiskey, too.

"Tarrin, look there," Gordon said.

She followed their gaze. A lone motorcyclist in the shadows, bike engine a steady chug, but the headlight off. Westerners and Thais flowed in front of the biker, other bikes and mopeds were circling toward the road, but that one remained motionless. Mazy felt a strange forlornness upset her equilibrium.

"That him, the one from the restaurant?" Gordon asked.

"I go see," Tarrin said, striding toward the dark corner. The headlight flashed to life and the driver gunned the engine. Tarrin broke into a run as the biker executed a tight turn. They caught a flash of turquoise and then it was gone, tearing noisily into one of the empty lots. Tarrin kept after it and Ginger gestured frantically for the vans to wheel around. The fleeing bike bobbed on the rough terrain but made the road, cutting in front of a tuk-tuk that screeched to a halt and nearly caused an accident. The biker was free, though, and his lone taillight sailed smoothly out of view.

Tarrin jogged back after catching his breath. "Blue Honda."

"Did you get the license plate number?" Gordon asked.

"No."

"You did more than these useless cunts," Gordon said, gesturing at Isaac and Ginger, who were opening the vans' doors.

"I was just getting these," Ginger protested. "So we can go after him."

"Go after him, now, in a pair of lumbering vans?"

"Sorry, Gordon," Isaac said.

"Right, we have ourselves a situation," Gordon said to them. "We are being watched. Don't know if they're onto Tarrin or onto us, but it doesn't matter. Amateur hour is now over, you got that? Keep your wits about you."

"Boss, this club is safe," Ginger said. "I've gone over the place. It's nice and private and I've already reserved the whole thing. You'll fancy the girls and they've got everything you like."

"Not tonight," Gordon said. "We can party back at the villa. Ginger, take one of the vans and go back there, collect as many whores as you think we'll need. If you see that cop on the bike, get rid of everything, you understand? Jump out of the sodding van if you have to. Think you can handle that?"

"On it, boss." Ginger climbed into the lead van.

"Oh, and Chester..."—Gordon used Ginger's given name when he wanted to drive home a point—"no messes, no extra-curriculars."

"No worries, Gordon."

"I need them clean and healthy."

Ginger grinned and slammed the van door shut.

Mazy felt her equilibrium sliding out of order. This last exchange terrified her. "Gordon, baby, what's going on?"

"It's about business. Nothing to concern you."

Mazy was the last to board the second van. She lingered as long as possible, staring at the road thinking about that vanishing red taillight and what it would have been like if it had been taking her away.

Chapter 11

There Be Monsters

"**W**HAT do you think, sis?" Trav said to the dog. She was lying on her favorite cushion on the porch; he was eating breakfast, eggs sunny-side up on toast. It was early morning after the near-miss outside the kickboxing stadium. High tide, and the waters journeyed swiftly across his palm-specked horizon. Looked like another beautiful day in this prison of boredom. "She gonna call?"

The dog looked at him with quizzical pity.

The villa was like a fortress from the outside, with its high walls cutting off the beach from the sand all the way back to the road. Its superstructure had a commanding view of the entire village, although Montri's rental house was shielded by a copse of palms and bamboo.

There were at least three of them in there, plus the Thais and Maze. And, recalled Trav, there would be a nighttime security man employed by the villa's management company who kept watch over the compound's open sea face.

And me with nothing but a busted hand. "A busted hand and a dog who refuses to hold up her end of the conversation." He threw her a piece of his morning toast.

Trav had ignored the villa throughout his stay. He hadn't been looking for memories coming to Koh Samui, and those were what the villa offered. He had stayed there for a week about eighteen months back, with Caroline and some of her friends, when life seemed devoid of cruel surprises, and the biggest decision you had to make was whether to do a seafood grill around the infinity pool, or get driven into town for some spicy noodles.

The decision to come here had been quick and desperate, with Chi-Man prone on the mat, choking on his own blood, and Kang sliding his finger across his throat as he regarded Trav with a cold hatred.

Trav had fled, taking just enough time to gather a bare necessity of belongings and as much cash out of his savings as he could from ATMs. His habitual compulsion had led him to sign up for far more credit cards than he needed, but that night it meant he had a lot of sources of instant cash.

In the wee hours, the airport check-in at Central was closed, so he had taken a taxi out to Chep Lap Kok with the idea of taking the first flight to Thailand, preferably. Almost anywhere would do, and maybe he should have just made a beeline back to the States, but America seemed too far away, not just physically but emotionally. Nobody was waiting for him on its distant shore.

Why Thailand? Because he had been there before. He could make himself comfortable there without burning through all his money, and he didn't know how long he'd be gone. Because he had this memory of Samui and a dog-eared business card with a number for an unobtrusive shack on the beach where he might stay for a while without anyone taking notice.

After haunting the arrivals hall for an hour in the predawn blackness, enveloped in a haze of painkillers, Thai Airways was among the first counters to open at five a.m., and by that point he knew that it would be suicidal to linger in Hong Kong for a minute longer. He paid in cash as his knuckles had begun to break out in pain.

Over the past few weeks he had grown nostalgic for that physical pain. Returning to the village on the quiet, south end of Samui had been survival instinct. Waking up every morning next to the villa where Caroline had admitted to sleeping with her boss had required a supreme effort at amnesia.

The villa and its memories, good and bad, had not been a part of his second life on the island. Until now.

He and Caroline and her friends had once occupied it as tourists, but the villa's purpose had become subverted by its latest, long-term tenant. Trav had always slightly hated himself for being a tourist. He found the idea of tourism, well, lame. His travels before meeting

Caroline had been purposeful: climbing Mount Kinabaloo, hiking the Gobi, making pilgrimage to the Potala Palace. He never took pictures or sent postcards. He traveled to live, to be exceptional. Just as a 'normal' desk job seemed an act of resignation in comparison with the adrenaline of gambling unseemly amounts of money on oil futures, being a standard tourist enjoying sun and Thai massage had felt like a letdown. He had forced himself to regard the villa, when he had stayed there, with condescension.

But now the villa housed mystery. For Trav, exiled to this shack, the dog his main companion, the banality of the *farang* tourist had become pretty appetizing.

The money was still plentiful but no more of it would be coming in. Even without having lost the securities firm a huge amount of money, simply doing a runner from Hong Kong like that meant he'd never get a job there, or probably anywhere else in finance, again. And his email inbox continued to pile up with lawyerly threats.

He had felt a change coming, and then he met Mazy and suddenly the villa and its memories were all he could think of. Standing on the porch, feeding the dog his breakfast, Trav now regarded the villa and its wall in a brand new way.

He thought about how much he missed the idea of Caroline. Not the woman herself; they had revealed too much to one another for that. But he knew that, even though the destruction of that relationship still stung, he wasn't cut out for this Lone Ranger, Hemingway macho act.

Grief washed through him. It had been a long time since he had mourned his lost parents and the unknown parts of his future that had been so abruptly ripped from his life. And he remembered what it was like to hoist Caroline above the gentle waves—*just over there*—and swing her around.

Most of all he could remember how, when times were good, Caroline's preternatural cool had calmed him down and given him some perspective. She had, in the early days, been forgiving, and that had made him feel at peace in a way that he hadn't known since his parents had died. When their relationship headed south, he had hated the absence of unconditional love. It made him cynical and unfaithful to her. Their final holiday at the villa had been meant to turn things around. They ended up screaming obscenities, the kind that had precluded any hope of his contacting her again.

Sorrow left him poleaxed. He slid to his haunches. The dog was sufficiently moved to walk over to where he sat on the porch floor and lick his salty tears.

Trav didn't know if he really liked Mazy or if it was just this combination of loneliness and repressed panic that had spurred him to chase her last night. Maybe it was just his natural penchant for mistaking risk for 'real' life. Maybe he was just reacting to her despondency: an unthinking act of biochemistry, instead of any thoughtful intent. He would have never pegged his attractive yoga instructor as being stuck with such an asshole, and from their exchange at the kickboxing hall she seemed absolutely terrified of the guy—or was he just inventing things to flatter himself?

But he did know that his time on Samui was nearing an end, and although he should probably just pack his bag and go somewhere else and start over, the idea had entered his head that he'd like it more if it was with this woman whom he didn't really know—and whom he had encountered only twenty-four hours ago, if for no other reason than she seemed lost. He could relate to that.

Lost and rambling within the insides of the villa, a place of sunlight and water and secrets. Within those walls, he and Caroline had once demolished their relationship in a fit of screams and revelations. Today, what disaster was taking place there? Had she kept his number? Could he dare walk over? There were at least three men inside the compound. Trav was keeping count.

Chapter 12

Blackout

ON the other side of the villa wall, Mazy phased into consciousness and knew, *knew*, that something was wrong. The physical memory of sexual intercourse felt strange, dulled by the more pressing sensation of being strung out and in immediate need of a drink. Underlining all of that, though, was something else, like a persistent bass line, a nagging sense of self-loathing that made her want to vomit.

Something had gone on last night. Another of Gordon's parties run amok. But she had weathered plenty of those, back when Gordon was a junkie and now when he was clean and preferred to encourage the downward spirals of others. She knew all the aches and this wasn't one of them.

She lay in bed, her stomach doing cartwheels and her pores dry, a fairly normal state of late, and tried to reconstruct the evening's depths. Music over the azure glow of the pool, drinking Johnny Walker Black from the bottle. Ginger and Tarrin fornicating with a new supply of Thai hookers in the pool, Isaac more shyly making out in the covered lounge seats by the beachfront. The girls were in various stages of intoxication. One of them had worn chunky fake jewelry, a necklace of colorful glass orbs. Why did she remember that? Oh yeah. Because Ginger had suggested it could double as a string of anal beads.

Mazy remembered the dinner and signing the papers. The kickboxing stadium—*whump* went her heart. Travis. The slip of paper wadded into a marble... Mazy lifted her head. Her purse lay on the floor, lips sealed, secrets intact. She hoped.

The orgy had gone on around the pool, but she had gone inside with Gordon, determined to help him come. She remembered pulling off his boxers and telling him it was OK, she'd make it remember how to get hard. She had tried gently using her fingers, but he had swatted her away in frustration, so she had taken his penis into her mouth. Mazy was pretty sure whatever damage he had sustained there was permanent but told him she could make it happen.

Mazy couldn't remember whether her ministrations had worked. That wasn't what was *wrong.*

The whisky bottle lay emptied on the floor, along with a few cans of Carlsberg. She feared relief meant a long walk outside, up the stairs to the kitchen, and another drink. The desire overcame the pain of getting out of bed, although she was momentarily overcome with a strange dizziness. *That's weird.* She slid into a short yellow kimono, surprised again at her body's acknowledgement of sex. It had been, she realized, a long time since the last. And...last night must have been rough. She parted the curtains, wincing at the bold daylight before braving it.

The villa was silent other than the sound of the waves caressing the beach and the gossip of kingfisher birds in the trees. She spied Isaac's black legs spread on one of the big covered futons by the villa's edge, where steps descended to the sand. Mazy assumed he was asleep or passed out there—it was the last place she remembered seeing him last night—but as she walked toward the stairs, he called her name, hiding his condition under his white trilby and sunglasses but the crack in his throat giving him away. But it wasn't his hoarse voice that gave her a nervous pause.

"All right, Maze?" It was the way he said it, with such weight.

"Not really." She meant it brightly, but it didn't come out that way. His wraparound shades masked whatever response his eyes might have betrayed.

"What's wrong?" he asked.

"Nothing. I'm cool. Just hung over, I guess."

"Quite a party."

"Look, I'm not in a chatty mood and I could use a drink."

"You, uh, you remember the whole thing?"

87

Whatever switch monitored her patience flipped. "You think I drink to remember shit, Isaac?"

"Sorry, Maze, I was just...concerned about you. It got a little, uh, extreme last night."

"Yeah, well, tell it to Oprah." She headed for the villa's main building, wondering what the fuck was Isaac's problem today.

What the fuck was *her* problem today?

I don't know but I am definitely not cool.

The top level was still. Fans dragged lazily over the lounge chairs and sofas. The stereo lay dark and mute. She judged by the kitchen, with a few dishes in the sink, that Lek had already made breakfast and gone to the market for groceries. At that moment, the loudspeakers that permeated the village outside coughed to life. Mazy braced herself for an hour-long barrage of hectoring from the same male Thai voice that blared throughout the village every day, forming a constant background noise to daily life in the villa. It must be one o'clock.

She poured herself a tall glass of orange juice and the last gulp of vodka remaining in the freezer. Equilibrium improved. She leaned over the black granite counter to see if there was any coffee left when one hand grabbed her arm and the other her rear. Mazy raised her arms and swung to the left, nailing Ginger's neck with her elbow with enough force to loosen his grip. She squirmed in his grasp, but he had the tail end of her kimono in his fist.

"Get offa me!"

He was absorbing her into his bear-like embrace. "You liked me well enough last night."

"Hell I did. Get off 'fore I scream for Gordon."

"Gordo's been out all day with Tarrin, love, and guess what? He's given you to me."

"Asshole!" Punching him in the jaw hurt her more than him. Ginger, his beady blue piggy eyes bright—*what is he* on?—just grinned. She scratched him next, drawing blood, and he shook her by her forearms so violently she couldn't scream.

"I'll be coming back for more," he said, throwing her to the kitchen's tiled floor. She fell on her elbows, kimono akimbo, looking like a bright butterfly pinned to a board. Thin black arms wrapped around Ginger and somehow pulled him back. "She ain't yours," Isaac said to him.

"Oh, yes, she is," Ginger said, shrugging him off. "And you know it, Isaac, I warned you."

Isaac, pushed against the counter, calmly pulled a cleaver out of the knife rack.

"Oh, is that the story, son? You going to chop me?" Ginger flexed his bulk, like a giant cornered cat.

"Just leave Mazy alone."

Ginger shook a sausage-sized finger at Isaac. "Massive error, my friend."

"We're all meant to be working together here, so let's act like it," Isaac said.

"Fuck you." Ginger started to leave but said to Mazy, "You stink, you know that, you skank? You smell like yesterday's dog puke."

Mazy, still on the floor, her elbow pronging currents of pain, burst into tears as Ginger stormed out of view. "What the fuh?" was all she could put together as words.

Isaac tried to help pick her up, but Mazy waved him off. She tried putting her weight on her elbow and it held. She was clear about her physical movements. *Breathe. Practice your* pranayama. Mazy breathed. She was on her hands and knees, cat pose, *bidalasana.* A way to move from the center. *Center yourself.*

Wearing nothing but a half-open kimono was likely to make this pose too much for Isaac, so she got to her feet and put her palms together to make a trembling *namaskar. Namah* meaning 'not me', a negation of ego or self; *om,* the sound of the universe; *kar,* the physical manifestation of *om. Breathe.*

Whatever was *wrong* was still wrong, Mazy realized, as she tried to clear her mind.

"Uh...Maze?"

She wiped tears from her eyes. "Isaac, tell me: what happened last night?"

There was a time when Mazy was not a helpless prisoner of drink and circumstance. Life had been as happy as these things go, and for a little while, delirious.

The problem with happiness is the way it blinds you. Happiness, she knew now, was a delusion or, at best, a temporary accident, and only an ignorant fool would believe it ever lasts.

Mazy became an alcoholic very deliberately in her late teen years as a way to forget about crouching in the snow behind the barn, peeing blood, after one of her foster dad's unwanted nighttime visits.

She hitchhiked halfway across the States to become an actress, during one of her subsequent bouts of bloody-mindedness. Her striking looks got her as far as the Hollywood porn industry, which she avoided only by sleeping with L.A.'s only straight male dance instructor in exchange for a few months of classes. He got her into yoga and a door opened.

For the first time in her life, Mazy became conscious of her own body, a thing until now that had been a despised necessity. She had always known the effect her looks had on men, and had occasionally put it to use, but she couldn't see why it worked. Looking at herself in the mirror just reminded her of the foster dad, and that was a memory she worked actively to banish.

Yoga, however, was all about self-awareness: the breathing, the postures, the way they made you think about everything, the way the instructors brought her attention to every part of her *self*, inside and out. Once she was willing to really look at her body, she could master it. She could be the one in control.

Her romances collapsed, one after another, like a string of poor jokes, but Mazy became the one doing the picking and the dumping, and, by her mid-twenties, she began to see the playground that life could be for a very attractive, self-possessed young woman. She got certified and sashayed her way into a gig on a cruise ship. The hours were long and the crew members were horny pests, but she liked the steady income and saw the west coast from Alaska to Acapulco.

One day, leading a class of retirees in a series of sun salutations, Mazy heard the clicks of a camera. Not a usual one-off sound from a passing tourist but a manic series of impatient notes. She inhaled back to center and beheld the *coolest guy ever*. She couldn't help the teenie-bopper phrase. Steve looked like a black-Irish mountain man on assignment for National Geographic magazine—which he actually was. He said he was moving to Asia for a few months, he had a couple of projects lined up all over, and was going to set up base in Hong Kong. Did she want to come?

Did she want to come? Mazy broke her contract, left a few weeks' back pay on the table, and waited just long enough to get a passport before following Steve to the Fragrant Harbor. She found work at a yoga studio in Causeway Bay and he managed to keep the projects going, one after another. He'd be gone for a few weeks at a time, and the waiting was something awful. His absence sent her into crazy depressions, more intense than Mazy had ever experienced. During those periods, she thought of nothing but the feel of his calloused hands and the acrid taste of cigars on his lips that she never liked but came to love.

Steve was life, and Mazy kept off the booze because she knew he would return. The mood swings became acute when she got pregnant —even the happy periods were so giddy they could tip her into anxiety about never wanting to be lonely and miserable again. It would have scared her, but the yoga was there to steady her. That had become her new fix. She glowed.

Mazy was surrounded by students and got hit on regularly, even by her colleagues, mostly Indian guys of amazing talent but far removed from their wives back home. Mazy didn't have real friends, though, and never quite connected with the women practicing in the studio. There always remained an unspoken mutual disdain or jealousy, something she could never put into words. It wasn't just her threatening looks; most women took an active dislike to her.

She knew she was a mongrel—it had said so on her birth certificate: Asian American. Whether from her mom or dad, Chinese or Korean or Japanese, Mazy never knew. She was a little too tall and pale, but with her sable hair and coffee eyes, she could blend among the Chinese in Hong Kong, at least until she opened her mouth and out came American English. Yet that feeling of separateness, whether in terms of language or empathy, was comforting, in its cowardly way. She felt comfortable in Hong Kong because it was anonymous and alien, and Steve and her yoga practice were all she needed. Until she got a call from a hospital in Borneo. It seemed like nothing to a man like Steve: just tripped over a clutch of roots and knocked his head. He had walked back to camp, cracking his usual jokes, developed a fever and was dead by morning. The shock was probably what caused her miscarriage the next week.

The stripping of delusion is a cold, thankless blessing. It reveals the truth in life, the sort of thing Mazy could philosophize about only in her moments of vodka-endowed clarity.

At first she sought refuge in her *asanas*, but you could only do backward bends and down-ward-facing dogs for so long. That still left a too many waking hours and, worse, the long, lonely nights to contend with. She couldn't face them by herself. The first time she got drunk it was like being enveloped in the mighty frozen arms of a long-lost friend, and Mazy decided the only way to live was to stay this way.

Just when she had it figured out, she met Gordon.

Chapter 13

What Rick Fury Would Do

TRAV bent over the laptop, a Chang perspiring on the table beside one of Montri's half-eaten catches of the day. The modest veranda was full today, about half locals, half tourists, and everybody was chatting about the incredible beachfront setting and the way the sun danced on the shallows. *Yeah, whatever.*

He pondered the next line of his erstwhile novel, about daring futures trader Rick Fury and his market nemesis, Lance Cutlass:

"Wow," Candy says as she removes her halter top. "You futures traders sure know a lot about money."

"I'll tell you a dirty secret about our tight-lipped industry," says Rick. "But first let me show you this."

Trav sighed and hit the delete button over and over. He switched to the Internet, where he could usually pirate the big villa's wi-fi connection—they hadn't changed the password, 'paradise', since he had stayed there.

If it was time to think about his next move, he'd better know what was up. The head-in-the-sand strategy, which had so far served him well, enjoyed a limited shelf life; plan B, scoring it big with the novel, wasn't looking too rosy either.

A quick Google search didn't turn up anything new, which was good, although his Facebook wall was littered with a mix of epithets, threats, 'likes' and snarky remarks, mostly dating from a month ago. A couple of scary-looking messages from the bank's legal counsel that he didn't dare open. About twenty journalists and private investigators wanted to 'friend' him; ever since Bloomberg had run a story about his disappearing from Hong Kong and being accused of rogue trading, Trav had become a popular guy among the bottom-fishers.

He checked West Texas Intermediate prices and reckoned most of his losses had probably been made up by now, but the duration of those contracts had probably left the firm a few mil in the hole.

"Pocket change," he murmured, finishing his beer. Trav had made the desk plenty of money over the past two years. He figured he was up, net-net. How could they sic a bunch of lawyers on him if, when all was said and done, he had made a profit for the firm?

His mobile did a little jig on the table. Trav didn't recognize the caller but it looked local, and for a moment he regretted giving his number to Mazy. It could be her, it could be anybody. It could be the cops.

It could be Kang.

"Hello."

"You said you're close, cowboy. How close?"

"I can see your villa," he said eagerly.

"Like if I have to find you, how do I do it?"

"You OK? They hurt you?"

"No time for chit-chat. You wanna help me, tell me where to go."

"Little house next door, behind the restaurant. I think you saw me go in there. When you—" But she had already hung up.

Dialing back that number was a bad idea. He thought about a text message, but no, the boyfriend might notice it. He tried to gaze at the sea, but he was too edgy now for tranquility. He paced around his corner of the veranda and ran his good hand's fingers through his lengthening hair.

Was she coming right now? Was he just an insurance policy, a possible bolt-hole if she decided to make a move? Would it be soon—how long were she and her psycho lover staying in Thailand?

His stomach did somersaults, half in frustration and half in excitement, in a way he hadn't experienced in a long time. She had actually called him. Was that a good thing? Did that mean she was getting the stuffing knocked out of her? How long did he have to stick around Samui to find out?

Trav closed his laptop, left some baht on the table and took a six-pack of beers to go. He might have a long wait. Sitting on the porch, prying off the cap of a Chang, he asked the dog, "What would Rick Fury do?"

Whatever the dog knew, she kept it to herself.

Chapter 14

Diamonds and Knives

Mᴀᴢʏ gave Lek two hundred baht to keep quiet about using the maid's cell phone and took a hot shower. She wasn't quite ready to process what Isaac had told her, at least not this straight. To hell with equilibrium: she aimed to get wasted.

She sat on a lounger in a one-piece bathing suit and her sunglasses, drinking Mazy's Amazing Thai Mojitos. Ingredients: Sang Som rum, the local hooch (80 proof version); local sugar cane juice, mint and limes, courtesy of Lek; sparkling water (just enough to dilute the sweetness and to give it some fizz); crushed ice optional. When she ran out of the mint and limes, she found they didn't actually add that much to the overall effect. Nor did it prove necessary to replenish the sugar cane juice or the sparkling water. Yes, Mazy's Amazing Thai Mojito, when boiled down to simple rum and some pressed dregs in her cup, was simplicity itself.

Now it was time to take stock, as she was safely buffered against practically any emotional reaction. Item number one: if Isaac were to be believed, her boyfriend, the gallant drug dealer Gordon, had decided to use her as a guinea pig. Apparently this new line of Ketamine he was developing included a nip of ephedrine, just to add a little stimulant to the downer, and some ecstasy to keep you lovey dovey. The street name would be K-Love.

Item number two: Gordon's methadone intake, meant to keep him off horse, had the unfortunate side effect of rendering him impotent most of the time.

"Very frustrating," Mazy told the pool.

And very unfortunate, because he was rapidly tiring of her. In fact, last night's bacchanalia may have been the tipping point. Leading us to item number three: Ginger. Apparently he had taken a generous portion of Viagra and had managed to do half the working girls in Chaweng and still wasn't sated.

Isaac had demurred on describing exactly how this exchange came about. She gathered that Ginger had been sufficiently high on coke to challenge Gordon directly in a manner regarding the boss's sexual capabilities, suggesting that Mazy's efforts were being wasted on the wrong gentleman.

"I guess that's item four," she informed the pool.

Item five: Gordon was not about to surrender his alpha-male status to his coked-up Liverpudlian heavy but was curious to test the effects of K-Love's alternative use—as a mickey to be slipped into the drinks of unsuspecting young ladies in the nightclubs of Hong Kong, Singapore, and Shanghai. He therefore suggested a swap, clawing back a third of Ginger's fifteen percent cut of the operation's revenue in return for access to Mazy—"C'est moi," she said—on a restricted and limited basis.

Which, clearing through the legalese, meant Gordon ordered her to blow Ginger so he could see whether she'd remember a thing, and she had obeyed. She had even hung out by the pool for a little while afterwards until throwing up in the Jacuzzi, at which point Isaac had deposited her soaking wet on her bed.

"Conclusions?"

Several. First, K-Love was a successful accessory for committing rape. The drug had made her pliant at the time and, even after being told of what had happened, the night now remained a blank. However, further research may be needed to test combining K-Love with different levels of alcohol intake.

Second conclusion: Ginger was pushing the terms of the agreement to believe it now gave him repeated access to Mazy, including in manners prohibited by the contract. More research might be required to determine whether Gordon gave a damn.

Conclusion number three: At some point soon, when she woke up sober, Mazy would have to make a decision. OD on sleeping pills and Jack Daniels in the tub? Slit her wrists in the pool? Run away to the cowboy? All of them would require time and privacy. Isaac was on guard most of the day down by the pool and the beach. Gordon had returned with Tarrin and was mucking about in the kitchen. Ginger was keeping an eye on the front entrance from up above. Now was not the time. Tonight, tonight would be the time.

Final conclusion: Mazy didn't care which outcome she chose. It was simply a matter of which would be the easiest to execute.

Mazy was at her most sober around dusk, before dinner. Gordon more or less insisted on it and she retained enough self-control to put off alcohol for a few hours. Then the only way to keep herself from going mad was to work through her practice.

Usually she waited for the sun to go down, but today she welcomed the heat and the sweat. Gordon, unusually, wasn't back yet. No one had seen him since regaining consciousness earlier in the day. He was probably out with Tarrin. Good. Mazy didn't want to deal with him. She began with sun salutations—well, sundown salutations today, moving lightly on her mat alongside the infinity pool. Isaac sat at the table, nodding his head along to Kanye West and Outkast tracks on the outdoor stereo, watching her go through her motions from behind his mask of sunglasses and white trilby.

Hands to the sun. Backward bend. Forward bend, palms beside her feet.

Tonight's the night.

Just breathe: right foot back in a lunge, then downward facing dog, hands and feet flat on the ground as her body formed a 90-degree angle upward.

She knew the Ketamine was inside the coconuts. So she'd need to get her hands on one of those and find a way to open it without spilling liquid K-Love. Gordon hadn't planned an excursion this evening, so she wasn't sure how to get it.

She'd figure it out. Upward facing dog, thrusting her hips forward and holding herself upright on her flat palms and outstretched toes. Plank position and a low push-up: hold.

They were making a ton of the stuff out at some shack in the interior. But Gordon's samples had been in the kitchen. Tarrin hadn't taken them back, she was pretty sure, so they must be here somewhere. The extra bedroom beneath the living area?

Back to downward-facing dog, right leg forward into another lunge. Left foot forward to a standing forward bend. Then hands raised high, another backward bend, and palms together in a prayer that she drew from the sky to her heart.

Namaste.

The villa had five bedrooms, arranged like a horseshoe around the pool, all facing toward the beach. Two formed the ground floor of the villa superstructure, beneath the living area and kitchen, partly hidden beneath the stairs.

These were dark, cavernous rooms with enormous wooden doors located on both the inside, opening to the pool, and on the outside, exiting to the garden and car park. Gordon sometimes used these as guest rooms; Tarrin had stayed over a few times. Normally all of the doors were kept locked and Gordon held on to the keys.

The other three bedrooms were made of glass, their floor-to-ceiling windows and sliding doors lined by white curtains or blinds. The two small ones, set just behind the outdoor table where Isaac now sat, were for him and Ginger. Across, on the Jacuzzi side of the pool, was the long master bedroom.

Mazy practiced for about ninety minutes, first vigorously and then concluding with relaxation techniques, until she felt more or less restored. The sun went down over the channel and the lights around the pool area glowed softly. Gordon had returned alone; the lights in the upstairs living area flashed on, followed by very loud James Brown remixes that drowned out the clucks of the geckos. That meant Gordo was in the mood to cook his own dinner, and he would be sending Lek back to the servants' quarters out front in the driveway, down where she lived with her husband Anurak.

Ginger wandered down the steps and stood there, arms folded, watching her wrap up with some spinal twists.

"What do you want," she said coldly.

"Boss wants you."

"I have to go take a shower."

"Boss wants you."

She picked up her towel and wrapped it around her shoulders. "Fine." She walked as widely past him as possible.

"I really enjoy your workouts, love," Ginger said just loud enough for her to hear.

Mazy ran up the steps to the living area. Gordon was practically dancing in the kitchen, peering into cabinets, slamming drawers, shadow boxing to the beat.

"You wanted something?" she shouted over the music.

"You don't look happy to see me, Mazy."

"I just worked out and I need a shower. I'm all sweaty."

He boogied toward her, one hand holding a coconut. "Give us a kiss."

Mazy pecked him on the lips but he shook his head. "What?"

"Is that a kiss?"

She had to be careful. She had promised Isaac not to let on what he had told her. And she didn't want Gordon to pay her extra attention. So she wrapped her hands around his lean, powerful shoulders, let his curly black beard tickle her chin, and she kissed him.

"I have a surprise for you," he said.

"Uh-hunh."

"Open it," he said, handing her the coconut.

"How? It's glued shut."

He practically dragged her to the island counter and picked up a cleaver. "Here, give it a good whack with the handle. It'll come loose."

She positioned the coconut on the counter and struck it twice. Then she turned the knife around and used the blade to pry it open. The coconut split abruptly in two and inside one of the rolling halves glinted a diamond ring.

Mazy plucked it with trembling fingers. She hoped Gordon would interpret that as excitement.

"Oh my God," she gasped.

Gordon leaned on his elbows like a conspiratorial schoolboy. "Well, what do you think?"

"I...I don't know what to say." Knowing this would irritate him, she quickly added, with an extra layer of girlishness, "Thank you. It's, well, you're right, I'm surprised."

"It's the most expensive ring at that jeweler's in town," he said.

He's gone completely mad.

"So?" he said.

"So, Gordon, I'm just the luckiest girl on the planet." She embraced him and looked at the stone. It looked like the real deal.

"No, I mean...so?"

The next horror dawned. "Um, well, I think, if you're asking me something, you need to ask."

"Right. Right." He bent down on one knee. Mazy couldn't believe it. "Oi, the ring."

She let him take it.

"Mazy, marry me."

Of course he wouldn't frame it as a question.

"Naturally," he said, "the wedding is contingent on a few things. One is the financial success of this operation."

"OK."

"Second is this. I have shown you by example what it is to take control of one's life." *Brother, here we go again.* "I need a mate who shares my strength, my discipline. You understand?"

"Yes."

"Tonight we will enjoy a fine Bordeaux with our meal, because this is a special occasion. But then you are not to drink any more, is that understood?"

"I'll try. Really, I will. I know I've got this disease."

"If you can't stop yourself, I'll have you tied to your bed and spoon feed you until you've cleaned it all out, all right?"

Mazy forced a bright smile. "Thank you so much, Gordon."

"Go on then," he whispered, holding up the ring, "say it."

"Yes, Gordon."

"Yes, what."

"Yes, I will marry you."

"Brilliant." He slid the ring on her finger. It was a size too small and got stuck at the first knuckle. "Bugger."

"We can get it resized at the store."

"Well, for the time being you can wear it on your pinkie." He switched fingers.

"It's beautiful."

"As are you, Mazy. Look, I'm cooking dinner. I've given Anurak a grocery list. He should be back soon and we'll get started."

"That's wonderful. So I'm going to take that shower now, OK?"

"By all means," he said, turning back to the cabinets.

She skipped down the steps, the knife hidden in the folds of her towel. At the bottom she paused. Ginger was sitting down to another game of cards with Isaac in the poolside gazebo.

Mazy, instead of walking to the cluster of bedrooms around the pool, turned back behind the steps and approached the two bedrooms on the ground floor of the main building. She tried both doors; both were locked, bolted from the inside.

She took the knife and slid it inside one of the door's cracks, hoping to catch and lift the latch.

The latch was easy to catch but hard to move. She paused in the darkness, unable to hear above the din of James Brown dubs. Mazy left the knife wedged in place and peeked around the stairs. The two men were still hunched over their cards. She ran back to the door and hauled the knife upward, trading strength for silence. It worked and the door opened.

She didn't dare turn on the lights, but she knew there was an emergency flashlight in all the closets. She found it and, making sure to first close the door, flicked it on. The spacious room didn't stir within her roving cone of light: bed, shelves, a painting of saffron-robed monks.

Mazy tip-toed into the bathroom, which contained a set of sinks, a rain head shower, and a huge, luxurious, white bathtub. Inside the tub: a milk crate full of coconuts.

She had to know, even though she was looking at coconuts in the bathroom of a locked guestroom. Mazy took one and felt for the telltale seam. She put it back, palmed another. Yep.

And were they all filled with little bags of K-Love, like grenades waiting to be launched against unsuspecting schoolgirls back in Hong Kong? Mazy put down the flashlight and used both hands to try to count the coconuts. She took them out of the crate in pairs, trying to keep track as some rolled around the bottom of the tub. How many teenage girls' lives would be shattered by this one mere crate's worth of Gordon's merchandise?

It dawned on her that she had been in here too long. She scrambled to put all the coconuts back. She had to bend all the way over the tub's wall to be sure, and at one point, knowing that a single errant coconut would create almighty trouble, she lit the flashlight to peer inside. Something lodged in the drain reflected the light. Mazy stretched and retrieved it, a small, egg-shaped piece of cheap jewelry, maybe blue or purple. She stood for a long moment, aiming the light on the discarded bit of glass that she turned around in her fingers, as if her brain had somehow stopped trying to identify things. Then she noticed the small hole—a tube, actually, for threading the stone, and she cast the thing away, knowing it was the prostitute's.

But what was a piece of her necklace doing here? The darkness of the bathroom was oppressive and she felt a terror unlike anything before. Where had Gordon been all day? She slashed the light around the room. The floors here were tile and clean. Spotless, in fact.

Mazy headed back to the bedroom. The bed was made, the sheets and blanket military tight. Like brand new, although she couldn't imagine why Lek or Anurak would bother tidying up in here. Had Tarrin spent the night? The floor was dark hardwood and cold against her bare feet. She knelt beside the bed, the wood hard against her knees, and peered beneath. Nothing. I'm losing it, she thought.

That was definitely a noise outside. She extinguished the flashlight and waited. The deep bass lines suddenly quieted and she heard the voices of the men, a little too low for her to understand the words, but that sounded like a snarling order from Gordon.

She wrapped two coconuts in her towel and crept toward the door. *Did I lock it?*

Now she heard Ginger said, "Checking, boss."

Mazy froze, not sure if she should dive for the lock or retreat into the bathroom—hide in the shower, in the tub? Maybe a closet, but no, those were in the main room, by the unlocked door. She saw Ginger's massive silhouette as he pressed against the window, trying to peer through the blinds. She ran and clicked the door lock. It sounded like a gunshot. Ginger pushed, then pounded on the door. It vibrated against her nose.

"What's that?" she heard Gordon call.

"I think she's in here. I heard a noise."

"This door's locked and only I have the key," Gordon said. "I don't think she could have gotten in there."

"Well, she didn't go on the beach. Isaac or me would have noticed her."

Gordon banged on the door. "Maze, you in there, darling?"

Mazy put her wrist in her mouth, too afraid to step back.

"You sure she's not taking a shower?" Gordon said.

"That's what Isaac says."

"Go upstairs and keep an eye out."

"It's dark, Gordon. I can see bugger-all out there."

"Just mind the entrance. If she's hiding in here, she might want to try to go out through the gate."

These were the bedrooms with doors on opposite sides, poolside and garden-side. She unbolted the far door and shut it as quietly as possible. She was now outside, on a narrow loggia where the bedroom doors faced the walkway toward the garage, a giant Buddha image carved into the wall between them.

Which way to flee? Across the garden to the parking lot? It was walled in. They'd see her if she tried to open the gate—she wasn't even sure where the control was. Would Lek or Anurak hide her?

Or go back up, for there were also stairs on either end of the walkway connected to the living space above—one near the kitchen, the other opposite, to the sofas and the TV—and which passed by the upstairs bathroom.

Geckos hooted.

The Buddha in the wall regarded her with cool indifference.

Her feet smacked on the sandstone steps, a ricocheting sound.

She came onto the porch overlooking the front drive and the road, and ducked to the right into a bathroom, just as Ginger's head appeared across the living room. She could only pray that he wasn't looking her direction as she pressed the door shut. Mazy flushed the toilet and used the moment of noise to shove the coconuts and the knife into the cabinet beneath the sink.

She washed her hands and opened the door. Ginger filled the doorway.

"What do you want?" conjuring anger to mask her terror.

Ginger eyed her the way a butcher might size up a piece of meat. "Nothing," he growled, turning away. "She's in the khazi," he called.

Chapter 15

K-Love

GORDON met Mazy only a few months after he arrived in Hong Kong. He had just cut a deal with a Chinese triad leader to supply high-quality cocaine and other delights to the children of wealthy expatriate financiers.

Mazy was, he said at the time, a high unlike any other.

Gordon would know. He had only recently dragged himself out of the habit of injecting heroin. Shooting smack was not the sort of thing his upscale clients in London had sought. They were mostly the children of City bankers and lawyers—coke, hash and amphetamines were the trendy school accessories. But one fragile teenage lad, destined for university in Leeds and dreading what the locals would make of his posh accent, decided he had needed to go down market.

Gordon procured him some junk and, in keeping with his admirable level of customer service, tested the quality of the product. And then went

on testing it, and testing it. That led to a regret-
table deterioration of business practices culmi-
nating in the arrest of several associates. He
also regretted to hear of the young student's un-
timely death in Leeds from swallowing his own
vomit while overdosing.

What Gordon learned from that episode was
that discipline was central to life and business.
That sorry student customer had lacked discipline, and look what happened to him. It
was through iron will that, shortly before leaving London before the Old Bill clapped him in
chains, he weaned himself off heroin at a clinic
administering methadone as a substitute.

"If you can't handle what I've got to sell, then
don't fucking shoot it, snort it, or swallow it,"
Gordon would tell his clients afterwards. "I handled it. I've done it all, and I've walked through
the fire. You wankers spending Daddy's money
know fuck all. So think of me as the warning
label on a packet of fags. This shit will fry your
brain, got it? That'll be a hundred fifty quid.
Now sod off."

The kids didn't quite know what to make of
this. Some figured he was joking, others were
terrified. Either way, most of them kept coming
back to Good Ole Gordo and his magic wares,
and Gordon enjoyed a peaceful rest at night.

He recognized the false promise of a high but
reckoned that you should enjoy it anyway while
it lasts. The strong control their desires. The
weak are consumed. Gordon was disciplined,
but even so, those heady days in Hong Kong

with this exotically beautiful American yoga instructor whom he had rescued from the bottle almost made him forget his work.

"You're so good for me," Mazy would say as they cuddled. She was following his example, having quit drinking for a time and pursuing her yoga teaching with a vengeance.

"You're no good for me," Gordon would reply, with a smile and a kiss, and she would laugh, thinking he was teasing her.

It was his discipline, his strength, he knew, that kept Mazy trapped in his orbit. His business again came under trouble, this time because he hadn't been properly minding the store. Gordon had to reestablish discipline over all facets of his life, and that included rebuking Maze when she started to complain about his unsavory working hours. After a few weeks, he came to realize that patient explanations wore him out. Best to simply shout at her until she shut up.

He had brought Isaac Alika with him from London, to see what the skinny bugger could concoct once he got his hands on some of Asia's raw materials. Until recently that had remained a work in progress, financed out of Gordon's profits, making Isaac a dependency, a ward.

He recruited Ginger in Hong Kong, the bruiser having flirted from one loser gang to another from among the disorganized amateurs whom Gordon was systematically replacing. A buyout took place, the triads preferring an amicable solution rather than a squabble over the expat market. One of the last dealers competing against Gordon retired to Bali and left behind his muscle, an unruly Scouser with Arnold Schwarzenegger's physique and Ringo Starr's accent.

The margins were, however, terrible—worse than London. The triads raised their stake again and again, until Gordon was left with practically nothing. The problem was not distribution, as he had managed to wheedle his way into capturing most of the market for the international schools. No, it was product. Too generic. He had nothing the triads needed. He was simply ruthless and organized enough to make it easy for the Chinese gangs to profit off the *gweilos*.

"What I need is an edge," he said to Mazy one night. This was about two months into living together and they were in his cramped flat, a four-hundred-square-foot concrete box in a Wanchai apartment tower with a view of other people's windows, as Mazy read a magazine and Gordon thumbed through the names on his cell phone. "I'm a business man. I should be living rich, not like a damned coolie."

"This apartment is worth a lot," she said. "Hong Kong's an expensive place."

He had regarded her with such loathing that the silly woman had the sense to shut her cakehole.

"I know people," he finally said, clutching his phone. "There's no way Gordon Wood is going to be stuck in this dump."

"I believe you," she said, giving him a kiss to assuage his anger, but he pushed her away.

"Don't patronize me, Maze."

"I wasn't patronizing you, Gordon, I was encouraging you. Don't be stupid."

"Stupid, am I?" He hit her. Not so hard as to be vicious, he gauged, but firmly enough to convey his frustration at her attitude.

The next night, after he and Isaac had spent the day thinking about the market and their next step, Mazy came home drunk. She even had the temerity to blame it on him, for giving her what she had coming!

For Gordon, this marked the beginning of the end. Weakness. He despised nothing more. Mazy had gone straight, under his tutelage and example, but now she was slipping back into her decrepitude. He knocked her about, just a bit, to drive some sense into her head, make her understand her lapse for what it was, but his efforts were fruitless. He caught her snogging a random bloke at Dusk Till Dawn; he put the eager Ginger onto getting rid of the man while Gordon took Mazy back home and delivered a savage beating with his belt. Her weaknesses compounded, however. Gordon had spent a week in Thailand, cementing some business connections, and by the time he returned to Hong Kong, Mazy had cut her teaching hours back to part time, to accommodate mornings spent unconscious on the couch.

Gordon had given Mazy so much: he had fed and clothed her, sheltered her, helped her out of her alcoholism. He had told her his life story (omitting the part about the dead nineteen-year-old in Leeds) time and again, to inspire her; yet with each lesson she seemed ever more withdrawn.

What had Mazy given him? Yes, Gordon would admit, it was nice to showcase this particular bit of crumpet. She was a damned attractive woman, mixing the best of vaguely Chinese eyes and structure with European skin as white as the finest cocaine. But the world was full of beautiful birds. Had she made him happy? Yes, Gordon would acknowledge that she had, initially, just as injecting heroin brought an initial rush of delirium.

But what she had given him, did it come close to what he had given to her? No, surely not. And now, he had gifted her so much more: the franchise to Chili Hut. An expensive diamond ring. A commitment—yes, a final attempt to show her what discipline was all about, a last chance for her to prove to him that she could also show strength of character and loyalty.

Gordon knew it was a mistake, helping others when he should be looking out for himself. But that's the kind of man he was.

Isaac Alika shared a similar sentiment: he knew he should look out for himself, too, but things had gotten, well, complicated.

Last night's spectacle had disturbed him in a way he had never experienced. Little things got to Isaac; he was touchy. Ginger's taunts,

Gordon's inflating sense of bossy self-importance. These things annoyed him, but he tolerated them because he was, deep down, imperturbable. At least, so he had thought, until he had fallen in...um...love, he supposed.

Emotions weren't his thing. Being mates, flirting with the ladies—not his forte. Isaac preferred the world of periodic tables of elements, molecular chemistry, beakers and bunson burners. Wizard of Ox, his old classmates had called him, after he reverse-engineered how to manufacture oxycodene and began dealing his wares on campus.

Uni had been great until the Wiz's hobby annoyed the local drug dealers, who suggested he either join them or end up in the River Don.

He justified his decision, he later told the police inspector, because he didn't know how to swim. Typically for Isaac, the cops had assumed he was taking the piss, so they beat him six types of purple.

He had seen people using. He used himself. It was Isaac who made Gordon aware of ket. This had become Isaac's drug of choice. It wasn't particularly addictive, so long as he didn't over do it, but the introspective trips it provided made it perfect for the anti-social. Although some people took it in moderate doses while clubbing or to have spaced-out chats with other users, Isaac was in it for the journey.

The first time he tried to explain to Gordon what it was like to go down the K-hole, he said an ambiance of isolation was key.

Isaac would turn out the lights in his room and stretch out naked on his bed, hands out, feet out, fingers and even toes splayed so no part of his body touched another. Sometimes he'd play dubstep, but at a very low volume, mostly to insure against street noise. Although it was easiest to sniff in powder form, Isaac preferred to inject it into his muscle tissue, building up to sizeable doses of one hundred milligrams or more, and slide on his eyeshades.

"Then what?" Gordon had asked.

Then...*everything.* Shifting out of his body. Seeing music play before him in spectacular color. Floating. Holding hands with angels. Conversing with God. The K-hole was a place of both peace and terror, but even the scary bits were like a dream in which you're half-awake, sort of knowing you can adjust the dial on the scariness, lingering among ghosts, gradually understanding that you are already dead because there's no such thing as dead anyway so what's to fear?

You knew it had been a good trip when, afterwards, whatever was labeled reality didn't feel right, and the rest of the day was like stumbling through a dream, and all you wanted was to get back in the hole.

"But the depression afterward's part of it," Isaac explained.

Isaac began to wonder what it would be like if he and Mazy used it together, just the two of them, maybe in his room, or maybe lying side by side on one of the loungers overlooking the sunset. They could spend an hour or two talking shite about their trips and he could hold her during the scary bits and tell her everything's going to be cool, you'll see, Maze, just let the Wiz take care of it.

So Isaac liked ketamine, and back in the UK he had spent a lot of time trying to make it. It was fiendishly difficult, which is why street ket is stolen from labs, hospitals or veterinary clinics, which deploy it as an anesthesia, rather than made from clandestine labs. Isaac figured it out, but obtaining or concocting things like methylamine, a mixture of carbon, hydrogen and nitrogen that created a noxious gas that corrodes metal, necessitated the sort of set-up and stability not usually associated with illicit manufacturing. It was, in fact, a police raid on the lab he had set up in Sheffield that necessitated Isaac's decision to follow Gordon out of the UK.

Gordo, for his part, had little interest in anything so complicated. Special K had to be stolen for resale, which merely added another layer of risk, and he preferred to stick to moving what he knew. Besides, Rohypnol was widely available—if you wanted to knock someone out and make them forget it, roofies did the trick.

But as he expanded his Hong Kong operation, the clamor for ketamine amplified. Gordo became aware of its alternative applications, and he began to think that, if he could tackle the challenges of ketamine, it would give him that competitive advantage and security against the triads. It was a question of marketing a hot new brand.

But what would be the hook?

That's when Isaac suggested that, with K-Love, users would really enjoy the experience before forgetting about it. For a short time, they'd be totally docile yet fully engaged.

That's what sold Gordo. Slipping drinks to girls would not only get them in bed but would get them to want it.

"It's meant to be beautiful," Isaac had suggested.

He was too disconnected from the world to bother thinking about what others might do with his creation. He didn't question Gordon, who had helped him slip out of the UK, and besides, no woman like Mazy would hang around with anyone too stupid or nasty. Or so it had been at first.

Isaac was normally unaware of other guys' girlfriends or short-time partners, but Mazy had a way of filling his imagination. He had once gone with Gordon to meet her at her studio, and he watched her through the door's window as she led her class through their yoga postures. She was engaged in a standing twist, hands clasped straight above her head, and every curve was on display. She then turned his way—she wore her hair long back then, and the pony tail whipped around—and Isaac was stunned by her blissful smile.

It's like she's tripping, he thought. *Heavy*.

Despite his own preference for K, Isaac chose ignorance when it came to knowing about Gordon's business plans. Nor was Gordon partial to sharing those details. Isaac suspected that the K-Love he had been tasked with developing could be used to spike drinks, but he told himself it was for conscious demand among real users.

It would have bothered him if Gordon had spiked one of the whores' drinks. Isaac dabbled in ladies if he didn't need to remember their names, because a man's a man and he needs to take care of business. But he treated the women with extreme courtesy; it was Ginger's brutishness that made Isaac come to hate the Scouse almost at once.

It took him a few turns to realize that Gordon and Tarrin were bringing hookers back to the villa as guinea pigs. Give them drinks laced with Isaac's test versions of K-Love, try different dosages, see what happened.

Even then, Isaac pretended it was still OK. No one got hurt, not really—they were prostitutes here to get fucked anyway, right? Besides, the girls seemed to have the times of their lives. Ginger and Tarrin had to make just the slightest suggestion, and the women would comply before inevitably puking and passing out. Then Tarrin would make sure his crew would collect the women, and Lek and Anurak would clean up the next morning.

Last night, Gordon had decided to test K-Love on Mazy—on his own girlfriend—on the closest thing to an angel Isaac had ever encountered in this so-called reality.

Isaac had wanted to protest, partly because it was a bastardization of a noble drug. Disrespectful. That's what he told himself.

Really, though, it was because it was going to render Mazy a physically numb, agreeable, spaced-out sex zombie for about an hour before she likely passed out with no memory of what had happened.

The worst, the most painful memory that Isaac wished like hell he could banish: Ginger, naked, with a thrusting hard-on despite having just finished with a Thai girl, walking through the open door to Gordon and Mazy's bedroom. His demands. Gordon's bargaining —like Mazy was nothing but a commodity, a bushel of wheat, a barrel of oil. And her lying there topless, looking around vacantly, examining her fingers, and hearing Gordon's suggestion, and smiling sort of sleepily before Ginger moved in.

And where had Gordon been? He had stayed for only a moment before flitting out, a dark look of determination on his face, and Isaac hadn't seen him the rest of the night.

And so Isaac found himself turned inside out in the so-called real world, without having taken anything other than a few puffs of a spliff. He was in a different type of hole, and the isolation that he had allowed to rule his life was spent.

Chapter 16

A Nice Romantic Dinner

"**C**AN I help?" Mazy asked at the top of the villa stairs.

Gordon was blasting Oasis and jigging around the kitchen, while Lek stood very stiffly at the counter, chopping vegetables, her face betraying no expression. Anurak, Lek's husband and the villa's driver and handyman, was setting the table for four; he too wore a look of flat stone, although he brightened into a smile at Mazy's approach.

"No, getting there," Gordon shouted back, opening the oven with a mitten. "This is going to be special."

Mazy had agonized over what to wear for this stupid dinner, not out of any particular obsession with fashion, for she was generally a simple, casual dresser, but because she wanted to draw no remark from Gordon. She needed to be seen to take the celebration seriously, but not overdo it. She settled on a red, off-the-shoulder halter top and blue jeans. She rarely wore makeup but tonight she put on lipstick, mascara and eye liner, and she used the blow dryer to feather out her locks.

The diamond ring sparkled cold fire on her pinkie.

Between showering and dressing, she had squatted before the safe in their bedroom closet, experimenting with six-digit combinations. His birthday, her birthday, the numbers that spelled out 'Gordon' on a telephone pad. After several attempts, the safe emitted an aggravated bleep. Cursing, Mazy stuffed the cubbyhole with a throw pillow from the sofa and shut the door, sagging against it and hoping no one had heard.

Then she went up to the kitchen.

"Dinner for four?" she said. "I thought this was just you and me."

"It is," Gordon replied, "but I want everyone to enjoy the toast."

She opened the fridge, feeling the usual craving, her spirits getting a little boost from the idea of a drink. A bottle of Veuve Cliquot had joined Gordon's collection of Chardonnays and Pinot Noirs—Gordon alternated methadone and fine wines. *Can't say the man ain't eclectic*, she mused.

"Why don't I do the Champagne, then?"

"What, now?"

"Sure, why not?"

"It's another twenty minutes at least before I get this roast sorted."

She opened the freezer and regarded with greed her remaining supply of vodka. "Well, this girl's going to need a starter."

Gordon frowned. "Not yet. You know the rules."

"C'mon, Gordon, please? Just one."

"It spoils the taste of fine Champagne."

"Then let's have the Champagne. Let me at least pour it."

He arched straight from the oven, eyes glowering. He hadn't changed out of his usual Thailand garb—camouflage shorts, grungy West Ham football jersey. "Are you arguing with me?"

Mazy shut the freezer door. "No, sorry. I'm just excited, I guess. Are you going to wear that to dinner?"

He glanced down at himself. "I'll change once this is done."

"Lek and I can handle things from here," she said. "Why don't you go wash up? Wear that nice blue shirt, the one I got you at H&M."

"Very well." He gave her a peck on the cheek. "You know how to cook a roast?"

"Of course," Mazy lied, having barely mastered the art of boiling water for tea. For a moment, she thought Gordon was going to call her bluff, for he regarded her quizzically, almost as though he suddenly had no idea whom he was looking at. He opened the freezer and took a moment to count the bottles of vodka and note their levels. "These will not have changed when I get back," he told her.

"I swear to God, Gordon."

Gordon grunted, walked brusquely past her and down the stairs toward the pool.

Mazy figured she had ten minutes, tops. "Lek, can you handle the roast?"

"Yes, miss."

Mazy strode toward the little upstairs bathroom across the wide living space, closed the door and ran the water as loudly as possible. She retrieved the knife and the coconuts. She hesitated, beginning to feel the panic in her stomach, wondering how to pull this off.

She had to trust Lek.

Breaking the coconuts in the bathroom seemed pointless, so she turned off the tap and carried everything in a hurried scamper back to the kitchen.

Lek was assembling ingredients for a salad; it was the sound of the first crack of the knife handle against the coconut that made her turn.

"Miss?"

Mazy placed her finger against her lips and nodded deliberately, eyes questioning. The maid nodded back and returned to her work.

Casting frightened glances across to the stairs —if any of the three men chose this moment to walk up, she had no explanation. She could handle a beating when she was drunk but not now, not sober...not *aching* for just one shot, knowing she had no room to sneak one in. Mercifully, after a few blows the coconut popped open in halves. There was no explosion of milk. A small, sealed plastic bag unfolded from within, half-filled with a clear liquid. Mazy had no idea how much or how little this was. Lek was staring wide-eyed at her work and hastily looked away again, and Mazy could tell the usually unruffled maid was nervous.

"You haven't seen anything," she said as quietly as she could over the loud music. "You're just making a salad, OK, Lek?"

Mazy searched the second coconut for its seal, hit there once, hard, and it opened. She picked up the shells and hustled them into the trash can under the kitchen sink. "I'm just cleaning up and you aren't paying any attention." She grabbed a sponge and cleaned up the island counter. "I need a funnel. Lek, funnel, you know? Please."

Lek pointed with a shaky finger at a drawer where Mazy found a crowded clutch of cooking tools, including a small tin funnel.

"Perfect." She fetched the Veuve and began to wedge the cork loose, looking at the two plastic baggies, and then at the top of the villa stairs. *Not yet...not yet!*

"Lek, glasses—Champagne glasses. Hurry!" She was practically weeping the words.

Lek ran to one of the higher cabinets and found the glasses. "Like this one, miss?"

"No, that's a wine glass—the flutes, the tall ones in the back."

Mazy pulled the cork and a cold crest of foam spilled over her fingers.

Lek scrambled to extract one, two, three—four flutes as the music inexplicably dropped off. Oh, no, Mazy realized as her heart leaped, it was because one of them was up here. He —they?—had come up and she hadn't heard them and they had crossed the living room to the stereo and turned the music down.

Gordon.

She stepped back to grab the baggies, still not spotting him, maybe it was just Gordo, but he'd be coming in now. "Get ready to pour," she hissed at Lek, who picked up the bottle in her unsteady hands as Mazy unsealed the first bag and began to empty it into the glasses. Her own hands were shaking like mad and most of the Love-K seemed to slop across the counter instead of going into the glasses.

"How about some Billie Holiday?" Gordon called.

"Oh I love her," Mazy shouted back. *Remember your* pranayama. *Breathe.*

Lek stared at her, mystified at Mazy's sudden pause in movement. Mazy allowed herself two quick inhalations. Then, her hands now steady, she poured the second baggie's contents neatly into three of the flutes.

"Did I hear the cork go?" Gordon asked, rounding the corner into the kitchen, his Android cell in hand. He was finishing up a text message, one of his innumerable communications that he called business but Maze suspected was more about football chit-chat.

"Yep," Mazy said, pouring the Veuve. "You're just in time, sweetie." Smiling, she handed him a glass, and he put the phone down on the table.

"Sorry, I got some on my hands. Lek, can you run the water, please?"

Gordon sniffed the glass and smiled appreciatively. "Nothing like a crisp champers, is there."

"Who doesn't love bubbly?" Mazy agreed. "You look handsome."

She had made sure to pour herself a particularly large portion, partly to identify her glass, but mostly because she sure needed the drink.

Gordon was dressed in a blue polo and white slacks, his dark curls pulled back into a budding ponytail. He almost drank, but then decided to wait, and opened the freezer to examine the vodka. Satisfied, he went to the dinner table as Ginger and Isaac filed up the stairs, both looking clean and dressed casually but nicely.

"A romantic dinner for us all?" Ginger wondered.

"Not tonight, lads," Gordon said. "Mazy, come here and show them your gift."

Mazy walked with her hand raised, fingers pointing down, to show off the diamond. "Gordon asked me to marry him."

"That's a surprise," Ginger said evenly.

"Yeah," Isaac said, looking startled. "Big surprise."

"That's my Gordon—never predictable."

"Expect the unexpected, always," Gordon said. "Hurry up with that Champagne. A toast, and then Anurak can drive you lot into town. Maze and me are having a nice romantic dinner here tonight."

"Brilliant," Ginger said, looking oddly pleased. Isaac frowned and accepted his flute in silence.

Mazy raised her glass. "Cheers!"

They clinked flutes and took some sips. Mazy knew she had to be patient. If Ginger and Isaac were going to leave, it didn't matter, but now she worried about the timing. Otherwise she needed them all to finish up quickly, simultaneously.

"I'd like to make a toast," she said. "To my fiancé, Gordon Wood, the smartest guy ever. Whoa, look out world."

Gordon shrugged and they sipped another round. Mazy waited for someone else to pick up the baton, but there was just an awkward silence. Gordon was admiring the way the bubbles teased his nose, Ginger's mind was probably focused on Chaweng barhopping, and Isaac was staring oddly at his flute, as though he had never tasted Champagne before.

"Well, another toast," Mazy said. "To Ginger and Isaac, who I hope to see at my wedding."

This time the ritual was perfunctory. Mazy took a deep gulp to steady herself.

"And to Koh Samui," she said.

"Enough," Gordon said, setting down his glass. "How'd that roast turn out?"

Shit! Mazy said, "Well, we were so excited, Gordon, I may have left the roast in there a little too long..."

Lek approached with the marinated side of pork steaming in its pan. "How this, Mister Gordon?"

He looked at it and nodded. "You didn't fuck it up."

Lek wobbled, not sure what he meant but hearing the f-word, so Mazy put a gentle hand on her arm.

"Good job, Lek," she said, and the maid smiled in relief and set the roast on the dinner table. "Well, this girl says bottoms up," and she drained her flute.

"Chin chin," Ginger muttered, following suit. Gordon wanted wine and scanned the interior of the fridge.

"Gordon," Mazy said, "don't you want to finish this delicious Champagne?"

"You have it."

Mazy forced her smile. "But, darling, it's for our toast."

"Bollocks to the toast," Gordon snarled. "I had mine, now I want some of this effing Burgundy, got it?"

"Got it," she said meekly.

"You're the bleeding alky, why don't you just finish it off for me."

Mazy stared at his glass.

Isaac stammered, "I-I'll have it."

"No, Isaac," she said. "You won't. That's Gordon's drink for our engagement and I think it would be bad luck for our marriage if you don't finish it, darling, isn't it nice?"

He sighed irritably. "Fuck's sake."

Ginger snorted. "You ain't even married yet, Gordon, and already she's nagging you."

Gordon shot him a cross look and swiped the glass from her outstretched hand. "Mind your mouth, Chester." He finished the drink. "Why don't you boys go downstairs, get Anurak. Mazy, sit down."

She obeyed and he brought her a glass of wine. Isaac and Ginger strolled across the living room to the balcony overlooking the drive, and down the steps leading out front. Gordon waved Lek away. "You can go," he told her, and she scampered away without a single word.

"Need a knife," he said, and Mazy felt her heart race again—where was the knife she had used to open the... Gordon returned with it, Lek must have washed it, and he proceeded to cut the meat while Mazy heaped salad on their plates. Gordon sat down opposite her with a strange heaviness. They raised their wine glasses and Maze had to force herself not to swallow it all at once. Gordon took just a sip and raised his fork and knife. "Well," he said. Mazy waited for him to continue but he just sat there, as though he were thinking hard about something.

"Gordon?"

"Yeah, OK," he said, absently chewing a bite of meat.

"Mm, it's really good."

He set down his fork and knife. "I don't feel too well."

"It's probably just the excitement. I'm all dizzy!"

"I feel strange."

He had such a question mark on his face that she nearly laughed. "It's not the roast, is it? It tastes fine to me."

Now he zeroed on her and Mazy's smile fluttered away. He looked angry. "You've done... something."

"No, nothing."

"Something's wrong. I feel..."

He stood up but his balance was off and his glass of Burgundy crashed on the sandstone. "My legs are numb."

"Gordon, maybe you should just lie down. I'll lower the music."

He lunged for her but she evaded him as she moved to the stereo, turned Lady Day down a few notches. Gordon stumbled to the circle of sofas, his hand clutching their fabric tops. "You."

"You want a glass of water, Gordon?"

He raised his arm. "I think I'm going to cut you... into a thousand little pieces."

Mazy backed up as he lurched toward her. "Gordon, you really should lie down."

"So many little pieces," he intoned. "Blood everywhere."

He's freaking out. What kind of dose was that, anyway? She didn't know exactly what ketamine was all about, but she had heard it was psychotropic, or something like that. Well, what's good for the goose is good for the gander.

"It's going to be all right," she said, trying to keep her voice easy. "Just lie down and listen to the music, Gordon."

He nodded then and slumped into the cushions. "Don't feel so good."

"That's it, baby," she said, already making to leave. She reached the top of the stairs, then ran back to the kitchen and pulled out the two bottles of Absolut. Mazy hurried to the villa steps and hesitated, looking back at the table. Gordon's cell phone. Without thinking, she tucked the vodka bottles into the crook of one arm, picked up the phone and stuffed it in her pocket, before leaping down the stairs toward the pool and their bedroom.

She hadn't risked packing her suitcase, but she had stuffed extra clothes into a backpack. She now added toiletries—tampons, toothbrush, combs, nail clippers—and stuffed her billfold inside her pocket. She slipped the two bottles of vodka into external pouches and she slung the bag over her two shoulders. Still barefoot, Mazy grabbed a pair of Converse sneakers on the way out.

Isaac was waiting for her at the edge of the infinity pool, his dark skin lit a bright blue by the pool lights, a tall ghost blocking her path to the beach. Maybe it was the weird lighting, but he seemed to be in a strange state of grace.

"Isaac," she said, "I thought you and Ginger were going into town."

"I don't think we're going to make it tonight, Maze."

"Well, um, Gordon's not feeling so hot, and maybe you should, you know, check up on him?"

"Gordon's down the hole. It's his first time but he'll come back."

"Hole? I don't know what you're talking about, Isaac."

"The K-hole, Maze, and it's like that, a maze, like you, an incredible puzzle, a mystery, a revelation."

"Wow."

"What you may not understand, Maze, is that I know the hole. I know the hole. The hole knows me. I'm guessing what, seventy, maybe a hundred migs? Ginge and Gordo, they're virgins, so that's a mega dose. They're in the hole. Me, I'm like the ship circling the whirlpool. I'm skimming the seas, I'm flying in the air, I'm dancing, but I'm not yet in the hole. I know, I been here."

"It was an accident."

He gave her a goofy smile. "Sure it was, Maze, sure it was. Big Ginge, know where I left him? Crying. Big man like that, crying. K-hole's scary, Maze. He'll find the beautiful place soon, because K's beautiful, but right now he wants his mummy."

"Isaac," she said carefully, "maybe you want to lie down, too."

"Maybe we can lie down together, Maze. There's so many things I want to say to you right now. But you need to use with me, yeah?" He opened his hand. "Snort this up and you'll be set. I'll show you so much, we'll talk so much, and it won't be scary, I promise."

"Isaac, I'm just taking a walk along the beach."

"OK, we can do that, too."

"No, Isaac, I have to go by myself, and you need to stay here."

"Maze," he said, his cheeks glistening with fresh tears, "I don't want to be here by myself, not with them. You have to...you have to *try* this."

"Sorry, Isaac," she said, making a sudden dash. His tolerance had kept him relatively lucid, but when he tried to follow her, his legs turned to rubber and he ended on his back upon the stretch of grass between the pool and the beach, staring up at the stars, the sound of the waves crashing through his consciousness.

Clutching her sneakers to her breast, her other hand on her backpack strap, Mazy ran onto the sand. Small white crabs scattered lizard-quick as she took off into the unlit littoral, a tongue of gulf water licking at her ankles. Something sharp pricked the ball of her left foot and she hopped along, cursing, wondering why she hadn't just put on the damn sneakers.

It was pitch dark here, no moon tonight, but the stars were enough for her to make out the sea and the beach, and the dark thicket of palms ahead. She didn't know exactly where she was going and she nearly crashed into one of the tables outside the beach restaurant. She glanced back, but no one was there. Mazy had to catch her breath. *Where the hell is it?*

The restaurant was dark; the Montris closed up at sundown. She barely made out a smaller structure alongside, and nearly strangled herself walking into a strung-up cord for laundry. Somehow she didn't think this was it. She crept into the nothingness, now stepping on nettles and sharp pebbles. Feeling stupid, she brushed off the soles of her feet and slipped on the sneakers. Then she felt her way forward again, each footstep causing an explosion of broken twigs.

A dog's bark shattered the calm and she froze, hands raised, but in such darkness she couldn't see them. She quickly looked over her shoulder, dimly made out the moving sea. Mazy was scared of big dogs, and that was in broad daylight.

What am I doing? She started to cry as the barking intensified. *I think I'm going to cut you into a thousand little pieces.* She could still go back. Come up with some explanation; spike a drink of her own from the coconut stash; blame it on Lek; blame it on Tarrin; she could go back crawling, could hold Gordon's hand and whisper sweet lies, easing him out of the K-hole, proving how much she loved him. It wasn't too late because she didn't want fangs to bite her in the dark...

A slender pole of yellow light appeared nearby. "Quit it, dog, what's your problem?"

Another light—from a porch, ten feet in front of her, and Mazy nearly fainted at the sight of the brown dog growling at her, teeth bared.

"Maze?" Then she saw Trav, standing there in shorts and a T-shirt. He petted the dog's head with the hand in the cast. "Easy, girl." He straightened. "That you?"

Mazy wiped her face with the crook of her arm and walked into the range of the porch light. "Hey," she said.

Chapter 17

Fumbling in the Dark

TRAV closed the front door, leaving the dog out on the porch. He wasn't sure if his amazement at Mazy's appearance should be tinged with joy or concern. Mazy looked all right to him, though. The twin bottles of vodka clinked as she shrugged her backpack off onto the kitchen table, next to his open laptop.

"Thanks," she said. "I really appreciate it."

"No problem. You OK?

She smiled a little too brightly. "You bet."

"You bet, but what?"

She leaned against the kitchenette, incongruous in her dressy red top—as though stopping by on her way to a cocktail party. The diamond was the brightest thing in the room, although he noticed it twinkled from her pinkie instead of her ring finger. "I guess not so OK."

"You hurt? That guy hit you?" He wanted to put a comforting hand on her bare shoulder but figured she might take it the wrong way. Or the right way. Or whatever.

"I'm not hurt, but at some point they might come looking for me. If not tonight then in the morning...but probably tonight."

"They?"

"Besides Gordon, there's Isaac, who I don't think's a problem, and Ginge—Chester, I mean. He's definitely a problem."

"Gordon's your boyfriend, the one with the beard and doughnuts for earlobes?"

"It's gross when you put it that way."

"It's just plain gross." Trav freed the Absoluts from the backpack and put them in the freezer. "I guess this is your rations."

"Pour a girl a drink?"

"Guess you could use one." He got out mismatched glasses from a cabinet. "I have some OJ, but not much."

"If there isn't enough, don't waste it on me."

Trav nodded, opening the fridge.

Mazy looked around at the Formica, the linoleum, the fluorescent light, the rattan furniture that never had the privilege of seeing a better day. "Quite the palace you got here."

"It's cheap," Trav said, pouring the last of the OJ into the two glasses. "And not really intended for entertaining guests."

He poured vodka, a shot for himself, a full glass for her.

"You know how to pour a drink," she said, accepting the glass.

"I'm not trying to get you drunk. I just figured you, uh, took doubles."

"You figured right, cowboy. Cheers."

He sat down, gestured for her to take another of the plastic chairs. "So, uh, now what? You want to talk about it?"

Mazy stood straight up again. "Your porch light still on?"

"Oh, right. That switch there."

She turned it off and crossed to look out the window beside the door, the one over the sink, adorned by flimsy wooden blinds. She peeked in both bedrooms. They each had one window, although his was half-filled with an air conditioner. Only the tiny bathroom stood without.

"Sure is bright in here," she said. "Look, Trav, I know this sounds crazy, and I'm sorry, but if you're going to let me crash, then I'd be a whole lot more comfy if we could kill the lights. I don't think Gordon knows this place exists, but if he comes looking for me the shades won't be enough."

"To hide the house in the dark?"

"Yeah."

Trav hadn't expected this—he didn't know what he *had* expected. Nothing, probably. Chasing her into town last night had been stupid and he had spent dinner in the marketplace across the road trying to forget about his idiocy.

"It's going to be pitch black."

Mazy set down her glass. "If this isn't cool, man, then you need to tell me right now so I can start running."

"No, no, it's cool. I just..."

"Didn't know what kind of viper's nest you'd just jumped into?"

He swung the Mac around. "I'll set this so the screen light stays on the whole time. That'll be enough for us to get around, all right? No one will ever see it. OK?"

She bit her lower lip and he had a first inkling of how scared she was. Trav sorted out the Mac. "OK, try the other switch."

Mazy turned off the light and the shack entered a cold darkness, except for the white square glow of the laptop screen. It didn't really shed much light past the keyboard, but it gave Trav a certain comfort. He heard Mazy glug her drink.

"Will the dog bark if they show up?" she asked, her face dim and ghostly.

"She barked at you, so, yeah, I guess so. But they'd have to get pretty close. And by then you'd want an alarm, right?"

"I guess so."

He had a thousand questions swimming through his head, but somehow he felt it would be wrong to unleash even a single one, especially in the dark. He had thought this black pitch might prove intimate or comforting, but it was too absolute. It was isolating. His eyes were adjusting and he could make out the outline of the window, but that was about it. And the silence grew suffocating, as they sat apart in the night. Half-familiar sounds came to him but at a strange proximity, as though the copse of palms and bamboo were closing in on the little house, driven by the barely audible rhythm of the tides.

The clock on the computer told him it was only a little past nine o'clock, which seemed early, and he wasn't the least bit tired. But it seemed weird to sit here in monastic silence—it sure was getting uncomfortable—and Mazy didn't seem in the mood for a conversation.

"Well," he whispered, his voice strange and awkward, "I guess it's bedtime."

"I don't want to give you the wrong idea," she replied.

"No wrong idea," he said, smothering a twinge of disappointment. *Well, that's one fantasy put to rest.* "There's two bedrooms. If you need the A.C. you can take mine."

There was a rustle outside and he heard her suck in her breath.

"Just the dog," he said.

Mazy eventually said, "I don't need the air-con, thanks."

Trav got up and felt his way into the bathroom, banging into the chair, flailing against the wall. He knew it was ridiculous to think these nothing sounds could travel, but they sounded terribly loud. Wincing, he slid shut the bathroom's folding sliding door and pulled the string for the naked bulb above. The tiled alcove was a harsh white and the toilet's flush roared.

As he brushed his teeth, he heard her crawling outside in the dark. He should probably be terrified if there were three men out there coming after her. And he was now totally sensitive to his own noise. The nearness of the villa loomed in his consciousness. But the house was set just far enough back from the beach, behind its defensive rim of foliage, to be invisible from the villa's top floor and, at night, impossible to find without knowing it was there.

How could he be scared when he had this woman here? He smiled at his reflection. *Dumbass like you, with a chick like that.* He had done it. Met the damsel in distress. Did some pretty cool tailing, like a Raymond Chandler hero. Tracked them into town. Avoided the bad guys, got close to her, flicked her his number —how slick had that been? Then the adrenaline moment outside the stadium, a chase, a getaway. And here he was, Travis Mitchell, ex-trader, ex-kickboxer, ex-fiancé, ex- ex- ex-, with the damsel having come to him for help.

Well, maybe for help, but taking Trav into her grateful arms didn't seem high on her agenda. He heard the squeal of the freezer door open and shut. Who needed the lights on to get drunk?

Trav exited the bathroom but left the door open a crack, to give them a modicum of light. The white ray found her standing alone with the bottle. She had put the glass in the sink.

"Your turn," he said. "Need anything?"

"Thanks, I'm good." She put the bottle down and reached for her backpack. "I can manage from here."

"You're limping. You sure you're OK?"

She kicked back her foot, looked over her shoulder at the sole of her sneaker. "I think I cut myself coming over here."

"Let's have a look."

"No, I'm tired."

"If you've cut yourself, you don't want to get an infection. Then you won't be running anywhere."

She sighed. "All right." Mazy dragged herself into the guest room, taking the bottle with her, and stretched out on her stomach.

There was a small reading light on the bedside table. Trav turned it around so it faced the corner and turned it on, providing just enough light to see the contours of a fuzzy night. Using her right shoe, Mazy nudged off the heel of the left. He slipped it off her foot and saw the gash on the round ball.

"Hang on." He went to the kitchen, half by feel, and found a clean hand towel in the drawer. He ran the tap into a plastic drinking cup and returned to the bedroom. She had shifted to one side so she could take a swig from the bottle.

"On your belly," he ordered her and she rolled back over.

Trav took the bare foot into both of his hands. "Give me the bottle for a sec." She passed it to him and he dabbed a dash onto the towel. She took back the bottle. "Lay still."

It was just a foot. It was just a cut. It was a thousand things more. He pressed the boozed towel against the wound, first gently, then firmly. She let out an oww and he heard the rustle of her clutching the pillow. He cleaned the wound as best he could in the near dark, first with the vodka, then with water.

"Don't move."

Trav knew there was a basic first-aid kit in the bathroom, on the shelf behind the mirror. He went there, the naked bulb inside casting a bright and harsh light. He took a couple of band-aids and returned to her waiting foot, hoisted straight up from the knee. He applied two of them tenderly, all the while looking at the curve of her foot, which connected to her ankle, which ran down that calf, shapely in her tight jeans, to the bend in her knee. From there her thighs lay slightly apart.

She had twisted her torso and was looking up at him, her expression masked by the darkness.

"Thanks," she said.

"You're welcome." He was still holding her foot. Massaging it. "Why do you drink like that?"

"Because I'm an alky."

"You couldn't have been an alky for long, or forever, if you were my yoga instructor a month ago."

She snorted, as though he had told a knee-slapper. "I guess I've been inspired lately."

"I just don't get why a woman like you ended up with that guy in the first place."

"Are you going to let go of my foot?"

"Oh. Yeah." He let go. "Hope it gets better."

She took another swig and those black sockets in her perfectly carved face seemed to bore right through him. "You want to fuck me, don't you?"

Trav stood up, afraid she would sense his vibration. Yes, he did want that, very much, but not like this, not when she was drunk, vulgar. Had it been just another girl, one of the Hong Kong party chicks he and Kar-wei picked up in nightclubs and took on Kar-wei's boat, then, yeah, sure. Get them liquored up and in the mood for a good time. But not Mazy, not when she was showing her ugliness.

"Good night, Maze."

"Good night, Trav."

He paused in the doorway. "Just, uh, knock if you need anything."

She nodded in the ray of light. "Sure thing."

Trav went to his bedroom and left the door ajar. He stripped down to his boxers and climbed into bed. His eyes were sufficiently adjusted that the meager portion of light from the bathroom was enough to navigate by. An alarm clock's red digital numerals floated nearby. He usually slept with the A.C. on, but tonight decided to forego it. Too noisy, and he wanted to hear everything going on—outside, inside. There was no ceiling fan in here, just a small portable one on the floor, and he put that on. Its low hum seemed to fill the room.

His eyes targeted the narrow opening of his door and once or twice he registered her moving around, heard her run the tap and later flush. Otherwise she moved silently until he heard the creak of the other bed, very faintly, and his eyes immediately widened as he remembered the big hole he had painstakingly carved from the bottom of the guest room mattress. She was lying on his cash-filled backpack and a parade of paranoid ideas jangled through his head. He wondered if she could feel the hidden pack. If she had knowledge of it. If he'd wake up to find her gone, the mattress's secret pouch emptied, the dog giving him that don't-blame-me look.

Wasn't this the part where she'd creep into his room, maybe feeling a little scared, or a little grateful, or just needing to be held? He entertained a few pathways this could take, his eyes flickering open and looking at the door. He lay still until he couldn't stand it, afraid to be heard. Then he flipped over, telling himself he was a ridiculous fool, or telling himself he was a hero, or sternly reminding himself that a gentleman has to live by a code, and say what you will, he was sticking to those principles from on high, but still, it would be nice if she just sought out, you know, some comforting.

The sound of the empty bottle banging onto the floor and taking about a million minutes to roll to a stop somewhere next door told him Mazy had already found whatever solace she required.

Chapter 18

Gordon Figures It Out

THE search mission never quite got off the ground last night. A heavy dose of ketamine on an inexperienced user was incapacitating to begin with, but Gordon suspected mixing it with methadone made it worse, perhaps even dangerous. He never made it off the sofa and awoke to the stink of his own vomit. It seemed to be everywhere, as though he had made a deliberate effort to coat his clothes, the sofa, the coffee table—anything within range.

It was early morning and the light was bright and intense. The sea burst silver with sunlight, adding to his dizziness.

He ached from having slept in more or less the same position, although sleep was not quite the right word for being comatose.

Gordon replayed what he could remember. Happiness, he remembered that, although the emotion seemed alien to him now. He had prepared a dinner for himself and Maze. A special dinner because he had given her the ring. The

JAME DIBIASIO

proposal had been completely spur of the moment, a surprise even to him. The last thing he remembered was the four of them toasting, and then pulling the chair back from the table, as if to sit—that was the most concrete thing in his mind, the physical weight of the chair in his hand.

Something must have been in the Champagne, and he wasn't sure who had put it there, but he had a pretty good idea of what it had been. Feeling strung out like this reminded Gordon of how much he sometimes missed heroin. He forced the notion from his mind.

His legs held him and he stumbled to the kitchen, drank some water. He patted his pockets but the phone wasn't there. The list of suspects shortened as he went down to the pool area. Isaac or Ginger could have gotten access to K-Love or something like it, but why would they spike the Champagne?

Ginger. Could have been. Jealous twat. Wouldn't put it past a Scouse.

Gordon knew that Ginger wanted Maze but couldn't have her. The sudden memory of two nights ago and the bargain he had struck with Ginge—it made him sick to his stomach all over again. He entertained the possibility that giving Ginger a taste of Mazy had been, perhaps, an error.

Shouldn't have let Ginge get the better of him —not that Ginger had done, understand. Gordon had traded her services fair and square. But maybe he should have just told Ginger

152

to sod off, because the brute might get ideas. Might make some smart remark about sexual performance. *Maze belongs to me.* Hadn't he proven it last night with the ring?

After that display, the notion that a covetous Ginger slipped the boss a mickey seemed far-fetched.

Same with Isaac. The chemist liked his drugs all right, and had an odd sense of humor. But he was a coward, and Gordon couldn't conceive of any scenario in which Maze would run away with him. Anyway, neither of the lads had been upstairs.

No, it had been Mazy who had opened the bottle. Poured the Champagne—with Lek, another suspect?—and had kept banging on about bleeding toasts. Gordon initially rejected the idea as preposterous. She wouldn't dare. And hadn't he sacrificed so much for her? Hadn't the ring been proof enough, as though any more were needed?

But Ginger had accused her of sneaking into the downstairs rooms, where Gordon housed a few samples. The room he had spent yesterday morning hosing down with Tarrin and two of his boys, entombing it in secrecy as the others had slept.

Gordon needed a few more facts before passing judgment. He'd start with Ginger. The bodyguard was sprawled beside the Jacuzzi, white skin rapidly turning red, snoring. Probably lucky he hadn't fallen in and drowned.

Isaac was propped up in one of the loungers at the far end of the infinity pool. He was awake, an empty water bottle in his hand. He must have been up for a little while, as he had changed into a clean set of clothes and now was turning his shades up at the sun. Gordon sat down next to him.

"Got any fags?"

Isaac nodded, fished out a pack and lighter from his shorts pocket.

Gordon lit up, enjoyed the drag, and felt an inch better. He wiped snot with the back of his hand and squinted at the brilliant waves. "So that was the product."

"Enjoy the trip?" Isaac asked.

"I don't remember, but there's sick all over me."

"Yeah, that can happen. Me, I went around the world. In fact, I'm not convinced I'm back, except everything feels so flat. Like going from color TV to black and white. So I guess it's all done and dusted, trip over."

Gordon eyed him skeptically. "Don't know what you're on about, but at least one of us had a good time. If Ginger doesn't get out of this sun, he's gonna get a new nickname. 'Scarlet', maybe."

Isaac chuckled. "He's always on about getting a tan. I'd let him get one, pasty bugger."

Gordon scratched himself, feeling sticky and prickly. "So were you awake last night? Cognizant of events?"

"To some degree, I suppose."

"Did she do it?"

Isaac paused then gave him a curt nod.

"You know it?"

"I know she's gone. I wasn't sure if I had imagined it from last night or not, but she ain't in your room. She just ran off. She was holding a pair of shoes, that part I remember."

"Fuck."

"Sorry, Gordon."

"Fucking cunt whore."

Isaac said nothing more. Neither did Gordon. He got up and went to his bedroom, automatically reaching into his pockets for the phone. Her stuff was still everywhere. This dizziness was driving him mental. He took a long shower, making the water first as hot as it would go, before turning off the heat and letting it go lukewarm. Feeling a little steadier, he went through the room, trying to figure out what she might have taken. Not much from what he could see, but women had so much stuff, who could tell? Her toiletries were still littered around the bathroom sink, her clothes still filled the closet, although when he opened one of the doors, a silk pillow popped out from below onto his feet. He looked it over, feeling confused and spaced out, and came to no conclusion.

Mazy's purse lay on the nightstand. He picked it up and shook its contents onto the untouched bed. Lipsticks, a flask (emptied), a money clip with a few hundred baht, a rolled up *Vanity Fair* she had brought from Hong Kong. Nothing. No diamond ring, either—he had gone out of his way to the Tesco Lotus supermarket to get it, some Chinese brand, cheaper than the Bulgari and the Cartier, but still, a carat's a carat. Gordon hurled the purse across the room. A white dot on the bedspread caught his eye.

He picked up a tight little wad of paper and opened it. A torn scrap; a telephone number, written in a man's handwriting. The number began +08 followed by eight digits. Thai landlines were seven digits, and 8 was the standard prefix for Thai mobiles.

For Gordon, this erased any lingering doubt that she had spiked the drink to do a runner. He had no idea, however, whose number it was. He always kept Mazy on a fairly tight leash. They had been on the island for over three weeks and he couldn't remember any time she had been allowed to wander around on her own. They had gone as a group into Chaweng a few times, mostly at night; a couple of rounds of golf; and once to the zoo. She had gone off on her own down the beach once or twice, but under someone's supervision...

The tourist.

No, now you're inventing fairy tales, he told himself.

Still, as he read and re-read the mobile number, he indulged the possibility.

Gordon tried to recollect the man called... Travis. *Naff sort of name favored by redneck septics.* She had certainly wasted little time striking up a conversation with him.

Gordon wondered where his phone had gone. He searched the familiar places in the room, and then nodded with the grim understanding that she had nicked it.

This delivered a cold shiver. Woke him up a bit more.

There were a lot of things on that phone. More than there should have ever been, Gordon knew.

The last thing he checked was the safe but its contents remained unmolested, and that's when he finally figured out the errant pillow. She'd tried to get in, probably to get her passport, but couldn't guess the lock code.

Knew him from her yoga classes, she'd said. Travis had looked like a military man, with that haircut and athletic build, but his right hand and wrist were cast in plaster, rendering him much easier to handle physically—a non-threat. Maybe Gordon should have interpreted the cast differently. *A man who takes risks, physical ones. Someone ready to do something very, very foolish.*

A man who hadn't listened to Gordon's generous advice.

A man with Gordon's phone.

Chapter 19

The Smell of Bacon

THERE was something bittersweet about waking to the smell of bacon, for it reminded Trav of Saturday mornings at home, the beginning of his father's two-day dominance over the kitchen. His imagination invented the sounds that should have gone with the odor —his mother closing a cabinet or opening the fridge, the beagle's excited nails scurrying on the kitchen floor. The relaxation of knowing there was no school today, that today he'd rise because he'd want to.

Indulging in such memories always ended badly. But sometimes, like now, he couldn't help himself, despite knowing it would end with that inevitable emptiness, that sense of the absences that he had learned to tolerate but never accept.

Except that really was the sound of a cabinet door, and that was the frantic stop and start of a dog.

He threw on a pair of shorts and opened the door.

Her back was to him, one hand working the spatula, the other holding the pan. She hadn't heard him stir. Mazy had let the dog inside, who stood quivering at attention as a tidbit of goodies passed down from this new human. She was wearing only a long tank top that revealed a peek at her white panties as she leaned to feed the dog. Her bare legs provided ample length for leaping dolphins. Her shoulders and upper arms were also tattooed in a dense web of Hindu imagery, reminding him of the shadow puppet show he had watched on the island. Mellowing brown bruises punctuated the spaces between the elaborate figures gracing either shoulder.

He was as taken with evidence of abuse as with the spectacle of her semi-undressed body in his kitchen. He'd viewed her physically before, from the couple of times he had taken her yoga class. Everyone in the studio reacted to her looks, even the other women. At the time, however, Trav had been dealing with the fallout from Caroline and pouring his focus almost entirely into the training. He had noticed the instructor but had deliberately ignored her and kept his thoughts on his mat, his hands, his position, his breathing. That had been enough.

Maybe, if back then, before everything had collapsed to shit, Trav had imagined her, barely decent, cooking him breakfast in his beach shack, he'd have been a helluva lot more diligent in his yoga practice.

She looked over her shoulder. "Hey, you're up."

"Morning," he said. He moved to scratch the dog on her head, but the dog's gaze never wavered from Mazy. *I don't blame you*, he thought.

"These eggs are about done. You want to set the table?"

The change in tone was too abrupt to process. The sunlight had obliterated the terrors of the night. "Sure. Smells good." He moved to the cabinet. There wasn't much in the way of the house's grab bag of dining wares.

"Okey-dokey, here we go." She turned the heat off the frying pan and laid the bacon onto a paper towel to absorb the excess fat. "I think I've cleaned you out, but I hope cooking breakfast makes up for that."

"We can get some groceries today." He was enjoying this bizarre domestic scene and he observed Mazy for some reaction to the suggestion, with its implication that her staying here might continue, but she revealed none.

The omelet seemed to contain most of his remaining supplies—onions, mushrooms, cheese—and filled most of its pan. Mazy divided it with the spatula and pushed the halves onto their plates.

"Coffee?" he said, but she had already made it. Its aroma mated with the sweet notes of bacon. He poured two mugs' worth. And so they sat at the table, eating bacon and omelets and drinking coffee and petting the dog, like a satisfied, domesticated couple, a distorted, magic-mirror reflection of a life that he had grown up with and, for a while, had also once seemed to have obtained.

"What do you think?" she asked, eating.

"Mm, delicious, yeah."

"You eat with that hand pretty good."

"Cast should come off soon. I had to learn to cook one-handed. You have no idea how many eggs ended up on the floor." He was about to pick up from last night's conversation, but her fork, instead of moving to her mouth, was rattling against the edge of the plate. Her other hand brushed tears off her cheeks, and Trav understood that she had invented this farce of holiday breakfast in a vain attempt to act like everything was perfectly A-OK.

"You all right?"

"Do I fucking look all right?"

He waited, no longer aware of the beautiful breakfast smells. He was wondering what had happened to Travis the Hero, because right now the leading man from last night was struggling for his next line.

He let her cry for a little longer.

"I'm sorry," she said. "I'm just a little, you know, frazzled."

"Gotcha."

"Your eggs will get cold."

She wanted normal? He'd try. "So what's up with those tats?"

The question made her smile, the first time he had seen her smile, not just sneer, and the beauty of it blotted out all thoughts beyond *Wow*. Mazy pointed to one shoulder. "This is Krishna. He was the avatar of the god Vishnu, whose job was to help preserve the balance in the universe. This guy"—other shoulder—"is Arjuna, a noble warrior king, who didn't want to fight a battle against his relatives. Krishna was serving as Arjuna's charioteer and had to convince him to do it, even though it meant killing his cousins and committing all kinds of atrocities, because it was all for the good of worshiping Vishnu."

"Kind of Job-like. Do it because God says your suffering doesn't mean anything, and who the hell are you to second-guess the creator of the universe, anyway?"

"Not quite. It's more like, this is your duty, your dharma, and if you don't follow it, things will get a lot worse."

"You a Hindu?"

"No, no. But I became interested in what it was all about. Most people, Westerners anyway, just think yoga's for exercise. I wanted an idea about the ideas behind it." Mazy shrugged. "Guess I liked it."

"But you believe in dharma?"

"Sure, I mean, I believe we're all here for a purpose. You aren't one of those people who think it's all random and pointless, are you? That's so, like, negative."

"I try not to think about it at all. Sorry, teacher. So...what's your dharma, then?"

She lowered her fork. "I think mine's expired."

"That's kind of random and pointless."

"No. Just misspent."

"Maybe it's to help people. You're a yoga instructor. That's a good thing, isn't it?"

"Yeah, it was. What got you into yoga anyway? You were new, weren't you?"

Trav nodded. "I was doing kickboxing, a lot of martial arts. My master had recommended it. I admit, I had a lot of doubts walking into your studio. I mean, I was used to sparring in the ring, pretty full-on stuff, doing real fights. Training was hard and tough. Yoga seemed like, I dunno, for the ladies who lunch."

"That's ridiculous. I mean, yeah, most of the students are women, but there's guys there, too. And look at the instructors. Almost all married, straight men." She fed another tidbit to the dog, saying to her, "Wow, you're hungry, ain'tcha?"

"I know that, now. Yoga's actually a great complement to Muay Thai training. It comes from the same source." He wanted to see her smile again. "But you know, it's a psychological switch. I guess I like the macho side to fighting. That feeling that you can walk into any bar and take care of yourself. With yoga it's like, I can't punch you, but hey, loser, check out my downward-facing dog."

"Yeah, OK, I can see where sticking your ass in the air might not get the reaction you want. But have you tried it?"

"Good point. It would probably freak the other guy out. Like, whoa dude, this guy's totally crazy."

"Better watch out!"

"Uh oh, here comes a tree pose!" he said, dramatically extending his arms upward, fingers locked.

She obliged him with a chuckle and maybe, he thought, a nice look. A moment.

"I haven't laughed for a while," she said. "Thank you. Things haven't been so funny."

"I guess not." He didn't want her to cry again, but the morning was going to end one way or another. "You want to tell me some of it?"

"Well," she said, "my boyfriend, or maybe he's technically now my fiancé, Gordon? He's a drug dealer. He mostly deals to the expats in Hong Kong, but he's got some *thing* going on with the Chinese triads, some kind of deal. Anyway, Gordon thinks of himself as like the Richard Branson of selling dope to rich white kids. Like he's a businessman. Entrepreneur, that's like his favorite word."

"And I thought my job was sleazy. So you're here on vacation or something?"

"That's what I thought at first, but I should've known better. Gordon's setting up a deal with a local gangster named Tarrin to develop ketamine here, and distribute it to Hong Kong and maybe some other places."

"OK."

Mazy sighed. "He made me sign these papers, that night you followed us."

"Just you. I was following just you."

Very quickly, she resumed. "I'm now the proud owner of this shitty chain of restaurants in Hong Kong called Chili Hut."

"Sure, I've eaten there."

"Yeah, well, Chili Hut went bankrupt, and Gordon used his drug money or maybe a loan from the triads to buy the franchise, which he's done in my name. Signed it over to me. Chili Hut's going to be a front to let him import drugs."

"And you're the fall girl if anything goes wrong."

"That's what I thought. Now I'm not so sure. Anyway, that's what Chili Hut's all about."

Trav finished his meal, pushed the plate aside. "That was really good, thanks." He was trying to process the word *fiancé*, although he noticed the diamond was no longer on her pinkie.

"You're welcome."

"So I take it the deal's off? You've left him?"

Mazy slumped her chin into her palms. "I've left him, but I'm not sure the deal's off. I've signed up and all."

"Why ketamine?" He had come across plenty of drugs in Hong Kong but not that one.

"Some people like it because it's like a psychotic trip or something. But it's also a date-rape drug. Gordon, he, uh, he sees the economic potential of both, but the primary market in Hong Kong is for loser guys to slip it into women's drinks."

"What else."

"What difference does it make?"

"I'm involved now. I need to know."

"Trav, no, no, man, you're not involved. Really. Stay out of this. Stay away."

"Little late now, isn't it?"

"I'm...I'm going to get out of here. Today. I've already stayed here too long."

"Well, Maze, as it so happens, I was trying to figure out my next move. Maybe we can, you know, team up."

She gave him a gentle look of condescension. Maybe it wasn't on purpose; she had probably disappointed so many men it had become a habit. "I'm sorry, Trav. I just, well, hadn't thought about anything like that. Tell the truth, I haven't thought about anything yet."

"Maze, listen to me. You're trouble, I know that's what you're going to tell me. Well, I'm trouble, too. I got trouble flowing out my ass like the goddamn river Ganges, OK? I know you must get hit on all the time so I'm not going to waste my breath on some corny line. I've been alone for a while now and I think you have, too, maybe not in terms of having people around you, that asshole boyfriend of yours, but alone as in—"

"As in what?"

"As in, like, a companion. A compadre."

She took his hand. "Travis, I can't thank you enough for what you've done for me. But I'm not ready for that. I don't think trouble plus trouble equals 'and they lived happily ever after'."

"I didn't mean it that way." He sighed miserably. "What I meant is—"

"I know what you meant," said Mazy, with sympathy. "But now I'm going."

A chime broke the tension. Trav looked at her backpack. "Your phone?"

Mazy blanched. "Not my phone."

Chapter 20

Tarrin Visits the Villa

TARRIN Niratpanasanarong arrived at Gordon's villa in a foul mood. He regretted having entered this crazy scheme. It was going to attract attention. It was already becoming a hindrance.

It had been two years since he had fired the Glock in anger. Two years since he had become the biggest *nakleng* on Samui, the one the police came to when they had a problem, the one who dealt with the clans in Phuket and Hat Yai and the syndicates in Bangkok.

He didn't want these bizarre foreigners to mess it up.

"Diversify," he said, mimicking Gordon's voice to himself as he pulled his Lexus up to the villa's gate and honked. "Export. Be big businessman."

He honked again and the gate slowly swung outward.

"Make big fuck money."

He snorted, steering the car into the drive, and reverted to thinking in Thai. Two servants outside gave him respectful *wais*, carefully keeping their gazes low, as he walked brusquely to the stairs that led to the villa's top floor.

The problem wasn't the scheme itself. It was partly that Gordon had no idea whom he was dealing with. Maybe he was a racist, like most whites, or maybe he was just stupid—also like most whites, in Tarrin's limited experience.

Tarrin had gotten his start as an impossibly skinny peasant teen sweeping the floor of the coconut-processing plant. The royal family had donated a hundred thousand coconut seeds, in a bid to revitalize the coconut industry on the island. As if Samui wasn't already drowning in coconuts! Anyway, it had kept a few families otherwise facing complete impoverishment from starving.

But coconuts were not going to be Tarrin's thing. No way. This was an industry in which they still used monkeys to collect the fruits from the trees. Trained them to tear off the coconuts and return them to the trainers in the palm plantations. Fucking monkeys! They wanted Tarrin to work as a janitor, cleaning up after the monkeys—subservient to the monkeys! No way was he going to stay long in this shit job.

Tarrin had not been tough enough to be a *nakleng*. He was not a good boxer; his shins and arms remained sensitive and flabby, not honed into an alloy. But he didn't see the point of wasting all that time on rituals and the circuit when all you needed to earn respect was a Glock.

A local gangster had tested him out when Tarrin was fourteen, wanted to see what the kid could do.

"You have to sacrifice something to get something," he big man had told him. Ha!

Tarrin still had the gun as a souvenir, a second-generation Glock 17, but these days preferred to go around with a third-gen Glock 30 subcompact that fired .45 automatic rounds, like the one currently tucked behind his back, beneath his Oakland A's shirt.

Oh, and that original big man who had given him the assignment? He now worked for Tarrin.

Meeting Gordon had been interesting, Tarrin had to admit, and the whole thing could still turn out well. Samui was a lucrative place to be on top. Not just coconuts! Tourism was benevolence made material. Tourists needed to buy things, so sell protection to the shopkeepers. Tourists wanted to ride elephants, so corner the touts! Tourists wanted to get laid—run prostitutes. Tourists wanted to eat fancy food—intimidate the importers! Tourists wanted to get a taxi or a tuk-tuk—take over the licenses!

Thais wanted all these things too, but the tourists were willing to pay the most, and their largesse made local Thais richer than in most of the rest of the country. So Tarrin could skim off Thai customers more, too. That was the beauty of doing business on Samui.

Of course, none of this was possible without the police and the mayor's office. But when money flows like the Chao Praya River, then such cooperation is not a problem. In fact, it is sought out. There was a time when, as Tarrin ascended the ladder, more bodies than usual were found in fields and streets. But Tarrin was the best at proving that such unpleasantness— the sort of messes that might frighten tourists —would be minimized if the authorities had to deal with only one real *nakleng* on Samui.

He didn't care whether someone was Buddhist or Muslim, either, and perhaps this had been his innovation, organizing crime regardless of religion or island clan. The authorities liked this, too. It kept the peace and meant nobody was going to make trouble on Samui. Personally, Tarrin thought the Muslims were like whinny dogs, and if his daughter ever so much as held hands with one of them, Tarrin would not hesitate to give his Glock another outing.

But she was a good girl, and Tarrin prayed every day to Kuan Im to continue to show his daughter Her mercy and love.

The goddess, however, had clearly not shown any benevolence to this *farang* woman, Mazy. Well, why should she? Had Mazy shown Kuan Im any deference? Had she tended the spirit house just inside the villa's driveway? No, she did not deserve such protection. And Tarrin knew what you had to do when a woman got out of hand. But he frowned on the sort of wanton punishments that Gordon preferred, not because he minded that a woman received a beating, but because Gordon was starting to irritate him. The Englishman talked about discipline but, in Tarrin's humble view, knew nothing of it.

Those who can't dance blame the flute and drum. A bit of Thai folk wisdom lost on the bearded *farang*.

Initially the partnership had worked well, when Gordon had remained overseas. But now Gordon and his men were here, making a mockery of the peaceful truce Tarrin had built with the cops.

Tarrin had initially welcomed their coming. Gordon had explained how ketamine worked, how to find it. The big white man, Ginger—a plain idiot in love with his own muscles, a type Tarrin had dealt with many times—showed how to serve it. Isaac, the skinny black *farang*, demonstrated how to make it. Very complicated. Isaac was the brains among them, even if Tarrin thought most Africans belonged in the trees, collecting coconuts with the monkeys.

Well, to call the man 'brains' was being nice. Tarrin did respect Isaac's knowledge, but the lab where they manufactured K-Love had fallen into chaos. Just like the party from the previous evening had spun out of control.

Gordon had blamed it on Ginger, but what difference did that make to Tarrin? He had called in two nephews to help them wash down the room, but the blood stains would never leave the mattress. So he had instructed another of his guys to get a new mattress, which they had taken straight from the store to the villa. They changed the sheets; the other ones would have to be burned or dumped into the ocean, along with the rest of the mess. By noon yesterday he had decided the room would hold up to scrutiny. Tarrin had spent last night explaining to the mama that the girl had run off with the sex tourist and he gave her a bit of money because missing girls, even teenage hookers, would inevitably mean trouble.

Then, this morning's visit to the lab. Tarrin had been looking forward to a break from Gordon and his sloppy friends, but the state of things had gone too far. They were going to be losing money at this rate. So for the second time in twenty-four hours, Tarrin had to pay a visit to the villa to clean up the foreigners' mess.

Ignoring the two servants, Tarrin walked past the Buddha image and up the side steps to the top of the villa's living area. He found the upstairs empty but the sofas splattered in vomit. Flies were buzzing over last night's virtually untouched dinner. Tarrin wondered if they were all dead and, for a moment, the idea lifted his spirits.

Gordon appeared at the base of the steps on the sea-facing side of the villa. "Tarrin. What brings you here?"

Tarrin adjusted his gold baseball cap against the sun's glare and descended, his chains clinking around his chest. "Lab. Big mess. We need Isaac again."

Gordon nodded. "Very well. He's just in the shower. We can be ready in a few minutes."

Tarrin looked around. The pool area seemed untroubled. "Somebody have sick last night?"

Gordon seemed embarrassed. "Ate something that disagreed with me. Lek hasn't started cleaning yet."

Tarrin didn't quite believe this.

Ginger appeared from his bedroom, wearing a polo and shorts, his white skin splotched with bright sunburn. Tarrin giggled.

"Go on, laugh," Ginger said without mirth.

"You look like Christmas tree," Tarrin said.

Isaac emerged from his room as well, dressed in a flowing cotton shirt, donning his trilby. "Morning, Tarrin. *Sawasdee krap.*"

"*Sawasdee krap.*"

Gordon said to Isaac, "Tarrin says there's some problem at the lab. We'd better get over there."

"Big fucking mess," Tarrin said. "Your turn clean up."

"My turn?" Isaac asked.

"We'll go now," Gordon interjected.

Isaac nodded. "Sure. I can go now."

"What about me?" Ginger said. "You want me to, you know, go looking?"

"Looking for what?" Tarrin said.

"Nothing," Gordon said.

"Where is Maze?" Tarrin demanded.

"Sleeping," Gordon said. "You know her. Too much to drink. Shall we go?"

"I call your phone," Tarrin said, as the three headed back up and out. "Why you no answer?"

Gordon felt his pockets. "No one picked up?"

"What do you mean, no one? Who should pick up your phone except you?"

"It's, well…"

Tarrin halted them at the villa's top floor. "Gordon, what happen here? You no bullshit with me."

Gordon shrugged. "It's nothing, Tarrin. Mazy, we had a row, she stormed out. She's taken off. She'll be back. That's all."

"And your phone?"

"Gone missing. It's here somewhere."

"She take."

"Maybe. What difference does it make? It's just a domestic between her and me. Silly non-sense."

Tarrin didn't reply. Best not to show his anger. He headed down the front stairs toward his car. He would love to get a look at that phone, see the names and numbers on it. Gordon had refused to let him have any contact with anyone in Hong Kong. Tarrin knew that once this deal got started, Gordon was nothing more than a middle man, a fixer. There was no way the Chinese would let him run something of this scale without their permission. And what was the advantage Gordon brought to the triads? Tarrin, of course—the Samui connection. But what if Tarrin could make that connection directly with the Chinese? Then…no more stupid Westerners needed. *Khop khun krap.*

So the girlfriend had finally run away. Probably not the first time, and if Tarrin interpreted things correctly, Ginger was going to go haul her back—if he could find her. Samui might be bigger than the foreigners realized. 'Like diving for a needle in the ocean.' But if Tarrin could get to her first, and get his hands on that phone, just for a few minutes...

In the Lexus, Isaac in back, Gordon in the passenger seat, Tarrin rang Narong on his cell. He explained the situation in Thai.

"What do I do with the girl if I find her?" Narong asked.

"It doesn't matter, so long as she stays alive. Have some fun. *Mai pen rai.*" He hung up, steering the car with his other hand. "My bookie," he told Gordon in English. "Thai people love gambling."

"Tarrin," Gordon asked, "could I borrow your mobile for a moment?"

Chapter 21

The Walking Dead

"**I**s there an American embassy on Samui?" Mazy asked.

Trav, showered and now dressed in fresh clothes, emerged from his room. "No, I don't think so. Why?"

Her backpack rested on a chair, looking impatient to be carried off, the remaining bottle of vodka snuggled in a side pocket. "Well, Gordon has my passport."

"I guess you'll have to report it lost when you get to Bangkok."

Trav heard the phone ring again, the second time that morning. Mazy jumped, which immediately set him on edge. She was wearing short cut-off jeans and fished a large smart phone from one front pocket. She just stared at it.

"Is it him?"

"It's his phone. I took it. I don't know why...I guess to piss him off."

"Does it say who's calling?"

"Tarrin. His local partner. Same as before."

She cradled the phone in her palms, paralyzed. It rang incessantly, filling the room with its demands.

"What are you going to do with that?" Trav asked. "If it's got a log of calls and numbers, the police would love to get their hands on it."

"Police?"

"Yeah, you know..." *riiing!* "the cops. Gordon's a..." *riiing!* "drug dealer, right?"

The damn thing finally fell silent.

"I hadn't thought about that," Mazy admitted. "I...I don't want to make trouble, or stay involved."

"The guy beats you. Look at you. You're covered in bruises."

"I fall down a lot," she said. "I have a drinking problem, in case you hadn't noticed." Her eyes were too defiant to give the line any credence.

"Mazy, you can bullshit him. You can even lie to yourself. But don't lie to me, 'kay?"

She put the phone in her pocket. "All I want to do, Trav, is get a ferry to the mainland and hitch a ride to Bangkok, so I can get the hell out of this country. You got a problem with that?"

"No," he said, irritated, knowing the decision was hers to make but feeling bitter, or maybe just disappointed, all the same. "Let's get going."

Then *his* phone rang, from the little nightstand in his room. They exchanged looks and he saw the fear in her face. It was infectious.

"You normally get calls?" she asked.

"Sometimes local sales pitches, they're all in Thai. Nobody else knows I'm here, or has my number." *Except for you, Maze.*

"You going to answer it?"

"Sure," he said, deciding the only way to calm her down was to show her that everything was cool. He didn't recognize the number but it was a local Thai mobile. "Hello?"

"Tourist," said a man, and Trav knew immediately that it was Gordon.

"Sorry?" he said stupidly, trying to hide his shock, but probably failing because he could see Mazy cringe.

"Travis," said the voice, hard and polished darkly like obsidian. "If you want to live, put her on the phone. Now."

"You have the wrong number." Trav hung up.

"That was him," Mazy said.

"Sales call."

"Who said something about lying?"

The phone rang again—same number.

"Don't answer it," she said.

Trav answered it. "You're too late," he told Gordon. "She's already gone."

"Don't fuck with me. I'm coming after the both of you. I'm going to get you. I have a knife and a Black and Decker hot glue gun, and I am going to take my time."

A Black and Decker—what?

"I'm calling you back." Trav hung up. "Give me his phone. Hurry up."

"What the hell are you doing?"

"Just give me the phone."

Mazy dug it out of her jeans pocket again. "I know the pass code," she said.

"OK, quick, pull up his contact list." Trav's mobile lit up again and he launched into speech before Gordon could say anything. "Listen, ass-hole," Trav began, watching as Mazy fumbled with Gordon's contact list. "I've got the goods on you and your little ketamine scheme. Mazy's long gone but she left me a little present, in case you came calling."

"I suppose I should be trembling at your feet, begging for mercy," Gordon said.

"You should be jumping off a cliff, douche bag." Mazy found the section he was looking for, showed it to him. "I've got a log of calls here, on your phone, Gordie, to all sorts of numbers. These are in Thailand...Hong Kong... Singapore. Wouldn't the Singaporeans love to know who your dealers are in their upstanding city?"

"Are you finished?" Gordon said.

"I haven't even gotten started."

"Then you might grant me the luxury of a comment. Everything you have told me is bol-locks and I know it's bollocks because you are a very stupid man with poor skills in dissem-bling. I also know it's bollocks because I know her, and I know what she is, and is not, capable of. So let me tell you something. You are stuck on this island and I am going to hunt you down and butcher you. I will spare the girl's life if she shows up at the villa, with my property, in the next hour. But you, Travis, you are the walking dead. As you Yanks like to say, have a nice fucking day."

He looked dumbfounded.

"Well?" Mazy demanded.

"I think we should go to the airport right now," Trav said, heading for her room.

"OK..." Mazy hadn't heard Gordon's side of the conversation, but she could guess what he might have said. "I told you not to answer it."

Trav was wrestling with the mattress of her bed. "He knew it was me. How'd he know it was me?"

"I have no idea. Lucky guess?"

Trav rounded on her. "You didn't tell him, did you? About me, about coming to find you?"

"Of course not!"

"So how'd he know my name? How'd he know he was calling my cell phone? The only person on this goddamn planet who has my number is you."

Trav went back to tossing the mattress as Mazy wondered how indeed everything seemed to have fallen apart. She felt her pockets, couldn't remember what she had done with the slip of paper he had given her.

Oh. Of course.

She bit her lip. "I might have left your number in my purse," she said. "It's at the villa."

"Great. Put your shoes on."

"Wait," she said, "I can't go to the airport without my passport. We'll have to take a ferry for the mainland."

"OK. But Gordon might know that."

"Then what are we waiting for? Let's just go," she said, squeezing into her Converse sneakers. "What are you doing?" He was ripping the mattress apart, improbably, with his hands.

"My stuff," he said, pulling a backpack from within the mattress. For a moment, Mazy wondered what she had been sleeping on last night. Too late now.

Trav took a wistful look about the house. "Computer," he said. "I'll need that."

Hurry hurry hurry, she urged silently as he unplugged the laptop and tried to insert it inside the backpack, not bothering to hide the stacks of Hong Kong dollars inside.

"Wow," she said. "Most people just use credit cards."

He stuffed a few errant bills back inside the backpack and slung it over his shoulder. "Yeah, well, most people aren't wanted by lawyers and triads at the same time."

"Interesting," she said, following him out onto the porch.

"Told you I was trouble, too," he said.

"I just figured you were lonely."

"Wow, feeling the gratitude."

There it was again, that word she had come to despise. Gordon's favorite. It stung her and hardened her a little bit toward this man, who was now kneeling by the dog, taking its head into his two hands, scratching her farewell: "Sorry, sweetie, I gotta go." Why were men always solemnly informing her of her lack of gratitude?

Easy one. To hide their own shortcomings.

The dog barked once, her tail wagging, expecting more bacon.

With the noise Trav instinctively looked up at the villa top, but trees kept it, and them, hidden from view. "Stay here," he told Mazy, "I'll bring the scooter around."

Mazy waited by the dog, accepting warm licks, wondering how likely she was to get fleas from this mangy outdoor animal. "You take care of yourself now," she instructed the dog.

The scooter's engine coughed and Trav backed it up toward her. "Here, wear this." Mazy caught the helmet. "They'll be looking for you, not me."

She stuffed her head inside the helmet and he helped tighten the strap under her chin. Trav rapped the top with his knuckles. "All set?" Mazy nodded and slid herself behind him on the blue Honda. The bike was a two-seater, but it was a tight fit. She wrapped her arms around his solid torso and her feet found the sideboard, but there wasn't enough room there for both of them so she had to angle her toes outward, resting just on the heels.

The scooter groaned under the extra weight but then dutifully carried them over a bed of brush and pebbles, away from the barking pleas of the dog, onto the stretch of wild grass in front of Montri's restaurant. The veranda was already busy with tourists. It was a splendid, sunny morning, a good day for an outing on Montri's boat. Trav paused at the roadside to let a knot of traffic clear—pickups full of construction workers, SUVs, some Westerners on a joy ride. Then he turned left, passed the villa's silent gate, and headed toward the western side of the island, oblivious to the man running after them on foot.

Chapter 22

News of a Funeral

GINGER wasn't good at gleaning answers from the locals. Maybe it was his intimidating size. He wore tight shorts, canvas shoes and a see-through tank top, in case someone didn't quite appreciate his sculpted build. A smile might have helped, but he wasn't in the smiling mood, not with half his skin burned to lobster.

He had spent nearly an hour wandering around the village outside the villa. He didn't give a rat's arse about the sun and the tropical breeze or the stupid picturesque islands and all that rubbish. His sunburn hurt and made movement stiff. It was a good motivator, though. All this hassle would make finding Mazy all the sweeter.

He had in mind something a little more exacting for her than a sunburn. Something more fun. Like they had enjoyed two nights ago. Only this time, he'd want her awake and alert. He'd want her to know what was going on. He'd want her calling his name.

But as he went from place to place along the beachfront, brusquely asking people if they'd seen the woman whose photo was on his mobile phone, Thais and tourists alike shook their heads and shrunk into themselves.

Eventually, he decided this half-baked search was pointless. The girl had done a runner. She'd be back. It was that simple. She had nowhere else to go. The only question was what Gordon would decide to do about her. Poisoning everyone with K-Love was ballsy, Ginger would give her that.

Judging by Gordon's increasingly erratic and ham-fisted behavior toward the girl, Ginger could guess what lay in store. Unless, of course, Ginger found her first. Maybe then he'd give her minge so much Ginge she wouldn't dream of Gordon again. She'd never want to be with another man. Sure as hell wouldn't be able to walk straight.

Frustrated with the stupid search, sour Thais and frightened tourists, the tropical sun scalding his already burnt skin, Ginger walked back through the village toward the villa, stopping at the seaside Thai restaurant beside the villa to buy bottled water. He took the bottle down to the beach and sat in the shade of a palm tree. The exertions of recent nights were taking their toll.

A loud *putt putt*. He watched a scooter pull out from behind the restaurant. Two people, white bloke driving, white bird behind him wearing a helmet and a backpack.

It meant nothing to him, and he finished the water.

Blue Honda.

That meant something.

Ginger tossed the empty into the sand and broke into a run, chasing the bike. It ambled onto the road and accelerated eastward. Ginger initially closed in, trying at least to read the plates, but the bike gained distance and he gradually came to a halt just outside the villa.

He scratched his carroty locks. Call the boss? And risk looking even dumber if it turned out to be nothing? This island was full of Honda scooters rented by foreign tourists.

Ginger needed to know more.

He headed back to the restaurant. He walked up the little pathway, beneath the poster of the somber Thai monarchs, through a hallway of junk—bicycles, mops, defunct barbecue, a washing machine—and back to the veranda. The usual tourists.

The young waitress recoiled at the giant *farang* striding across the restaurant.

Ginger ignored her and walked across to the steps leading down to the beach. To his left was the village with its little restaurants and boat rentals that he had already canvassed. He turned right, in the direction of the villa. He noticed a small, dilapidated house—a shack, really. He had never realized it existed, practically nestled against the side of the villa wall, hidden behind a copse of trees and patches of bamboo.

A brown mongrel lay curled on the cushion of the rickety rattan furniture on the porch.

Ginger walked up to the porch and the dog growled, but he wasn't afraid of dogs and the dog declined to challenge him. Ginger couldn't see through the windows, because it was too bright outside. He knocked on the door and waited a moment. Nothing. He tried the door-knob and it opened outward.

"Hello?"

Hearing no response, he stepped inside. The smell of bacon lingered. The dishes and pans lay in the sink, on the table. The coffee machine was still on. The bathroom was empty but wa-ter droplets remained on the sink and the mir-ror, and the shower curtain was slick. Jutting from the little trashcan was an empty bottle of Absolut.

"Maze," Ginger said.

He moved into one bedroom where the bed had been stripped and the mattress thrown against the wall. Ginger tilted it, saw a big hole carved into its bottom. He stuck a hand in there, but it was empty.

The other room's bed was unmade. There was a closet which was empty except for a hamper still containing some laundry—two pairs of a man's boxer shorts, some T's, a pair of socks. Ginger checked the drawers and the cabinets, but nothing belonging to the man or Mazy was still here. He wondered how they had done it. Missionary? Doggie style? Maybe standing up, that's how Ginger would have liked to do it, standing beside the bed, Mazy on her back, feet resting on his shoulders as he pounded her hard enough to split the bed frame.

His penis, despite its recent Olympic trials, grew firm and he considered jacking off. But as he got started, the Mazy in his head laughed at him. *Is that all you've got?* She would say it like that. She never gave him anything but cruel sneers. But check out these pecs, these arms! Why did she always favor a skinny geezer like Isaac? Why did all the girls dismiss him or shudder at his glance? Ginger had lost count of all the women he had banged, but the fact was the fact, he was pushing thirty and had paid for them all—except for Mazy, who didn't even know he had done her. Did that count? Maybe, but not as much as if the man in this shack had done her. That would count proper.

He snapped back into the room, his erection nowhere in sight.

Whatever the events of last night, they had left in a real hurry.

Ginger knew there were only two ways off this island: airport or ferry terminal. A local fisherman might be persuaded to take them to the mainland, but he doubted Mazy had much cash, or the ready connections to make it happen, although the strange man was an unknown factor. But the only way for her to leave was by sea: Gordon kept all of their passports locked in his safe, because Gordon was a paranoid bastard. Ginger remembered making a spluttering protest at having to surrender his

British passport, but now he admired Gordon for the precaution.

That meant no airport for Mazy.

There wasn't much for a tourist up on the west side of the island. The road led through some quiet developments, a lot of seaside shacks like this one, and then you arrived at Nathon, the administrative center for Samui, a place for the mayor to kick up his heels and the cops to count their bribes. Tarrin had said he had connections there, had told a few colorful stories. Including one about the time he and one of the cops on his payroll had taken the ferry to the brothels on the mainland.

Ginger burst out of the house at full sprint.

Gordon understood that Tarrin was unhappy—not just pissed off, but upset at Gordon, who had, he knew, let things begin to slip—so he remained quiet as his Thai partner drove them toward Lamai. Instead of turning left into the island's interior, however, he made a right toward the aquarium and tiger zoo at Orchid Resorts.

Isaac, in the back seat, said, "Gordo, tell him the one about Mazy and the tiger."

Tarrin's eyebrows levitated.

"Another time," Gordon said.

"Tell me about Mazy and the tiger," Tarrin said.

Gordon sighed. Tarrin wanted payback for having to sort out yesterday's emergency clean-up. "When we first came to Samui I treated her to a visit because you know what she's like, the moody cow. There's a bit at the end of the tour where for eight hundred baht, they let you sit in a cage with a Bengal tiger and get a photo. Don't know what they feed the tigers to keep them all docile like."

"Ketamine, man," Isaac said from the back.

"Would you shut it?" Gordon snapped. "Anyway, Mazy was her usual self, sweating so much vodka I'm surprised she didn't intoxicate the bloody tiger. She wasn't meant to do anything except put her arm around it, with the trainer there, but does she ever do anything sensible? Does she ever just do what she's told? No, not our Maze. She gives the tiger—and we're talking about a fucking gigantic tiger—she gives it a hug, both arms, full on fucking half nelson, I'm telling you. Well, it was chaos. Crazy bint's lucky to be alive."

"You, too," Tarrin said with a smile. "You are lucky."

Gordon didn't know what to make of that. Best to let it pass, for now. "The tiger had the last laugh. Turned around in its cage and nailed Mazy with some kind of horrible piss."

"Yeah, I had to take her home in a taxi," Isaac said. "Gordon wouldn't let her in the van."

Tarrin giggled.

Gordon turned around in his seat. "One more word from you and that tiger's going to be snacking on Nigerian oysters."

"Sorry," Isaac said, his voice small.

As Tarrin drove them toward the zoo, Gordon remembered what Jaidee had told him right after Isaac had taken Mazy back to the villa. The tiger was a female. Gordon knew that's why Mazy had ended up getting pissed on. A male tiger would have rolled over and let her scratch its belly. She had a way of making fools of men, human or otherwise.

Tarrin parked the Lexus in the aquarium's sandy parking lot beneath the tall cotton trees. He told Gordon to wait, but Gordon wasn't going to do that. He was feeling charged after the exchange with Travis. He needed to pace, feeling like a big cat himself, but not one of these pathetic beasts stuck behind bars, taken out to be stroked by giggling tourists, kept on a constant drip of who knew what they grew in the hills nearby. No, he was on the prowl.

Gordon liked the feeling; too much sun and snorkeling was turning him soft.

"I'm coming with you," Gordon declared.

"Then you just be quiet," Tarrin warned.

The aquarium and zoo was a sprawling complex. Signs pointed to one show featuring sea lions, another Bengal tigers. Tourists milled around beneath the trees outside among a few makeshift stalls selling Thai sweets and ice cream.

But Tarrin did not head for the entrance. Instead it was a long walk in the hot afternoon in the direction of the Orchid Resort's beach. As they neared the far end of the zoo complex, Tarrin stopped outside a discreet service entrance.

He made a brief call on his phone. The service door opened a moment later. Jaidee stood there in a dark shirt covered with the image of a tiger, dark jeans, and black Wellingtons. He smiled and gave Tarrin a *wai*, clasping his palms and making a short bow. He deigned to give Gordon a nod.

There was a brief exchange in Thai. Tarrin handed Jaidee a written note. The janitor looked at it blankly. Tarrin said something else and Jaidee turned the note around, and Gordon realized the man was illiterate.

So why give him instructions in writing?

Jaidee nodded and Tarrin said, "We wait here."

"Jaidee," Gordon said, "mate, I need to use your phone. Your mobile."

Tarrin translated this.

"Phone?" Jaidee said in English.

"Yeah, mate, your phone. Talkie talkie. Let me use it."

Jaidee had an old clunker of a Nokia, but the way he handled it was as though it were a block of gold.

"I'm not going to steal it," Gordon sneered.

Tarrin seemed bemused by the exchange and he spoke gently to Jaidee, and the attendant reluctantly gave Gordon the phone before turning back inside and slamming the door.

"Would you excuse me," Gordon said, walking away from Isaac and Tarrin, further into the parking lot simmering under the high sun, leaving them in a narrow strip of shade along the concrete wall.

Gordon dialed Heinz's number from memory, just one of two that he knew by heart.

The phone rang several times until, finally, the other side picked up and he heard Heinz's voice, his thick German accent creeping through the receiver as a whisper. "*Wei*, hello?"

"Master Heinz, it's me, Gordo, in Thailand."

There was an awkward pause. "Why are you calling me *now*?"

"I need some information about a guy giving me a toothache."

"I can't talk now…wait…hold on."

"Where are you? What's that crashing sound?" Mid-day, Heinz should be at his gym, or maybe out for lunch, but the background was rattling with a steady, annoying metallic chiming.

"Gongs. I'm at the funeral."

"They're making a right racket." Gordon said.

"It's a Chinese funeral, *ja*? Didn't you hear, the son of *laoban* is dead."

"I have no idea what you're on about, Heinz. I've been in Thailand the past few weeks, putting together this deal. The boss's son?"

Heinz sighed like he would at one of his more hopeless students. "You heard about Chi-Man, who got knocked out in that fight."

Gordon raised a hand to shield his eyes against the noonday sun. "Chi-Man's dead? Kang's son, the nerdy one?"

"Seriously, you didn't know?"

"I've been focused on things here." He knew the excuse wouldn't impress Kang. Kang's was the other number he had committed to memory. "I need to give my condolences to Kang. Send some flowers."

"Why are we having this conversation?"

"I need you to get a name for me."

"Not now. Kang's a wreck... they're lining up to throw dirt onto the coffin, the whole family. Gordon, I can't keep talking. It's disrespectful."

"Just be quiet for a moment and let me finish, yeah? There's a man I need to know about. An American. Was a student of Mazy's at Indra. First name Travis. That's all I've got."

Heinz said nothing.

"Heinz? You heard that?"

"What phone is this you're calling me on?"

"A local mobile, a burner."

"How secure are we?"

"This phone's safe for a one-time call."

"Wait."

Gordon stood in the heat for a long moment, listening to the distant buzz of traffic, seeing tourists milling near the covered entrance around the corner, observed Isaac and Tarrin make small talk. The ordinariness of the day meant nothing to him; he was excited, his stomach churning in anticipation.

Heinz came back, the background noise more distant. "Tell me about this guy."

"I don't want to say too much. He's become a problem, that's all, and I want to know something about him, like his last name and where he works and who he shags. Can you ask around Indra's? They must have a registrar with his name on it. Can't be too many bleeding Travises doing yoga in Hong Kong."

"Travis Mitchell. It could be Travis Mitchell."

"You know him?"

"Know him? I trained him."

"Well, he's here now, making a nuisance of himself. I can handle him, but it would be useful to have some extra leverage. What can you tell me?"

"He's hard."

"He's *hard*? We must be talking about the wrong bloke. This Trav puts on airs but airs is all they are."

"Trav. *Ja*, that's him, that's how he calls himself. He's my protégé."

"Bollocks."

"Be careful with this guy, Gordon, I'm telling you."

"Careful? I'm going to tear him apart. Besides, he's got a broken arm or wrist or something."

"You remember once, when I used to train you, I told you about the perfect fighter. The one I would create to put in the ring and create a phenomenon."

Gordon rolled his eyes. "Yes, I remember."

"Karate for the mental discipline, the focus, the awareness. Muay Thai for the street-fighting skills. And Brazilian jujitsu, for the grappling techniques, because every street fight ultimately ends up a mess on the ground." Heinz sounded lost in the reverie of his own dream.

"Yeah, yeah, got that. What of it?"

"That's this guy, Gordon. Trav Mitchell. He had the jujitsu. He came to my dojo. Black belt, second degree. I helped him add the Muay Thai. He's some kind of finance guy, wanted the boxing to do some white-collar fights. But he's better than that. He's aggressive, he's skilled. I had a word with friends of ours, got him on a new circuit. The *real* circuit, the one I thought you were going to do before you disappeared into whatever shit you do now."

Heinz was referring to underground mixed martial arts, an up-and-coming illegal blood sport favored among Hong Kong's keener gamblers. Gordon had trained hard for it, but the methadone treatment had brought on dizzy spells whenever he worked out too hard. It had been a while since he had sparred with Heinz ...and who had taken his place as the master's favorite student? Travis fucking Mitchell!

"I can handle him," Gordon said. "I just need to know how to make him come to me."

"Gordon..." Heinz sighed. "You are good, I've seen you. But this guy...you want my advice, let me speak to Kang. He's going to want to know."

"I don't want Kang involved. Not his affair. Nothing to do with business."

"The tropics are baking your senses, my friend," said Heinz. "Kang wants this guy. He's involved."

"What are you talking about? What's Kang got to do with this?"

"You have *scheisse* for brains, you know? Trav's the one who fought Chi-Man. Kang's son. The fight was fixed; Trav was to take the fall. What does this guy do? One right hook, pow, breaks Chi-Man's jaw, sends him to the mat, eyes go vacant, nobody home. A beautiful punch, incredible reflexes. I had to go through hell on bent knees in front of Kang. You know what he's like, and who can blame him? He may run some controversial enterprises, shall we say, but he's a father, too. Not only that but he lost a huge amount betting on the fight. Big loss of face in front of everybody. Chi-Man's been on life support for a month until two days ago. Now they're putting him in the ground. I'm looking at this very moment at a family of very pissed off tria–uh, businessmen who are going to want to find Trav. You know what these guys will do."

"Then Kang will be grateful when I deliver Trav's balls on a platter. I got the picture. So tell me how to get to this guy, how to make him come out into the open?"

"He's in Samui? You know that for a fact?"

"He is for now, yeah."

"What does Mazy say?"

"She's, uh...I prefer to keep her out of this."

"She doing him? That it?"

Gordon hissed, "No, that's not fucking it."

"OK, settle down. Where is she now, and give me a straight answer."

"I don't know," Gordon said.

"What does that mean?"

"It means what it means. I don't know. What's she got to do with anything?"

"Kang will want to know."

"Leave him out of it, Heinz." Gordon gritted his teeth and added, "Please."

"You know how it is, Gordon. *Dumm gelaufen!* —shit happens. I got to go. They're going to slaughter a chicken over the grave. This is the best part."

Chapter 23

Bad Karma

JAIDEE once had dreams of becoming a zookeeper. As a little boy he watched the men in their green uniforms *inside the pens*. There was bravery, but there was also the rapport they enjoyed with the cats. It was a communion with power that a peasant kid from the islands could only dream about. It sure beat pre-dawn rises to mend his aunt's fishing nets.

When the landlord sent thugs to kick them off Uncle's land—something about official papers with chops and signatures, but by then Jaidee was old enough to recognize theft—he was lost. Uncle had died, Auntie was just a wizened hag, his brothers were crewing a fishing trawler and his sister had married and left.

The tigers found him. Jaidee had gone to the wat for food the monks prepared for the indigent. The local newspaper was posted behind a plastic frame. Jaidee couldn't read but he saw the photo of a tiger, and stood entranced.

A monk translated for him: 'Samui zookeeper loses arm to tiger.'

Great—there's a zoo! Right here on Samui! And not just any old park, but a tiger zoo! He had never realized this.

Getting the janitor job turned out to be a lot harder than he had reckoned. Something about qualifications, an education. Why was he surprised? Any man who stepped into a tiger's pen would have to be a great man already. But there were ways. Jaidee visited the local loan shark, who was beginning to advance him a few baht to cover his dice games. How about a bigger loan so he could bribe his way into the job? The loan shark, sensing a stable but probably not quite sufficient income stream, agreed.

The job involved mopping and waxing the floors of the aquarium and picking up the trash in the amphitheater. He immediately hated the aquarium, a dark and brooding place surrounded by soulless creatures: huge eels, practically blind but always hungry; giant sharks in open-top tanks that sped around in silent restlessness, their fins occasionally smacking through the surface and splashing him; massive round, ugly deep-sea creatures that he couldn't even name, things that were all mouths, beady eyes, and appetites.

Nor was he that interested in the noisy, irritable birds, the flashy parrots and cockatoos that featured in the bird show. Jaidee did, however, quickly grow interested in the very pretty young women who worked in the back of the compound all morning, training with the birds for the afternoon entertainment. Especially Nongmook, the prettiest of them all, with her creamy complexion; why she wasn't a model in Bangkok instead of a bird handler hamming up for foreign tourists, he couldn't explain.

What transfixed him, though, even more than Nongmook, were the big cats, emperors of the jungle. He envied the young fellows under the wing of Chittilai, tiger trainer extraordinaire. After a while, Chittilai let Jaidee clean up the stage after the show, and he worked hard to win Chittilai's attention. Jaidee used any excuse to approach the stout, striding trainer—asking him if he'd like another soda or juice, offering to polish his boots, telling him how amazing he had been this afternoon on stage.

After a year or so of groveling, the trainers let Jaidee start cleaning up the pens. They gave him a few tips on what to look for in the stool, in case anything was wrong with the tigers and leopards. Initially, Jaidee took to this new responsibility with zest. He never stopped harboring the hope that Chittilai would pick him from obscurity and let him join the other apprentices who appeared with the handler on stage in the tiger cage. When he wasn't so exhausted at night as to allow a little daydreaming, it usually involved guiding the great animals through hoops of fire just as Nongmook would be watching.

In fact, only recently had he approached Chittilai and stammered out a request, but the trainer had only laughed at him, a deep belly laugh, with his hands on his hips, and the other two young men under his tutelage joined in. "What do you know of tigers?" Chittilai had demanded. "Where's your degree in wildlife biology? Where's your knowledge of animal behavior and anatomy? Where's your bribe to the union?"

There followed a week later a chance encounter with Nongmook. He rarely saw the troupe of girls, who showed up early in the morning, shared breakfast from one of the stalls outside, and spent several hours a day drilling with the birds before doing the show and then leaving. Jaidee had been cleaning up the main hall where tourists waited to have their snapshot taken with a tiger, piling up plastic chairs and cleaning off tables, when he saw Nongmook in a corner by herself, holding her phone and crying.

His chance! She must have broken up with her boyfriend!

But he remained paralyzed for several minutes, and then she noticed him staring at her, and with a look of utter disgust strode out to the parking lot without so much as a *sawasdee ka*.

By now, Jaidee's enchantment with the cats was fading. Chittilai had made clear that Jaidee was too poor, too stupid, too ignorant, and too hick to even dream of becoming an animal trainer. Scooping mounds of warm cat shit with his hands as flies attacked him in that airless heat lost its appeal once Jaidee realized it was about as close to interacting with the cats as he was going to get.

The cruelest cut: the tigers, his idols, were if anything more haughty than Chittilai. Despite his cleaning their cages and refreshing their water, the cats flicked their tails at him with an awful combination of menace and disdain, and the females liked to torment him by turning around in their cages, raising their haunches, and striking him with their spray. It would take him days and multiple baths to get the disgusting scent off.

About three months ago, after finishing his chores, he had found Chittilai in the aquarium zoo's office, looking at a computer. The trainer had waved him over. "So you want to play with the cats, Jaidee?"

What's this? Had the abuse and scorn been just a test? Jaidee had smiled brightly, suddenly eager to reclaim his dream. "Oh, yes, Khun Chittilai."

"Take a look at this."

Jaidee was not traveling on the digital highway, and had only the faintest idea of what the Internet was. When Chittilai showed him a white screen full of blue scribble, he had to admit to the trainer that he couldn't read.

The humiliation didn't end there, either. "These are news headlines," Chittilai said. "I did a search for 'tiger' and 'zookeeper', to show you what this job is all about."

Chittilai proceeded to read the headlines out loud.

'White tiger kills zookeeper as tourists watch.'

'Tiger kills zookeeper in Japan.'

'Tiger in unlocked cage kills Shanghai zookeeper.'

And then he played the videos from something called YouTube, accompanying them with his cackles.

Screen after screen the trainer showed him, everywhere cats devouring zookeepers, as though a great conspiracy had been unleashed upon the unsuspecting world. And not against just any random humans, but the humans who, in most cases, had been feeding the cats for years. Simple people, faithful for decades to their own murderers.

Chittilai laughed at Jaidee's perplexity. "You're not one for the tigers, Jaidee. They'd tear you to pieces. You're not man enough. Now go home, get out of here."

Jaidee had done just that, burning with humiliation. But maybe Chittilai had a point. His back hurt from always bending over. He couldn't seem to wash the stench of tiger spray from his skin anymore. Finally, the other night, Granny had kicked him out of the shack, waving a hand in front of her scrunched up nose.

That was it for him. The veil of boyish naivety had been lifted.

Jaidee hated those fucking cats.

But a job was a job and he wasn't competing with the monkeys to harvest coconuts or getting sick on a hellish fishing boat. He depended on every baht. So he kept toiling there, a man made servant to beasts, until one day soon after the Internet debacle, the gangster named Tarrin, whom everyone had heard of or sort of knew, had approached him with an idea to earn some extra cash using his access card and willingness to work the late shift.

At first, Jaidee thought he had died and joined the Buddha. Tarrin paid him more baht than he had ever held in his entire life for one raid on the pharmacy for the little bottles of liquids that Tarrin wanted. He couldn't understand their names, written for him in Latin letters, but could compare the characters 'K e t a s e t' from Tarrin's little note to the characters on the labels. And although illiterate, Jaidee knew these were anesthetics for the big animals.

Tarrin had described to him precautions against getting caught, like injecting the contents into a plastic bag with a zipper and replacing the bottles with tap water, so no one would miss the supply.

Until, of course, one day one of these arrogant zookeepers gave a lion or a tiger an injection, thinking it was going to put them to sleep! Maybe it would be Chittilai's duty, and then it would be *his* name on the Internet: 'Bald trainer devoured by Samui's Bengal tigers.' For a time, Jaidee had worried this was against religion, but then figured if a cat was going to eat Chittilai, it had nothing to do with him, and Jaidee could be nothing more than an agent fulfilling the trainer's karma. Who knows how turns the Wheel of Law?

So the money was good and his actions didn't seem to be contradicting the Buddha, and maybe were helping hasten fate for zookeeper and beast. Then there was the sex. Jaidee was not a virgin—that's what brothels were for, and they tended to take any excess baht he accumulated—but the servicing that Tarrin's ladies were able to provide was beyond anything Jaidee had imagined. These were not the hags of the shacks in the mountains, but pretty young women with fine skin, almost as good looking as Nongmook. His bonus, Tarrin called these occasional excursions.

But the good life had come with strings attached, namely these loud, boorish foreigners whom Jaidee didn't like or trust. He didn't speak their language, but he knew when he was being laughed at.

And he didn't like the way they mistreated the woman, Mazy, gorgeous, perfect Mazy, even prettier than Nongmook, if such a thing were possible. Jaidee adored her silently from afar as though she were a pearly bodhisattva, Kuan Im in the flesh. True, she had turned out to be almost as accommodating as the prostitutes, at least with Gordon, and Jaidee was pretty sure that Nongmook was not such an enthusiastic consumer of Lady Song. So Mazy wasn't the embodiment of Kuan Im. Still, his breast was filled with raw anger whenever he saw the way *farangs* like Gordon hurt Mazy. She must have committed a terrible sin in her previous life, to deserve a boyfriend like that.

Then he heard about the lab in the forest that the African *farang* was said to have built, and he realized that he wasn't just stealing anesthetics for Tarrin's local purposes, but for something that was surely real trouble. The foreigners were bad luck.

Jaidee was, therefore, not happy to see Tarrin show up at his place of work with Gordon and Isaac. Tarrin seemed at home anywhere, regardless of dressing like a hip-hop singer. He had the stroll of a *nakleng*, a tough guy, and everyone on the island seemed to know him. But that aura of confidence didn't cover Tarrin's associates, small potatoes like Jaidee. Quite the opposite, he knew. Having Tarrin anywhere near the zoo, and asking for him, would put Jaidee in a bad spot, particularly once the switch involving the anesthetics was eventually discovered.

Something about the K e t – whatever, that stuff, something wasn't quite good enough, so Tarrin now handed over to Jaidee a new set of Latin-language characters. The gangster didn't need him to steal anything right now, but Tarrin wanted to know if the zoo kept this new type of medicine in stock.

Jaidee walked through a dim corridor past some administrative rooms to the lobby of a veterinary clinic, a fairly sizeable complex. In the center was a reception area where a lone woman sat, absorbed in her computer, surrounded by five doors leading deeper into the clinic. Jaidee couldn't read the signs, but he knew what they said: 'Exam rooms', 'Boarding /bathing', 'Radiology', 'Surgery'.

The last: 'Lab/Pharm'. As nonchalantly as possible, Jaidee strolled in that direction and, checking to ensure no one was looking, swiped his card to get in. The lab was empty and so was the pharmacy behind it, which also required his electronic passkey to access.

This new name began like the previous drug, and was branded Ketavet, and the zoo had it. Lots of it.

Jaidee slipped back outside to the parking lot to report the good news. Tarrin and the foreigners were waiting for him. He told Tarrin what he had seen and Tarrin smiled and nodded, and said something to the black man, Isaac, who also smiled and nodded. Jaidee also smiled and nodded. Then he held his hand out to Gordon.

The foreigner returned his Nokia but showed Jaidee the phone's chip in his other hand. Gordon said something and Jaidee caught "sorry" as he snapped the chip in two and proceeded to pulverize it with his sandal heel.

Gordon said something and Isaac handed Jaidee a hundred baht with a look of apology. Jaidee didn't catch the "cost of doing business" remark. He looked at his useless phone, then at Gordon, who was already walking back toward Tarrin's Lexus. Tarrin grunted neutrally, indifferent to Jaidee's troubles, and followed his foreign guests.

Jaidee thought about karma real hard. Karma and hungry tigers.

Chapter 24

Big Uncle

B IG Uncle Kang didn't weep. He had scattered an offering of oranges. He had burnt the paper money. He had buried his number-three son on a hill overlooking Tolo Harbor, marked by a freshly made, horseshoe-shaped limestone grave ornamented brightly with ceramics of the Eight Immortals. He had endured the wailing of his wife and of Chi-Man's mother, one of Kang's mistresses. He had accepted the long line of supplicants come to offer a kind word and stay in Kang's good books. He had eaten the lunch in a daze, unable to taste the food.

He did not weep. He seethed.

Kang retired to his limousine, surrounded by bodyguards, ready to be whisked to his New Territories mansion, one of several he owned in Hong Kong, and the most private. He wished to be left completely alone.

"Dai Bak," said Heinz in a gravelly German accent.

"Dai Bak does not wish to be disturbed now," said one of the bodyguards, placing a hand on Heinz's thick torso.

"I have news you'll want to hear," Heinz said in Cantonese. "About Travis Mitchell."

Kang, half bent as he entered his limo, halted and stood back up. His small circular sunglasses and tall white fedora, brim low, could not hide his taut fury.

"You dare mention that name to me?"

"He's in Thailand, sir."

Kang hesitated, and then said, "Get in."

Heinz joined Big Uncle in the back of the limo. Both men wore traditional all-white funeral gowns and headbands, sitting like a pair of ghosts in the dark interior. Kang removed his headband and said, "Speak."

"He's had some kind of encounter with Gordon Wood and his girlfriend, Mazy—you remember her, the very beautiful—"

"I remember."

"I got a call just now from Wood. He asked me what I knew about Mitchell. Didn't know who he was, they never met in Hong Kong. Mitchell escaped to Koh Samui, and I think Mazy's run off with him. Wood didn't say so, exactly, but that's what I think happened. He's jealous, wants to find Mitchell and kill him, I suppose."

Big Uncle sat very still, breathing noisily through his nostrils.

"Wood also says he lost his phone. I don't know what's on there. I don't know if it has anything to do with any of this. But I thought you should know."

Kang never used a phone except to speak with his daughters, so he was not concerned about that, but it did show Gordon Wood was sloppy. Wood had been a useful tool to consolidate the Hong Kong expat drug trade, which would make it now quite easy for Kang to acquire it and swallow it whole. Wood could choose to work for him if he had any sense, although this episode was now inclining Kang toward disposing of the Englishman. All he needed was the Thai connection, and then the ketamine operation would be his, too.

But there was more at stake here than Gordon Wood. Gordon Wood was a louse on a dog's anus. That was all he was, as far as Big Uncle Kang was concerned. What was at stake here was honor.

More than losing face, he had lost his son. Chi-Man was not going to be a triad; he hadn't had the gumption. He had always wanted to be as tough as his older brothers and be like his father, although Kang knew Chi-Man had been better suited to managing the accounting books for the family's legitimate businesses of real-estate developments and nightclubs. But the young man had felt the need to prove himself to his father, and had insisted on pursuing martial arts diligently, if poorly. The fix was meant to ensure Chi-Man's honor as much as make Kang some money.

Travis Mitchell had been instructed to lose the fight. He had been promised compensation. He had disobeyed, costing Kang over a million Hong

Kong dollars. More than the money, it cost him respect.

The other bosses had been there. Three-Eyed Lin, Fattie Chow, Spectacles Wong, and the syndicates from Hong Kong Island, Shenzhen, and Zhuhai.

To see Chi-Man sucker-punched by a duplicitous *gweilo*. To see Kang's number-three son fall unconscious before Kang himself. The *gweilo* had recognized his mistake at once and had fled. He beat Kang's men to his apartment by maybe half an hour, and the airport by a lesser margin, but his trail had gone cold. The news stories about his perfidy at work, which emerged soon after, had only confirmed his unworthiness.

Kang was embarrassed to have ever entrusted anything to this Mitchell—not in person, of course, but via Heinz. This Mitchell: a disgrace to the human race. A piece of vermin needing extermination.

Kang said to the fight promoter, "You were right to bring me this information."

"Yes, Dai Bak." Heinz was fluent in Cantonese. The big German touched the door handle but Kang raised a finger.

"This Travis Mitchell is not to be the affair of Gordon Wood."

"Wood's out to kill him. He wants to serve you as well as himself."

"I want Mitchell brought back to me alive."

"Brought here, to Hong Kong? Dai Bak, if I can say so, I think that is a dangerous operation. Kidnapping across borders is not the same as kidnapping in one's own territory. This asshole's caused enough trouble already."

"What I want," Dai Bak said, "is to squeeze the life out of the wretch with my own hands. Tell Wood."

Kang made a small gesture with his hands, dismissing Heinz, who silently slipped out of the limo and shut the door. Kang touched the button signaling the driver to go. He felt the limo effortlessly glide down the mountain road. Heinz overestimated the trouble of transporting an unwilling person to Hong Kong; a private plane was all that was needed.

Perhaps the promoter was still sympathetic to Mitchell; he had, after all, helped train him. Kang could understand the bond of loyalty between master and student, even after the student's spectacular betrayal. Still, there was logic in wishing to avoid a mess here. Kang had other headaches right now. Police, prices, rivals, new pressures from the mainland. It was a delicate time in his empire.

His fortuneteller had interpreted the Way of the Tao when Kang had knelt before the temple in his garden this morning and put himself in the hands of chance. His oracle had read:

The Han dynasty began with the fall of a great city;
Two generals strove to be the conqueror,

One threw up walls around it, but the mightiest
Could break them down to claim his throne

"Seize your opportunity!" advised the fortuneteller. "Troubled by a tenacious opponent?
Strike while the iron is hot! That's what the
fortune is telling you."

His physician, on the other hand, yesterday
had told him to get some rest. Settle the nerves.
Maybe take a holiday.

Take action? Or rest? Maybe he could achieve
both.

Big Uncle Kang called his secretary and told
her to get his private jet ready. He was going to
Koh Samui.

Chapter 25

Woodchopper

"**C**AN'T this thing go any faster?" she shouted.

"No!" Trav had the scooter throttle maxed. The Honda had only a 100cc engine and the weight of a second person and their backpacks forced it into a slow, whiny grind as they took a hill.

"Some escape."

Trav didn't dare take his eyes off the road, even though Mazy's complaint sparked a bud of anger that flowered into a vision of his squeezing the brakes. *Oh, I'm sorry, yoga guru; here—you drive this thing.*

They were on the main ring road that circumnavigated most of the island, but at this point detoured through the interior's hilly quilt of forests. The road was lined with the detritus of tourism—advertisements for elephant rides, *wats*, and scenic waterfalls. Traffic was busy; and for the third time, assailing an incline, a car honked and blew past them, its windy wake causing the scooter to shudder.

"Careful!"

"What do you want me to do, hit the turbo button?"

The road leveled out, to his relief. They passed a gas station, followed by a low-slung building with a rusted tin roof, a stadium for buffalo fights. Country was turning to town, and Trav knew they were almost there. They closed in on a small temple and a school, and then the view opened on their left, down past the scrub and trees, to the bright sea. They descended toward Nathon and the roadside buildings thickened into something like a port.

Trav hit the brakes to avoid a group of women in sarongs crossing the road, heading to the outdoor market. He gunned it and turned left again until they were on the beachfront street, the ferry terminal's twin piers of covered pontoons stretching silently into the calm ocean waters. A four-storey Seatrans ferry loomed above the tallest building along the shore.

"That's our ride," he said, wanting to accelerate but held back by traffic. Nathon wasn't a particularly bustling spot, far from it, but the road was a knot of pedestrians, cars, pickups and tuk-tuks. They posed a noisy contrast to the quiet dive shops and day spas along the sidewalk, their entrances shaded and mute beneath protective awnings.

A local bus peeled into traffic from a station just before the ferry bridges, and Trav sped into the empty space.

"Ferry's over there, not here," Mazy said.

"I know, but I gotta park somewhere."

He found a space nestled among a row of scooters and motorcycles and killed the engine, feeling somewhat deafened. The ride had provided too much sun and wind, too many noxious clouds from passing vehicles or dust kicked up alongside the road. He knew he needed to move fast.

Mazy slid off and fumbled with the chinstrap. "Let me," he said, but she pulled away. "Fine, whatever." Trav retrieved his backpack from beneath the seat.

She removed the helmet and shook her hair free, then tossed the helmet to him. "Here you go, cowboy."

Trav didn't bother with putting it away inside the seat pouch. He just stuck it on a handlebar. Mazy was already jogging around a column of busses through the closed stalls of an empty night market that lay between them and the ferry pier.

The Seatrans ferry horn shook the seafront.

Mazy broke into a trot.

Trav followed but in his desperation to keep up with her tripped on an uneven sidewalk and tumbled chin first.

He picked himself up, a little dazed, his chin on fire, and kept running, his hip not quite working right, his back feeling pinched. As he ran the kinks worked themselves out but the pain across his face grew intense, as though fanned by the wind, and he knew he was bleeding a torrent. He could feel the sick cold flow

218

from his chin and was aware of splatter marks appearing on his T-shirt. But none of that mattered to him, not as he watched Mazy distance herself, the sun lighting up her scything arms and legs and glinting off the bottle of vodka sticking out of her backpack.

Mazy! He wanted to shout her name but it was all he could do to regain his own rhythm and rejoin the race.

A shiny black van screeched alongside her at the edge of the piers. She veered off course and Trav knew this was bad. Her narrow room to move was sliced thin as the van drove onto the sidewalk, jumping excitedly along the uneven pavement blocks, until it came to an abrupt, rubber-burning halt beside her and the passenger door swung open, clipping her legs as she tried to sprint past.

Trav accelerated, his view of her blocked by a man jumping out from the passenger side. He was white and sunburnt, and very big, a bodybuilder with a tight- fitting tank top and a pate of cropped brassy hair. He closed the door and Trav could see Mazy crawling on the ground, like a swimmer struggling to keep her head above the angry waves.

Muscle Man slowed to a jog until he was standing right over her. She twisted onto her back and tried to kick him, but Muscles grabbed her foot and twisted it a little further. Trav heard her frantic yelps. He jettisoned his own backpack and ducked into a tackling position like an NFL linesman, chin buried on his chest, and slammed against the big man, aiming to hit where it hurt, shoulder into the guy's kidney.

For a one-on-one, Trav preferred to bring a fight down to the ground as quickly as possible, particularly since he was currently a fist short. He was careful not to crush his cast as he followed Muscles' tumble to the pavement. The big man fell, *oomph*. Trav sprawled himself atop him, going into a simple mount, resting his weight upon Muscle's huge chest. He took a punch in the ribs, but the big man lacked leverage.

Trav inched himself upward and used his own chest to smother Muscles, sliding his left hand under the man's neck to increase the pressure. Muscles bucked, using his sheer size to fight back, and kicked up from the waist. Trav was still trying to get the right hold and lost control. A flurry of sneakers as Mazy scrambled away. Then he was thrown—on the cast, no pain—and there was an arc of blood, more blood spraying from Trav's opened chin, and Muscles was trying to return the favor, spreading his bulk over Trav to suffocate him into submission.

But Muscles didn't know how to defend in jujitsu and Trav got his legs around the man's relatively thin waist and locked it with his feet. Trav thrust his good hand up and landed a choke hold. Muscles' little porky eyes lit up in shock as Trav squeezed and pushed the big man's torso back, not so much lifting it but forcing Muscles to pull up so that he could breathe. The guy was huge, but he didn't know how to escape Trav's guard position, not with Trav's fingers cramping his trachea. A huge white fist tried to peel away Trav's choke hold, but Trav used his locked legs to shake Muscles off balance.

If Trav had use of his other hand, he could have finished it right here, but it was all he could do to keep Muscles from regaining the initiative and it became a question of who'd tire first. Both of them paused when Mazy walked up and swung her hands in the air, legs apart, inhaling into a back bend—*She's doing a goddamn yoga stretch?*—and then exhaled with a *pah!* as she levered her body into a sharp squat and brought down the bottle of Absolut onto Muscles' upturned forehead.

Trav used his last juice to increase the chokehold, but it probably didn't matter. Muscles was done. He let out a kind of sniveling cry and crumpled, nearly crushing Trav, who maneuvered the man off to the side where he curled up and bellowed, hands covering his face, his white sausage fingers leaking vodka-thinned blood.

Mazy regarded her handiwork with numb austerity. "Woodchopper pose," she said, "good for hamstrings. Great anger release." She melted into tears.

Trav was now aware of the driver of the van, but the man, a slender Thai in a white short-sleeved shirt and dark slacks, was not a threat. The driver was immobilized in shock. Muscle Man sobbed in pained confusion as he raised himself onto his hands and knees. Trav considered a Muay Thai kick, but it wasn't necessary. Muscles clambered back into the van, groping for handholds, blind from the flow of blood. Trav grabbed him by the waist and heaved him into the passenger seat.

"You bitch," Muscles gasped.

"You and Gordon can go fuck yourselves," Mazy hissed, looking at the angry abrasions on her calves. "You nearly crippled me."

"Anurak, help," Muscles said to the driver before he fainted in the seat. Trav rolled the van door shut. The driver snapped out of his shock and gently drove the Alphard forward.

She was still shaking. "You OK?" Trav asked her.

"Son of a bitch clipped me good." Her hands may have been shaking but her eyes steadily observed the van's departure. "But yeah, I'll live."

The van slumped back into the street.

"I guess I underestimated yoga," Trav said. "That was pretty badass." But Mazy didn't hear him—she was already limping furiously toward the ferry gate. Trav hefted his own backpack and mustered the energy to follow.

The Seatrans ferry horn sounded again. Mazy accelerated into a hobble, but it was too late: the ferry was pulling away from the pier, spouting a greasy cone of smoke.

Trav caught up with her and tried to present a brave front. "There'll be more ferries," he said.

"When! When we're already dead?"

"It's going to be OK. Let's check the schedule."

"We have, like, hours. Minutes. Before they come back."

"Just wait here." He walked back to the ticket office, its outer wall covered in posters. He ran a finger down the timetables. Not good. "There's another one leaving today."

"And?"

"More like tonight."

"Great."

"Look, after what you did to that guy, I'm guessing he isn't coming back. Who was that, anyway? One of Gordon's men?"

She nodded absently. "Ginger. His real name's Chester, but everybody calls him Ginger." She walked back to the low-set fringe of town. Trav tried to keep pace.

"He's a piece of work," he said.

"He's a fucking asshole."

"I can see that."

"We shouldn't have let him go."

"What, we should torture him in broad daylight in downtown Nathon?"

Her voice flattened in an ugly way. "Why not."

Trav realized how lucky they had been. The streets were sleepy, but not empty, and there was a thin stream of people, tourists and Thais, who had disembarked from the ferry still milling around. The van, by blocking Mazy off, had also hidden the fight from view. Except, Trav thought, for one man, a Thai, who was walking directly for them.

But he wasn't coming from the pier, where there would have been a clear line of sight of their fracas, but from across the street. He was tall and hipster thin, wearing an unbuttoned paisley shirt that showed off his brown compact abs. He boasted a long mane of hair and a greasy attempt at a mustache, which gave him a louche confidence. The breeze off the ocean ruffling his feathered hair made him look like some kind of 1970s porn star.

"You know this guy?" Trav asked softly.

"No."

The man stopped about ten feet from them and outstretched a long, thin arm and an expectant palm.

"Your phone, give to me."

"Excuse me?" Mazy said.

"Who are you?" Trav demanded.

The thin Thai's other hand reached behind his flapping shirttails and he pulled out a Beretta pistol and pointed it at them.

"Phone. Mobile. Give me."

"Are you a robber?" Mazy asked.

"Maze, just give him the phone," Trav said, feeling his hairs stand at attention. He'd had enough adventure for one morning. He took an instinctive step backward, as though an extra foot would slow the bullet.

"Now," snapped the Thai man.

"Or what?" she demanded. "You shoot us in the middle of the day? Look, there's people over there. You can't shoot us!"

The man didn't seem too bothered. He shrugged and aimed directly at her. "Five. Four. Three."

The guy didn't care, Trav thought, which meant he was either driven by something scarier than the prospect of jail, or didn't seem to think jail was a serious possibility for daylight murder.

"Maze, give him the goddamn phone."

"Shit." She reached a trembling hand into her pocket.

Chapter 26

A Bowl of Noodles

For Major Win Arpornakun, inspector of the Samui Tourist Police, Region 8 Surat Thani, the problem with fighting crime today was hemorrhoids. It didn't seem to matter whether he was sitting at his desk or riding in the brown-and-white. Face it, he reasoned: when your ass is on fire, it's hard to concentrate on solving cases.

He preferred to walk than ride. Sitting in one place for too long was a ticket to hell. He would usually fill in reports while standing up, writing on top of the filing cabinet. But he especially felt the urge to stroll when it was time for lunch.

The food in the canteen was free to members of the force, and it would have been churlish not to join his colleagues there. Afterwards, though, he would direct his bulging belly out onto the street of Nathon, down towards the crystal blue sea and the front street with his favorite hawker stand. Sometimes as he went, he would whisper to himself the country saying, 'Don't eat lying down, you will become a snake in the next life,' as though it were a mantra. Lying down and eating at the same time was unhealthy because you might suffocate. Logic, extended liberally, suggested that sitting to eat was only slightly less dangerous.

The doctors had warned him off the fiery dark broth that Mrs. Phueng conjured in her curbside stall. Doctors. Well. They gave him these supplements of bran. What was bran, anyway? Win had once tried it while a university student in America. It had diminished his regard for foreigners.

No, for Major Win, the best way to conclude lunch in the canteen was with a nice bowl of Mrs. Phueng's chili-laden noodle soup with crispy pork. The most important question of the day often revolved around the choice of noodle: flat and wide or thin and long? Soft glass vermicelli, or hard and crunchy?

Win's office was in the main police station, two blocks back from the ferry terminal, a tall, dingy concrete structure behind city hall that doubled as a barracks, which explained the lines of white undergarments drying off on the balconies of the upper stories. There was a Tourist Police box near the terminal itself, manned by his juniors. Win's job was to liaise with the Provincial Police for matters more serious than lost passports and pickpocket victims.

It was nothing like the detective work he had done as part of Bangkok's Metropolitan Police force—officers did *not* dry their underwear on the upper floors of the Royal Thai Police Head-quarters. But the politics of yellow shirts versus red shirts had gotten in the way of his career, and when the prime minister's office changed hands, Win had found himself on the wrong side. They couldn't sack him, particularly given his local fame and his clean reputation among the corps and Bangkok journalists. So: a promotion and transfer to Koh Samui.

After the constant nervous energy of Bangkok, Samui might as well have been the Sahara. Or Antarctica, as Win's wife, desperately missing the shopping malls of Bangkok, liked to describe it nearly every day.

He'd endured three boring years. Local population—fifty thousand, with plenty of transients, plus the ebb and flow of tourists, both foreign and Thai. He tried to maintain a little of his big-city pace. Every month he treated the officers among the provincial police and the counter-terrorism unit to dinner. He'd gotten to know the hotel operators, the tour guides, the villa owners. He had a passing acquaintance with the coconut farmers and the fishermen's union, and he prayed, occasionally, at all the wats and the mosques, too. He knew most of the representatives of the property developers, though never came close to the families themselves.

He knew the gangs, country versions of the crude toughs who ran the streets of Bangkok. He knew the fences and the fronts, had an inkling of the way hash and other things floated around, came in and out.

But Win wasn't on vice or homicide, not anymore, not on quiet Koh Samui. His Metropolitan Police days had given him plenty of experience in crackdowns. But such things were no longer his business. Mostly, therefore, he ate. His nagging wife ate. There wasn't much more to do than fill in paperwork and get fat.

Win did face some serious crimes. From time to time, more regularly than the authorities admitted, isolated foreign tourists, usually women, washed up dead. Local perverts or desperados were usually to blame, although occasionally the foreigners brought spats and violence with them. Such cases were as exciting as it got for tourist police, but lately things had been especially quiet, which was good for the economy but not so good for his waistline.

Samui was no paradise for a cop—just a purgatory. Without cases, there wasn't much else to occupy one's mind. The idea of his chopsticks immersed in a knot of broad, flat noodles in Mrs. Phueng's spicy dark pork broth—now that was something to think about. Which Major Win did as he walked out of the police station's front gate and ambled toward the water, his brown uniform taut around his spherical belly.

Mrs. Phueng was there, of course, immune to the sweltering heat of her portable kitchen, and she greeted him with respect. He gave her his order. She knew his curious habit of eating while standing, and she served the soup inside an extra bowl, so he could hold it comfortably.

"Delicious," he said, slurping down the fiery broth, feeling the sweat prick his neck and the bald patch beneath his officer's hat. "Your noodles are still the best in Koh Samui, Khun Phueng," calling her by the standard honorific. He shared with Mrs. Phueng heat upon heat there, steaming soup beneath the mid-day sun, watching people get off the ferry: young foreigners shouldering bulky backpacks, local Thais with bicycles, caged chickens and big plastic bags full of new possessions bought on the mainland.

A loud screech prompted him to gaze up from his meal. A black Toyota van had come careening to a stop just before the terminal. Major Win considered the prospect of a ticket for illegal parking but gave a mental shrug. Not really his beat. And the noodles were good. They were going to give him dragon bum and inflame the hemorrhoids, he knew, but those were going to hurt anyway, so why deprive himself?

He saw a white person behind the van hit the ground. A woman with dark hair. She seemed to be scrambling. The erratic driving, falling down...probably drunk or on drugs. Now that was his beat: disorderly foreigners. Maybe the chance to collar a dealer. Win had no problem with *farang* people but, like most police officers, took an unsympathetic view to their involvement in drugs in Thailand. The country was already awash with amphetamines, cocaine and hashish, and it didn't need pampered Westerners adding their own dirty habits and criminal connections to the local mix.

Win thanked Mrs. Phueng and dabbed his lips with a tissue. The white woman had gotten up and seemed fine, but Win saw no harm in extending his daily peregrination across the street to have a closer look.

But then he saw something more interesting, which gave Win pause. Someone else was walking toward the van from further down the street, a skinny Thai man with long hair and a shirt open down the front. Win recognized the man as Narong, one of Tarrin's boys, whom the Provincial Police suspected of murder but had no hard evidence against.

While watching Narong strut toward the pier, Win missed whatever transpired at the van— he thought he heard a cry or a shout, but a glance caught nothing. As Narong approached the noodle stand, the van trundled off, leaving two foreigners, a man and a woman, standing there holding backpacks. The foreigners moved toward the ferry but the ferry's horn bellowed and the ship heaved off. The white people stopped. Narong was now crossing the street. Win handed Mrs. Phueng a twenty-baht note and ambled after Narong.

As he crossed the front street, he saw Narong pull a gun on the two foreigners, which set his heart racing. This was not usual, not even for a *nakleng*. The arrogance of it infuriated Win. *As though we are nothing. As though cops don't count.*

But he knew that if someone wanted to spend enough money to make a gun charge go away, it was possible. It had happened to him in Bangkok.

Win drew his own service revolver, now hurrying, and got on his walkie-talkie and called for backup.

Narong must have sensed Win's clumsy approach, for he turned to face the policeman, hiding his pistol back behind his shirt. Flashing Win a naughty grin, Narong bolted. Win considered shooting him, but it was too risky, and even if his aim were true, the fallout would be harsh. 'Tourists panic at Samui ferry shooting'—not the kind of headline the commissioner would be pleased to read. He made a half-hearted effort to chase Narong but quickly got winded.

Well, job done, foreigners saved...but questions persisted.

They were at the ticket stand.

"Excuse me," Win said in fluent English—he had a bachelor's degree from the University of Portland, which he put to use regularly. "I need you to answer some questions." His uniform was obvious, but he tapped his badge to make sure there was no mistake.

He noticed the woman immediately: striking, like a model or a movie actress, dark hair on pale skin, Caucasian from a distance but something Asian in her eyes. The man was more ordinary, although obviously in good shape, his congenial looks marred by the strange slant of his nose, the sure mark of a boxer.

Win would have expected anxiety, or resignation, or relief. But his presence just made the foreigners tense, and the bloody gash in the man's chin and fresh dark stains on the woman's shirt suggested something was wrong. And that's when the man said, "We're late for the ferry, sir. Sorry."

"Yeah, we've got to go now," the woman added.

Win looked at the pair of pontoons penetrating the turquoise panorama, framing the now-distant vessel.

"But the ferry's gone," said Win. "And I saw you miss it."

Chapter 27

Bad Monkey

GORDON followed Isaac and Tarrin down a trail along the side of the road, through a forest of palm trees. Isaac had made this trek enough times to know the way, it seemed. The tight military formation of the palms revealed they were walking on a plantation, not through natural jungle.

The land undulated here in a patchwork of lighter and darker greens, interrupted by bare white patches of limestone hills. They were not, in fact, far from the southern coast, from Lamai and the zoo and the villa. But this was another world here, the brooding village world of isolated rural Thailand.

They might as well have driven from the busy coast for days, Gordon reflected, not for twenty minutes, to wind up here.

Tarrin's car was parked at a nearby garage, sited in an interior village never visited by tourists, the kind of place where children played naked in mud puddles; the kind of place, Gordon had noted, where the locals spoke warmly to Tarrin, knowing exactly what kind of man he was, and accepted a coin or two from him with a smile and a *wai*. If Tarrin didn't come from that particular hamlet, he probably came from one just like it.

The lab occupied a storehouse on a coconut plantation. The building had lost its use and been left derelict, its windows boarded. One of Tarrin's skinny youths squatted by the door, keeping a lazy eye on the little clearing surrounding the building. To one side leaned a trio of trash cans, contents overflowing to the point of spilling all over the ground: empty cans of beer, soiled condoms, needles, rubber tubing, cans of kerosene, Styrofoam containers from fast-food restaurants or food stalls.

Small grey macaques screamed and hooted along the storehouse roof, and more sauntered around the trash bins. Tarrin kicked at one beggar that came too close and the swarm hooted and scattered but did not retreat.

The kid watching the door stood and opened the door for them.

Isaac had spent the first two weeks of their time on the island assembling the lab. He had worked with Tarrin to get the right equipment or jerry-rig a substitute. It didn't require anything too fancy: buckets, a kerosene heater and camp stove fuel, a freezer, hydrochloric acid, filters, tubes, lithium batteries, matches. That was for the mixing. The other half of the storehouse had been restored to a twisted version of its original purpose: housing coconuts.

Tarrin had recruited some village children to put it together, help Isaac hook up the electricity generator out back, and to dig a deep pit where they'd bury the noxious chemical runoff. Outside, the smell of fumes had been mixed with shit and the stench of general dereliction; inside it was nauseatingly intense. Gordon knew at once these kids hadn't been taking care of the waste properly.

The interior was split, with the lab in front. A pair of naked bulbs strung along the lone beam running through the ceiling provided dim light for the two teenage boys who were handling the mixing. A large mattress was incongruously propped against a wall, its exposed side heavily stained by the color of rust, but somehow a lack of dust made it look as though it had been placed there only recently.

"So what's the problem then?" Gordon asked.

Through Tarrin, Isaac tried to get them to explain what had gone wrong. This was where the stolen Ketaset, kept in the freezer, was transformed into K-Love. This was where Isaac's genius was being realized. Ground zero for the introduction to the world of what Isaac had regarded as a superior trip, and what Gordon knew was, in fact, the world's most incredible date-rape drug.

The squalid lab wasn't in fact Gordon's main point of interest. He left Tarrin and Isaac there to walk through a door into the main area. The room was big and dark, but suffocating, hot and awful. A single fan was all there was to battle the fumes of glue, which is why the quartet of young girls wore facemasks and nothing else. Their skinny, sweaty brown backs bent over the central table as their nimble fingers worked with knives to open the coconuts, replace the milk with little plastic baggies of K-Love, and then glue them perfectly shut. Their spiritless black eyes occasionally communicated some mundane emotion, or flitted nervously to the old village man with flecks of a white beard, who hovered around them with a machete stuffed in his belt; or to another of Tarrin's goons, a dusty man in grease-smeared overalls, who was now urinating against the wall where he kept a crowbar propped.

It wasn't pleasant, Gordon acknowledged, squarely meeting the bitter gazes of those prematurely aged brown eyes, but what about England's dark Satanic mills and all that? China, the modern-day workshop of the world, was pitted with poisoned rivers and cities of slag heaps. The price of enterprise. The price of innovation. Besides, he wasn't forcing any of these young adults to work here. They wanted the money, the grubby little bitches. Or their parents did, at any rate, but that wasn't Gordon's affair.

He moved to examine the huge pile of finished coconuts. The old man with the machete stepped back with timid deference. Most of the husks bore unnatural ridges and clefts, but you couldn't tell unless you were looking out for defects. The long, hard hairs obscured the coconuts' deformities. When he shook them, the K-Love made enough of a sloshing noise to satisfy him. Samui had been exporting coconuts around Southeast Asia for decades, centuries. Who was going to care if a Thai restaurant chain in Hong Kong wanted to buy coconuts wholesale from here?

There was a second pile of coconuts, however, and this merited his attention. These specimens were meant to be finished products, but their assembly had gone wrong. Their fissures had been reopened into dark gaping gashes.

Gordon examined these failures with disappointment. He wordlessly dropped a maimed coconut back onto the pile of fellow defects and returned to the lab, where Isaac had removed his shirt and wrapped it around his head to cover his nose and mouth. He was kneeling by his mixing contraption, stirring a bucket with a thin stick, checking the temperature on a thermometer.

Chili Hut. Gordon shook his head at his own misplaced generosity. He had given it to Mazy to make sure, if the Hong Kong police ever did get wind of the operation, it was under a name other than Gordon Wood's. He had intended to distance himself entirely from it. He was ready to let her run the business, and if it ever turned a dollar again—unlikely—she could keep it. He'd pay the debts to keep the front going. What mattered wasn't selling pad thai and shrimp cakes to the Cantonese, but signing for the coconut shipments.

Gordon had momentarily lost his senses by asking her to marry him. He didn't really want to analyze this turn of events, for he didn't want to learn which hurt more: foolishly letting his guard down because of his cursed generosity and his expression of love for her, or her betrayal?

Nor was Gordon in the mood to explore the question of what had really led him to the rash marriage proposal in the first place. Lying in bed, impotent in her care, and then trading her services to the insatiable Scouse—the image of it flashed through his mind again, as it had so often these past twenty-four hours, and he banished the memory with a wince. When the time came, and that time was coming soon, Gordon would deliver a reminder to Ginger of his place in this organization.

This nagging train of thought, having intruded into his work, combined with the retching stench of the lab and the pointed eyes of these naked children, caused him to lose his patience. "Well, what's the fucking problem?" he snarled.

Tarrin seemed to take this personally. He raised his gold chains and shook them. "Who you talk to, Gordon?"

"Isaac, not you, mate. Isaac! You're the bleeding chemist."

"Something about the Ketaset wasn't mixing as well as we thought. If it gets out of the plastic baggie, it acts like a solvent on the coconut wall."

"Oh, brilliant. So what have you created, may I ask? A ketamine derivative or Drano?" *Whatever it is, Maze's given us all a good dose of it.*

"Don't worry, chief, it's not going to unclog the old drains. But in this concentrated liquid form, it's not reacting well to the coconut. That's me guess."

"And you think this new version, the Ketavet, will do the trick?"

"Sure thing," Isaac said from behind his makeshift facemask. "Ketavet's almost a hundred percent the same chemical structure, but it's got a different pH and is a little less acidic than Ketaset. All we need to do is change the pharmacological brand, amp up the heat on the mixer here when we put in the MDMA, tighten up the rubber bands on the baggies, and Bob's your uncle."

Gordon nodded and exited that particular little corner of hell. The smell lingered outside but at least there was a breeze. Monkeys picked through the piles of garbage. One cheeky macaque noticed him and, in a display of rude bravado, leapt on a nearby female and stuck its penis inside her, keeping its gaze firmly on Gordon the whole time. But Gordon no longer saw the raping monkey; he witnessed instead the vision of Ginger, drawers down, moving in on Mazy with his quivering wet dick. Drug or no drug, she had acquiesced, and happily, near as Gordon could tell. He would know. He had been lying beside her, sourly impotent, until he had left in a fit of disgust, determined to get some of his own elsewhere if need be.

Sodding Scouse. Ungrateful, deceitful whore.

To think he had then gone out and bought that silly ring. For that slut!

The female macaque screeched and shoved the male away, but the damned creature kept grinning at Gordon, as if to say, *Whaddaya think of that?*

Well, Mazy had better be back at the villa by the time he returned. Maybe he'd spare her, if she really squealed for forgiveness.

Gordon lifted a discarded soda can and hurled it at the offending monkey.

And if Ginger said another uppity word back to him, Gordon would have Tarrin take care of him. One less loose end; one final lesson in respect.

Chapter 28

Names and Numbers

THE quietude of Nathon belied the inside of the police station, a narrow, grimy building that bustled with noise and havoc. It seemed to Travis like part community center and part circus, where the Thais came to complain, beseech, and harass one another. The cops mostly maintained rehearsed expressions of calm indifference as they shuffled among the hapless and the indignant.

The policeman, Win, had led them through the bustle, belly first, parting the throngs of beseechers like an amiable sea lion. Trav thought they would stop at a window with an English sign that read "Tourist Police", where there was another foreigner waiting, a young bearded backpacker. But no, he and Mazy obediently followed the fat policeman past that, to a flight of concrete steps that led upstairs to a somewhat more subdued floor of cubicles, lazy fans, stacks of paper and a few ancient looking computers.

"Please, sit," the cop bid them when they reached what appeared to be his desk, a large, paper-strewn plastic table. He was an older, beefy man, weathered as dark brown as the uniform that bulged uncomfortably around his prodigious belly. Major Win eased with a grimace into his chair and flicked through Trav's passport. Trav tucked his backpack beneath his seat, desperately wishing he had locked it in the motorcycle seat.

"So, Travis," the policeman said, addressing him in a casual, American-accented style, "you two are going to the mainland."

"Yes, sir."

"For a day trip."

"Yeah."

"And you, young lady, have no identification?"

"I lost my passport yesterday. I'm on my way to the US embassy in Bangkok. That's why we're in a hurry."

"Lost your passport, I see. How long ago?"

"What?" Mazy asked stupidly.

"How long ago did you lose your passport?"

He's testing us, Trav thought. *He doesn't believe us…and why should he?*

"I'm not sure," she replied. "I had it with me when I went shopping in Chaweng two days ago, but now it's gone."

"What's your name again?"

"Mazy."

"Any other ID?"

She shook her head. "Sorry."

"Not even a driver's license?"

"Mine expired a while ago. I live in Hong Kong so I never bothered to get it renewed."

"So you have a Hong Kong I.D. card."

"I guess that's gone, too," Mazy stammered. "I mean, my purse is gone. Everything was in there. Credit cards and everything."

"I have mine," Trav offered. "My Hong Kong I. D., I mean."

"I wasn't asking you," Win snapped. "Do you know who was that man with the gun?"

"No idea," Trav said. "We never saw him before."

"What did he want?"

"Money." It was a lie, but shouldn't a mugger want cash?

"Really?" Win asked. "That's what he said, he wants your money?"

Trav nodded.

"In daylight, surrounded by people, this man points a gun at you for money."

"I guess he's desperate," Trav offered. "Maybe he's a junkie."

"His name's Narong and he's not a junkie," Win said.

Busted. Trav felt his stomach sink.

"In fact, he's got plenty of money already," the cop continued. "So why don't you tell me the truth? How do you know him? What does he want from you?"

"We really have no clue," Mazy said.

"Who was in that black van? The one that drove off. You, mystery miss, you seemed like you were hurt. Some kind of struggle."

"Van?" Mazy asked. Trav was impressed by her manufactured puzzlement.

The cop sighed irritably. He shifted uncomfortably in his chair. "Look, you two, I can keep you here for a long time, OK? You want to see the inside of a Thai jail?"

Trav shook his head. "No, sir, we don't, but we haven't done anything wrong. We're just tourists. She needs a new passport. That's all."

Win stood up and did a little jig behind his desk, as though he had ants in his pants. "That's all you're going to say?"

"That's all there is to say," Trav replied.

"Open your bags."

His face tensed. "But...may I ask why?"

"Open them."

Mazy obliged, showing the meager contents she had taken from the villa. The cop rummaged idly through her possessions, pausing to peer at the diamond ring, and pushed the bag back to her. She seemed oddly calm to Trav.

But why shouldn't she be? She wasn't the one carrying a backpack stuffed with an inexplicable amount of cash.

"So, um, can I go?" Mazy said.

Gee, thanks for the show of solidarity, Trav seethed.

The cop ignored her. "OK, Travis, your turn."

He was stuck. He could refuse, but this wasn't the United States, and he didn't think defiance would get him far. But as soon as the cop saw his backpack stuffed with baht and Hong Kong dollars...

Mazy was done. She wanted out. She had to get a new passport, a new life. She was practically about to bolt out of her chair and run back to the ferry pier. All she needed was...what, for him to get stuck in this spider's web?

Trav sighed and said, "Look, sir, you're right. That guy, Narong you called him? He didn't ask for money."

Win sat down again. "Good, Travis. What did he ask for?"

Trav said, "Well, I've got something for you, sir. Something you're going to like. Maybe we can do a deal."

The cop exploded. "You think Thai cops are all corrupt, huh? You think you rich Americans can just pay me off and get away?"

Trav raised his palms in supplication. "No, no, no. Sir, no. I'm not trying to—for crying out loud—no, I'm not trying to bribe you. I want to give you something for your job. Maze, give it to him."

"What?"

"The phone. Give it to him."

She petulantly dug into her pocket and put Gordon's mobile on the desk.

"What's this?" Win demanded, still angry.

"This, sir, is the mobile phone of an Englishman who's here to manufacture and deal in ketamine. It contains a lot of interesting phone numbers, and probably a useful log of his calls.

Hong Kong, Singapore, other places. This phone can tie together an operation that's still being put together. You can use it to bust it up."

Win slammed both fists on the desk. "What is this bullshit? You think I'm some kind of stupid hick cop?"

Trav turned to Mazy. "You gotta show him. Please."

"I don't know anything about that phone," she said. "It doesn't belong to me."

"It belongs to Gordon. Your fiancé, remember?"

Now it was her turn to flare up red, but whatever she was about to spit out halted at the tip of her tongue.

Trav said, "Officer, you can see she's got a few bruises. These men have hit her. They're violent, dangerous. We were on our way off the island, for good. If they track either of us down, they'll hurt her again, and maybe kill me. All I'm asking is that you let us get the heck out of here. That man you saw, Narong? He wanted this phone. Can we make a deal here?"

Win picked up the cell. "You say these men are foreigners."

"Yes, sir."

"So how do they know a local troublemaker like Narong?"

"Gordon's partner is a Thai," Mazy offered. "But I never saw Narong before in my life."

"We don't know him," Trav said. "All I can guess is that Gordon really wants to get his hands on this phone. It must have a lot of important information on it. You saw it, officer. They'd shoot us in broad daylight to get this phone. Whatever's on there means nothing to us, but just having it is like a death sentence."

"So why do you have it?"

That stumped him. Trav waited for Mazy to reply, but she just shrugged.

"Please," Trav said, "I'm begging you, just let us go."

"Two four eight," Mazy said, "nine six."

Both men stared at her.

"That's the security code," she said. "Gordon thinks when you move your finger around phone numbers that way, it makes a 'G'."

Win grunted and input the code. The phone's screen flashed to life. He scrolled through text messages for a long moment. "Not much here."

"Try the phone log," Trav suggested. "Or the address book."

"It's that little symbol with the little green head," Mazy added.

"I know how to use a smartphone," Win growled. He put the phone on the desk so they could all see the screen. "Show me."

His thick finger sent names careening across the small screen. She leaned forward and pointed out one of Gordon's cronies. "That guy, I think he gets pot from triads in Hong Kong... That guy's got some kind of deal going in Singapore, I'm not sure what... That's Isaac, he's here on the island. He built a lab somewhere in the jungle."

"A drug lab on Samui?" the cop wondered.

"I haven't been there. But they're stealing ke-tamine from the tiger zoo and then mixing it into something different."

Win scrolled through more names. "Tarrin," he grunted.

"Yeah, Tarrin," Mazy said. "He's Gordon's local partner. Helping supply stuff. You know him?"

The cop nodded.

"Then you know we're not bullshitting you," Trav said.

Win scrolled through more names. "Tell me more. Who is this Gordon?"

Mazy leaned forward to see the screen. "Gordon Wood. He's been renting a big villa on the south side for the past few weeks. He's from Hong Kong. He's organized the whole thing."

"And you're marrying this man?"

"No. He just thinks I am."

"I can't just have you leave Koh Samui," Win told them.

Mazy sat back. "You have to let me go. They've threatened my life."

"I don't have to let you go anywhere if you're a material witness to drug trafficking."

Trav said, "Look, officer, I know you can keep us here for as long as you want. I'm asking you, though, to let us go. You've got the phone. If we stay here, we're dead—Heinz?" He thought he had seen the name flash on the screen. "Hey, go back. Holy shit, Heinz."

"Who's Heinz?" Win asked.

"My trainer, back in Hong Kong."

"Trainer?"

"I do a little kickboxing. Just amateur stuff, for fitness."

"That how you hurt your wrist?"

"Yeah."

Win continued down through the alphabet.

And there it was, under the Ks.

Trav buried his face in his hands.

Gordon's entry: Kang.

Chapter 29

Out on a Limb

THE deal was this: Major Win would let them leave Koh Samui but not Thailand. He confiscated Trav's passport and sealed it in a sturdy manila envelope, to be couriered to Bangkok once Win had received confirmation that Travis and Mazy were in the company of Surat Thani's Provincial Police. That department had been notified that it was to receive two American nationals on an evening ferry, and they were to be immediately transferred to Win's friends on the Bangkok Metropolitan force.

In turn for getting them off the island, though, they were going to have to serve as witnesses, which meant they were going to have to remain in Thailand. They were given numbers to call on a daily basis, to let the cops know of their whereabouts. Moreover, the US embassy was going to be notified and asked to postpone giving them new passports, a stipulation Win made clear was within the powers of the Royal Thai Police.

While the police made their arrangements, Mazy and Trav remained separated in barely furnished interrogation rooms, undergoing Win's questioning. Mazy, the first to be escorted away, had left Trav with a withering look. But he felt if anyone should feel aggrieved, it was him. The cut on his chin continued to throb, even after a policewoman had cleaned it and applied a bandage, a constant reminder of his sacrifice.

In the end, he had to show Win the contents of his backpack—the thing he had hoped to prevent with the phone gambit, earning Mazy's ire in the process. But the game had been up as soon as the policeman had appeared on the ferry pier, Trav now reckoned. And besides, Win may have saved their lives.

So he went step by step, telling the policeman several times over about how he had abandoned his life in Hong Kong because of a stupid mistake in a late-night illegal fighting session, knocking out cold the third son of a triad boss named Kang—yes, almost certainly the same Kang as the one on Gordon's mobile phone—and that's why the cash was mostly in Hong Kong dollars, not Thai baht. He told Win about the little house rented from the Montri family and showed him, sheepishly, the thrilling adventures of Rick Fury, kick-ass futures trader, and his nemesis Lance Cutlass.

Whatever conversation Win later had with Mazy, Trav could only guess.

He then had to sign a lot of documents, all in Thai. Win didn't bother to explain them and

Trav could have been signing away his future first-born, for all he knew, but he didn't see how he had much choice. He even caved on his one absolute demand: he had made it clear to Win that he could stay in Bangkok, or be deported to America, or sent almost anywhere, so long as he wasn't sent to Hong Kong. But Win told him that Trav was not in the position to make demands, absolute or otherwise.

"Sympathy and a buck-fifty'll get me a soft pretzel on Fifth Avenue," Trav mumbled as he put his John Hancock to one unintelligible indenture after another.

Kang. Frickin' Kang. If Gordon had found out Trav's identity, and was connected to Heinz and Kang, then surely the Chinese gangster must now know where Trav had gone. That made this little tropical island of paradise a death sentence for him. It probably made Bangkok unsafe, too, but he'd now have to take things one step at a time.

Win seemed pretty competent, and not just because of his fluent English. His questioning, the way he jumped on all of Trav's little inconsistencies, made clear Win's intelligence. He knew what he was doing. So did the way he appeared to stick by the rules, like making sure the Americans were obliged to remain in the country, and the way he set about enforcing them, without falling back on the sort of brutal solution that Trav had feared, such as throwing the two of them in jail 'for their own protection'. At least in Bangkok they'd have a reasonably free run of things.

And, presumably after making a few calls or Internet searches, Win seemed to accept Trav's story about the cash. He hadn't taken a single dollar or baht, Trav was pretty sure of that. Win returned the money and the computer, keeping only Gordon's mobile and Trav's passport.

Of course, Trav knew that there was a very likely chance that Kang wouldn't be the only one to figure out where he had fled. He dreaded checking his email again and began to brace himself for a new deluge of legal threats from his former employer. He wondered if there was a criminal charge by now.

So: Kang. The lawyers. And maybe even Gordon's Thai partners—just because Win was a straight arrow didn't mean word of the two Americans hadn't leaked throughout the police station, and Trav wasn't confident that each of Win's colleagues shared his rectitude.

For all of those worries, he was getting off the island, he still had his cash and his computer, and Trav found himself thinking mostly about Mazy. He wasn't sure if he wanted to kiss her or kill her, or if he should be worried about her ...or about whatever venom she might direct his way. He suspected she blamed him for remaining trapped on Samui, and maybe she was right. He'd spoken up about the phone to save his own skin, and that had led inexorably to her revealing her story to the police. She had a direct connection to Gordon and the cops were going to want to know all about that, and exploit it. She could be held as an accomplice, but Mazy didn't seem the kind who liked being pinned down, whether for love or malice.

It was with a strange mix of nervousness and relief that Trav found himself back at Win's desk, cradling the backpack, waiting for the policeman to reappear with Mazy in tow. She seemed to have shrunk into herself, and avoided looking at him as she took the chair beside him. Win made a final phone call while standing behind his desk, all in Thai. He looked older now, too, for the past few hours had been as grueling for the cops as it had been for the reluctant witnesses.

"We're on the eight o'clock ferry," Win told them.

"Gordon might be watching it," Trav said. "He could follow us."

"I'll be with you," Win said, "all the way until my colleagues in Surat Thani take over, and they'll be with you all the way to Bangkok. You don't need to worry about your safety now."

His desk phone rang as a junior officer appeared with a face bright with urgency. Win held up a calming hand as he took the call first. The major's tone remained neutral as Morse code but his eyes darkened and his jowls formed a scowl. The first conversation over, he received the young cop's breathless report. The junior was skinny and wore thin wire-rim glasses, and to Trav looked like he belonged more in front of a computer than wearing a badge and carrying a revolver. The interns at the Hong Kong brokerage had more swagger than this guy. Yet whatever he was saying to Win made the old cop age a few years.

Win dismissed the young officer and said, "Something's come up. I won't be able to go with you after all."

"What's going on?"

"Nothing to concern you. Unrelated incidents that require the police. Our force is limited and I can't be everywhere at once."

Trav glanced at Mazy. She had turned sheet white. He said, "So what about us?"

Win offered a fatherly smile. "You are getting out of here."

He escorted them downstairs, accompanied by two junior Tourist Police officers, including the young nerd. "This is Officer Suan," Win said. "He will go with you."

"Hello," Suan said, his English as uncertain as his poise.

"I know you must have a lot going on," Trav said, "but we'd really feel a lot more, uh, comfortable if you could come with us. No offense," he added for Suan, although it wasn't clear Suan had followed the meaning of the conversation.

"Officer Suan is a very capable officer," Win said. "He'll look after you."

They walked outside. After hours inside the stale police station, the fresh air was a revelation. Cops were everywhere in the courtyard fronting city hall next door. A police car waited on the street, its blue and reds filling the evening with frantic color.

Win paused to go over arrangements one last time. "I've given you the names and IDs of the officers waiting for you in Surat Thani. You have the number to call in case there's a mix-up. You understand what you can and can't expect when you reach Bangkok. I'm sorry I have to go, but you'll be all right."

"Thanks, Win," Trav said, meaning it. "I know you've gone out on a limb."

"I usually never say this to the tourists I help," the older cop said, "but I hope to never see you on Samui again. I mean that in a nice way."

"Yeah, us, too," Trav said, but knew that, if he had ever been given the privilege of speaking for Mazy, he possessed it no longer.

Whatever plans Win had for Gordon, Trav didn't ask. The fat old cop backed into the waiting seat of the police car. Before he had even closed the door the car was on the move, its siren crying *whoop whoop*.

"This way," Suan said and the three of them turned a corner. They could see the oceanfront waiting a few blocks away, a cone of light around the ticket station, and the dark hulk of the ferry.

"You all right?" Trav asked Mazy as they set out, but she just stared ahead.

Chapter 30

Souvenir

Mazy ached for a drink. Everything today had been so horrible, the grilling from Win worst of all, being confined to that room for hours with nothing but her own pointless story to tell, over and over again. For a while, she found strength in her rage at Travis for throwing her to the sharks. At least it had been something to focus on other than what a lousy job she had made of her own life.

Mazy never considered herself one for delusion, but Win's relentless hammering had made clear just how much of her recent life had been built around self-willed blindness. The interrogation had left her no room to hide—not from the police, of course, for she had nothing concrete to answer for to them; nor from herself.

–What's your relationship to Tarrin?

None. He's Gordon's business partner.

–Where's your passport? Your driver's license? Any ID?

Gordon took them, locked them in a safe.
Burned them, for all I know.

–What's your relationship to Gordon?

Ex-girlfriend.

–Ex?

As of last night.

–And before that?

Girlfriend.

–You always let your boyfriends steal your ID?

He said it was for safekeeping. I decided to
believe him.

–Why did you leave him?

Because I thought he loved me, but he only
loves himself. He's gone insane, or maybe just
reverted to his true self. He threatened to kill me
and I believe him. He used me as a guinea pig
for his date-rape drug. He made me do...things
...with another man whom I hate. I let all of this
happen to me because...because I'm worthless,
so please can you let me get out of here so I can
find the nearest bar?

Win was smart, and he had quickly figured
out that she was just a bit player in the bigger drama. He wanted details: about Gordon,
about Isaac, about Ginger, about Kang. But
all of that required her to dig into her own relationships, her own standing with those men,
and all the self-loathing that she had managed
to keep suppressed—through booze, through
yoga, though stubbornness. She mined fresh
seams of a hateful lode.

For a while, sweating in that airless interrogation room, beneath a single naked light bulb,

perspiration dampening the bits of her T-shirt not already covered in Ginger's blood, she maintained her poise by seething at Trav.

Win took a break and sent in a female officer who asked Mazy to sign a statement. That's what finally cracked her. A statement. *Why?* Because she was a rape victim, the policewoman told her. They wanted to send her to the hospital, run some tests, search her insides for evidence, take photos of her bruises.

She had stopped listening beyond the word 'victim'. The tension of the past forty-eight hours cracked like a storm cloud. She had held on long enough to ask for a few minutes alone and then sobbed her guts out. The delusions that had provided her emotional bedrock for the past few weeks—months? longer?—had been coldly stripped away. The blinders had been removed. What she saw was ugly and pathetic.

What filled the emptiness in her soul was hatred. Mazy was surprised that she was capable of such a hate. *But I'm a teacher.* The words came back to her now as mockery.

Mazy told the policewoman that she was not going to sign a statement.

She was more cooperative when Win returned, answering his questions as best she could.

The cop had given her a few minutes to herself in the ladies' room before taking her back to Trav. He was a hard man, but not unkind.

Win knew he had pulled the string that had un-spooled her knot of delusions. Maybe he felt sorry for her.

The new hatred inside her chest turned anx-iously cold when Win told them he wouldn't be on the ferry with them. What was the expres-sion he had used? "Unrelated incidents that re-quire the police."

Gordon. Tarrin. She felt their invisible hands as though they were clutching her heart.

Once they boarded the ferry, Officer Suan gestured for them to share seats inside, along-side the window, and took up his position in the row behind them. The interior was lit in harsh fluorescence that made everyone look bleached. The windows were dark. Outside the modest lights of Nathon receded, leaving Mazy to contemplate the pitch darkness of the South China Sea at night.

Trav asked her if she would like something to drink or eat. She assumed that he correctly in-terpreted her silence as hostility, but she didn't know who to direct it at anymore.

Suan gave Trav permission to fetch something from the little bar at the other end of the hall. He returned with a pair of Singha beers in big plastic cups and a steaming cup of instant noo-dles.

"We can share these or I can get you an-other one," he said as she wordlessly accepted the beer. Mazy closed her eyes and practically downed it in one gulp. Trav had taken perhaps three sips before she rested her empty cup in her lap.

He was astonished, but then he said, "Would you like another?"

"Yes, please." It was the first thing she had said since being reunited with him in the police station.

"You want any food?"

She shook her head, and he went and bought her another beer. She was able to take this one more slowly.

"I know you're angry at me," he said. "I'm sorry if I've got you stuck in Thailand. But I didn't see any other way out. And besides, it was just about the truth. It was the right thing to do."

She heard his words, silently accepted them, but forming full sentences seemed beyond her.

"And you're safe now. Gordon's going to go to jail and then you'll be free to go wherever you like."

Mazy granted him a faint nod.

"For what it's worth, I think I'm in bigger trouble than you now. Kang's going to find out I'm here, if he doesn't know already. Remember, I told you about how the triads want me? Well, I was in this underground fighting ring, mixed martial arts. Big gambling thing for a certain class of people in Hong Kong. Heinz, who I guess you know, he was my trainer. He's the one who sent me to Indra to add yoga to my regimen. Anyway, he got me into this thing and I was like, cool, because I...I wanted to show off, be seen as a tough guy. Seek a thrill. Live hard."

"I get it," she said.

"I thought that was what life was all about, you know, for real men. But I didn't know what the hell I was doing. I thought I was this super cool guy, Steve McQueen in Hong Kong, making shitloads of money trading oil futures contracts, training hard, fighting at night in these underground matches in front of seriously connected guys.

"There's a saying gamblers have about knowing who at the poker table is the stooge. If you can't figure out who's the fall guy, then that means the fall guy is you. I should have figured it out last year when Caroline left me. She wasn't perfect and she wasn't faithful, but it's only recently that I've come to realize that it was my ego bullshit that led to the whole thing falling apart. Then I started getting reckless at work, putting on these crazy positions. My boss, Wally, had the final authority and he knew how to intimidate the risk guys, and I just poured a river of BS into his ear and he liked me and bought it. But I didn't know what the hell I was doing. Now it turns out those positions lost the brokerage fifty million bucks and they want to sue me, maybe arrest me.

"Same with the boxing. I've done martial arts ever since I was a teenager, and I'm all right—medium. But I got in this jag, like I just had to win at everything, be the best, be the man. Especially after Caroline left. I had nothing else to do, so I just poured myself into the training, thinking I was the incarnation of Bruce Lee or something. Then Heinz gets me into these night fights, and I win one, and then on the next one he tells me—tells me, doesn't ask—tells me I gotta lose; no matter what, I gotta lose. And I'll get paid some money, under the table, quite a bit of money, if I just take a dive and don't make it look obvious. I don't know anything about this kid, a Chinese guy named Chi-Man.

"I get into the ring, we do our three rounds. The kid was in good condition but had no moxie, you know? No killer instincts. He was mostly defense, had no idea how to get inside, work the angles. I thought I had every intention to do what I was supposed to do. For Heinz, not for the money. And I wasn't even thinking about what, or who, was behind this, I just knew a fix must be in among those guys who did the gambling. We're in the ring, third round, a minute left, and I knew it was time to make a move, get it over with. But..."

Trav fell silent, his soliloquy apparently over. She turned from the window. He was staring at his hands, the right one still in its dirty, raggedy cast.

"But," she said, admitting to being interested.

"It pissed me off. It was like they thought I belonged to them."

"And so?"

He raised his right hand. "And so I clocked that son of a bitch under the chin with the best upper cut I got. He went down and didn't move.

I recognized Kang across the ring—the yellow fedora, he always wears it. He stood up and made a movement like slitting his throat, and I knew instantly just how badly I had messed up. I literally fled the ring, got my keys and wallet, didn't even bother to change out of my boxing gear. Ran to my apartment, got my passport and a few things, maxed out every credit card on the ATM, and went straight to the airport. It was only after I bought the first ticket out of Hong Kong that I realized I had broken my hand knocking out Kang's son."

Mazy put her hand on his cast. "You said it when we met. You're a dumb son of a bitch." To her surprise, she smiled as she said it.

He let out a sad little laugh. "Yeah."

"But you didn't learn your lesson, did you? Now we're both stuck."

"When I saw you at that beachfront restaurant, should I have just minded my own business? Have I made everything worse for you?"

"Way worse," Mazy said, with a little smile. She knew then that Trav had been getting around to this, a sort of apology, even though if anyone had to say sorry or thank-you or admit to a lifelong addiction to bad choices, it was her.

"You asked me why I drank like I do."

He nodded. "When you came to me last night. I wasn't sure...how much of that night you'd..."

"Remember? All of it, Trav. I remember all of it." She closed her eyes. Being forced to say it to Win—maybe that had dislodged something

inside of her. Rolled a burning stone of remem-
brance down the cold slope. "I learned to drink
to forget. Then I met a man and I fell in love."
She could feel him tense. "The yoga had always been there, something that kept me steady
when I tried to quit drinking, but never enough
for me to just be happy, and eventually I'd have
to get a drink. With this man, I was able to forget about the past without having to get myself
smashed. It was as if I could live a real life."
She gripped Trav's fingers. "I followed him out
to Asia. I thought life was this, like, real, ac-
tual thing. But it's not, Trav. At least not for
me. And when he went away, there was nothing
left."

She considered mentioning the pregnancy,
the miscarriage. No, that was too much; some
things were best left undisturbed. "At first, Gordon was a substitute for that man," Mazy said.
"And the yoga—that, I had kept. Yoga helped
a lot, because there's no time for thinking. It's
just about emptying yourself, being in the now.
I guess the first time I hit the bottle again was
right after the first time Gordon punched me.
Getting numb was so much easier than trying
to survive in real life. Pretty soon letting him
hit me and getting drunk had become my new
substitutes. The truth is, the reason I came
here for so long is that I got fired. When you
went to Indra, you were probably in the last few
classes I taught."

She finished her beer. "That's about as much
talking as I think I can handle," she added.

"I'm sorry," he said. "And I appreciate your telling me, when I know it really isn't any of my business."

Mazy kissed him gently and he looked like an amazed boy.

"That's for not minding your own business," she said.

"You're welcome."

She kissed him again.

"And that's for helping me escape Gordon and Ginger."

"You're definitely welcome."

He moved in, hungry to put his lips on hers, but she pulled away. "I like you, Trav. I really do. That's why when we get to Bangkok, we're going to have to go our own ways."

"That makes absolutely no sense."

"I'm sorry." Mazy turned away from him. She finished her beer in one gulp and gazed out at the blank night, because that was what she figured the rest of her days were going to be like.

Chapter 31

Reception Committee

TRAV returned with more beer, her fifth and his second. She was sitting upright, her eyes a little glassy. Outside the bright string of lights revealed the approaching mainland.

"Where's Suan?" he asked, noting the absence of the young policeman.

"Bathroom."

He had tried to occupy her in more conversation, then had no choice but to accept her three kisses of affection as her last word. It was a hell of a thing, sitting next to the most beautiful woman in the world, pouring yourself out to her, and having her accept you with a loving kiss before rejecting you. Part of him wanted to throw a tantrum, hurl the beer cups over the heads of the other passengers, tell her to snap the hell out of this pointless black funk and realize that they could get through this together. Trav wasn't sure if he should despise himself for fetching her one round of brew after the next, but he did it because it's what she asked for, and she seemed to have reached some kind of temporary solace.

A hell of a thing.

She finished her beer as he was halfway through his and got up to use the bathroom, remarkably steady considering her intake, leaving Trav alone with their bags. The shoreline lights drew near and the ferry's horn boomed. She was back. "They've closed the bar," she said.

"My turn."

Trav let her finish his beer, noting the empty space where Officer Suan had parked himself for most of the journey. He walked through rows of passengers to the rear toilets, arranged between the ferry's two flanks. He opened the first unlocked door and was surprised by the weight behind it. He let the door slide outward and Officer Suan tumbled face first to the floor, a bloody rag stuffed in his mouth. The impact cracked his glasses.

Trav backed up. "Oh shit." The ferry shuddered against the pier. Suan's head lolled in sync, but the cop made no effort to get up. Trav turned to run back to Mazy, but Narong was there, carefully positioned out of kicking range, casually aiming his pistol at Trav's chest. Narong grinned, revealing several gold fillings.

"Get off ferry. I go behind you and the girl. You try run away, pow-pow." He was wearing an electric-blue Adidas jacket over his other outlandish clothes, and put the pistol inside a jacket pocket. It jutted out obviously.

"You're making a mistake," Trav said. "There will be cops everywhere outside, waiting for us." He gestured to Suan. "Waiting for him."

Narong motioned with his chin. "First you put cop back."

Trav considered taking his chances but saw only bad endings. So he lifted Suan, surprised by how warm the body was, how it kept hold of vitality for these lingering moments. Maybe the cop wasn't dead yet, although he seemed pretty … He told himself not to think as he propped the policeman into the tiny bathroom. He gently lowered the eyelids and placed the broken glasses in Suan's passive hand.

Maybe someone could have come along and surprised Narong, given Trav just an inch of an opportunity. But no one came. The journey was over, they were pulling into the docks, and the crowd was busy gathering packages and bags and swarming toward the stairs in the opposite direction. Trav pushed the door shut and Narong gestured with the gun for him to go join Mazy.

She was waiting for him, holding their backpacks in her hands. "Where's Suan?" she asked, but then she saw his forbidding expression and saw Narong a few steps behind with the snub rectangle protruding from his blue jacket's pocket.

He took his backpack from her and put it on.

"What do we do?" she whispered.

"I don't know. Suan's dead."

They stepped into the slow flow of passengers making their way toward the gangplank. His mind raced through ideas, but he had none—Narong was armed and fearless, and Trav didn't want anyone to get shot. Narong must have been watching them closely and snuck onto the ferry at the last minute. He wouldn't know anything about the arrangements Win had made, wouldn't know there were Provincial Police on the pier waiting to receive the two foreigners.

Would he?

Mazy's fingers weaved through his. The pressure of her grip expressed the same terror he felt, but her skin also gave him a little electrical jolt of happiness. Holding hands, they walked down the gangway together, moving from frigid air conditioning to the moist heat of the Thai night. He looked furtively for brown police uniforms. The plan had, in fact, been for Suan to escort them to a police box near the Surat Thani ferry station. Which meant there was a gap between the pier and the cops.

Four Thai men blocked their way at the end of the gangplank. They wore hip-hop blue jeans or track pants, and loud T-shirts, with baseball caps or trendy flat caps. Mazy's grip on his hand tightened to the point it hurt, but he would have endured far more to receive her touch.

"This way," said Narong behind them.

The gang of men surrounded Trav and Maze. They tore her from him. The men pushed and pulled them to the parking lot, its sparse lamps casting long shadows behind a van, its side door open. He struggled to reunite their flesh, to again feel her fingers locked with his. He threw off one thug, then another. Someone slammed a pistol butt on the back of Trav's head. He was unconscious before he hit the ground.

Chapter 32

The Darkness, Absolute

WHEN Trav went down, she knelt beside him, but feet kicked her and arms dragged her and then a hand with a rag appeared in her face. She screamed and fought, but they were too many and everything got muffled and confused. She cowered beneath Narong's raised pistol butt, her hands upturned in a plea. He seemed satisfied and lowered the gun. Her hands were pinned behind her and she felt the bite of hemp on her wrists. Her nostrils swelled with exertion. Then she was manhandled into the van, where they had already deposited Trav.

The worst part of the ride, which lasted ten minutes that felt like an entire long night, was that she had no means of clearing the tears from her eyes. They blinded her, but perhaps it didn't matter. She could only hope they'd be quick and not rape her first. But now that death was imminent, Mazy found that it was no longer something she was prepared to welcome.

The van bobbed its way along a gravelly lane through a thicket of forest. They stopped amid pitch darkness. Narong, who had been sitting beside her, gestured with his gun, and she stumbled out of the van and fell on her knees. They lifted her up. They were by the sea. Moonlight illuminated the white crests of the waves. Men hoisted Trav's supine form out of the van and onto a dark pier. A speedboat undulated next to it. Lights came on inside its cabin.

The men chatted quietly among themselves for a moment. Trav was lifted onto the open rear of the boat, beside the cabin's sliding doors, and his hands were also bound. They threw a tarp over him. Then Narong gestured with the gun for her to embark. She stepped next to Trav. Narong brushed past her into the cabin, followed by one of his cohorts, while a third kept a hand around her arm. A fourth man, remaining on the pier, tossed their backpacks onto the boat.

So they were going to be drowned and fed to the sharks. Would it be with weights? Would they be shot first?

Narong's companion piloted the boat away from the pier, its engines purring softly, leaving the last two men on shore. The van headlights spun and rapidly disappeared in the opposite direction. The lights of town retreated off to the side. They drifted past a jetty of boulders and past lines of fishing boats, their whitewashed hulls ghostly in the moonlight. After they cleared the shallows, the pilot gunned the engine and the boat leaped. Mazy and her guard both nearly stumbled overboard.

Narong stuck his head out of the cabin. "Inside," he told her in English. He gestured for her to sit in the corner while he eased into one of the cushy stools beside the pilot. Her guard hunkered down, one hand holding the wall, keeping watch on both her and the unconscious Trav outside.

The boat continued to accelerate over the waves, which transformed from tame to formidable as they entered open water. Their wake sliced a trail of eerie foam across the black sea. The boat heaved and pitched, going airborne one moment, crashing to the surface the next. Each hit shook her to the core. Mazy wondered if it would be possible to simply make a beeline for the rear of the boat and jump—let the waters take her. More dignity in that, perhaps, than what lay in store.

It was tempting. Very tempting.

But then she'd see Trav's body and had a sense that if staying alive might, somehow, impossibly, give her a chance to sway Gordon, convince him that it was all her doing, maybe Trav would get off with just a savage beating or a lost limb. So she sat there and bounced off the floor and winced every time they smashed into the next wave.

Mazy couldn't hear a thing over the roar of the engine and the pounding of the surf, but the jostling revived Trav. She could see him kick and squirm between each violent impact against the ocean.

"Help him," she said to Narong, but the killer just chuckled and left Trav to endure the ride however well he could.

The ordeal was exhausting but impossible to sleep through. It seemed to stretch on forever, the interminable leaps and collisions, the screaming thrust of engines, the high sprays of water against the cabin windows and the accumulation of bruises. Trav stopped wriggling and eventually settled into a fetal position, braced against a rear corner where he couldn't bounce around so much, until the end finally came and the engines cut to a slower pace.

They must be in the middle of nowhere and Mazy assumed this was where they'd dump Trav and maybe her, too. If she could feel any relief it was that the men kept a close eye on her but not a lecherous leer. They didn't size her up that way. Rape wasn't on the menu, at least not now, not in the boat.

In a way, that reassurance meant that when the ride was over, circumstances could change. The easing motor, the return of her hearing, the cessation of the mad hurtling into the sea, all meant they were one step closer to disposing of her, one way or another.

She tried to get some sort of bearing through the window but saw nothing but the impervious night. The boat continued to decelerate. The sea had become gentle again. Narong and the pilot conversed in low tones, and consulted what

Mazy assumed was a GPS screen. She had tried to get a decent view of it, in the hope it would reveal some useful information, but it was hidden from where she crouched.

Now the engines were quieted almost completely and the boat moved with care and finally came to rest. The thug watching over Mazy moved outside and clambered along the side of the craft, handling ropes. They were docking along another pier, lit by a sole fluorescent light on a pole.

The guard came back and scooped Trav over his shoulder.

"Trav?"

He stirred at her voice but whatever passed through his lips was unintelligible. The guard threw him like cargo onto the dark pier, then climbed out and lifted Trav again.

"Out," Narong said to her, as usual his pistol showing the way.

The pilot helped her stand and climb onto the wooden pier. She was beneath the light and around her could see nothing. The darkness here was absolute. She could hear the ocean and could barely make out a wall of trees of some kind. The pilot held her arm, more to steady her than to command. He and Narong took a few minutes to tie the boat properly to the pier. All three of the men—Narong, the guard, the pilot—turned on big, industrial-sized flashlights.

Narong gathered up Mazy and Trav's backpacks and held their straps with one hand, his

JAME DIBIASIO

flashlight with the other. He went first. Mazy was bid to follow, the pilot just behind her with a flashlight of his own. The guard came last, Trav over one shoulder, his flashlight in the other hand.

The pier's wooden slats were rotting away and she had to mind her step. The three circles of light revealed they were walking through a mangrove. Mazy had never seen one of these before, and it creeped her out: a forest of tall, spindly trees with trunks that ended in a confusing spidery thicket of right angles disappearing beneath murky water.

Where the boat lay moored was ocean, but almost as soon as the water hit the mangrove trees it was becalmed. Within just a few steps, the water adopted the stillness of a pond. She could faintly hear the tops of these tall trees moving in the breeze, but she could feel nothing stir down below. The airless silence was terrifying. The tree trunks glowed a sickly white in the flashlights' cones of illumination. The waters shifted below with a milky opacity.

They walked on.

There seemed to be no bird life in here, despite the abundance of trees. If there were birds, they dwelled high up in the leaves. Down here at human level, walking along the decaying pier, the trees seemed lifeless, propped up on an arachnid-like array of black branches that extended into the deathly calm waters. There were mosquitoes, though, plenty of them. The swarm thickened the deeper they went.

And there were other things out there, too. Mazy caught the men's fear. Each quiet noise prompted the pilot to jerk his light here and there. Sometimes his beam caught something that reflected a dull yellow glow. Two somethings. Many little somethings, all silent and alert.

"What's down here?" she whispered.

The pilot responded in Thai.

Narong translated. "Crocodile."

The pilot whispered something else.

"And snake," Narong added. "Big snake."

"Where the hell are you taking me—" she said before the plank gave out and she fell chest first into the dark knot of menacing tree legs. She gasped as she hovered in mid-air, the pilot having grabbed the back of her shirt. Before it could tear and allow her body to complete the journey, they pulled her back.

Narong said something uncomplimentary in Thai and she nodded. 'Watch your step,' probably. *Good advice. Maybe for once in your life, girl, you should take it.*

The pier zigzagged into the haunting infinite and time seemed to slow down. It wasn't about minutes or even pace; it was measured in insect bites. What distance was required for the mosquitoes to bite an entire arm? How about one arm and both ankles? Their incessant whine filled her ears as they dive-bombed her in waves.

And just like that, it was over, and they were on solid ground. The three shifting flashlights outlined a trail of soft black mud and sand that ran left to right, with the ground swiftly rising up into a cliff before them. Trees—real trees—grew thickly here, and the forest was alive with the hoots and hollers of insomniac birds.

They didn't walk far. They took the trail to the right. The guard's breathing turned to a laborious wheeze as he tired of his burden. It was with relief that he finally lowered Trav to the ground, not very gently, and stretched his arms. They had moved a little further inland, hugging the cliff, and arrived at a cave. Its mouth yawned blackly. The crisscross of light beams didn't get too far inside before the emptiness enveloped them.

Narong stepped inside, picking his footing carefully.

"No way am I going in there," she said, but the pilot pushed her in the small of the back and she stumbled inside. There was an immediate screech and deafening flutter and she fell to her knees. Bats! A startled swarm blasted past them, dozens of them screaming their irritation at being disturbed.

"Just gets better and better," she muttered, shivering.

A little further inside the guard and Narong set about lighting a fire with charcoaled wood that lay beneath an orange tarp—this cave had been pre-stocked with supplies. The fire didn't take long to get going and while the smoke stung their nostrils and eyes, it would keep away the bats and the bugs. And the fire provided a welcome light and heat, for the cave was damp and chilly.

There were a few plastic storage bins in there. Narong opened these and pulled out some sleeping bags and a few cans of beer.

"Please," Mazy said.

Narong tossed a rolled-up sleeping bag to her but she said, "Beer."

The killer nodded and pulled the tab. Mazy gestured with her shoulders, indicating her bound hands. With the guard holding her steady from behind, they undid her hands and retied them in front of her. Her arms screamed in pain and she used the brief moment of freedom to flex her wrists, noting how they had swelled. Then the ropes were tied on again, but at least she could hold the can in her trembling hands up to her parched lips. She chugged the beer, causing the men to gasp, and that helped remove some of the edge of pain.

She scooted beside Travis, who was semi-conscious. "Trav, you OK?"

He groaned, his eyes fluttering. His skin felt cold.

"Please, you need to cover him up and keep him warm."

It took all three of the men several long grunting minutes to get Trav inside a sleeping bag. They also retied his wrists in front of him. His good wrist was circled by angry welts and his arms were also swollen. Mazy knelt beside him and rested his head in her lap. His shirt was still damp from getting soused in the back of the boat from the leaping waves.

"Don't die on me, cowboy," she whispered as she worked little sips of bottled water into his mouth.

"Maze," he whispered, hoarsely.

"Shut up, stupid, and drink."

So they weren't going to kill them, at least not here, not yet. That was something. She murmured it into his ear.

He managed an "OK" before falling asleep. She stroked his hair and traced her fingers along his sun-browned face. The gauze had come off his chin, revealing a purple gash, and she could feel the lump on the back of his head where Narong had clubbed him. His breathing was even, though, and he wasn't running a fever.

Narong had gone outside. He spoke on his mobile in a long, low-pitched stream of Thai. Then he returned and watched them indifferently, stroking his slinky mustache, not caring to reveal his orders yet.

"Can I have another beer?"

They were out of beer. The guard revealed the supplies contained a half-full bottle of Lady Song. He unscrewed the cap and offered her a sip. Mazy clasped the guard's hands and guzzled down huge gulps. The guard was surprised and jerked the bottle away, whisky splashing on her face and chest. She licked off what she could.

"You crazy bitch," Narong said, sauntering inside the cave.

She wiped her mouth with the back of her bound hands and said nothing.

"Now you go back," Narong said, exchanging the cell phone for the pistol. "Up."

Mazy clambered upright, exhausted but feeling a little warmer inside. She bent over to wake Trav.

"No him. You only."

She regarded three pairs of hard faces flickering in the firelight and gently eased his head onto the ground. "I don't want to die," she blurted.

And then, as Narong and the pilot escorted her out of the cave, leaving the guard to stand watch over Travis, she ached with the certainty that she didn't want Trav to die either, and that if they killed him, it would be worse than dying herself.

Chapter 33

The Big Time

MAJOR Win had not stuck around to watch the departure of the two Americans and Officer Suan. But as they sped into the darkening hills, a familiar but unwelcome tingle troubled his stomach. This was not hemorrhoids or Mrs. Phueng's spicy noodles. It was a gut feeling he had learned to trust in the alleyways of Bangkok.

The timing was improbably tight. A knifing in Chaweng, a fire in Bhoput, a home invasion of a villa in Lamai, all called within five minutes. Samui had never seen so much vice and misfortune distilled so neatly. The phone call had been from the colonel. Not enough men to handle it all. And the Lamai robbery involved breaking into a villa rented by a party of Germans. If the island's police had an unofficial mandate, above all, it was to suppress news of bad things that happened to tourists. The colonel was emphatic: Win had to handle it. Personally.

He had walked around the villa a little too an-grily, glass from the shattered door crunching beneath his shoes, as a junior officer snapped photographs. He took the statements of the frightened Germans. Two young Thai men, wearing bandanas to partly cover their faces and wielding steel pipes, broke in around seven-thirty, interrupting the tourists' dinnertime. Lots of carrying on, threats, one middle-aged man got thrown around a bit but, in the end, they took a few wallets and that was it. No jew-elry, no watches. A lot of smoke for such a tiny fire.

The other incidents were also slapdash. The arson was done in a rush, in an alley behind a restaurant frequented by backpackers, with no motive Win could see. The restaurant owner was angry and perplexed, and let it be known she had been diligent with both her regular protection money to the local gang and some red-packet money for the cops. Best Win could tell, the whole thing was a diversion. Similarly the knifing involved a youth sprinting through Bhoput's Walking Street, a night market full of foreigners, who randomly slashed at an old man serving ice cream. The wound was superfi-cial and the attacker just kept running, leaving screams in his wake.

Win needed evidence, not a hunch. Tarrin was his best guess. The gangster was notori-ous among Samui's police force. The odd spate of crimes had nothing to do with Tarrin's usual M.O. He was into all kinds of rackets, including drugs and prostitution, but he was crafty and methodical. And seeing Narong holding a gun in broad daylight at the ferry pier, and knowing that Narong was Tarrin's go-to tough—it was too much of a coincidence.

He finally returned to the station to file his paperwork when another report came in. This one was worse, but different. Another body of a Thai teenage girl had washed up near Lamai beach, the second that month. They were going to take her to the morgue at Samui Government Hospital but the ambulances were tied up, so she was rotting outdoors.

Win and a colleague drove as quickly as they could, the siren's wail cutting through the congested roads for the second time that day. The corpse was being kept in a refrigerator lying on the beach, commandeered by the police arriving on the scene from a nearby seafood restaurant, and still plugged into its generator. They opened the fridge's door to show him. She had been in the water for at least two days, Win guessed, looking at the shriveled, fish-nibbled remains still partly wrapped in seaweed. Severe knife gashes across her body. Teeth smashed in, finger and toes missing.

He sighed. From his training in the United States, he knew what this called for: a proper inquest by a coroner and a pathologist, with a quick turnaround for lab results. In Bangkok such resources could occasionally be made available. Here, though...a body lying in a seafood restaurant's upturned fridge...

"Let's get her to the morgue," he said. At least there would be lights there.

It took a while and Win stayed with the corpse, even though technically she wasn't the responsibility of the Tourist Police. But the local coroner didn't object to Win's looking her over once they placed her on the cold steel slab: his main job was to identify signs of drug and alcohol use, so the authorities could protect themselves from blame whenever tourists drowned or injured themselves. Prodding around the cut-up remains of what was probably a local hooker was not part of the job.

The girl had resisted; that would explain the rut in her neck, caused not by a knife but the attacker, Win guessed, tearing at a necklace.

"Hit the bars from Lamai to Chaweng," he told two Provincial cops who didn't look very interested in what he had to say. "Find out if any of the girls have gone missing in the past forty-eight hours." Win knew from their slouches they wouldn't try very hard. A shitty end to a shitty night. He washed up and went home, the dead girl and the two foreigners competing for his mind's attention.

Awake beside his sleeping wife, he considered the possibility that one of his people had tipped off Tarrin to Win's plan to get the two Americans off the island. Tarrin had the resources to throw together enough ad-hoc incidents to distract the police. Tarrin had the foresight to scare the daylights out of tourists. Which meant he knew to target Win. But did that have anything to do with the murdered girl—the second one to wash up like that in as many weeks?

The telephone rattled in his bedroom. His wife had once grown used to these late-night emergencies when he had been on the Metropolitan force, but this had never happened before on Samui: a murdered cop. She had gone off to make him black tea while he sat on the edge of the bed, receiving the news, amazed that things could get even worse.

He had dressed in his uniform and driven to the station. It was open twenty-four hours, but late at night was usually a sleepy void. Not this morning. A small group of Tourist and Provincial officers had gathered around Win's office. Some kept up a stony demeanor while others smiled nervously or wept, but the news of Suan's death put them all in shock.

Win tried to calm them down, remembering some of his old speeches from his Bangkok days —speeches he had thought he'd never have to make again, certainly not whiling away his final years of duty on Samui. The life of a policeman always involved a measure of risk, and Samui life offered its fair share of trouble, with its transients and its drunks, but this blatant violence, the deliberate murder of a policeman, was something he thought he had left behind in the capital.

Then there was the matter of the two foreigners, who had failed to appear before the Provincial Police station on the mainland, itself a stone's throw from the ferry pier. At this point he didn't know if this was a case of abscond-ing *farang*s, or kidnapping. But he assumed the latter.

As he consulted with his superiors in Surat Thani and his colleagues here in the Provincial Police, Win's initial hunch about a series of di-versions to separate him from the foreigners, leaving them vulnerable on the ferry, hardened into conviction. He still had no evidence but had little doubt where to begin looking: with Narong, which meant ultimately with Tarrin.

Yet the whole thing still perplexed him. The gangs could be vicious among their own, but murder or anything to attract police attention was rare. Crime gangs and police preferred to maintain a certain peace, because they both de-pended on tourist money. So what did it mean if Narong had dared pull a gun in open daylight, a mere two blocks from the Nathon police sta-tion? What impunity did he think he possessed for such a serious crime? Why was Tarrin so desperate to get the two Americans? What made him or his buddies—or at least their boss—feel invulnerable, even after murdering a Tourist Po-liceman, in uniform, on duty?

Win shook his head at the implications. This sort of thing was normal in Bangkok, a viper's pit of overlapping loyalties. But Nathon wasn't Bangkok. Money and power were what drove those corrupt relationships. The corruption on Samui was mild and generally productive. It kept the peace, it reassured the tourists, it kept the bureaucrats in Bangkok off the locals' backs, and it allowed everyone a chance to make some money.

For someone to murder Officer Suan in such a foul manner could only mean the stakes had just risen, exponentially. There wasn't much on the island able to generate such immediate riches. Most crime here centered on ways of siphoning off the lucre of tourism. There were also a few discreet valleys where cannabis grew and then found its way into Bangkok, Hat Yai, and Malaysia. Small-time stuff, really. No. this had to be new, and the only thing Win knew that had a chance of altering the rules of the game was something like what the two Americans had described.

He typed his report standing up, computer keyboard resting on the filing cabinet top. Then he logged an all-points bulletin throughout all of Surat Thani province for Tarrin and Narong.

It wasn't yet dawn.

Win downed his second cup of coffee and met with the colonel in charge of the Provincial Police. Technically Win had nothing to do with Colonel Siri or his department, which handled serious crimes, but the old man respected Win's city experience, and the two were amiable colleagues.

The Colonel listened to Win's story and decided Win should run the case. Never mind that you're only Tourist Police, he had told Win: it's one of your own lying in a mainland morgue.

Win couldn't help but feel a little tweak of electricity as he left Siri's office. He walked back to where some of his Tourist Police colleagues were erecting a modest shrine to Suan, aged twenty-five; years on the force: one and a half. It all felt so depressingly routine for Win as he handed them their assignments. But he had to stifle a grim little smile. After three years of helping *farang*s fill out reports over lost purses and drunken brawls, Major Win Arpornakun had an important, live case to solve.

Chapter 34

Little Pink Pills

JAIDEE arrived at Orchid Resorts every morning before dawn. Lately, thanks to some memorable nights out, courtesy of Tarrin and the *farang*s, he had needed the aid of some *yaa-baa* to roust him from the snores of Lady Song's embrace. Balance sheets were not Jaidee's forte, and he knew that most of the money he was making from Tarrin was now being spent on the little pink pills that tasted like chocolate, but the amphetamines were turning into necessary fuel.

This morning, like several others of late, he found himself reaching for the plastic box of Tic-Tacs that had been converted into his supply cabinet. Usually dousing himself with the hose of cold water in the backyard of granny's country shack was enough to wake him. But the idea of getting through the entire day feeling so knocked about was too much. After popping one of those sweet little darlings, the rest of the morning went a lot faster. Before he knew it, he was pulling his scooter into the rear parking area at Orchid Resorts and trading his sandals for a pair of rubber boots in the janitor's shed.

His routine was to start with the areas behind the scenes where the performers, zookeepers, and administrators would soon be busy. He'd go through the aquarium and the amphitheaters last, making sure they were clean enough before the first visitors were admitted at nine o'clock, a little under five hours from now.

The complex was not without other humans at this hour. The cats were nocturnal and required supervision, and there was the constant threat of robbers. A guard out front, near the visitors' entrance, would be propped up in a plastic chair, a blanket around his shoulders to ward off the wee-hour chill, an aging pistol holstered in his belt. He was usually asleep. There was always at least one zookeeper or handler on the premises as well, sometimes doing the rounds, or just playing computer games in the office, keeping half an eye on some video monitors.

The interiors were mostly still. The birds were settled in their hooded cages. The eels retreated into their watery holes. Only the sharks seemed alive in those cold, awful dens, damned to keep swimming lest they die, their black, remorseless eyes taking in the same sights over and over again, minute after minute, their sleek bodies silently slicing the water as the creatures inched toward madness.

Outside, the big cats were active, including the leopards and jaguars, but the Bengal tigers were the biggest animals in the compound. The resort kept a series of cages in the visitor's area and a larger outdoor area out back, hidden from view, where the tigers were trained by Chittilai and allowed more space to roam.

At this time of morning, Jaidee knew by routine, the biggest male, Chao Fa, "Crown Prince", was doubtless on the prowl. Tigers were solitary and Chao Fa liked to pace among the females. The other, slightly smaller male not of Chao Fa's bloodline—for he had sired one of the cubs—was named Klaew Kla, "Daring and Brave", but was neither. He was sneaky, and always sniffing around Fa Ying ("Celestial Princess") or the other tigresses. As soon as Chao Fa got wind of Klaew Kla's machinations, he'd confront him with a powerful bark and occasionally wallop the scamp, who'd invariably cringe and retreat.

This morning, however, the tigers would have to wait. Jaidee began his usual routine with the mop in the administrative offices. He worked his way down corridors in the fake fluorescent light, the only sound the trundle of his bucket wheels and the slap of his wet mop against the tiles. Then came the most important part of his routine, the veterinary clinic. He made directly for the lab, feeling his heart beat a little harder.

He knew at least one of the zookeepers would be down the hall in the office area, and they might fancy dropping by the clinic's boarding room to check in on any of the animals in the ward's care—there was always a cat in there, recovering from illness or a wound, sometimes just in isolation, sometimes recovering from a minor surgery. The boredom of those dark pre-dawn hours often drove anyone working the late shift to seek out company, even if it was an unconscious leopard or a drugged-up cockatoo.

Jaidee waited but heard nothing. The door to the boarding/bathing room was shut. Only ghosts trod with him now. He swiped his electronic access card and entered the lab, his mop and bucket rattling noisily in tow.

Accessing the lab's well-stocked pharmacy, however, required overcoming two more hurdles: the locked door itself, and then the locked glass cases that enclosed the tiers of shelves of liquids, pills and gels, all neatly arrayed like rows of soldiers.

Tarrin had instructed Jaidee to take photos of these locks with his mobile phone, and then taught him how to pick them. The door had a deadbolt, which was the harder one for Jaidee to crack, but Tarrin had shown him how to use a tension wrench and a pick to listen for the pins falling into place, which turned out to be easy in the intense quiet before sunrise. The wafer locks on the glass cabinets sprang open to the simple combination of a pair of straightened paper clips and a screwdriver, all of which he kept in an apron pocket.

He searched for the new type of tranquilizer, found the supply, chose a bottle at random, and poured its contents into the empty water bottle he kept in a pouch on the front end of the bucket. He replaced the Ketavet with some of the cleaning water, screwing on the top extra tight. He lingered over the pills for a while, admiring their shapes and colors, wondering if any of these were *yaa-baa*, or something like it. Maybe Tarrin would know. Jaidee took out his phone and began taking pictures of the pills and their labels. Then he heard a thump.

He straightened but could move no further. His ears strained to discern more, but he only heard the piercing silence and the sound of his heart. He didn't realize that he had ceased breathing. Thump and voices, distressed. He could make out no more. Jaidee shoved the phone in his pants and hurriedly shut the glass cabinets one by one, each making a harsh clang louder than the last. His jittery fingers fumbled to return the locks to their previous state. Crying now, and a male voice, harsh but pleading. Jaidee flicked off the pharmacy light and pushed his mop bucket out, the ungreased wheels squealing in noisy protest. He pulled the door and it clicked shut as two figures fluttered past the lab door.

Jaidee ran his sweaty palms over his pants. He gripped the mop tightly and guided the bucket toward the door. He wasn't supposed to be in the lab but could play dumb—no one would doubt him if he stammered some confusion over what rooms to clean. But better to get out of there unseen.

He pushed his way into the clinic entrance and hurried into the corridor linking it to the offices. Two figures stood pressed against the hallway's wall, writhing, pale legs hoisted, one pink sandal on the floor and the other dangling from a toe, just below where panties wreathed the ankle. From the way she was crying, it wasn't clear to Jaidee that Nongmook was in distress. She was sobbing and sighing and her right hand clung to a fistful of Chittilai's black T-shirt, while her left spread itself across his broad back and then wriggled down inside his jeans.

Maybe it was the *yaa-baa*. Maybe it was the stink of tiger piss that he couldn't seem to shake. Something in Jaidee snapped, as though this final humiliation had been aimed directly at him. Consumed with rage, he hefted the mop with both fists down near the dripping rag end and launched himself across the corridor. He had meant to crush Chittilai's neck but missed and whacked the back of Nongmook's arm, the one groping the trainer's buttocks, and her moans turned to a sudden shriek. Jaidee's mind was beyond sympathy and he swung again.

Chittilai disengaged himself from Nongmook in time to catch this blow on the shoulder—it knocked him to his knees. The girl collapsed in a crying heap, bare legs akimbo. The trainer raised his big arms to take the third blow, but the mop was heavy and clumsy in Jaidee's hands, and he slipped on the pool of water gathering around his feet. The blow was a mere glance and Chittilai sprang and knocked the mop from Jaidee's grip.

JAME DIBIASIO

"*Ai heea!*" the trainer raged, calling Jaidee an iguana but meaning a cunt. Chittilai felled him with one punch that sent the janitor airborne for a good length of hallway. On his back, Jaidee kicked his feet in an attempt to scramble out of harm's way. The trainer lifted the mop and snapped the handle over his knee. He discarded the sagging wet cloth strands and whacked the broken end into his other palm as he walked slowly but surely toward Jaidee.

The beating didn't take long. Jaidee was reduced to a quivering heap on the floor. Only the increasing pitch of Nongmook's wail finally convinced Chittilai to stop. He delivered a final kick and returned to her. Jaidee's senses were red and dim, and all he could really fathom was that he was bleeding from the nose and mouth and that all sorts of bits of him were sparking in pain. But Nongmook's laments penetrated his mind and he started to realize that he had broken her arm. As the fog of madness thinned and he processed what he had just done, Jaidee rolled to one side and puked.

"I'm sorry," he gibbered through his bloodied mouth. "Nongmook, I didn't mean... I..."

"Shut up," Chittilai hissed as he knelt beside her. "We need to get you to a hospital," he said to Nongmook. He took her good arm to pry her up. She was in shock, shivering, and he tore off his T-shirt to wrap it around her shoulders. "You want some water before we go?"

She nodded and the trainer liberated Jaidee's water bottle from its bucket pouch.

"No," Jaidee said, half rising. "Don't drink that." The words were barely intelligible.

"*Yet pho*," she hissed back—'Screw your father'.

Chittilai unscrewed the top and put the bottle to her lips. "Drink up," he said.

Time jerked and ran, seized up, kept going. He had wheeled the gurney into the corridor. It was usually used to transport drugged cats in and out of the clinic, and since a big male like Fa Chou weighed nearly 220 kilograms, it could easily handle the burden of two humans.

Jaidee had tackled Chittilai first. He didn't know how he had done it—the man was so big and heavy, from his thick neck down to his bulging biceps and calves. The trainer had taken a good swig from the water bottle after Nongmook. He might still be alive, but Jaidee wasn't interested in double-checking. There was a lot of foam around the mouth and the eyes were dilated, and maybe the breathing hadn't exactly stopped, but it sure had slowed.

Anyway, lifting Chittilai was like wrestling the big statue of Buddha in the temple by Granny's shack. Finally, Jaidee winched the trainer into enough of an angle that he was able to grab the man's ankles and hoist him all the way. That left him gasping for breath, and every inhalation delivered a sharp series of cracks through his ribcage. He suspected a few items in there were broken. Thank the gods for *yaa-baa*; Jaidee had already taken a handful of pills from his Tic-Tac box, because he sensed he'd need every little bit of help to get through this damnable morning.

He later would have no recollection of handling Nongmook. But she was harder, so much harder on him, even though her body was feather light and seemed to float in his arms. After quaffing the liquid, she had simply receded into herself, quivered for a little while, and then—and by this time Chittilai had fallen into convulsions—she released a slow line of dribble that snaked down from the corner of her mouth. Her eyes remained open the entire time, fluttering along as her mind ventured to mysterious destinations. She must have finally settled on one of those brilliant interior worlds because by the time she was lifted onto the gurney, her eyes stared with complete stillness.

Chapter 35

Unexpected Visitors

GORDON woke with the dawn. He had left the curtains open in his giant bedroom and had been rousted by the sun sparkling on the restless sea. He propped himself on his elbows, not used to being alone. He was usually an early riser, but he missed the hump of Mazy—definitely not an early riser—breathing quietly beside him.

He donned his swimming trunks and went outside and took in the eternal view: the contrasting blues of the infinity pool, the channel, the nearby islands, the sky. The palms protected the compound from the morning sun's direct glow. Local fishermen's boats floated nearby, their ancient motors wrapped in tarp, their long propeller shafts lifted out of the water. There was no sound but that of the wind ruffling through the trees and the waves shushing onto the beach. If only Gordon could achieve such tranquility.

But no entrepreneur ever had it easy, he reasoned. The van driver hired by the villa had returned Ginger yesterday with a smashed face. Gordon had called Tarrin, who had arranged for a nurse to visit and take care of the stitches. The bodyguard may have been a hardened thug but he also cried like a baby. More than that, he had admitted to losing Mazy and Travis at the Seatrans ferry pier.

"He suckered me from behind," Ginger had mumbled through the gauze, but this hadn't assuaged Gordon. He had tried to communicate something else but Gordon had lost patience and told him he might as well keep his wounded mouth shut.

Ginger's eyes still knew how to express themselves, so Gordon warned him he'd stick pencils in them if they didn't regard him with a bit of respect. Not after such a failure. So Ginger had contained his anger and stomped off. That had been the end to yesterday.

The good news was that Isaac had reported progress at the lab, and production of K-Love had resumed. Tarrin was due to come by later this morning with new samples.

For now, there was nothing to do but wait. It was to be a hateful interlude. Business was business, but without anything concrete to focus on, Gordon couldn't shake the disgusting images that paraded before his eyes. Ginger and Mazy. Mazy and Travis. His own humiliation.

Gordon practiced his tae kwon do sequences for an hour. Normally he would have had Ginger put on the pads and lead him through kicks and punches, but now his supposed bodyguard was no doubt still asleep, as lazy as he was becoming useless. Perhaps Gordon could employ him to intimidate puppies and kittens.

The workout ended with laps in the pool. That kept his mind empty for a while, but afterward, as he lay drying in a lounger under the sun, he wondered how he was going to track them down. Where could she go without a passport? Nowhere except the US embassy to get another one. He could, therefore, find her in Bangkok. But Bangkok was a big city where Tarrin lacked reliable connections, and Gordon couldn't exactly camp outside the embassy wall all day.

He wondered if Tarrin could hire someone to do that, hang out among the hawker stalls opposite the embassy entrance on Wireless Road, a local who could avoid attention, while Gordon waited for the lookout's call in a nearby hotel. If the Samui operation was a success, if the first shipment were made, he could afford to leave, at least for a few days, before the coconuts hit the docks in Hong Kong.

Children emerged from the surrounding plots of land to play in the water and give one of the water buffalos a bath. Isaac appeared in trunks and his white trilby and slipped upstairs to make coffee. Gordon followed him in time to see Lek shoo Isaac away from the counters, where she was putting the final touches on a spread of eggs, toast and a platter of fresh mango, pineapple, rambutan, and yellow watermelon. Gordon told Isaac to get him a coffee, too. Ginger stumbled upstairs, his mangled face zippered in stitches. Lek gave him yoghurt and a concoction of fruit from the blender that he could sip through a straw.

"Do you have to suck that so loud?" Gordon snapped. "It's a straw, not your todger."

Isaac guffawed. Ginger glowered back but managed to lower the volume on his intake.

"It's good to see you up and about, Ginge," Gordon said, "but you've been a disappointment to me."

Ginger hurled the fruit blend across the kitchen and bright mush exploded against the wall, sending a terrified Lek scurrying. "Think yer so smart," he managed.

Gordon arched an eyebrow. "It speaks."

Ginger slurred, "I know where they been hiding."

"Let me get this straight. All this time you know where Mazy went."

"Tried to tell you."

"He did, boss," Isaac said. "He did try to tell you."

"Shut it, Isaac," Gordon snarled. "Ginger, what do you want to tell me."

"Too late," Ginger said, giving Gordon two fingers.

"Really? After everything I've done for you?" Gordon's pitch climbed a notch. "The opportunities afforded, the path to sure wealth cleared, the messes I've cleaned up?"

"Messes?"

"You know what I'm talking about, Ginger, messy messes, egregious cases. Now look, I appreciate you put yourself on the line, physically, for the sake of our business. Gotten a bottle in the face, ruined your pretty looks. So let me take this opportunity to reveal how generous I can be. I'm upping your stake to fifteen percent, Ginger. And that's all out of my bit. Because loyalty is the number one thing I value, loyalty ...and gratitude. That's all I ask, all any entrepreneur can ask of his colleagues. So if that's perfectly all right with you, mate, can you calm the fuck down and tell me where she is."

Ginger thought it over. "Said where she been, not where she is."

"Fine. Show me, now."

Ginger walked downstairs toward the pool. Gordon followed him onto the beach and left, eastward, into the bright sun. Ginger moved sluggishly but with determination, leading Gordon past idle boats and the Thai kids and their water buffalo. They neared the beachfront restaurant on stilts and its handful of makeshift tables from the polished stubs of tree trunks. Gordon felt a tightening inside as Ginger turned inland and guided him to an anonymous shack a little ways back, surrounded by trees, where a mangy brown dog watched them from the porch.

"He been staying in there," Ginger said.

Gordon nodded, now seeing it unfold. Travis Mitchell had been right under his nose the whole time. It was like another poke in the eye.

Gordon opened the door and found it un-
changed since Ginger's visit yesterday. He
picked the empty vodka bottle from the trash,
rummaged through Travis's discarded clothes
as though he were a dog seeking the scent, or
a psychic picking up a vibration. But Gordon
received no further clue.

"If it's the last thing I do, Ginger, I'm going to
make a mince pie out of that cunt."

The dog stood in the doorway, wary, its tail
down and its ears standing tall.

He picked up a big knife from the sink. Gordon tested the tip with a finger. Plenty sharp.
"Nobody makes a fool of me."

"Or me."

Gordon snorted. "If you was doing your job
proper like, you'd be gutting that Yank like what
you did with that whore."

Ginger's expression was one of surprise.

"Oh, yeah, I know all about what you like.
Who do you think cleans up all of your messes?
But you can't chase down a stupid girl without
getting your face bashed in."

"I just..."

"You should be here hanging that septic by his
own intestines. Instead you let a bleeding yoga
instructor beat you to a pulp."

The dog had wandered onto the porch and
now began to bark.

"This enterprise needs for you to get results.
Pull yourself together, for fuck's sake." Gordon
strode out to the porch. The dog got one whiff
of him, folded her ears and turned tail.

Someone appeared beyond the palms, running along the beach in an urgent herky-jerk: Isaac, apparently trying to track them. Bloody hell, now what? Isaac would never notice the house set back in the copse, so Gordon shouted his name and walked out to meet him. Isaac hadn't run more than five minutes, but he was already a sweaty bugger. He hadn't put on his shades, which was unlike him, and his eyes were wide, borderline hysteric. Isaac's perspiration wasn't just from the tropical sun.

"What is it?" As they met, Gordon noticed Isaac's lip was swollen and glistened with a dab of blood.

"Gordon, we've got company. These Chinese blokes. They've taken over the villa."

Chapter 36

Zooprise

"Sir, you're not going to believe this," said the duty officer.

Win was standing at his filing cabinet, eating leftovers from yesterday's fried rice and drinking limpid tea from a thermos. This was the first break he had been able to take in hours, and his hemorrhoids were acting up. *Must lose weight*, he was telling himself as he tipped the bowl to his lips and sucked up the rest of the rice.

Win smacked his lips, hoping some word had come of Tarrin's whereabouts. He had sent a patrol car to the man's known house; nobody home. "Report."

"It's the zoo. There's been a...a..."

"A what?"

"Deaths, sir. Two people, maybe employees, are being...eaten. By the tigers. Sir."

Win lowered his bowl and spoon and closed his eyes. Of all the days.

"This should go to the Provincial Police."

"We got the call."

"The tigers get loose?"

"I don't think so. They're in their cages, from what we understand."

"Who's available?"

"All units are on the Suan case."

Win didn't bother hiding his irritation. How many disasters could they handle? But he couldn't understand it. A dead cop, kidnapped foreigners, Tarrin's gang wreaking terror, a dead Thai prostitute. None of those things seemed to fit together.

So why not throw tigers into the mix?

Still, he reasoned, it was possible there was a connection. Maybe this was Narong's way of disposing of the two Americans.

"All right," he sighed. "Who's closest to Orchid Resort right now?"

The duty officer had the roster at the ready, but Win already knew the answer. Car Three, sent out to find the drug lab that Mazy had described.

Something else she had said suddenly pierced his thoughts.

"Wait," he said to the duty officer, rummaging through his hand-written notes on yellow pads. No time to go through the tapes. His fat fingers snapped through the pages of scribble. What was it she had said, about one of Tarrin's associates? Met him at a trip to the zoo. An illiterate peasant. Some kind of janitor.

Met him at the zoo.

Win didn't have a warrant to search the villa where Wood was staying, but the request was making its way through the judiciary machinery. He hadn't sent a car there, not yet; better to start with Tarrin or Narong. But perhaps that had been a mistake.

"I'll take this call myself," Win said.

Tarrin angled his Lexus toward the villa's driveway. The car shook with the beats of The Notorious B.I.G.'s "Mo Money, Mo Problems". It was another postcard day on Koh Samui and Tarrin was in especially high spirits.

He had received the call from one of his sources in the police department. Yes, the foreigners were there. Singing like a pair of myna birds. It would be easy for something unfortunate to happen to them while they rotted in a Nathon jail...but wait, Major Win was playing with an ace up his sleeve. He was going to get the Americans off the island, out of Tarrin's grasp. He was going to escort them personally to the mainland.

Tarrin couldn't let that happen, not if Mazy had Gordon's phone. That would be like letting a river of gold go undammed.

Even Narong knew his limits. He was not about to take on Win face to face. Other cops could be bought or intimidated, but Win was too much trouble.

But what if Win couldn't be on the ferry? And so began Tarrin's frantic organizing of the loose association of men who worked for him into a small army of troublemakers which he then loosened on the unsuspecting tourists of Koh Samui.

It had paid off. Narong had called him around eleven last night. Yes, they had the girl, and the man with whom she had run off. But no phone.

Tarrin wasn't sure if this gave him an advantage. The phone was Gordon's link to the Chinese. Tarrin knew it would be difficult to remove Gordon completely. Isaac had the K-Love recipe in his head. It could now be replicated, of course, or Tarrin could simply deliver the Ketaset raw; it would serve the market well enough. But the coconut scheme required someone knowledgeable on the other side.

The Chinese could handle it easily enough, so again, Tarrin was back to that link. With it, he could squeeze Gordon out of the Samui end of the chain. Without the Chinese connection, Tarrin's profits would continue to be pinched by the middleman, and he'd have to continue putting up with foreigners sticking their big noses into his affairs.

So he didn't have their contacts. But he had the woman and her lover, and the knowledge that Gordon's phone was now in the hands of the police, an interesting fact that, revealed at the right moment, could serve as leverage, at least until Tarrin paid enough bribes for someone inside the force to steal it for him. The question for today, however, was how much the girl and her lover would be worth to Gordon. What would Gordon be willing to trade to get his hands on them?

Bets, in Tarrin's opinion, should be hedged.
And so he had told Narong to send him the girl,
but hold onto the man, at least for now. Keep
him in reserve, until Tarrin had deduced their
value.

He had met them at dawn at an isolated private beach on the southwestern tip of Samui.
A typical longtail boat had cut across the sap-
phire vista, coming from Koh Tan or one of the
other small isles that hovered to the south. A local fisherman manned the motorized tail, while
one of Narong's men crouched protectively behind a sour-looking Mazy. She had been seated
up front, her skin and hair sparkling from the
dousing of ocean waves received on the ride
over, her bound hands braced against the plank
seat in front of her. Whatever protests she had
felt like shouting were muffled behind the rags
stuffed in her mouth.

The fisherman had eased the prow onto the
shallow bank and the guard carried her to Tarrin's Lexus. She started to writhe and kick
when she realized where they were going to de-
posit her, and Tarrin had to help shove her into
the trunk.

Tarrin, now traveling alone, drove up to the
villa gate with his unusual cargo and honked.
After a moment, the automatic gate began to
slide open. Before Tarrin could move the car
inside, however, a strange man emerged, Chinese by the look of him, with pale skin and a
jagged haircut. The man wore a flowery shirt
and slacks, as though on holiday, but he was

clearly not here to enjoy the sun and sand. At least not with that bamboo staff in his hands.

The man rapped the edge of the bamboo stick on Tarrin's window. Tarrin lowered it. "Hey, don't no fuck my car," he snapped in English.

The Chinese man thrust the tip of the bamboo onto Tarrin's face, retaining taut control so that the tip only whispered against his cheek and stayed there, without wavering.

Tarrin was impressed, but he didn't flinch either. Samui was his turf and he had nothing to fear so long as he was on it.

"My name Tarrin."

This seemed to register with the Chinese man, who retracted the bamboo staff and waved him in. Tarrin made a show of examining his window, which was smudged but not damaged. The Chinese man didn't respond, but he didn't attempt any lip, either. Tarrin decided he had made his point and parked the Lexus next to a shimmering white stretch limousine. It was the first time Tarrin had seen one of these outside of Bangkok.

Someone here wasn't too concerned about keeping out of sight. Someone here carried himself with confidence. Top-line luxury was this person's habit.

Tarrin had a pretty good idea who had come to pay a visit to Gordon's villa. Maybe he didn't need the phone at all. The cargo in his trunk would suffice.

He smiled. Today was his lucky day. Feeling cocky, he threw the car keys at the Chinese, who caught it. "Don't lose," Tarrin said over his shoulder.

The fountains gushed along either side of the walkway. Tarrin glanced up and saw another Chinese guard prowling along the upper floor's balcony, keeping an eye on the road. Tarrin bowed and *wai*ed the bas-relief of the bodhisattva Alokeshvara carved into the face of the villa's outside wall (the one that Gordon and his entourage mistook for the Lord Buddha). Then he proceeded up the stairs to the villa's top floor.

The second Chinese guard met him at the top of the stairs. This one was squat and chubby, with a bowl-shaped haircut and a caved-in face that even a mother would struggle to love.

He dug into his pocket and pulled out the diamond ring that his men had taken off the girl. He held it up so it caught the sun.

"I'm Tarrin. Tell you boss Mr. Kang now I come."

Chapter 37

Carving, Boat, Search, Sword

GORDON asked Isaac, "Who let them in? The gate's locked; there's a wall."

"No clue, boss. I was watching the footy highlights and heard this commotion. I ran to the balcony, but the gate was already open and they came in this white fuck-off limo."

"Chinese?"

"Three of them—two Bruce Lees and a Confucius type in traditional kit, with a goatee and a yellow fedora."

Gordon's heart rate doubled. "What did he say to you?"

"He knows you. He knows you're here. He just said, 'Where's Gordon?' in this posh accent. 'Where's me old China?' Like that. They got me on my knees when I said you'd gone out. Knocked me about. I said you'd gone off this way. On foot. He said to fetch you. What kind of Chinese guy uses the word 'fetch'?"

One who's used to having people fetch all sorts of things for him. "His name is Kang. You call him Tai Bak."

"That's Kang?"

"Congratulations, Isaac. You've just met the hardest triad from Hong Kong and so far lived to tell the tale. We'd better leg it."

The three of them ran back to the villa, Gordon turning a jog into a run, the others panting to keep pace. He took the short set of steps leading from the beach to the villa's pool in a single leap. One of the goons awaited them, a thin, agile man in a flowery shirt and a bamboo staff that he pointed at Gordon's chest, signaling him to halt. Gordon obeyed and in a quick glance observed the scene: a second Chinese, a squat man of vaudevillian ugliness, also armed with a bamboo rod; Tarrin, on the other side of the pool, reclining in a lounge chair in the blingy splendor of baggy jeans, twisted baseball cap, and gold chains. And the centerpiece of the tableau, moving down the sandstone steps on the far end of the compound—gliding, it seemed, as though having mastered the art of levitation—in a flowing black Mandarin-style gown, sleeves turned out in white, with yellow slippers, round sunglasses and Western-style yellow fedora, smoking a long cigar that was most likely a Romeo y Julieta robusto, was Kang himself.

Tai Bak raised his hands like wings, as though prepared to embrace them all, and he practically danced around the edge of the pool. He had a tummy and was, after all, past what could be politely termed middle age. It was the English upbringing—Marlborough, Cambridge and all that—which had allowed him to indulge in the eccentric. That and the understanding people around him had gained long ago that deriding his habits led to their children returned with broken arms, or mistresses handed back minus a digit or two.

Gordon waited for the man's joyous approach but found no charity observable in Kang's face. His eyes may have been hidden but the lines parenthesizing his mouth were deep and haggard, and his lips parted in a snarl.

"Mr. Wood."

Gordon managed a slight bow. "Tai Bak. If I had known you were coming, I could have made arrangements, cleaned up a bit."

"Tai Bak," Ginger echoed through his mauled mouth, he and Isaac nodding their heads.

"I have no need for your housekeeping skills," said Kang with a gummy English accent that the Queen would envy. "At any rate, I understand your organization has suffered infiltrations, defections and loss of focus."

So Heinz had told him everything; Gordon would remember that for the next time they met. Kang's arrival was unsettling. But worse, he realized, was Tarrin's presence. What had transpired between these two? How did they even know each other? *The phone...Mazy.*

But he maintained a level demeanor. "I wouldn't say that, Tai Bak. In fact, we begin shipments this week. The contracts for Chili Hut are sorted, the lab's working, the product's there. It's all good. Mazy's done a runner, I guess you know that, but she's just a stupid bint who doesn't have anything to do with this."

Kang spread his hands over his heart. "Indeed. Well, then, Mr. Wood, I suppose I owe you an apology, for I must be grossly misinformed."

"No, Tai Bak, that's not necessary," Gordon said. "I mean, you're right to wonder. I'd wonder, too, if I were in your position. But I have news for you which I think you'll like."

"Do tell."

"Would you care for something? A glass of water? Tea, something to eat?"

Kang's mouth smiled like a wolf would smile as it contemplated its prey. "No, thank you."

The thin goon's bamboo shaft was still tautly poised an inch in front of Gordon's chest. Throughout the short dialogue, it hadn't flinched. Gordon put his palm against it but knew better than to push it out of the way.

"Could we, er, possibly relax?"

The thin man waited for Kang's pert nod before lowering the rod.

"Why don't we all sit together," Kang suggested, gesturing to the gazebo. "Your Thai friend, Mr. Tarrin, has already introduced himself. A most interesting fellow."

They sat: Gordon with his back to the beach; Kang, enjoying the panorama; and Tarrin, his chains jangling as he jauntily swung one leg over the bench. Ginger and Isaac tried to join them, but the two Chinese guards interceded. The squat goon with the unfortunate face blocked Isaac, while Ginger and the tall

Chinese entered a silent tussle, noses an inch apart, trying to maneuver around each other.

"Mr. Wood, you mentioned you bring me news," Kang said. "You have me astir with curiosity. Please."

Gordon said, "We're getting close to finding Travis Mitchell. I know about him, Tai Bak, and what he did to your son. Allow me to extend my condolences. You don't need to dirty your hands with this bloke. You don't need to remember his name. But he's going to remember yours, believe me, once I've got him. Your name will be the last thing he ever hears in his misguided life. That's my pledge to you. Thought you might like to know that."

Kang was half listening, half focused on coaxing the cigar to life with some robust inhalations, and Gordon grew uncomfortably aware of just how tenuous the value of his services had become.

"You honor me with this offer," Kang said.

"Believe me, Tai Bak, the honor will be mine."

"And in return for this generous service?"

"Nothing. We're in business together. I just want to let you know my intentions. In case that's why you've come."

"I see." Kang inhaled slowly and blew a perfect ring of smoke, letting a long trail of ash hang from the edge of his robusto. "Yes, I see."

"The rest of the operation is fine."

"Of that I have no doubt, if that is your word. I am most impressed by your local associate."

When Kang's robusto pointed his way, Tarrin broke into a smile. "We have good talk."

"Yes, we certainly did," Kang drawled. "I gather, Mr. Wood, that a certain item of yours has gone missing. An item that perhaps contains some digital information that it should not."

"My phone. Yeah, well, Mazy bolted with it. But it doesn't matter."

"It doesn't, of course not."

"Tai Bak, believe me, a business operation doesn't go tits just because a girl does a runner with my phone."

"I'll be the judge of my concerns," Kang snapped. "I gather you have lost the phone, which you have certainly used to call all manner of people whom should not be so contacted; you have lost a woman whose name is on certain contracts and who knows everything about this operation —no, keep silent now; and you have no idea where to find Mitchell, or anything about where they've been and whom they've encountered."

"It's just a girl."

"Tarrin here has some news that I do find truly interesting. Tarrin, say it again, what you told me."

Tarrin adjusted his baseball cap. "Mazy and loverboy go police. Nathon Station. This one," he said, indicating Ginger, "he get beat up, run away. Mazy give phone police. Take ferry to Surat Thani."

Gordon's face darkened into a single thought: *No gratitude.*

"So you see," Kang hissed, "it's not all right at all. But I do appreciate your desire to work with me in harmony. As of right now, you no longer work *with* me, Mr. Wood, but *for* me. These are my terms. You may continue to liaise with Tarrin from Hong Kong for the import and distribution of K-Love, and keep ten percent of the proceeds. Tarrin's stake rises to thirty-five percent."

"Ten percent! This is my operation. I've set it up. I've got the chemist. I've got the supplies. I've got the distribution. The original deal, Tai Bak, was thirty. Just because this girl runs off doesn't mean you can just change the terms of our agreement."

The triad lord puffed on his cigar. "But that was before I had any inkling of your local business arrangements. At any rate, Isaac here will happily serve as a chemist working for me, won't you, lad?"

Isaac's eyes flicked between the two Chinese bodyguards. "Reckon so."

"You see, Mr. Wood, you don't need all the overhead expense of so many employees," Kang said, crushing his cigar on the tabletop, at which point the ugly thug whirled away from Isaac and whacked his rod against the back of Ginger's knee.

Gordon leapt to his feet but then froze, seeing Tarrin point his Glock at him. The Thai shook his head and Gordon sat back down. Ginger curled on the ground under a barrage of damp thuds as the two Chinese guards beat him with their staves. Tarrin's laugh was thin and sugary.

Kang said, "Let me tell you, Gordon, if I may be so informal, a story from long ago, because the older a story, the more timeless its moral. In the state of Chu there lived a soldier who loved his sword very much. One day, while crossing a river, he accidentally dropped it into the water. Thinking quickly, he took out a knife and carved a marking on the side of the boat, to indicate where the sword had fallen. Then the boatman carried on taking him to the far bank."

The goons by now had knocked the fight out of Ginger. They discarded their shafts and each took one of those giant legs in their arms. They grimaced with the weight as they shifted the body toward the pool.

"Upon reaching the shallows by the shore, the soldier plunged into the water beside the mark on the boat, searching for his lost sword. This story has been since distilled into the four-character expression *ke zhou qiu jian*, literally 'carving, boat, search, sword'."

The goons had pushed Ginger onto his belly and into the pool head first, each standing at the edge holding an ankle. Water came to life as the Scouse flailed like Ahab's great white whale.

"This is a typical *chengyu*, one of the many delights of the Chinese language, both classical and vernacular. You would probably know nothing of the grace of a language that, perfected over two thousand years, can distil such a wide range of philosophy and poetry down to a mere four characters. Every child knows *ke zhou qiu jian*, and the story behind it, which highlights what happens when one refuses to accept that circumstances have changed. The soldier leaves a mark to find his sword, but is oblivious to the fact that the boat has moved. And so he never recovers his beloved totem."

Splash splash. It was all the two bodyguards could do to keep hold of his ankles, but Gordon could plainly tell the man was weakening. Across from the table, Isaac hid his face in his hands.

"I trust, Gordon, that you can see how this idiom applies to your current situation."

Ginger's struggling faded to sporadic jerks. The bodyguards stood erect. They weren't fighting anymore. They were just holding his quivering legs.

"That," Gordon said, "is the stupidest fucking story I've ever heard." He looked at the unresponsive round sunglasses beneath the yellow brim. "If you want my opinion."

"Gordon," Isaac hissed, his eyes bright with panic.

Kang scowled. "It applies so ever more precisely to your situation."

"Nobody's going to shed a tear for Ginger's passing," Gordon said. "But I would have appreciated your letting me handle my men my way."

"You've lost the plot, I fear. Tarrin here tells me that, according to you, Mr. Wood, Chester Collins engaged in certain, ah, proclivities.

Things that required our Thai partners to work hard to cover up."

Chester Collins was drowned. The two goons let go of his ankles and his body floated face down like a giant jellyfish in the becalmed infinity pool. The pleasured shrieks of village children punctured the air as the kids hit the beach.

"I don't know what got into him, Tai Bak. I know he was becoming a liability."

"A liability, exactly. Behavior of that sort is bound to attract attention that would impede operations. Sand in the wheels of commerce, you know. And there's the question of discipline. And finally, well, a matter of taste."

"I'm sorry you had to hear anything about that," Gordon said.

"As am I, but I am even sorrier that it may all be a lie."

Gordon tipped his head. "Come again?"

"Your partner Tarrin doesn't seem to believe you, Mr. Wood."

"What do you mean?" Gordon asked, a hint of squeal in his voice.

Kang drummed his fingers on the table. "I mean, on top of everything else you've fouled up, like disobeying me by putting my number in your phone, and then letting it fall into the hands of the police, you seem to conclude unspeakable nighttime goings-on with the local whore population by cutting one open with a knife and then blaming it on Collins."

Gordon stopped breathing. The sight of Ginger's floating corpse seemed to flicker and a terrible buzzing filled his ears.

The moment passed. "Ridiculous," Gordon said. "Ginger was a psychopath. That's the real story, then? You think because one of my boys got a little overexcited when it came to the girls, you can run this operation without me. Fine. It's all yours, mate. I quit."

"There's no quitting in this life, me old China," Kang said, a posh man usurping a poor man's expression. "For how much longer have you taken this villa?"

"What?"

"For how much longer do you have the lease for this villa?"

"Four or five days, something like that."

"I compliment you on its taste. Rather surprising for a low-class predator of schoolyards and drugged prostitutes, I must say. May I presume that your errant lady friend had a hand in its selection?"

"What are you on about, Kang?"

"I am taking this villa for my holiday. You are going to the airport and returning to Hong Kong, where you will be met by one of my people with simple instructions regarding the distribution of the first shipment of K-Love, instructions that even you should have little trouble understanding and following."

"What about Trav Mitchell? Don't you want me to find him for you?"

"I have a feeling our Thai friends will have more success at that."

Tarrin put his pistol away. "Sorry, man," he said to Gordon, but his eyes weren't sorry at all. Isaac wouldn't return his gaze, and Gordon was left wondering how, with a snap of the fingers, he had lost everything, how he had let her humiliate him, with Ginger, with Trav, with every little bloody thing.

"You'll be sorry," Gordon replied, "when you're the one who has to deal with that viper bitch of mine."

"You mean Maze?" Tarrin asked, grinning for no reason that Gordon could fathom.

"Yes, I bloody well mean Maze. Who else would I mean?"

The Thai gangster giggled. "She in my car."

"What are you on about?" Gordon gawked at the Thai gangster, struggling to process the words.

"Oh, dear, all this time in the trunk of your car," Kang said, "in such beastly heat. How inconsiderate of us. Gordon, you'd like to see your girlfriend, wouldn't you? She and Travis Mitchell have been in Tarrin's custody since last night." He pinched two fingers; something flashed. A diamond ring.

Gordon was going to be sick.

Chapter 38

Dance

So this is pain.

S Trav had achieved enough sustained awareness to allow a sliver of cogitation. Despite enduring a full-body battering, it was the throb of his cleft chin that awakened him. The bandaging from the police station had come off somewhere along the way and the naked cut jangled like ice on fire. The bump on his head and the countless bruises on his abused corpus were just so much background noise.

He could control the pain just enough, just enough to turn sardonic. *I guess this is the part where I say I feel so alive.* Then a slight movement would amp the pain, twist the flaming blade, adjust the glowing tongs, and it was all he could do to breathe.

Yes. Breathe.

Easy there.

He forced himself to relax. To accept the multiple aches and lancing jabs. *That's just part of me now.* Breathe and relax his face, the hardest, but he could start with the brow, and then the eyes, and finally the jaw. Relax it even as it burned. Then his neck and shoulders, loosen all the knots, and so on down his torso and through his extremities.

Be there in the pose, Mazy had once exhorted the class. Lose yourself, said his karate *sensei*, for if there is effort, you have already limited yourself.

Don't think, just do, Heinz had told him about a thousand times, usually about at the point when Trav was about to collapse from exhaustion.

That had always been his problem, thinking. Thinking about how cool he was. How this trade was going to rock. How being the tough guy in the ring was going to floor the nightclub babes. And then, just as he was feeling cocky, he'd screw up and the sparring partner would connect. What was the constant source of this undirected thrusting? What were the lacunae in his biography, who were the ghosts in his dreams, whispering his name? Despite everything, he reeked with mediocrity and despised himself for it. This wasn't suppression of the ego: it was another form of indulgence, and maybe it explained why he had no job, had no novel, had no fiancée, had just about nothing anymore except this cut up body and a cord of hemp around his wrists.

Even Mazy, about as fucked up a girl as he'd ever met, didn't want him.

Images and sounds flicked through his consciousness. The touch of fingers on his face. *Don't die on me, cowboy.*

Mazy. Where was she? Where were any of them?

Trav opened his eyes.

He was in a sleeping bag, curled on his side, and it was dark and dank. He moved his head to get a better look, and paid the price—everywhere. But at least nothing was broken. He could move. He was in a dark pit of some kind, with the entrance behind him hovering like a ragged hole of light that was too bright to regard directly.

Trav heaved himself into a sitting position. He was in a cave, alone. A small campfire nearby had long since gone out. Bottles of liquor and squeezed-out cans of beer littered the hard ground. The chill of damp was everywhere, coating the liner of the sleeping bag with perspiration.

He had no idea what time of day it was. Someone had liberated him of his watch over the course of the long night. His hands were sore but the horrible blue swelling of his wrists had abated. Trav vaguely recalled they had been bound behind his back, but now they were clasped together before him. The hemp rope had been fixed with the expert fastness of a fisherman's knot.

Trav wriggled all of the fingers on his right hand. The cast had been due to come off later this week. He tried to prize loose the rope against the cast but no luck. He put both hands on the ground, put some weight on them. Protests, but they were all right. He arched his buttocks up but his chin, enduring a rush of blood, forced him down. The hands were fine. He squatted, stood erect and missed the stalactites by a few inches. His jeans crinkled under layers of filth.

He stumbled toward the cave's mouth, holding his bound hands to shield his eyes from the glare. He could make out only the bleached outlines of outside: a clearing, trees. He stooped and ducked his head out the entrance. A somewhat smelly landing of flat, sandy ground, surrounded by forest. The noise of a neighborhood inhabited by birds. The instant heat of the unbroken sun. And to one side, a short, stocky Thai man, standing before a thicket of brush, legs splayed and trousers down, his pelvis reverberating in that time-old manner of killing boredom with a wank.

Trav ducked back in the cave, but there was no time to map out a plan. He needed a weapon. Remembering Mazy's bludgeoning of Ginger with the bottle of Absolut, Trav scrambled back for the discarded Lady Song. He picked it up with his tethered hands, and his unwitting sneaker sent a crumpled tin can hurtling against the cave wall. He cringed but kept going, folding into a crouch by the cave entrance. Had the man heard him kick the can? Trav peered around the corner—man's not there; oh *shit*—ducked back inside.

Look back. Anything. Gun? No. Man's on the move. Trav lifted the bottle. He could practically hear the muscles and tendons creak. He was stuck. He was thinking too much. He was holding his breath—bad. *Breathe.*

A tiny movement. A shadow. Outside, on the sand. He could touch it if he just extended his hands. The shadow wobbled. The man was on the opposite side of the cave wall. Lowering into a crouch just like Trav's. But betrayed by the sun, and maybe realizing it.

Trav breathed through his nose. In. Out. In. Out. The neck of the bottle, already slick with dew, grew slippery in his grasp. The brightness from outside made his head spin. He trained his eyes on the ground. He could see only a tiny slice of the man's shadow. It vibrated, fell out of view for a second, or was that just his eyes?

He blinked, the shadow was still there, scarcely moving. Trav could wait. He could breathe; he could focus on that scrap of grey on the sand, even as the pulse from his chin played bass chords in his head. He could— The man, when he attempted to creep forward, was loud and clumsy. Fingers clasped an edge of the cave mouth, sandaled feet pressed into the ground, but most of all, the man had been holding his breath and now he exhaled as he moved, and in that moment it was as if he had cupped his lips and shouted at the top of his lungs. Trav slammed the bottle against the fingers, not to break the glass but to deliver a sharp rap. He jumped out of the mouth and the man was already on his knees, moving to clutch his mangled digits.

Trav popped his knee into the man's face, got him in the eye. Maybe uncorked the cheekbone and the bridge of the guy's nose. A quick jet of blood as the man's head flinched back against the cliff wall. He slumped as though snoozing on a sofa. Trav knelt beside him. Young guy, almost a kid. Floppy hair, hip-hop chains, chunky silver earrings. Been born somewhere else to some other set of parents, could have been a sophomore studying biology. Now he lay unconscious with a broken face.

Trav had to free his hands. There could be more of these guys. Would be more. He tried edging the rope free, but no luck. He looked at the man's smashed fingers, bleeding on top, two of them clearly bent unnaturally, and got an idea. Trav began to bang the cast against the sharp end of a rock in the cave's mouth. Nothing. He swung harder, then sawed. The next man was there.

It was the killer from the pier, with the gold teeth and the glittery flip-flops, the greasy mustache and the purple pants. The 70s porn star had emerged from the brush, from some path that Trav hadn't spotted. Narong stopped and stared in amazement. Trav hit the cast a third time, hard, and it ripped and crumbled. Narong lifted his floppy shirttails. Gun in the waistband, pressed to the man's skinny brown stomach. Narong smiled and the sun caught his golden fillings.

The crushed cast left a millimeter of space but that was enough for him to shrug off the rope. Trav wasn't thinking. He was just in motion. Narong had the gun in his hand. He was raising the gun at the man hurtling toward him. Point blank. *Bang.* Trav didn't feel it. He knew the look in the man's eyes, though. Panic. Trav delivered a roundhouse kick that connected with Narong's outstretched hand and sent the gun flying. It was only as Trav returned to a boxer's stance that he realized he was bleeding again and there was a horrible, shrieking wind in his left ear.

Narong slipped out of his flip-flops, preferring to fight barefoot. He grinned, gestured. *Let's dance.*

Trav was already in motion. He didn't trust his hands, didn't know what the right one could do. Instead he kicked—one, two, three roundhouses, each pushing Porn Star back. Narong defended with his arms, each a block of wood. Like the wooden practice dummy in Heinz's dojo. Only this dummy knew how to deflect Trav's ankle, spin him around, kick back. Narong pirouetted, golden teeth rotating in and out of the sun. He drove Trav back to where they began, but one kick proved too ambitious and Trav got in close, sprang and kneed him square in the chest.

Narong rolled out of immediate harm and came up on his haunches. Trav circled. Narong grimaced as he touched his breast where Trav had nailed him, but then he flashed that mad, lustrous smirk. "You die time."

They engaged again, this time Narong attacking with his kicks but trying to get closer, to get inside, sensing Trav's reluctance to engage with his fists. Trav kept his left up, caught a hook with his left and turned the tables, angling Narong's arm to the side and popping him in the temple. But it was a feeble hit and they sprang apart.

Narong leapt again and now he was going all out on Trav's right side, kicks and punches. Porn Star wouldn't be able to keep it up much longer at that rate, but as Trav became conscious of his trepidation to use his right hand, his defense grew desperate, and Narong had him backed up against the cliff wall. Narong's knuckles found the jagged rut in his jaw and a hundred light bulbs burst.

Now the man had broken through Trav's defenses, and he was taking solid hits to the kidneys. Trav defended with pushkicks, trying to create any kind of distance, any sort of breathing room. He switched to a low kick against Narong's inner calf but the man had bones of iron.

The onslaught had, however, left Narong winded and his punches slowed to the point that Trav broke out. Literally ran, forgetting his footwork, making the mistake of showing his back, and he paid the price with a kick that crashed into his hip and sent him face-first to eat sand.

Rolled over. Narong took his time. Strolled. Enjoying it but breathing hard. It was a good performance, but Trav knew the man was spent. Narong gestured again. *Get up, asshole.*

Trav winced as he got onto his hands and knees. Mistake. Narong wasn't waiting for a gentleman's duel. Hard kick, Trav got a defensive arm up just in time to save his head, but it threw him onto his back. He crawled, kicked sand, scared.

Narong chuckled. His teeth sparkled, darkly playful. He was getting his wind back. He pranced, shadow-boxed for Trav's entertainment.

Trav sprang up. Skipped the hands and knees part. Straight to his feet. It cost him about everything he had. Every ounce of juice. But he didn't want to get kicked again.

And he was standing up.

"Let's dance, asshole," Trav said, assuming his stance.

A flicker of doubt crossed Porn Star's face. Trav didn't attack; he was too tired. He waited.

It came and this time Trav switched from Muay Thai to karate, clasping his hands and catching Narong's fist. The kicks came but too late to prevent a twist. Narong's kicks forced Trav to free his hand. The wrist wasn't broken but it must have been sore. Trav was inside. Four elbows: slash, smash, slash, jump, his favorite combo, could have ended the fight. But no juice. Narong got his hands on Trav's waist, threw him into the brush.

Trav crashed through a harsh thicket of branches and thorns, down a sudden incline and head-first into water. That surprised him, and he got a mouthful that sent him into a spasm of choking. He fought to clear his head of the water. Not much time to take in his surroundings, lying head down like that, but he took note of a wooden walkway, of spindly trees, of the sudden hush of the mangrove. *Where the hell—?*

Narong loomed above him. The man was panting but still smiling.

"Dance, dance," Narong said. "Disco!"

Trav wanted to collapse against the ground, but as soon as his core muscles wobbled, the back of his head dipped into the brackish water. He was stuck in a partial, upside-down sit-up. He was alive and Narong would have to find a way to kill him. Maybe just waiting for him to give up and drown was enough.

He tried to roll out of the way, but Narong bent down and grabbed both of his ankles. That fucking smile.

Trav attempted a sudden sit-up that might end with a surprise head butt. It was a desperate action and he was too tired to pull it off quickly. Narong laughed and, pressing on his calves, gently pushed his body down a few inches deeper. Now it was all he could do to simply keep his head out of the water. His hands flailed beneath him, striking submerged branches and bramble.

He gulped air and went under. Came up. Maybe for the last time. Looked at the brown hands on his legs. The rocks and the mud. The dark canopy high above, the absence of sunlight. No light, no hope, nothing except Narong's lost pistol lying equidistant between their hands on Trav's right side.

They both noticed it at the same time. Eyes locked—bodies moved. Narong's fingers curled around the Glock's nose, Trav's found the hilt. A silent tussle. Weight came off Trav's right leg. Kick. Not much, just enough. The gun sailed, plopped into the water somewhere. Narong laughed, just back to the status quo, except as his hand fell on Trav's leg and pushed him further down, Trav's hand found a rock and he curled forward. Narong had let himself extend too far for the gun and he wasn't paying attention.

Travis smashed his nose. Narong pulled back, let go. Trav slid into the water but his other hand grabbed hold of Narong's flashy shirt, pulling him down. They flailed in the milky opacity of the mangrove waters, hands on each others' throats, but Trav had a rock in his other palm. By the time he was done, the water was clouding darkly with blood and bits of Narong's skin and hair.

Standing in the mangrove in a widening nebula of blood like that creeped him out. He was suddenly aware that he was exposed. To what, he didn't know—that was what was so frightening. The faded grey planks of the rotting walkway beckoned beyond the spidery tangle of branches.

Every footfall was a slow step into an unknown clutter of nasty underwater roots. He
wasn't even sure how deep the water was, or
what he was standing on. His foot got snagged.
He looked back in a panic as something from
below tugged at Narong's body. Screaming but
not knowing he was screaming, Trav wrenched
his ankle free at the price of yet another jolt of
pain. But he was clear and he hauled himself
onto the walkway. Narong's body kept jerking.
Porn Star was breakfast. Travis was alive.

Maybe she was, too.

Chapter 39

Strange Homecoming

HALF dead or half alive? And which should she prefer? It didn't matter. Time was endurance, tolerating being bent like a fetus, hemp around her wrists and a filthy bandana stuffed in her mouth. The battering from Samui's imperfect roads while trussed inside the trunk of Tarrin's Lexus had been terrifying, but just lying in her coffin, sweating her way to death, was a hell unto itself.

Mazy couldn't say for how long she had lain in that black sauna after Tarrin had parked. She had felt the car gently rock as he closed the driver's door. She had registered the digital coocoo of the door lock. Some muffled voices, impossible to decipher. Then, nothing but to stew, literally, in her own juices. The morning had grown late and the sun had long since assumed its mighty position. Falling unconscious was a relief, but something, some discomfort, a sharp serving of pain, continuously brought her back to awareness.

She missed the opening of the trunk. Only gradually did she wake up to the brightness, to hands unbending her, and to the sweetness of fresh air. Air—incredible. She sucked it through her nostrils greedily and paid the price with a round of coughs that nearly did her in. Death by tropical breeze.

The light was too intense for her to make out anything of her whereabouts, and she was too weak to do more than try to wobble on her own legs. A woman's voice twittered nervously, but Mazy couldn't decipher the words. They were leading her from the gravel of a parking lot to a series of sandstone steps rising out of a few inches of water. Water cascaded on both sides of her, leaving her aching for the touch of water droplets on her skin. As she approached the giant Buddhist image that hovered closer before her, Mazy realized she was back at the villa.

Tarrin was there. The woman's voice—that had been Lek's. Now Lek's husband was up front, opening one of the doors to the twin guest bedrooms that formed the ground level of the villa's main building. So who were these two men half-dragging her between the lines of fountains? She couldn't quite make them out, the light was too bright, but they seemed vaguely Asian without looking like locals.

They took her into the guest room. Its elegant, spare furnishing remained crisp and untouched. Anurak had opened the opposite door that would lead to the inner courtyard. The men carrying her wore beige slacks and floral short-sleeved shirts. One was stubby, the other leonine, and they were Chinese.

"I can walk," she said, only it came out a mumble. Her lips were parched and she could barely speak.

They led her outside to the shaded porch, behind the great staircase that connected the courtyard to the villa's top floor. They were in the part of the garden that embraced the buildings within the compound walls: magnificent palm fans, frangipani trees with their fragrant pink flowers, gorgeous hibiscus, lascivious orchids, gardenias opening in little carroty surprises—

She breathed it all, loved it all, missed it already.

They walked to the bright open infinity pool, the open sky, the lounge chairs and the hedge, the steps opening the villa to the beach and the sea. It was morning and the tide was high and swift. The neighboring islands were still there, silent blue sunbathers, and she wondered which one was where they had in all likelihood let Trav Mitchell die.

Gordon was standing by the sliding glass doors of their bedroom, expression hidden behind sunglasses. Dark curls, the slightly wild beard, the big silver cones filling his earlobes, the cargo shorts and the West Ham T-shirt. It was like nothing had changed. Almost nothing. He stood quietly with his hands thrust in his pockets.

Isaac was there, too, sharp as ever in his summer whites and snappy trilby, wearing the wrap-around shades that could not hide the signs of a beating that marked his lips, nose and cheeks.

What a strange, subdued pair.

And then there was the visitor, a pot-bellied older Chinese man sitting in the shade of the sala, struggling to light a cigar against the steady breeze off the beach. The long Chinese silk garment, the yellow fedora, the little round John Lennon sunglasses. She hadn't met Tai Bak but she knew who he was.

Lek scurried up with a wet hand towel. "She need rest," Lek said.

"Water," Mazy sort of said.

Tarrin made a grand gesture. "See," he said to Kang, "Tarrin get her."

"Hey Maze," Isaac said, quietly. "Good to see you, mate."

Gordon said nothing.

Kang finally ignited his cigar and he reclined on the bench, stoking the flame with a few sharp inhales before indulging in a long drag that he blew out in a fleetingly perfect ring.

"So I see, Khun Tarrin," he eventually said. "You have proven your resourcefulness. I was right to liberate you of incompetent help, was I not, Mr. Wood?"

Gordon remained silent, and Mazy got the sense that he and Isaac had as much freedom right now as she did.

"Oh, and I believe this is yours," Kang said, revealing her ring in his palm.

"Keep it," she said.

Kang tossed the ring to Tarrin. "For services rendered. See that she recovers. I'll want to interrogate her when we get back."

The two Chinese escorted her into the master bedroom. They dumped her without ceremony on the bed and left. Lek helped Mazy roll onto her back and applied the dripping cloth to her face.

"Water," Mazy croaked, and Lek squeezed water out of the cloth into her mouth. She dabbed Mazy's lips and gently pushed errant hair out of her face. Anurak appeared with a tray bearing more water, along with fruit and some fried corn fritters. They exchanged Thai murmurs of concern as Lek helped Mazy sit up and drink.

She was ravenous and attacked the sliced rambutan and mango with gusto, until sweet, sticky ichor covered her fingers and spilled down her chin. They left her like that. The curtains covered the floor-to-ceiling windows all around the bedroom and the air conditioner's hum blocked out the sounds from outside. It felt so strange to be back here now, as though Gordon had never hit her, menaced her, drugged her, let Ginger force himself upon her. As though she had never spiked their drinks, lied through her teeth, hidden in terror from them, run away, suffered a humiliating police inquisition, been kidnapped and beaten, witnessed what they did to Trav.

She wearily got up. Everything hurt and she was exhausted, and she knew if that triad boss wanted to hurt her, she might not be able to stand it. But it felt unreal, even the bruises and the cuts. What felt real was how she stank, how she needed a long bath. How she longed for a drink.

Mazy parted the curtain by the sliding door and found the strange Chinese man in the floral shirt with the awful bowl cut loitering outside. He seemed annoyed by her presence. When she began to open the door, he held it steady, allowing her only a crack, and she realized that he was there to see she stayed put.

"Beer," she said. "*Bejau, m'goi.* Vodka *hou-ah.*" Anything would do.

The man nodded and shut the door.

Figuring the guy might take a while, Mazy shed her clothes and examined the cut on her foot. It was filthy but didn't look too bad. She closed her eyes and tried to remember what Trav's hands felt like on her, but she had been too drunk and distant, even though it was just two nights ago. She hated the sorrow she felt.

Mazy opened the closet. Her clothes were still there. So was the safe, but now its door was open and the interior empty. Only Gordon knew the lock code, and she suspected this emptiness had something to do with Kang's arrival. She wandered around the room, going through the drawers, but didn't find anything of use.

Time for a pee and a bath. Mazy picked out a clean pair of panties and a bra and carried these through the heavy sliding door to the giant bathroom, then dropped her garments and screamed. Ginger was there, reclining in the white claw-footed bathtub, his red mangled face looking right at her.

Ginger didn't flinch. His eyes were leveled at her but didn't see. The horror movie that was his face—not a twitch. Despite his huge size, he seemed shrunken and almost little, swallowed in the womb of the vast bathtub.

The shock had caused her to pee on herself. Suddenly feeling her nakedness, she picked up her garments and covered her crotch. She took a tentative step inside, trying to hold her bladder from an all-out eruption. Even though he must be dead, she was terrified of him, of his corpse. What was it Kang had said to Gordon, something about freeing him of incompetent help?

She had to go desperately, but she couldn't see herself sitting on the toilet just beyond Ginger, with nothing to look at but his torn flesh poking over the tub's rim. Cringing, she dashed through the bathroom to the far set of sliding doors that led to the outdoor shower. It was covered and hidden by three walls, the missing fourth extending to a small pool that was also walled but open to the sky.

Mazy had loved showering out here, beneath the rain shower head, exposed yet protected; she had tried to make love to Gordon here, hoping the venue would excite him out of his methadone impotence, so that he would be happy and embrace her as he once had; but now, running the water as hot as the plumbing would allow, she squatted above the drain and urinated, feeling tawdry and scared.

Chapter 40

The Zoo

ISAAC reluctantly followed Kang, Tarrin and one of Kang's bodyguards—the tall, handsome one —out to the parking lot. He kept trying to think of an excuse to get out of there, but his imagination failed him.

Wizard of Ox. What a joke. Isaac had escaped a few sketchy moments, in Sheffield, in London. He had taken his share of beatings and endured threats. Joining Gordo and heading to Hongkers had seemed like such a relief: A new start. Interesting business ventures. Bit of dosh. Birds. And the freedom to explore a few personal psychotropic interests. Brilliant.

Violence always hovered at the edges of an illicit business, but it still managed to surprise and frighten him. He was an explorer, a pioneer. Not a thug. Sure, Ginger had been a dull brute, and Gordon had hinted that the man possessed darker tastes. But to see him murdered like that...in daylight, for fuck's sake! Right here at the villa, where they had killed time over cards, brought back pros for some fun, had some laughs.

Even that, however, Isaac could handle. But seeing them pull Mazy out of the trunk of Tarrin's car...this same car where he now sat in the front passenger seat. She had looked emaciated, like one of those victims of a third-world refugee camp. Isaac thanked God for bringing her back, but she was in a poor state. He didn't want to know what they had put her through. And yet he wanted to know. He wanted to stay behind and take care of her, be there when she woke up and...

And what, regale her with tales of heroism? No, Isaac hadn't done anything to help anyone. And he didn't have a plan to get her out of there, just the two of them.

Instead he got into the front passenger seat of Tarrin's car.

Anurak opened the outer gate. Tarrin backed the Lexus out to the road, past the shaded patch that didn't quite encompass the white stretch limo. Kang and his bodyguard occupied the back seats. They were going on a little field trip.

What fun.

Kang had said he wanted to see the whole operation, now that he was getting directly involved. He wanted to understand the set-up. Know his partner. Sniff it all out. Jesus, that guy had a way of banging on. Uppity Chinese bloke who thought he was Winston Churchill. Or Prince Philip. Some posh white colonial tosser.

Tarrin drove east toward Lamai. Twice he made a call on his mobile but didn't seem to get an answer. The second time he hissed something in Thai which, to Isaac, sounded like cursing. Something was going on. Isaac guessed Tarrin was trying to reach Jaidee, tell him or warn him of their visit. From what Isaac could tell, Tarrin hadn't said anything to Kang about the janitor, but Kang clearly wanted to see the source of K-Love. That meant they were heading either to the zoo or to the lab. Isaac remembered how Gordon had smashed Jaidee's mobile chip, in a spate of sheer meanness. He considered reminding Tarrin, but didn't see the point.

Left, into the mountains, meant the lab; straight and then right would mean Orchid Resorts. They passed the intersection. So the zoo then.

The tree-lined road turned dusty and they saw the ocean glitter not too far ahead. They passed the signs featuring tigers, sharks and cockatoos. Tarrin parked amid a row of cars lined up out front of the tall white walls of the complex. Two amphitheaters draped in blue tarps dominated the area; the resort lay ahead, closer to the water. It was mid- morning, and the place was still fairly empty. But not tranquil. Isaac spotted the two cop cars immediately, brown and white cruisers. And an ambulance, backed up to one of the service entrances to the zoo. A television station's van was parked nearby and a scrum of cameramen and presenters had formed a line just beyond the police.

"What a zoo," Isaac muttered.

"Yes, here zoo," Tarrin said.

"No, I mean...never mind."

"We go lab now," Tarrin said.

"No," Kang said. "We have nothing to fear from the police here, have we, Tarrin? Are we not free men?"

Tarrin either didn't understand Kang's babble or was pretending, but he kept both hands on the steering wheel.

"Come," Kang said, opening his door. "In Hong Kong I go about in public as I like, provided I have the necessary escort. You surely enjoy a similar sense of freedom, Khun Tarrin, given the status you enjoy, as you have conveyed to me."

Tarrin stared into the rearview mirror with utter confusion.

"Move it," Kang barked as he slid out into the hot morning.

The four of them gathered in an incongruous knot. Tarrin locked the Lexus with his remote. Police were starting to crisscross the visitor's entrance in yellow tape.

"Isaac," Kang said, "this is the source of the ketamine, yes?"

"Yes."

"And so there is someone on the inside who sources it for you?"

"Yeah."

"This is the individual Tarrin has been tele-
phoning?"

Isaac shrugged. "His name's Jaidee. He's a
janitor here."

Kang touched his fingers together. "I see. So
this business venture then rests on the shoulders of a peasant illiterate with a mop, bucket,
and privileged access."

"Tarrin and Gordo pay him enough, I guess,"
Isaac ventured.

"And then how does the ketamine reach you?"

"Tarrin or one of his gang. They get it from
Jaidee here, I think, and then take it to the lab.
To be honest, I've only been here a couple of
times before. Twice. Once just as a visitor, and
once when Tarrin and Gordo came by a few days
ago."

The deep lines around Kang's lips twitched.
"So this operation is...rather informal."

"Reckon you could say that."

"Informal and amateur. Well, we'll see to that.
Tarrin's not my only friend in Thailand. Do you
get that, Tarrin?"

Tarrin seemed edgy, his eyes darting from
one policeman to another. More cops had
emerged from inside with paramedics, escorting a stretcher with a blanket covering a body.
They loaded the corpse into the rear of the ambulance. The handful of visitors at this hour
and the hawkers with their little one-man stalls
stared and watched. A man in a blue suit,
presumably representing the resort, conferred

nervously with one cop, a hefty older fellow with a bulging belly.

"Tarrin," Kang said, "where is this Jaidee?"

"Don't know. No answer. This no good. Go lab now."

"No, not yet," Kang replied, walking ahead, the bodyguard at his side. "I want to see what this place is all about."

Another cop emerged from the service entrance, escorting a man in working clothes, hands cuffed behind his back, his head hung low. The line of reporters surged toward the man in custody, stretching out their microphones and tape recorders. Two officers tried to keep the whirlwind of reporters at bay but the throng knocked the suspect to his knees, out of Isaac's view. This just encouraged another eruption of camera lights and flashes.

Kang and the bodyguard closed in on the minor melee, with Tarrin and Isaac several paces behind.

The fat policeman, the one who appeared to be in charge, noticed the two Chinese first, eccentrics who didn't belong there, not at that time.

"Uh, guys," Isaac ventured, but Kang ignored him.

The older cop helped the suspect get to his feet as other officers pushed back the mob of journalists. The handcuffed man's eyes glassed over Kang and the bodyguard, who meant nothing to him, but then he saw Isaac, and he smiled.

"Jaidee," Isaac gasped.

The fat cop noticed the smile and now spotted Isaac and Tarrin. He broke free, handing Jaidee off to a colleague, and waded through the press pack.

He was coming for them.

Tarrin knew he should have gone to see the fortuneteller more recently—like, yesterday. Things had been going well until he got those phone calls. And then Kang had insisted on seeing the operation right away. Another foreigner sticking his nose into Tarrin's affairs.

But as his grip on the situation came loose, Tarrin knew he had no choice but to take Kang to see the zoo and the lab. Narong was dead. That was the first alarming call of the morning. Narong was dead and Trav had emerged from the swamp like a ghost and taken the boat.

He had reassured himself that a direct connection with Kang was the right move, even if it meant lying a little about Trav Mitchell, telling Kang he was still in Narong's possession. Tarrin could sort that out later, no problem.

Seeing Orchid Resorts crawling with police and reporters, though, couldn't be good. Tarrin would have preferred they skip this. It wasn't worth it. He suspected that Kang was using the situation as a test, to see just what Tarrin was made of, what level of privilege he enjoyed on Samui. If only he had consulted the fortuneteller! Then he'd know how to play it.

Instead, Tarrin meekly followed Kang out of the car and walked toward the zoo. It was crazy, a murder scene. The reporters moved in a pack, oblivious of whom or what they crashed into. They were screaming and shouting, and Tarrin could make out only the head of an older policeman and the bowed form of the man under arrest. He recognized Win. Shit. Tarrin knew Win was just tourist police, theoretically a non-threat, but the old man was smart and Bangkok-savvy. Tarrin's spate of crimes had outwitted Win last night, but a dead cop had been found on the ferry, one of Win's. The supreme confidence he had enjoyed this morning driving to the villa crumbled.

The reporters called out the name of the suspect. They wanted him to speak. They wanted him to look at their camera.

"Say something to the people of Samui!"

"Janitor, look this way!"

"How does it feel to be a murder suspect?"

"Did you kill them before you fed them to the tigers?"

What madness!

Then Isaac said, "Jaidee," and Tarrin's stomach twisted and the ground collapsed from beneath his feet and everything spun.

He couldn't believe it. He should have just turned and ran. Gotten in the car, and Kang could go to hell. Jumped back in his Lexus, pumped up Jay-Z's "Show Me What You Got" until he couldn't hear any of those reporters, and burned rubber. Jaidee. The bastard was looking right at him, smiling as Thais do under strain, but also because the janitor seemed to think he was looking at friends.

The cops had Jaidee. It didn't matter for what. Feeding somebody to the tigers? Jaidee was being taken in. The janitor was too stupid to know what to say, what to hide. He was going to spill everything.

Tarrin wasn't worried about going to jail. He had plenty of money and lots of interesting friends, but he knew that the K-Love adventure was over. Maybe Kang didn't know it, but he didn't matter. The big time, taking his syndicate international, was going to have to wait. Cops would find the lab, which would lead them to Isaac and Gordon. Tarrin was protected. Too many layers between him and the physical evidence. Right?

He turned away and headed back to the car. He had seen enough. Time to go somewhere quiet and think. Tarrin walked, careful to maintain his pimp roll, letting his jeans fall halfway down his ass, baseball cap turned smartly to one side. He was still the baddest motherfucker on Samui. He pointed the keychain at the Lexus and opened the locks.

"Tarrin, freeze."

He paused, his fingers almost touching the door handle.

"I'll shoot you," Win said.

"Put that down, old man, it looks too heavy for you."

"You're under arrest."

Tarrin made a face. "Me? For what?"

Win had come closer, and two more police officers were hurrying to catch up. Another had taken hold of Isaac. Several reporters broke from their pack and ran, shoulder-held cameras recording everything. Win said, "Two counts of kidnapping, one of accomplice to murder of a police officer, and too many counts of conspiracy for me to keep track of."

"You're just a tourist cop," Tarrin spat. "You got no authority. And besides, I didn't do any of that stuff."

"Cuff him," Win said, keeping his service revolver trained on Tarrin as another police officer made him spread his hands on the roof of the car.

"He's armed, sir," said the officer, easing Tarrin's Glock from his waistband.

"And one count of illegal possession of a firearm," Win said. "Frisk him."

Tarrin endured having a man pat him down. The cop's fingers dug deeply into Tarrin's pocket. He was about to launch an insult when he remembered what was in there.

The cop held up Mazy's diamond ring.

"I think I recognize that," Win said. "That's evidence. Bag it."

They pulled Tarrin's hands back, one by one. *Snap. Snap.*

"Old man, you can't prove anything."

Win holstered his weapon and pulled a plastic baggie from his utility belt and enclosed the Glock. "I'll bet forensics will have a lot of fun with this. But what I'm really going to enjoy is getting you to explain how you ended up with the *farang*'s ring. Book him for the murder of a police officer."

Tarrin looked around, knowing that this would destroy his credibility in the eyes of the triad. But he was now surrounded by the mob of reporters.

"That's Tarrin!"

"Tarrin, what's your connection to the zoo murders?"

"Did you order Chittilai fed to the tigers?"

The mob sparked Tarrin's frustration. "What are you assholes talking about?" By then Win had dragged him over to a brown and white. They were taking him in. He stared sullenly from the caged rear seat, not believing that this was real. But it was real. He'd get off, of course, but the favors he'd have to call in, the promises he'd have to make, the money he'd have to pay... And the very public nature of this whole thing was going to leave some of the elders around here embarrassed.

"Tarrin!" shouted reporters at him. They were mobbing the sides of the car. "Why'd you do it?"

Win squeezed his plump body into the front passenger seat. A younger cop took the wheel. Win craned his neck and Tarrin met his gaze with sullen hostility.

"Are those two foreigners still alive?"

Tarrin mustered as much bravado as he could. "I think you've gone senile, old timer."

Win sighed. "You're going to jail, Tarrin, but if you cooperate, I'll make sure the judge knows about it. So where are they, the two Americans?"

Tarrin rolled his eyes. "You crazy old buffalo. You think I'm scared of you?"

Win gave him a jaded, patient expression. "All right. The station." The driver put the car into gear. "Let's stop in Lamai for a snack on the way back."

"Yes, sir," said the driver as the cop cruiser slid away from the pack of reporters.

"Old Sopawadee's stand by the market. She makes those glass noodles in oxtail soup."

As Win radioed in his catch, Tarrin saw another cop easing Isaac into the other police cruiser. The car drifted gently down the road, nudging past the press pack, and then sliding past Kang and the bodyguard. The two Chinese were standing in the shade of a tall silk cotton tree. The triad had lit a cigar and was watching Tarrin's departure in studied nonchalance. The bodyguard was touching numbers on his mobile phone. Kang lifted his fedora and granted Tarrin a sardonic bow.

Scenery whizzed by. Tarrin contemplated his ruined ambitions, but even so, something else perplexed him. Something he couldn't put his finger on.

What was the deal with the fucking tigers?

Chapter 41

Six-pack

THE upstairs of the villa was at peace. The sea breeze drove the ceiling fans in lazy loops. Below, the fountains leading to the driveway were still running, adding a soothing hiss to the melody of birdsong and the hush of the wind in the palms. Lek had finished her morning duties and had retreated to the servant's cottage. Gordon sat on one of the balcony loungers overlooking the pool and the beach.

He was anything but at peace. She was down there, in their bedroom. Laughing at him? Dreading what he was going to do to her? He burned to know, to see her.

Kang had been explicit when he left with Isaac and Tarrin. "Leave her till I return," he had said. "For the time being, she is my property. Perhaps I'll give her back to you."

He had left the clown down there to enforce his writ.

Gordon had watched them leave in the Lexus, leaving the stretch limo behind to occupy half the parking lot. Anurak and Lek had disappeared. Gordon had run down to the pool area, seething. *His property? Where the fuck did Kang get off?* But the clown was there, standing like a bloody terracotta warrior, and Gordon decided he had had quite enough of Tai Bak.

Sullen, he had retreated upstairs. Watched the longtail boats go by. Listened to the fucking birds.

He had awoken this morning with a business empire of his own creation. It wasn't even lunch yet, and he had nothing but an ungrateful ex-fiancée down there, in his own room, whom he couldn't even approach; a dead bodyguard; and a chemist who had leapt into bed with the triads. And to add insult to injury, Tarrin had somehow gotten his corrupt little fingers on Travis Mitchell.

Gordon wrestled with his few bad options. Swallow his pride and work for Tai Bak Kang? Never. Just pack it in, head back to Blighty? Maybe. Probably.

He held in his hands the items from his safe. Tai Bak had insisted on seeing them; he too liked order and control. Inside had been the passports for all four of them—Gordon, Mazy, Isaac, Ginger—along with some cash, Hong Kong dollars, sterling, Thai baht. Tai Bak had instructed Gordon to burn Ginger's into a fine ash and scatter the dust into the pool, but he hadn't done it yet. He thumbed through the passport, looked at the stamps, looked at the Scouse's photo. Didn't the big thug look like the type to chop up pros? He shagged enough of them, for fuck's sake. That's what Gordon had told Tarrin as they put the bloodied mattress in the back of a pickup truck.

It took Tarrin's boys till dawn to scrub down the bedroom. The mattress had absorbed most of the blood but her body had contained a surprising amount of it. Well, she wouldn't be around to laugh at a man's inability to get it up. She would not be gossiping with Tarrin's gang about the way Gordon begged her to get him hard, or how he wept when she couldn't. And when she called him a faggot, he had told her if it was anal she wanted why didn't she just ask for it. So he gave it to her. Beat her into submission on the bed and ripped off her necklace. Oblong glass spheres flew everywhere, bounced hard against the floor. One he shoved up her anus, which stirred a hint of wakefulness in his penis, and he was almost able to mount her.

Too bad for her he couldn't.

Ginger, having his fun with Mazy. Isaac in K-Love la-la land. The other girls unconscious. Useless, the lot of them. Tarrin, the only sharp pencil in the box, had already left. Gordon had called him back. Yeah, he had said, Ginger got carried away again.

Tarrin hadn't let him down. It had been Tarrin's suggestion to mutilate the body so it couldn't be identified. He had stayed there past dawn to make sure the mattress was replaced, that the room was spotless.

And now this. Tarrin, the final betrayal. He too was under Mazy's spell, Gordon could tell. The harpie had ruined everything, made a fool of him. The whole bloody business with the phone was what had done it. Brought Tai Bak here. Gotten Tarrin's lot involved. Tipped off the police. Knifed him in the back.

"After everything I've done for you," he said aloud.

That was why he stayed at the villa instead of bolting for the airport. That was why he risked angering Tai Bak.

He heard voices below. Leaning up on his elbows, he saw Mazy at the door of the bedroom, arguing with the clown. This could be interesting. Gordon sprang to his feet and hurried down the sandstone staircase.

"...you know? Beer? *Bejau*?"

"Later," the clown said flatly.

Gordon approached them. Mazy regarded him with suspicion and withdrew inside the doorway. She looked gaunt and haggard, despite having showered and changed into a clean set of T-shirt and cutoff jeans. Gordon couldn't help but let slip a smile. He knew what torment she was going through.

"It's all right," Gordon said to the clown. "Go on up and get her a drink. I'll stay here and make sure she doesn't go anywhere."

The clown shook his head.

"Your orders are clear, then," Gordon said.

"Go away," Mazy said. It came out a whisper.

"Do you want a drink or not?"

"Not from you."

"Hm. We'll see."

Gordon was halfway up the stairs when the clown's mobile chimed to the tune of a Cantopop song. "*Wei?*" Gordon paused to listen. The bodyguard said, "*Hai, hai,*" and a few other words in Chinese. The clown noticed Gordon observing him. In English, he said, "Tai Bak call, I go pick up. Tai Bak say you stay here, no touch girl."

"Of course," Gordon said, locking eyes with Mazy. She seemed distraught and slid shut the glass door and disappeared behind the curtain.

As Gordon returned to the villa's top floor, the clown walked around the side of the villa toward the garage and the awning that partly shaded the limo. Gordon strode to the outer balcony and watched the clown say something into the garage then get into the limo. Anurak came outside to open the gate. The limo required quite a bit of maneuvering, but the clown managed to get it out in one piece. Gordon watched it speed up along the road and hurry through the village like a giant enamel coffin. The car was so white and so massive that it was easy to track as it turned away from the coast. Bits of the limo flashed through the palm and scrub until it had finally driven completely out of view. Then Gordon went to the kitchen and selected a solid chef's knife. The blade was carbon steel and the long handle was a composite of laminated wood and plastic resin. He tested the tip on his thumb: it was blunt and needed sharpening, but it was a good knife.

Whistling "Colonel Bogey's March", Gordon placed the knife in one of the bulky pockets on the side of his shorts. The handle stuck out and he twisted it so he could cover the blade with the pocket's lip and button it fast. When he walked, with his hands at his sides, his knuckles brushed the protruding handle. He tried covering it with his T-shirt but the arrangement was awkward. More natural just to leave it in there. He checked in the upstairs bathroom's mirror. Standing at an angle, the knife wasn't really noticeable if you weren't in a noticing mood.

From the fridge Gordon took a six-pack of Chang tinnies, bound by a set of plastic rings. Still whistling, he went down to their bedroom and knocked politely.

She brushed aside the curtain. "What do you want?" she said through the glass.

Gordon hoisted the beers, arched his eyebrows in suggestion.

"Go away." She left him with nothing but the drapes.

"Maze, I just want to talk. We should talk, don't you think?"

Silence. Stillness.

"I mean, I thought...ha! I thought we were about to be engaged. Get married. Get rich together. Get a little place back in England, maybe near the sea. You love the sea, don't you? Wouldn't that be nice? Have a few little nippers of our own. Isn't that what normal people do when they get married?"

She had been there the whole time. She thrust back the curtain. "There's nothing normal about you, Gordon," she shouted through the glass. "Leave me alone."

"You heard the man. You're under Tai Bak's protection. You have nothing to fear from me." The six-pack swung slightly like a pendulum from his fingers and he noticed her eyes follow it. "I know I owe you an apology, Maze. Several apologies, I reckon. I've been under massive stress lately, yeah? All that's been going on. So close to realizing our dreams. Maybe I haven't been myself. And my methadone treatment. What it does to me. Any bloke would go a little bit mad if he had to deal with what I deal with, Maze. Hear me out. Go on, love, open the door and have a beer. That's it."

She opened the door a crack, and then some more, enough to extend a hand and take hold of a beer can. He let her tug it free of the ring. She lifted the tab and sipped tentatively, her eyes never leaving him. He remained still, his other hand down by his waist, blocking her view of the knife handle. She took another sip, and then a gulp, and her greed for alcohol took over and she downed it.

Chapter 42

Bad Paradise

GORDON watched as Mazy brushed stray beads of beer from her chin and licked them off her hand. She crinkled up the empty tinnie and said to him, "OK."

Gordon followed her into their bedroom. "Bit gloomy, innit." She shrugged, but he didn't turn on the lights. The muted shadows suited him, too.

"Get him out of here," she said, pointing to the bathroom.

"Tarrin's sorted it for tonight, after the sun goes down. One of those longtail fishing boats and two blokes with choppers. Another beer?"

She shook her head. "It'll make me have to pee. And I don't want to go back in there. Let me move to another room."

Gordon walked into the center of the room, beneath the roof's high arch. There was a long L-shaped sofa, a coffee table, a big TV set into the wall. Behind the king-sized bed stood a partial wall, the back of their closets; the bathroom entrance was behind that. "Tai Bak's command. Besides. This room, Maze, has been ours for the past month. Our sanctuary. Our paradise."

"Paradise... where you drugged me and let Ginger rape me?"

"We were all drunk and on drugs, babe, you know that. Come here and let me apologize properly."

"Fuck you."

"Now we're getting somewhere. I should say the same. You spiked my drink, all of our drinks, with far more than I gave you. Nearly killed us, you did. And on the night I had proposed. I fucking love you, and this is how you treat me." He could feel his temper rise. He had to keep her lulled, approach her gradually. That was the way to do it. But something in him, that part of himself that haunted him, wouldn't accept this. It was greedy for the hot glow of release. "You whore around behind my back. Pick up random strangers. Travis bloody Mitchell?"

"He's got nothing to do with this and you know it."

"How many times did you fuck him in Hong Kong, eh, Maze? Think I don't figure these things out?"

"Just get out." She pointed to the exit. "I had nothing to do with him or anybody else, and I still wouldn't if you weren't such a...a ..." Her eyes widened and her hands began to tremble, and he knew she had seen the knife handle sticking out of his cargo pants pocket, and maybe the bulge of the blade outlined against his thigh. She screamed, but she was exhausted and he was fast. Gordon caught her and slapped her face with the back of his hand. The blow unspooled her across the bed. He was on top of her.

"You ungrateful whore."

The knife was now in his grasp. She squirmed and yelled her face purple. He hit her again, adjusted his position atop her. The knife blade licked the edge of her cutoffs, just below the flesh of her rump.

"Better hold still... hold the fuck still or this knife'll carve your cunt into little bloody pieces."

She was still screaming no no no, but he was thinking yes yes oh yes as he wedged the cold tip of steel between her jeans and her bare thigh. He sawed at the denim and severed the strip covering her crotch, exposing her white panties. He couldn't control the pressure once the denim surrendered and he knicked her thigh, eliciting hysterical screaming.

"That's what you get for making a fuss. Now shut it. Stop fucking moving. I'm going to do you and you're going to beg for it."

"No," she sobbed, but her body seized, paralyzed.

Gordon moved more carefully this time, sure she wasn't going to do anything rash so long as he held the blade so closely against her. He lifted her panties and sliced them open. Then he shifted so that the knob of the knife handle touched her vagina and he began to screw it in.

"Hard, innit. The way you like it. I know. I've tried. I've tried to be man enough for you, because I love you, but you have no pity, no compassion, no gratitude. I'm going to love you now, and you're going to fucking cry. Pleasure and pain. Pleasure first. You enjoying that? You like that hard long wood in your cunt? Well, enjoy it while it lasts, love, because after this it's going to be the other end that goes inside."

She was begging him through muffled blubbering, but his other hand had taken hold of one of hers and his fingers were applying a pressure point to the webbing between the thumb and forefinger. Squeezing it just so delivered a white pain that drowned out what was going on down below. If she squirmed she had either this crippling shot of pain or she had the blade. Gordon put his lips near her upturned ear. "Tell me how much you love me."

She whimpered something.

"Say it loud and clear."

"I love you."

"You want me to do you."

"Please...let me go."

"You want me to do you." He withdrew the knife handle from inside her and deliberately drew a fine red line across her thigh. She scrambled wildly, but he pinched her hand and she begged him to let go. "You want me to do you."

"Do me," she gasped, "I want you to do me."

He pointed the knife's tip. "I'm going to fucking do you." Outside there was a mechanical scream. The curtains rose up like the billowing cape of the devil and the air exploded in glass and shrieked in flame.

Chapter 43

Speedboat

TRAV had left Narong and the youth with the shattered face. He could have lain on that pier forever catching his breath. But it wasn't just the terror of seeing the crocs get at Narong's corpse. And it wasn't the dawning of hunger, or the beginning pangs of pain from the previous night's abuse. It was the sense that if he was going to find Mazy, he probably didn't have much time. He assumed she was dead, but if there was a chance—

Anyway, the awful mangrove was short on charm and comfort, and long on mosquitoes and crocodiles. He stumbled down the zig-zagging pier, wondering how long it would take to get out of there, his blown-away ear filling his head with an incessant buzzing.

And then the mangrove opened and he was walking along a pier into open sea. The speedboat was moored there. The chubby pilot was inside, enjoying the shade, with headphones covering his ears. He was nodding along to a song. He looked up as Trav's shadow crossed his face. Trav must have looked like a ghost; he certainly felt like a walking cadaver. The man leapt up but the headphones were plugged into a CD player embedded in the console and they yanked him back before the cord popped out. Thai country music flooded the cabin.

Trav jumped into the boat, punched him once and threw him into the rear. The pilot scrambled out of the boat, onto the pier. He was unarmed and held up his hands in supplication. Trav checked to see the keys were still in the boat's ignition. He saw also that his backpack and Mazy's bag were still inside. There was a GPS on the console, too. Enough.

He untied the boat from the pier. The pilot had scrambled back and watched helplessly as the ghost calmly took his boat. The pilot touched his jaw and winced. Trav freed the boat, pulled in the ropes, fastened them in place. He pushed the boat off the pier with his hands. It bobbed uncertainly. The water here was more ocean than mangrove. Trav started the boat. He had only a little experience with these things— from the days when he and Kar-wei would take Kar-wei's speedboat out, a little something Kar-wei had spent his bonus money on. Lift some girls the night before in Privée or Beijing Club, take them out on Kar-wei's Pussy Express, as he privately called it, and jolly around Sai Kung or southern Lantau. Somewhere get 'stranded', one take his girl onto the forward deck, the other try the little cushioned seats around the table, and...

Another life. An irrelevance. But Trav had handled the controls from time to time. He tried the speedboat's throttle. It was stiff, and as he tried to figure it out, he realized he was going backwards. He nearly crashed into mangrove before he wheeled the thing around. Even then, it was disorienting; going backwards, the steering wheel went in the opposite direction of where he wanted to go. He banged the side of the boat into the pier, shaking it.

The pilot, a mobile phone in hand, ran down the pier into the dank tangle. *Maybe I should have killed him, too.* But it wasn't a thought he relished. He hadn't had time to internalize it, think it through. It had been kill or be killed. It was too raw. But he knew that, no matter how justified, he wasn't a killer. Porn Star was going to haunt him.

Reflection would have to wait. Trav figured out how to shift the throttle to get the boat powered in the right direction. He looked at the gauges. Fuel looked OK. The others he didn't know much about.

Then he had to figure out where the hell he was. He turned on the GPS and spent a while trying to make sure he understood. He still wasn't sure; reading a boat GPS wasn't like a car's. He didn't have a robotic female voice advising him of a left-hand turn half a mile ahead. Everything was in Thai script. If he interpreted the curves correctly, however, he wasn't far from the southern coast of Koh Samui.

Trav wondered how long he had been out. Clock said it was about 10:45 in the morning. For a while, then. He had a sense they had taken Mazy while it had still been dark.

There was a first-aid kit and he took a few minutes in the little bathroom to examine his chin, to feel the bump on the back of his skull, and then, last of all, the ear. He didn't want to look at it but he had to. Half his face and neck was caked in blood; all of him was layered in mud. He cleaned himself up as best he could and looked again. The chin cut was nasty but not immediately fatal. The ear... He sucked in his breath and forced himself to prod with his fingers. The pain was incredible. There was just a hole there, a black nothing amid the filth. The buzzing in his head wasn't abating.

He tried a little humor. *Just got the cast off, right buddy? And now straight back to the doc. Hey doc, remember what you told me about getting into fights? Well, you're not going to believe this one.*

Hmmm.

Well, partner, it sure goes with that crooked nose of yours.

Might be funny later. Like in a couple of years from now.

One last thing before going: he was starving. He ransacked the cabin. There was a fridge with water, sodas, beers and little hotel room-sized bottles of whisky. He figured he'd save the booze for Mazy, if he ever found her, and downed the water. There were some chips and candy bars; he devoured them. The snack left him even more hungry, if that were possible, but he felt the sugar rush. That was it: time to drive.

The pilot had a set of wraparound shades suspended above the console. Trav wore them. They rested in a slant, one side loose because there was no ear for the stem to catch. But that was a mighty fierce sun, and the heaving water reflected it with glee.

Trav pointed to open water and pushed the throttle. It was an ornery stick. He had to push a button inside the grip to unlock its motion. The button sometimes cooperated, sometimes didn't. And the waves. This was really open water. Cruising around Sai Kung's calm bay hadn't prepared him for proper ocean. The waves were big and hard. He vaguely recollected getting bounced around the back of the boat last night. Another century ago, he'd have thought, but his body's aches suggested otherwise.

He wasn't good on the water. He didn't know if he should take the waves head on or go alongside. Hit the throttle as they struck, or relax? As he rounded the edge of the little island where Narong had maintained their hideaway, the seas got more aggressive, and he spun out. Nearly capsized the boat. Jesus, this was scary. He knew he wasn't thinking straight. *Just cool it, bud.* But he couldn't. He needed to go. He needed speed.

What he believed to be Samui appeared on the horizon. The GPS seemed to confirm this. At least the lines on it conformed to his assumptions...or maybe his hopes.

Trav considered going straight to Nathon. Find Win, tell him about the murder of Officer Suan, the kidnapping, that Mazy was missing. But then he began to wonder why these men had been so relaxed about murdering a policeman. Why they had been able to catch him and Mazy with such ease. Trav still believed Win was on the up and up, but maybe his colleagues were not. No, the cops weren't going to be of much help. The only one who might know where to find Mazy was Gordon.

Trav hardened his soul as he bumped and banged his way toward the approaching landmass. Maybe in this condition, he was no match for Gordon. But he was willing to find out. He was ready to do whatever it took. He'd killed a man today to save his own life. He was ready to do it again if it would save Mazy's.

The closer he drew to the land, the more convinced he was that it was, indeed, Samui. He could make out features that he recognized from previous excursions on Montri's longtail boat.

The channel between Koh Samui and Koh Tan was busy with similar tours and a few commercial fishing trawlers. He had to slow down just to make sure he didn't crash. He had a close call with another speedboat that seemed to come out of nowhere, and the throttle jammed and Trav's boat spun around in two complete circles.

It was all he could do to keep it from spilling over, and was probably saved more by the luck of the waves than his own effort. The other boat circled around to check on him. Trav waved that everything was OK. He gave an apologetic *wai*. He didn't know what else to do; there wasn't any time. He gunned it for the looming coast.

Yes, that was it. He was coming at the village at a hard angle. Along this stretch of beach, the villa was the tallest structure. It stood slightly apart from the cozy camaraderie of the village's cluster of beachfront restaurants and piers. The roof of the villa's main structure was a vast, handsome brown quadrangle, fronted by minia- ture copies covering the lower bedrooms and the sala. As he drew closer he could see right through the open top floor, at the greenery of the forest on the villa's landward side. From here it would have been difficult to make out people, unless they were standing on the beach or along the compound's edge, but there were none.

He knew the channel here was going to be shallow, but he wasn't sure just how shallow. During the evenings, at low tide, he could walk far out, maybe a quarter of a mile, with the water no higher than his thighs. During the mornings, the tide was high and the waters ran swiftly.

Boats came and went, often moored just a few feet from the beach, and he wondered if he was driving a flat-bottomed craft. Maybe—he had seen similar boats along the coast. There was also a trench dredged from the center of the village out to the channel, to allow boats ingress and egress at all times of day. Perhaps best to try the trench. Park in the village, walk over?

But the villa was gated and probably guarded. The only way in was from the beach. There was a longtail boat not far from the villa's front, tethered on a long rope to the eager bow of a palm tree. It couldn't be that deep.

Why not just go in? The sooner the better. And if nobody was home, well, he could consider popping back into the boat, maybe try his luck in Nathon.

His heart racing, his destination now at hand, Trav nudged the throttle forward. He was impatient. His mind raced with the unimaginable. Mazy. He said her name aloud: "Mazy." It was a mantra. He breathed her name, each exhale to convey it from his lips. He'd cut the speed when he drew even with the dredged channel. He reached that point. The throttle jammed.

Panicking, he jammed the trigger. It cut back, but he was now racing over the shallows and the villa rose hugely in his view. Trav pulled the throttle back, way back, too much. The boat spun out again. He wrestled with the wheel. The window was filled with bright blue, bursting fingers of silver, bright everything, then the verdant darkness of forest. He had reduced the speed but not cut the speed and the spinout had taken him straight there. He was still going.

He cut the speed entirely, pulling the throttle back all the way, the nose of his boat approaching the few stairs connecting the beach to the compound like an open smile. He braked but it was too late, and he knew it. He was screaming in terror, utter terror the likes of which he had never known, not even when he thought Narong was going to drown him, because then he had been fighting, concentrating, he had been trained for that. Not for this, not for crashing the boat onto the beach, hitting the stairs at an angle.

A terrific thump and spinning lights and a crump so loud it blotted out the buzzing in his head. Airborne for a glorious second before hitting the infinity pool, but that wasn't the landing, that was more like a trampoline, a stone skipping along the surface of the sea. By this time Trav had no idea what had happened; he wasn't in control, he wasn't a witness; there was only the paroxysm of insentient horror as the boat sailed into the roof of the master bedroom.

Chapter 44

Revenge

IT was the coughing that brought her back to awareness, but not to understanding. One minute she had been on the bed with Gordon on top of her. That was then. Now she was lying on her back on the floor, thrown against the wall by the television, staring up at bright blue sky through an enormous tear. Above her dangled slats of wood, ready to follow the cloud of glass and rain down. The walls were gone, save for a few bent steel bars; the furthest one still clung to a fold of curtain, which billowed in the surprising sea breeze. Gordon lay nearby on his side, his skin embossed with a hundred tiny gems of silently sparkling glass.

And behind her, where the false wall in back of the bed had stood—the closets were back there, and the entrance to the bathroom—there was a speedboat, its canopy smashed, its white fiberglass charred and cracked. The rear wall was partly collapsed, showing the bathroom and the stretch of pool water that ran between it and the villa's outer wall—the only structure apparently intact.

She blinked and coughed. Dark black smoke was rising from beneath the boat. Its engine was going to catch fire. Or maybe it already had. She couldn't tell. She couldn't hear a thing.

Mazy tried moving, just her hands and feet to start with. They seemed OK. She should have been more careful as she got to her knees and palms, because the ground was a moonscape of debris that bit. She realized she was bleeding all over and had to repress the urge to scream. Breathing was the most important thing.

Her muscles were wobbly and when she raised her head, everything wheeled into a flickering spin. She touched her head, felt dampness and dull pain, but her fingers didn't identify any kind of significant wound.

Sound popped back into one ear, a male Thai voice, calmly berating her, cutting sonorously through the crackling of fire. She couldn't believe it. In her woozy state it was as though God were Thai and he was urging her on to something incomprehensible.

Mazy looked around for her shoes but, amid the wreckage, couldn't make out a thing.

Gordon moaned and rolled over. He looked bad, and he coughed some blood. But he was alive and his eyes were open, casting about for something to recognize.

Mazy wanted to get out of there, she knew that much, but moving seemed so difficult, so clumsy, and fraught with danger. The stun of the extraordinary still fogged her senses, but a narrative began to take shape. This boat had sailed into the bedroom. Gordon had been on top, about to put the knife into her. That may have saved her life, judging by the look of him.

The boat—there was motion. A hand. Then another. "Trav!" She thought she called his name. It came out muffled. He appeared in the aft of the boat, carrying, of all things, his backpack.

He saw her. He looked like something out of a zombie movie. Half the skin on his face seemed to have turned a slick raw color. His clothes had been reduced to scraps. The cut on his chin pulsed purple. He stumbled and toppled out of the boat.

"Trav!"

She moved toward him, heedless of the way the ground sought to cut her up, ignoring the intonations of the disembodied Thai voice, but something grabbed her ankle. She thought she had twisted it but no, she realized as she flopped onto her belly, it was Gordon's hand. She looked over her shoulder at his blazing eyes. She kicked herself free and he seemed unable to pursue. She scrambled to Trav and, cupping his upturned face, kissed him as fiercely as she dared.

"That hurts," he said.

"Oh my God, Trav."

"But I liked it."

"I promise I'll keep doing it if we get out of here."

"If," he said. "I think I crashed the boat."

"You sure did."

"Some rescue, hunh?" He laughed but had to stop because it wracked him in pain.

"Oh, Trav," she said, blinking back tears. "My stupid cowboy."

"This is all very touching," Gordon said behind them, slowly rising to his hands and knees. "It's really quite...reassuring to know that you have ...come back, Travis Mitchell." He was now more or less standing. "Tourist in bloody paradise. Sticking your nose where it don't belong, taking what isn't yours."

"You fucking monster, get away from us!" Mazy screamed.

Gordon drew himself erect. His entire body was covered in twinkling glass. He was a walking bleed, and he could only shuffle his feet, but approach he did. "You've thrown your life away for this worthless bird. A nice piece of tail, I'll grant you that. But a more dishonest, treacherous, hateful cunt you'll never meet."

Trav managed to say, "It's over...get lost..."

"Just leave us alone!" Mazy shouted.

Gordon kept coming. "It's over. Oh, I see, Trav, thank you for filling me in. Missing details. You've won the girl, you've destroyed my villa. Well done." He was only a few feet away now. Trav's own leg lay bent the wrong way and Mazy realized he may have broken some ribs as well. She scanned the floor desperately.

Trav's ravaged face looked strangely calm. "She's too good for you," he said to Gordon even as she pulled herself away.

"That so, Trav? You know all about her, eh? You know this slut's lying, cheating ways by heart now? Look, she's just abandoned you. Let me tell you something, you cunting little fuck, you know fuck all about her. I bet you don't even know her bleeding name." Trav's quizzical expression caused Gordon to giggle. "Look, there she goes, crawling like a baby to get away from you. She knows you can't help her now, not lying there all broke like. One minute it's all, 'Oh Trav, darling,' and now she's back to saving her own skin. Treacherous cow." Gordon now loomed directly over Trav's prone body. "So tell me, Trav, what's her name?"

"Mazy."

Gordon giggled again. Drops of his blood sprinkled Trav's torso. "That's not her real name, mate. You've basically just killed yourself over a girl and you don't know her real name. That's kind of pathetic."

She was scrambling away from them as fast as the savage ground and her smarting skin would allow. Gordon knelt beside Trav, who surprised him by hitting him with the backpack, knocking him back on his rear. The effort had taken everything out of Trav, though, and he collapsed.

"Her name," Gordon said as he knelt beside Trav, "is taken from a rapist foster parent from Twatsberg, U.S.A." He seized the backpack and sent it skidding through the smoke into the bathroom. "Which is why she hates to be called Esther—"

Trav took hold of Gordon's throat. It was slippery in his grasp, but Gordon choked, his own hands reaching for the attacking arm. Gordon put one hand on Trav's face and began to steadily pry his neck free. Trav cried as Gordon bent his arm back.

"A fighter to the end. That's perhaps the only thing I like about you, Trav." Gordon twisted and Trav screamed, his torso heaving as Gordon snapped his wrist. "But you know, I'm really going to enjoy this." He raised his other hand in a fist—then his entire body froze; he quivered; his mouth opened and a thick roll of blood and spit flowed down his chin.

Mazy, grunting, twisted the knife between Gordon's shoulder blades. Gordon's body sagged and she lost her grip as he rolled over into a jerking heap.

"Come on, cowboy," Mazy said. "I have to pick you up. Can you get up, baby? Come on. Come with me."

Trav didn't respond. She somehow dragged him up, lighter than she had expected. He was a bundle of weakness, a solid man no longer. His head lolling in her arms. More smoke was rushing from beneath the wrecked boat and she could feel heat coming from there.

"Who's talking," he mumbled.

"Just that Thai man on the loudspeakers. Come on, help me, baby."

"The bag," he gasped. "The money."

She carried him toward the pool, his dying words buzzing in her ears. It was slow going because of the glass and debris. She thought she saw the canary fabric of her sneakers, blown across the sandstone patio by the force of the boat's entrance. Beyond them, on the beach, villagers had gathered to see what had become of the crashing speedboat. But they were reluctant to walk up the steps onto the compound.

"Somebody call an ambulance," she shouted at them. "Help us, please help us." She lay him down on a patch of grass. "Hang on." Mazy hobbled over to her sneakers and put them on. The cuts in her feet burned, but wearing shoes amid the wreckage of the villa was better than remaining barefoot.

On the beach, more people had gathered— kids, teenagers, all gawking. And all Thais. Didn't anyone understand "help"?

Mazy reached Trav and said, "Cowboy, this is gonna hurt." He cried out when she sat him up. "I'm sorry, baby," she said, "but you gotta do this." Somehow she got him to cross to the relative safety of the *sala* on the other side of the pool just as the speedboat's engine exploded. A column of smoke and debris shot upwards. Ash and small bits of everything rained onto the pool, plopping and pinging like hailstones. Flotsam rained on the roof of the *sala*. The villagers tentatively moving toward the pool scattered back to the beach.

"You're going to be OK," she said. *Please be OK.*

An agonized moan was the best he could do.

"You're going to be fine, damn it. We just have to get you to a hospital, OK? Stay here, I'm going to get the phone."

As she got up, she saw Anurak and Lek standing at the top of the staircase, staring in amazed terror. Beneath them, floating down the sandstone steps, was Kang, trailed by his two bodyguards. Kang paused to regard the scene.

"Bravo," he said, clapping. "I am indeed impressed. Travis Mitchell, you continue to wreak destruction and death wherever you tread."

"Leave us alone," Mazy snarled.

Kang ignored her and wafted past.

"Don't touch him!" she screamed, but the bodyguards had each taken her by the arm and she was out of strength. Her knees surrendered and she crumpled in their grip. "He's hurt bad. He needs an ambulance."

Kang walked to where Trav lay. "Yes, I can see that."

The bodyguards half-dragged her to stand behind the triad boss. "I came here to avenge the murder of my third son," Kang said. "To cleanse the earth of a man with no integrity or honor. A man who humiliated me, out of malice or stupidity."

"Leave him alone, Kang," Mazy implored. "Look around you. Look at those people." The neighbors had grown in number and two men were now walking from the beach to the edge of the compound. "You're going to kill him in front of the whole village?"

Kang didn't bother to acknowledge the villagers. "There are some decisions that are not about our petty wants and whims. There are matters of law and justice that must be obeyed. Your lover killed my son. Betrayed me, embarrassed me. I have no choice." He studied her for the first time. "I had the impression, from all the fuss, that you were Helen of Troy incarnate. I had half a mind to stick you in a Macau brothel. But honestly, I can't see it."

"He's suffering, Kang, can't you see that? Look at him. Please, don't kill him."

Kang smiled. "As you wish. No point in beating this rather dead horse."

The bodyguards let Mazy wriggle free and she prostrated herself across Trav's body. "Trav, Trav..."

"Yes, he's quite dead already," Kang said. "And as you say, with half of these coconut farmers joining our merry festival, I suppose I won't put you out of your misery, Miss..." He paused to retrieve a booklet from the pocket of his silk gown. "...Esther Parr." He flicked it at her. It banged off her cheek and fell to the ground. Her passport.

"Ms. Parr, as much as I would enjoy leasing that body of yours for a dozen paid screws a night, I do not wish to make a scene. If there's one thing I can't stand, it is making a scene, which is the resort of the mawkish and the crass. And we seem to have attracted an audience. I suggest you avoid Hong Kong forever more, lest it cost you your life."

The three Chinese men walked back to the villa's top floor as a cluster of village men and women surrounded her, chatting in concern, throwing in a few words of English. One tried to pull her to her feet, but Mazy slapped the hands away. She hovered over Trav and wept. In stillness, the slash of his crooked nose gave his face a sense of motion, but he didn't react when teardrops touched his burned cheeks. Not even a flicker.

"Told you to stay away from me, cowboy," she whispered.

Glancing over her shoulder, she saw the master bedroom's remains blown to hell, the crust of the boat blackened and billowing smoke. Behind it, however, the bathroom and shower area appeared intact. She couldn't see Gordon from here. Somehow she didn't quite believe that he was dead.

And then Mazy heard the wailing of sirens above the steady sermon of the loudspeakers. It was time.

She got to her feet. The villagers were scurrying up and down the villa steps, Anukrak and Lek calling back and forth, but there was nothing they could do about the smoldering boat in the ruined bedroom. Mazy brushed past the villagers and plunged into the smoke, unable to keep it from burning her eyes. The heat inside the ruins was still intense. It occurred to her that the boat might have more fuel ready to explode. But she wasn't leaving without the money.

The ocean breeze was already thinning the oily smoke, but even so she had to slow down. The cuts on her feet reminded her of their presence with each step. Gordon was still on the floor, limbs at strange angles, his skin blackened from the explosion. He wouldn't have been recognizable without the knife sticking out from between his crisped shoulder blades. Mazy moved between Gordon and the burning shell of the boat, toward the bathroom, and there was Ginger, grinning demonically, and she couldn't help but scream.

His monstrous form remained seated in the bathtub, untouched by the crashing boat but unable to escape the leaping flames; his hair was burning and his eyes had melted out of their sockets. The skin had fallen away around his face, leaving the ghoulish smile, like a parting gift.

The backpack had survived the explosion, lodged beneath the big plaster tub.

Mazy tugged it free and ran. The villagers standing around Trav's corpse called to her but no one would stop her. She barreled through the crowd of gawkers on the beach. Too many people. She bolted off to the right, away from the restaurant and Trav's shack.

She ran until the pain in her feet was too much. No one had followed. She veered into a wooded area, hoping to quietly slip back to the refuge. She was tripping through mud and brush when she stumbled across the backside of a water buffalo, enormous this close up. She didn't have to muster a sprint, instinct took care of that. The buffalo was tethered to a tree via a hook in its nose, which yanked it hard before it could trample the intruder. Its angry snorts filled her ears as she made it to a desolate gravel path. Civilization at last.

It took some patience, some waiting around, but shortly after nightfall Mazy returned to the shack hidden among the trees. The firemen and police had long since come and gone from the villa next door. Its high wall brooded like a mausoleum, but Trav's little shack was not lifeless. The dog greeted Mazy with a tail wag and an eager wet nose, and if the stray had any questions about the previous master of the house, she kept them to herself.

Chapter 45

Chicks and Buffaloes

MAJOR Win Arpornakun of the Tourist Police accepted the offer of Siri, the Provincial Police colonel, for a drink after work the next day.

Win leaned against the bar at a Nathon karaoke joint, under the red neon lights advertising Singha and Lady Song, as another off-duty officer crooned his way through a country tune. The colonel preferred to sit on a barstool but Win's backside was tormenting him, as usual.

"You did a fine job, Win."

"I appreciate it, sir, but it was mostly luck. In fact we might have prevented some of the killings if it weren't for the incident at the zoo. That's what I thought at first, because the units I had to divert were those closest."

"The ones heading for the villa."

"Yes. But then it turned out that the zoo tied everything together."

"This janitor, he was the fulcrum."

"More a cog, I'd say, sir. Just a temple dog. He went crazy when he saw the heavenly flower he fancied with that zookeeper."

"The girl, Nongmook, and Chittilai."

"Yes. After he attacked Chittilai and the girl, they drank his water, but it was actually an animal tranquillizer. It takes about 200 milliliters of that stuff to sedate a Bengal tiger. Imagine what drinking that pure stuff would do to a human."

The colonel began to peel the label off his bottle. "Did it kill them outright?"

"The mortician said the girl was dead within minutes, but Chittilai, well, he was a big man, tough." Win paused. Nongmook had come from a village near Surat Thani. Informing her parents had been a bad piece of business.

"So the janitor fed him to the tigers alive?"

"Apparently. We can't quite tell from the videos. The thing is, Colonel, we didn't know the janitor was stealing the drugs. The zookeepers shot one of the tigers with a ketamine bolt. We think it might have been one of the bottles that had been replaced with water. We're not sure but it didn't stop the tiger. All we know is the tiger got so much ketamine from eating the people, later he just keeled over. But that was several minutes after they shot him. It was as they were checking the ketamine—because they needed another round—that the staff noticed something was fishy with the way the bottles were arranged."

"Incredible. This used to be a peaceful island, you know. Not like Bangkok."

"We haven't finished with the cows, and here come the buffaloes. As we were questioning the janitor, he just spilled it all out, about stealing the drugs for this operation. And, of course, I had just heard the same story the night before from those foreigners, but they had talked about Tarrin and Gordon Wood and a lab in the hills. The woman had mentioned the janitor and the zoo, but I hadn't been paying proper attention."

"The woman, the one eaten by the tiger?"

"No, the American one, the girlfriend. You should have seen her, Colonel."

"Not one of these fat, ugly Western girls?"

"No, sir. Like a chick seducing a croc."

The colonel closed his eyes and murmured in approval.

"So who shows up? Tarrin and the black foreigner, the one who blends the ketamine into this new rape drug. And they were with the Chinese gangster, Kang."

"You didn't arrest him?"

"We didn't have a charge. Tarrin was wanted for murder, and we had the janitor's testimony about giving Tarrin drugs. We knew there was a connection to Gordon, but it was Isaac's presence that gave us probable cause. Then we found the American girl's ring on Tarrin's person. It's a match with the American girl's ring from our police file. We've got him on kidnapping and for killing Officer Suan."

"What about Kang?"

"Too many steps removed."

The colonel finished his beer. "You're right. It's not unusual for those triads to come to Thailand. They have powerful friends."

"But I think we got the one killing the girls."

"I thought the girl was missing."

"Not the American girl—the Thai girls. The prostitutes."

"That's good. Can't have bodies washing up and frightening tourists."

"I think it's good because at least two Thai women were murdered."

"Of course, of course."

"We found a mattress at the drug lab, stained everywhere with blood. Tarrin says Gordon did it when he had trouble, you know, performing. I wish we had the resources to run blood samples here, to be sure, but I showed the foreigners' passport photos to the mama-san who ran the bar where the girl worked. She ID'd Collins, said he'd been the one who bought out a couple of girls that night."

Siri didn't seem very interested in this part. "But what about Kang?"

"Nothing solid. The girl's testimony, Mazy, that's it. Isaac is cooperating, but he had nothing specific, just circumstantial. Gordon was the only real link to Kang but he's dead."

Win paused, remembering this morning's interrogation of the chemist. Isaac had begged them not to throw him in jail. He explained everything he knew, which as far as the drug lab went, was plenty. Win would note the cooperation when it came time for a trial, but he had told Isaac in plain terms that there were probably twenty years in a Thai cell ahead of him. Isaac had wept, but Win remembered those teenagers slaving in the lab's fetid heat, breathing piss and chemicals through every naked pore. Village children. He didn't feel an ounce of pity for Isaac.

"Well, get Mazy to testify," said the colonel.

"That's the problem, sir. We don't know where she is."

"These people blow up a villa and create all sorts of mayhem, killing one another, and you don't know where she is?"

"Her face is everywhere. At immigration, at the ports, with all the hotels, the airport. We don't have her real name. When I took her in, she had no identification. The name she gave us was false. The other American, Trav, was the only one with a passport."

"Another dead foreign buffalo on my island."

"Yes." Win shifted his weight to the other leg. "Her name was Darunee."

"I thought you said we didn't know her real name."

"I mean the murdered Thai girl. She was from Isaan, been on the island maybe six months. I thought you'd want to know that she had a name. Darunee."

The colonel shrugged. "Girls like her go missing in Bangkok every week."

Win nodded. He had dealt with plenty of vulnerable children and young adults, kids with no future and not much of a past. For a time, he had fought against the police force's general indifference; nothing angered him more. Win wanted to tell Siri he was a mediocre asshole but knew what would come of it, and he was too near to his pension—the sort of thing that a young firebrand could ignore, but not an old vet.

"So what about the dead American?" Siri asked. "Didn't he know the girl's name?"

"He barely knew her, just called her Mazy. Didn't even know her last name when I asked him for it." Win signaled the bartender for the bill. He wanted to go home to his wife and get some sleep. But he admitted to being stumped. He recalled the young woman in his office, her knock-out beauty, the way she had made even him catch his breath. "She could have been any-body," he said. "Imagine, a girl like that."

It took her a day and a half to leave. She had meant to stay longer and recover, but the old man, Montri, hadn't liked her staying at the house. She made up a story about Trav being out for the day, but the locals were on edge af-ter seeing what had happened at the villa. The management of the villa hadn't been too happy, either. It was probably best to sneak out be-fore Montri started asking questions. She knew Trav had liked the old man, though, so she left a thousand-baht note on the pillow, walked a mile or two down the road, and hitched a ride with a couple of construction workers in a pickup.

Her first stop was Chaweng, the only town big enough to get lost in. She needed more than grooming. She needed a makeover. A real change.

The options at the airport were limited, but there were no limits in Thailand on moving around, not with the sort of currency she was in possession of, so she picked the next flight to Bangkok and paid in cash. She figured she could make a proper choice from there. But she was thinking India or Sri Lanka. Get her yoga back up to scratch, live cheap, and then...who knew? With Trav's money, maybe she could find a nice spot back home and open her own yoga studio. Something near the water. Santa Barbara, or maybe Venice Beach. Yeah, that sounded good.

She allowed herself one luxury. She was still sore and didn't want to get cramped into economy. So she made it business—'Royal Silk' class—at least to Bangkok.

The Thai Airways flight attendants noticed her, sure. They privately gaped and gossiped about the stunning *farang* with the long legs and the ultra-short, platinum blonde hair, who never removed her big black sunglasses. She could have been a movie star, although the lacerations that covered her arms, thighs and face were certainly strange.

The other strange thing about the glamorous passenger was that her only possession seemed to be a filthy backpack. Not even a smart purse.

Later, the stewardess serving in business class would Google the name from the manifest, but nothing would come up.

When the plane lifted from Samui International, all of the passengers with a window seat stared wistfully at the receding tropical paradise, trying to hold on to their holiday as long as possible. Everyone except for the blonde woman, who stared straight ahead with a stony resolution, eyes hidden behind her shades and her thoughts veiled with them.

Once the plane assumed its cruising altitude, the stewardess brought her a tray bristling with drinks.

"Good day, Miss Esther," she said, having practiced all of the business-class passenger names. "Can I get a drink for you? We have Champagne, beer, wine and spirits."

The passenger hesitated.

"I think I'll just have an orange juice."

Go here to be the first to know about new thrillers, crime stories, and mysteries coming from Water Street Crime.

mailchi.mp/waterstreetpressbooks.com/ waterstreetcrimemailinglist

Get the Water Street Crime Starter Library
FOR FREE

Get four, full-length ebooks—***BLOODY PARADISE***, ***FROM ICE TO ASHES***, ***TROPICAL ICE***, and ***SING FOR THE DEAD***—plus two introductory short stories by the author of ***STAINED FORTUNE*** and lots more exclusive content, all for free!

Building a relationship with our readers is the very best thing about publishing.
We occasionally send newsletters with details on new releases, special offers and other bits of news relating to Water Street Press.

And if you sign up to the mailing list we'll send you all this free stuff:

1. A free ebook edition of the exotic thriller ***BLOODY PARADISE***—"...a spicy thriller..."

2. A free ebook edition of the crime thriller ***FROM ICE TO ASHES***—"designed to shoot the ice down your spine..."

3. A free ebook edition of the eco-thriller ***TROPICAL ICE***—"...well-spun, tautly written..."

4. A free ebook edition of the delightfully noir-ish mystery ***SING FOR THE DEAD***—Foreword Reviews' Gold Medal winner

5. A free copy of two introductory short stores from the author of **STAINED FORTUNE**—stories from the childhoods of two his most intriguing characters, Alvaro and Pablo.

6. Advance notice about the release of new Water Street Crime novels.

You can get all this and more,
for free, just by signing up at

**mailchi.mp/waterstreetpressbooks.com/
waterstreetcrimemailinglist**

Did you enjoy this book? You can make a big difference for our amazing Water Street Crime authors.

Reviews are the most powerful tools in our arsenal when it comes getting attention for our books. Much as we'd like to, we don't have the financial muscle of a New York publisher. We can't take out full-page ads in the newspaper or put posters on the subway.

(Not yet, anyway).

But we do have something much more powerful and effective than that, and it's something that those publishers would kill to get their hands on.

A committed and loyal bunch of readers.

Honest reviews of our books help bring them to the attention of other readers.

If you've enjoyed this book we would be very grateful if you could spend just five minutes on Amazon or the online vendor of your choice leaving a review (it can be as short as you like).

Thank you very much.

About the Author

JAME DiBiasio is author of the thrillers *Gai-jin Cowgirl* (Crime Wave Press), as well as the non-fiction *The Story of Angkor* (Silkworm Books). He is an award-winning financial journalist and founding editor of *AsianInvestor*. He can be found on Facebook, Twitter, and Instagram.

ALSO FROM WATER STREET PRESS

Ready for more thrills?

We suggest **Stained Fortune**, by Joe Calderwood, the first in his Clint Kennedy Crime Series.

THE CLINT KENNEDY CRIME SERIES, #1

JOE CALDERWOOD

STAINED FORTUNE

"...GREED, MONEY, DRUGS... AN ENGROSSING THRILLER..."

Have you read all the books in the Water Street Crime collection? Check out Water Street Press at this link and see all the amazing books we have to offer:

www.waterstreetpressbooks.com

Stained Fortune

Enjoy this excerpt from STAINED FORTUNE, *the first book in the* CLINT KENNEDY CRIME SERIES *by* JOE CALDERWOOD.

Chapter 1

I had not planned on ending up back in jail. But when the rewards are great, the risks are often greater.

I remembered how it felt the first time I'd entered jail, the edge of fear that seemed to jab at my nerve endings like the tip of a knife—a sensation I did not find completely unpleasant. Ambition had landed me here, certainly, but I couldn't discount that the nearly carnal satisfaction of an adrenaline rush didn't have something to do with how high I was willing to aim, or how far I'd go to meet my goals.

The other inmates—six in the cell of the Mexican jail I was led to—were hard-pressed to contain their desire to pounce on me as I took my seat among them on the cold, damp concrete floor. Child molesters, rapists, robbers, murderers, assorted minor scam artists—my new compatriots, their hair gelled to porcupine points at the top of their heads, dusty feet in battered flip-flops, dark and shining eyes assessing me.

The prison housed hundreds in cramped cells like this, dungeons with a toilet as the feature at the center of the room, a dank, brown liquid coagulated at its base and a metal seat for seven or more prisoners to use—no privacy and no toilet paper. Weeds sprouted from the cracks in the concrete floor, and the small, damp room smelled of body odor and spent bodily fluids. It was clear the toilet didn't get a lot of use; the inmates pissed wherever they stood.

Pedro, Luis, Gustavo, Manuel, Jose, Carlos—I was the only one with white skin among the mix of Spanish, Mayan, and Mexican prisoners. Most spoke Spanish, or Mayan, with only a spattering of English among them, but I spoke enough Spanish to make myself understood, and to understand that their conversation was about me, and irreverent.

Fortunately for me, Mexico—unlike America in these early years of the new century—was still an aspirational country. My new prison friends appreciated American men like me: they didn't resent my fresh, new, costly clothes or my expensive haircut; they enjoyed the appearance of money, and their proximity to someone who looked like he had a lot of it.

Chapter 2

The intent to make my fortune was what had landed me in jail the first time, but make my fortune I had, in spite of the temporary obstacle of incarceration. At just thirty-four, and with a fat bank account, I'd moved to Mérida, in the Yucatan, "The White City" named for the common color of its old buildings, and for its cleanliness. I'd bought and restored an eight-bedroom colonial mansion for my home. I spent my days drinking beer by my pool, reading a book or watching an old movie on TV, and feasting on the local dishes my houseboy, Pedro, prepared for me—*Poc Chuc* and *Papadzules*. My nights were spent drinking Scotch and making the rounds of restaurants, art galleries and the symphony that made up the vibrant cultural life of the city. The Mérida population includes the largest percentile of indigenous persons in Mexico—Mayans, most of whom were still struggling to reach even the lowest rung of the ladder their Mexican neighbors sat upon—and so I took it into my head that I would help them in their rise, though perhaps in an even more practical way than I'd been helped in mine: I'd bought three additional old colonials, each smaller than my residence, though just a few streets away, and was in the process of combining them into one building and restoring it as a school for Mayan kids. It was a deeply and not surprisingly satisfying way to spend my time, and my money.

Taavi, for one, wouldn't have been surprised. Maybe he was the one who put the idea in my head in the first place—roused himself from eternal sleep and whispered it to me in my dreams. That would have been something he would have done, if at all possible, and who was to say it wasn't?

In any case, my life was paradise, and it wasn't enough.

Who's to say what's "enough"? What is plenty for one man is paltry to another. I had wads of dollars in my pocket and stacks in my safe and rows and rows of numbers on my balance sheets, but when it came to thrills, I was poverty-stricken.

About three months after my move to Mexico, in the early spring of 2008, I volunteered as a worker for the Yucatan elections—the one hundred and six "municipal presidents", or mayors as we call them in the U.S., that were to be elected that May. Those few weeks of volunteer work consisted mostly of answering phones in various campaign headquarters, posting yard signs where they were permitted—and sometimes where they were not permitted, approaching area business people with a fundraising pitch on behalf of the resident power brokers and decision makers. You could call me a "people person". From the time I was a kid, I could always pick out the ones who would be most beneficial to know. I worked my ass off for the local pols and, by the time the elections were over, I had a whole new group of friends. Politics is an inherently dirty business and the pollution among the Mexican political class is deservedly legendary; I figured someone in that crowd could get me into a little bit of much-needed trouble.

Chapter 3

My trouble came with a name: Alvaro.

I met Alvaro—met him *formally*—at the victory party for the candidate in Mérida's Third District. He—Alvaro, not the candidate; the candidate was a forgettable little puke who would later be indicted for removing his opponent's advertising materials and exchanging cash for voting cards—was a solid six feet tall, with a body of lean muscle and a head of wavy, thick black hair. Even at first glance he seemed too lithe and graceful—too *physical*—to be a politician. Periodically he'd throw an arm around the smaller but exceptionally beautiful man at his side; the way he looked down at his companion, the smile he gave him, made me wonder if they were a couple. Both of them were surrounded by the circle of spectators who'd gathered around Alvaro, a crowd of men and women who looked up at Alvaro less as just another guest at the victory party but as if they were his fans. There were a few people among that crowd who looked too alert and wary to be simply guests; they looked like Secret Service guys if Secret Service guys routinely dressed in Irish linen guayaberas.

"Do you know who that is?"

"What?" I turned to the Mayan who'd been on the candidate's PR team. I didn't catch his name, but he looked enough like Taavi to draw me to him when I'd first arrived at the party and he'd taken it upon herself to give me the lay of the land—point out the important people I might like to know.

He gestured now toward Alvaro with the hand that held his frothy cocktail. "You think you recognize him, don't you? He's Alvaro Moreno, the bullfighter—not as well-known as his brother, Oscar, but Alvaro's the one who stabbed and killed the Intimidator."

I nodded. "I've never been to a bullfight in my life."

Chapter 4

"Politicians and bullfighters, there is no difference between them," Alvaro told the crowd. "If you are a bullfighter, the bull is your opponent. He is the one you are trying to beat in the race, the one you do not want to lose the election to, hmmm?" he continued, and the people around him chuckled. "And everything a bullfighter does, every move he makes, is to do one of three things—distract his opponent, so the opponent is confused and can't fight back as well; anger his opponent, so the opponent makes a stupid mistake; cause injury to his opponent, so the spectators will see the bullfighter is strong and his opponent, this massive animal, is weak." By the time he finished, the people around him were laughing in earnest. He didn't need to twist to one side as if to dodge attack, his hands holding an imaginary cape, to keep his audience captive; that flourish at the end was all showmanship.

But when he'd twisted he'd ended up directly in front of me.

I stretched my hand out to him. "I'm Clint Kennedy. New to the area—"

Alvaro put up a hand and let his black eyes wander over my white skin, blonde hair, blue eyes. "New to the area? Who would have guessed such a thing?" he asked, sending the people who were still gathered around him into another gale of laughter.

I might have been put off—distracted—by his greeting, but that was just what he wanted.

"I've never been to a bullfight. I'd love to see you in the ring."

"You would?" he laughed, and he grabbed the beautiful man who'd been standing near to him and kissed him on the neck. "Then what do you say, Javier? I fight again in, what is it?

Two weeks? Should we invite this Mister Clint Kennedy to be our guest?"

Javier shrugged, but he smiled as well. "I think Mister Clint Kennedy would like that, Alvaro."

"Then that's what we will do!" Alvaro boomed. He reached out at last to take the hand I had offered him. "Pleased to meet you, Clint. Call me Alvaro—and this is Javier, my brother-in-law."

Brother-in-law, I thought as I began to loosen my hand from Alvaro's grip in order to shake hands with Javier. *This relationship might be more complicated than I assumed...*

But I didn't get to either finish the thought or offer Javier my hand. Alvaro kept his fist tight over mine and yanked me toward him to whisper in my ear, "I know who you are, Mister Clint Kennedy."

www.ingramcontent.com/pod-product-compliance
Lightning Source LLC
Chambersburg PA
CBHW051515250626
47156CB00001B/100